CHRISTOPHER BLAND is a former Chairman of the BBC, BT and the Royal Shakespeare Company. He is married with a son and four stepchildren. His first novel, *Ashes in the Wind*, was published by Head of Zeus in 2014.

Also by Christopher Bland

Ashes in the Wind

CHRISTOPHER BLAND

Cathar

HEAD of ZEUS

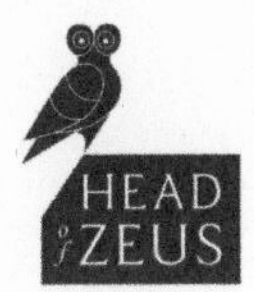

First published in the UK in 2016 by Head of Zeus Ltd.

9 7 5 3 1 2 4 6 8

A catalogue record for this book is available from the British Library.

ISBN (HB) 9781784976064
ISBN (XTPB) 9781784976071
ISBN (E) 9781784976057

Typeset by Ben Cracknell Studios

Printed and bound in Germany
by CPI Books GmbH

Head of Zeus Ltd
Clerkenwell House
45-47 Clerkenwell Green
London EC1R 0HT

WWW.HEADOFZEUS.COM

For Archie, Georgia, Jamie, Tara and William

'Tuez les tous... Dieu reconnaitra les siens'

– Arnald-Amaury, Papal Legate, on being asked how to distinguish between good Catholics and heretic Cathars after the fall of Béziers

'How can people manage to bear the pain when they are burning at the stake?'

'God takes the pain upon himself, of course'

Cathar conversation from
The Records of the Inquisition

'Le Catharisme n'est plus aujourd'hui qu'un astre mort, dont nous recevons à nouveau la lumière fascinante et froide, après un demi-millénaire d'occultation'

Emmanuel Le Roy Ladurie,
Montaillou

The Washing Pool

THE REFLECTION IN the water reminds me of the man I am now – there is no one to tell me of the man I was twenty years ago. It is a battered face that stares back at me from the water. Scar tissue from a deep cut that runs along one jaw, a single eye, still blue, the other socket sealed by skin that has grown over the place where my right eye used to be. There is a long scar diagonally across my back from a wound that, years ago, took many months to heal.

I have lost an eye. I have lost my right arm.

I see my face once a week in the clear water of the washing pool, and only then when no one else is there to ruffle the surface with their splashing.

The washing pool lies outside the village. The women grumble about the walk and say that the water from the well could be diverted to create a basin inside the walls. I am the only man who goes there regularly, although I doubt whether the others would bother to wash more frequently even if the pool was closer to home.

It is quiet there in the early morning, and I have the place to myself for as long as I need to strip and wash thoroughly from head to toe. It is there that I see my face, there that Beatrice saw me naked, made a joke about limbs they had overlooked. When I turned my back on her she gave a little gasp, and I remembered the healed wound under my right shoulder, a wound that nearly finished me, leaving a scar that I have never seen. Beatrice didn't turn away, watched me dry and dress myself.

'I can see it's hard to dress with one arm,' she said, and smiled as she rode away.

Whoever built the washing pool did a thorough job. The spring is protected by a little stone hut with a timbered roof, and the water flows out along a shallow groove in the natural rock for twenty yards, then drops from a spout into the basin below. The basin is of stone with a rounded lip and a stone floor, a perfect square. The water is four feet deep, and because it is built on a slope there is a steady flow, the water leaving by a second spout on the far side to run off into a series of irrigation channels. There are poplars around three sides of the basin, one long stone bench, and the water is always cool and clear.

Once I saw a young roebuck drinking from it in the very early morning, his front legs splayed out so he could reach the water. He wasn't nervous, finished drinking as I stood there, then trotted off towards the woods.

I feel better after my weekly visit. Some of the men in the village make jokes about my past and the need to wash my sins away. Or suggest I go there because that is where the women go.

Sitting on the bench to dry myself and my clothes I can see the path that leads across the fields and into the woods, a path I know well, as do the other shepherds. Beyond are the foothills of the Pyrenees and the good summer grazing, and beyond that on a clear day the peak of Puymorens, snow-covered until the end of May.

The path is my escape route should I need one again. After two long sieges trapped inside castles, I prefer the valley in which I now live. It is a comfort to know I can slip out of Montaillou at night to the safety of Catalonia.

It is also comforting to know that Montaillou has survived the wars, the skirmishes and the so-called Albigensian Crusade unscathed. Throughout the thirteenth century there has been fighting somewhere in the Languedoc, ranging from pitched battles and lengthy sieges at one extreme, and at the other small raids by marauding bands, intent on survival, and with no other skill but the sword. Religion has always been used as a cloak to justify these conflicts, but the real driving forces have always been the same. Land. Money. Power.

Montaillou is Cathar, its heresy generally acknowledged at the subtle, subterranean level of Occitan rumour and gossip that vanishes into thin air when challenged. The church is full on Sundays and holy days, tithes are collected and returned to Carcassonne, and our priest uses the heresy of his flock as a means of consolidating his power.

Is he Cathar? When it suits him, is the answer. The visits of the Cathar Perfects are discreet and infrequent, limited mainly to the consoling of the dying. All in all it is a curious arrangement, in a sense reflecting the dualism that is the centre of our Cathar faith.

Montaillou is the ideal refuge for me. My missing arm and eye ensure that I am no longer regarded as a threat, and not many in the village are aware of my skill with the crossbow. So here I am, not unnoticed by the Inquisition (they make it their business to notice everything), but categorised by them as no longer dangerous. They sent me to Compostela, and I have the precious certificate to prove that I completed the penitential journey. As I look into the water, the scars on my body bear witness to the existence of evil. I have to look elsewhere for evidence of the existence of goodness, and there have been several moments in my life when the struggle between God and the Devil seemed one-sided. Nevertheless, I am still here. I am Cathar.

1

Avignonet

MY FATHER AND *I were both knights; our sworn allegiance was to Bernard de Roqueville, and we lived in a small castle built on a spur in the valley of the River Baise.*

Beaufort (it had a grand name, but was not much more than a fortified farmhouse) was a four-square building with a tower at one corner in which a staircase led to the first floor. We and our close servants lived on that floor in three rooms, eating in the largest where there was a fire which we kept going day and night except during the summer. We spent most of our time in that room, in winter the only warm place in the building.

Our cattle were brought in at night to the ground floor from the end of September to early April. Their bodies helped to warm the place, which had a not unpleasant smell of milk and cow dung and hay and the steam from their hides. Most of the time my father and I were glorified farmers, making sure that the men looked after the beasts and themselves.

There were three families working for us, twenty-four souls in all; my father's right-hand man, Michel, lived with his wife and four children in Beaufort, and the rest in two dwellings built up against the walls. Beaufort was surrounded by a seven-foot wall; the only gate had a dovecote above it with a low-pitched, red-tiled roof, and on top of that flew our flag, day and night.

I looked after the pigeons, four hundred or more of them, making sure they were fed and watered and setting traps for the rats that were their main predators. The occasional sparrowhawk would appear and try his luck, but I learned to wait until the hawk had made a kill and was gorging on the ground. Then I'd use my crossbow at close range, usually to good effect.

Once a young sparrowhawk managed to squeeze through the entrance under the eaves. I was in the courtyard when this happened, saw the pigeons exploding out of the dovecote and heard the noise of the wings and the frantic calling of birds trying to escape. I climbed the ladder, opened the trapdoor and there was the sparrowhawk feasting on one of the three pigeons he had killed. He looked at me with fierce, unblinking yellow eyes, then continued with his meal. I watched him for two or three minutes as he gripped the bird with his talons, his curved yellow beak tearing into the soft breast of the bird. I had never been so close to a wild hawk before and felt sorry that I had to destroy such a fearless creature. For several days afterwards the pigeons were unsettled, didn't lay and twenty or more birds never returned to the dovecote.

The inside of the dovecote had three hundred small chambers set into its walls, and there the pigeons nested, laid their eggs and reared their young. They were used to me bringing them water and grain, and made little protest when I took away the squabs. The pigeons were an important source of food for us all, the eight-week-old squabs in particular, although we would eat the older birds too when they had come to the end of their useful lives. I collected the droppings once a week and we used them to fertilise the vegetable garden. The constant murmuring of the pigeons was a reassuring sound that you could hear in the courtyard all the day long.

Roqueville itself stood three miles away from Beaufort at the end of a semicircle of hills open only to the east. It was a fertile valley thanks to the River Baise, producing enough grass for the summer grazing and hay for the winter out of earth that was dark brown, almost black, heavy under the plough. Most of the land was pasture for cattle; we left the rearing of sheep to those who lived closer to the Pyrenees. The valley had been cleared of its woods a hundred years before, but enough oak and ash had been left to provide shade for the cattle, and the wooded hills gave us firewood and charcoal. There were little vineyards on the higher, stonier slopes of the valley, one of which was ours; we produced a hundred barrels of red wine for our own use and sent ten barrels up to Roqueville as part of our dues.

Our role at Beaufort was to act as sentinels. Our position gave us a good view of anyone approaching along the rough track which ran parallel to the river. We were expected to deal with any small armed bands that might appear; if a serious force arrived we were to withdraw to Roqueville, bringing our cattle with us if we could.

My father and I both had armour, a helmet, a shield and a horse; we knew how to carry a lance, and regularly practised swordplay on foot and on horseback with each other and with the sergeant-at-arms at Roqueville. As it turned out, all of my later fighting was on foot or behind castle walls, when in the mêlée of scrabbling, cursing, shouting bodies it was hard to distinguish friend from foe, never mind remembering the parry in octave or the disengage in prime. I never used my lance, and soon learned that the most useful weapon, on horse or on foot, was the crossbow, at which I became quick and accurate, as the sparrowhawks learned to their cost.

We did have a coat of arms, Argent, on a Bend Sable Three Pheons d'Or, three golden arrowheads. My father had them painted on his shield. Our crest, a cockerel with a pheon d'or on its breast, led a precarious existence on the top of his helmet until it was sheared off in the skirmish at Avignonet. The arms and the crest seemed, like the lance, to have been designed for the pitched battles of fifty years earlier, although they came into their own at tournaments, which continued a curious parallel existence to real warfare for many years.

I was knighted on the eve of the great tournament at Chauvency, organised by Louis, Count of Chimy. Bernard de Roqueville had been invited, and brought with him a forty-strong retinue: knights, esquires, soldiers, his armourer and his herald. Three of us were chosen; we had a ritual bath the night before, kept vigil until dawn in the small church at Chauvency, even though two of us were Cathar, and were formally dubbed knights by Bernard de Roqueville in the morning. I remember his words very clearly:

'You should be hardy, courteous, generous, loyal; ferocious to your enemies, frank and debonair to your friends. He only has a real right to knighthood who has proved himself in battle or in the tournament. You can begin to earn that right today through deeds that deserve to be remembered.'

Bernard made me the traditional present of a magnificent woollen cloak, dyed purple, with the Beaufort cockerel embroidered at its neck.

'That's my wife's needlework. She doesn't do that for everyone.' I kept the cloak for several years, wearing it only on the grandest of occasions, until it was destroyed by moths.

The tournament was held in a large field around which the great men had put up their tents, vying with each other to make the best display with their armorial flags and coloured pennants and the most noise with their musicians and troubadours. I had never before been out of our valley, never before seen such a spectacle – the clash of the jousters, the snorting, whinnying horses, the shouts of the spectators, the trumpeters calling for silence as the heralds announced the names, dignities and armorial bearings of the combatants.

The jousting was serious and dangerous; after three days there were many wounded and two men dead. I fought only on the first day, reserved for the newly knighted. I was excited and I was frightened, frightened that I might be killed or maimed, even more that I might disgrace myself by swerving away at the last moment.

I was confident about my horse, less so about my aim with the lance, and uncomfortable in a full suit of armour. My father had helped me choose from the racks of tournament lances – 'Choose one with the straightest grain, less likely to shatter or splinter' – and he supervised the Roqueville armourer as he strapped and buckled and bolted me into my armour.

My first joust was against an equally inexperienced knight from Artois, and after we had each broken three lances, both remaining in the saddle, it was declared an honourable draw.

The heralds made much of the ten quarterings of my second opponent in the afternoon, dwelling briefly on my coat of arms. My father reassured me as I waited to mount and enter the arena: 'That only tells you about his ancestors, nothing about him. You've a good horse; just keep your eyes on the tip of your lance and line it up with his midriff. Start at a slow canter, and make sure you are at full gallop as you come together. When you are two lengths away crouch down in the saddle and push your lance forward at the last moment. All the lances are the same length, and you want to strike your opponent before he strikes you. Otherwise you will both be unhorsed.'

I was fortunate; my enemy's horse was reluctant, barely willing to break out of a trot. I galloped into him, held my lance steady and struck him out of the saddle. He lay stunned on the ground; I dismounted and stood over him, waiting for him until he recovered and formally yielded. I was entitled to his horse, which I certainly did not want, and to his armour, which looked to be German and a good deal finer than mine. But the desperate look in his eyes when the forfeiture was announced by the heralds made me forgo the privilege.

This earned me great applause from the spectators and kind words from Blanche de Roqueville that evening at the feast, which was held in a great tent close by the jousting field. Three hundred of us sat down to an endless meal, punctuated by troubadours, jugglers, short masques, speeches at random that few could or wished to hear, and later the occasional squabble that relived an incident or insult earlier in the day.

Blanche de Roqueville was seated many places away from me, but close enough that I could hear the troubadour who sought her out and sang tributes to her beauty:

'Lady Blanche, your virtue and wisdom and beauty,
Your elegant speech, your sweet laughter
Draw me to you with a pure and loving heart;
In you lie all my happiness, all my desire,
I cannot find another one as fair'

he sang, and as he sang I fell in love for the first time. Hopeless, appropriately so, for courtly love was meant to be passionate, pure and unrequited. I was happy for the moment just to gaze on her red lips, her black hair, the golden headdress that framed her oval face, and tried to remember exactly what she had said to me on her way to her place at dinner. 'Good knights make good beginnings': it was something like that; she rested her hand for a moment on my shoulder, which still burned from her touch at the end of the feast.

My father and I rode back together; he had acquitted himself well in the final series of mêlées which ended the tournament, and from which the Roqueville band had emerged victorious, although with several wounded men to carry home. My father was unhurt; his strength with sword and shield was legendary, and, as a young man – he told me as we rode along – he had earned a living from tournaments.

'It was possible in those days, if you were determined and lucky. Geoffrey de Goncourt and I fought in twenty tournaments in nine months, and between us unhorsed and ransomed thirty knights. We went as far as the River Loire in search of glory and treasure. In those days you were what you got. I began with poor equipment, and a slow horse. Only my sword was fit for a knight.'

'Did you ever fight in a battle?'

'The only real battle, more of a skirmish, was in Flanders where I fought for the Normans against the Flemings, and had my horse killed under me. I fought in my next tournament on a borrowed, sorry nag but came up against a weak opponent on a strong horse that became mine. I came away from that day with two warhorses, a palfrey and harnesses. Later at Lagny I captured ten knights and twelve horses in a single day. I couldn't do that now. Fewer tournaments, better organised. And I relied on my strength; you're a better swordsman than I am. I battered my opponents into submission. Anyhow, that's what built Beaufort.'

It was the longest speech I heard my father make, and would have sounded boastful coming from anyone else. I asked him about my vigil.

'It's no sin for a Cathar to pray in a Catholic church; it's your prayers that matter, and there's no need to pay any attention to the priests and their mumblings.'

We were both Cathar, Credentes, believers, as were all our men, as was Bernard de Roqueville, as was my mother, who died giving birth to me. According to my father she received the Consolamentum on her deathbed and died a Perfect, making him swear to bring me up as Cathar, a Bon Chrétien. Which he did his best to do.

Our beliefs are not set down in detail in any book. Most important, to me at least, was the recognition of the equal and opposite forces of Good and Evil. I had seen enough of the latter in the Languedoc to be a convinced dualist, as the Catholic Church called us. Beyond that, Cathars held that the material world was in a sense unreal, that final salvation could only be achieved by becoming a Perfect, and that as many as nine lives were available to achieve that state.

We hated the Catholic Church, its Pope, cardinals, bishops, priests and monks. As they hated and sought to exterminate us. They tortured anyone they suspected, burned at the stake any Perfect they caught and gave currency to a tissue of lies – orgies, child sacrifice, sodomy – about the Cathars. They would even dig up corpses if they had been denounced as Cathar and burn them at the stake, as if to show that the long arm of the Church could reach beyond the grave. All this made them easy to hate.

The Perfect Guillaume Authie once told me, 'You can choose between the Cathar church, which flees and forgives, and the other, which fetters and flays; the former holds to the straight path of the Apostles, and does not lie or deceive, the latter is the Church of Rome.'

Not too much was expected of us as Credentes. To tell the truth, to confess our sins to a Perfect at reasonable intervals, and to take the Consolamentum, the last rites of the Cathars, on our deathbed if we could find a Perfect in time, was all that was asked. If you were determined to become a Perfect in this incarnation, you were expected after the Consolamentum to go through the Endura – that is, to eat and drink nothing until you died. This had little appeal for me. I always planned to take my chance on eight more incarnations.

The Perfects were different. They too were expected to tell the truth, and they did, which made them wonderfully forthcoming witnesses for the Inquisition, although they were tortured first anyway. They could not make love, eat meat or eggs, although fish was permitted, they had to pray many times a day and fast three days a week. Several times a year they had to fast for forty days and forty nights.

These were good men, risking their lives to look after us, normally travelling in pairs, and wearing dark blue or dark green cloaks when it was safe to do so. I always felt a better man after spending a few days, or even hours, in their company, although this was a feeling that was not easy to maintain once they had departed.

For a number of years when my father was young there was a tacit acceptance of the Cathars in our part of the Languedoc. There was no attempt to seek us out, no burnings, a policy of live and let live, although that couldn't last forever given the passionate Cathar denunciation of all that the

Catholic Church stood for. In the end it turned out not to be about dogma or belief but about money and power. The growing refusal of Cathars to pay tithes hit the Church where it hurt most, in its money bags.

When the Papal Legate Peter of Castelnau was killed on his way back to Rome by the men of Raymond VI, Count of Toulouse, Pope Innocent declared a crusade, a crusade accompanied by the full panoply of indulgences – forgiveness of sins, cancellation of debts, and, most important of all, the promise of land and treasure confiscated from the Cathars. All this for forty days of service on the mainland, without crossing the Mediterranean to the much less hospitable Near East.

It took time for the long arm of the Church to reach our backwater in the valley of the Baise, but reach us it did. It began with a demand from Toulouse that Bernard de Roqueville pay the ten years of tithes he owed – we all owed – to the Bishop of Pamiers. When Bernard sent the messenger packing there was an uneasy calm for three months, and then the Church returned with a well-armed force of a hundred men, commanded by one of de Montfort's nephews.

They took us by surprise at Beaufort, passing us at first light and on towards Roqueville before we could warn them. They discovered our sentry, one of the older herdsmen, fast asleep and didn't bother to kill him, but took most of our beasts on their way through. The gates at Roqueville had been closed, but they were not able to bring in their cattle, and half the herd was collected by the crusaders and driven back down the valley to Carcassonne. All this in a single day, without any killing, although two of the Roqueville herdsmen were badly beaten when they tried to prevent the round-up. We had spent the day ingloriously behind the walls of

Beaufort, guarding what was left of our herd, aware that we had failed in our duty.

Bernard de Roqueville was a choleric man at the best of times and stealing his cattle was not to be tolerated. A few days later he arrived at Beaufort escorted by four of his men and asked to see my father on his own.

Bernard had rarely visited Beaufort, never in my lifetime that I could remember, and would always send for my father if there was anything to discuss. We would both go to Roqueville for the great feast on New Year's Day; other than that, six months or a year could easily pass by without meeting Bernard.

It was the day our lives began to change. Bernard sat at the table in the big room upstairs, his back to the fire, picking at the bread and cheese that Michel had put in front of him. There was red wine in our only silver goblet, untouched until the end of the meeting. He was wearing a leather jerkin over a brown linen shirt, linen trousers tucked into high leather boots, and before he spoke he took off his gloves and laid them on the table, straightening the fingers as he did so.

'I've learned that the Inquisitors, Stephen of St-Thibery and William Arnald, will be crossing the big river at Avignonet in four days' time. I want you and your son,' and here he looked at me for the first time, 'with three men that you can trust, to kill them.'

'Kill unarmed Dominicans…?' My father's question trailed off.

'They both carry weapons, they'd be long dead otherwise, and they're never without an armed guard of four or five men, Italians, loyal to them and to the Pope. These two are bad men; they've tortured and burned Cathars in this part of the Languedoc for two years now, and it's time it ended.'

'Why us?'

'You and your son for two reasons. You failed to warn us when they came for our cattle.'

My father tried to protest.

'I know, I know. Nevertheless they came past you. More important, I trust you to do this and to keep quiet about it afterwards. I don't want it traced back to Roqueville.'

So it's all right if it's traced back to Beaufort, I thought, but said nothing.

Bernard stood up, as did my father. He took a long drink from the goblet of wine and offered it to my father, who finished what was left. This seemed to seal what had been discussed. Then Bernard clasped my father's shoulder for a moment and left the room.

We stayed where we were, silent until we heard the clatter of hooves as Bernard and his escort trotted out under the dovecote and back to Roqueville.

'We don't have a choice,' said my father. 'It will be your first taste of real fighting.'

I was excited. Bernard had made it clear that these were not unarmed innocents. The excitement lasted while we prepared; my father selected Michel and two of our strongest men, all sworn to secrecy, although the fact that we would be away for a week was bound to cause gossip and speculation.

'Lances?' I asked.

'Useless for what we're going to do. Sword, crossbow and twenty bolts will be enough. No shields.'

I noticed he had brought his crested helm.

'We will kill them all,' he said, seeing my surprised look. We got our horses ready, packed enough food and wine for three days and set off for Avignonet at dawn the next day. We trotted through country that was new to me, drier and less fertile than the Roqueville valley. We passed several hamlets, and in each of them streets emptied and doors were bolted on our arrival. We looked threatening, five men in chain mail carrying crossbows and swords, clearly bent on a mission which each hamlet hoped would not involve them. We were spoken to by no one, even in those places which my father knew to be Cathar.

We arrived a day before the Inquisitors were due, in good time to see the lie of the land and plan our tactics. The big river was fordable in only one place, a mile outside the little village of Avignonet, and the track either side of the ford led through oak woods, providing good cover at that time of year.

'They should be here around midday tomorrow,' said my father. 'We'll watch the crossing from first light.'

We made a camp in the woods on the south side of the ford, lit a fire and ate the dried beef, bread and cheese that we had brought with us from Beaufort.

'No wine,' my father said. 'We'll need clear heads tomorrow.'

We slept next to the fire on blankets over pine branches; the smell was clean and resinous, but I found it difficult to sleep, although my father next to me was gently snoring within minutes of resting his head on his saddlebag. We took it in turn to guard the horses, which we had tethered at the edge of our small clearing. In the morning we had a breakfast of bread, water and dried apples, mounted and listened carefully while my father told us what to do.

'We'll take them in the middle of the river, where the water comes up to a horse's belly, where they will be at their slowest. We won't charge, the river's too deep, and we want them to think we're peaceful travellers. Michel will watch the ford from the edge of the wood, the rest of us will stay back until the signal. Leave the Inquisitors to my son and to me – that way you'll avoid excommunication.' I laughed at my father's little joke; the others all looked too stern to smile.

It went much as my father had planned. Michel gave a long whistle when he saw them on the far side approaching the ford, and the five of us trotted down to meet them. There was a narrow band of mist along the river, and by the time the Inquisitors and their escort reached the river only their heads and shoulders were visible.

They drew their swords as soon as they saw us; the Italians were slow to get out their crossbows. The two Inquisitors both wore white tunics with the crusader's red cross, which made them easy to identify. I shot one of the Inquisitors from close range with my crossbow and my father cut down the other. The bolt didn't kill my man, although blood stained his white tunic so I could no longer see the red cross; he plucked at the bolt with his left hand, tried to draw his sword with his right, then groaned and toppled into the water, disappearing under the surface as my horse trampled him down. The skirmish turned into a wild mêlée of shouting, hacking men, in which it was hard to distinguish friend from foe in the mist that shrouded us all from the waist down. It was not like the tournament at Chauvency.

Two of our men were soon on foot, one because his horse had thrown him and bolted, the other to deal with one of the Italians who was trying to remount. The splashing of the river as we milled around, the neighing of the terrified horses, the cries, grunts and groans, the clanging of sword against sword, seemed to last an age, followed by a strange silence when it was all over. At the end I was shaking, not with fear but with relief, exhausted by a fight that had lasted no more than ten minutes in all.

Our men killed three of the five-man escort, but two of them managed to turn back towards Avignonet; I brought down one of their horses with two crossbow bolts in quick succession as they were leaving the river, and Michel finished off the rider, but the other got clean away.

'We'll not catch him,' said my father. 'The river will take care of the bodies, and we'll have their horses and the pack mule. They owe them to us for the cattle they stole.'

He was holding his shoulder as he spoke; he'd been caught from behind by one of the Italians with a heavy sword that had gone through his chain mail, inflicting a deep cut. Michel killed the man before he had a chance at a second blow.

'It's bleeding, but not badly. It didn't break the bone. I've had many worse.' My father had taken the tunic from one of the Inquisitors; I tore this into strips and used them to bandage the cut.

One of the men had lost two fingers, but these were our only casualties. We trotted back to Beaufort, our men pleased with themselves; I was unable to share in their pleasure. I had killed for the first time, but it had been a less than chivalrous contest in which I'd shot a man before he had a chance to fight. The image of the Inquisitor drowning under my horse's feet took a long time to disappear from my dreams.

We were all uneasy about the man who had got away.

'I don't think it makes much difference,' said my father. 'Even if we had killed them all it would have been clear this was a Cathar attack. Bernard would always get the blame.'

Back at Beaufort I dressed my father's wound, which seemed clean enough, although I had to pick many strands of his shirt out of the cut before bandaging it again. Then he sent me off to Roqueville to tell them what had happened at Avignonet.

Bernard seemed pleased.

'That was a good day's work – a pity you didn't kill them all, but this will bring the Inquisition up short. You'll stay the night, dine with us?'

It wasn't really a question. That evening I sat at his right hand and was waited on by his wife, Blanche, whom I had not seen since the tournament at Chauvency. She seemed pleased to see me, asked after my father, and plainly knew where we had been and what we had done. She looked beautiful in an embroidered crimson gown, her hair held close to her head by a gold clasp, then flowing down her back almost to her waist. It was said she was a Perfect, and I noticed she ate no meat at dinner. Although we did not speak of the ambush, it would have been clear to most of the assembled company (there were perhaps forty men in all sitting in the Great Hall) that something momentous had happened.

When I got back to Beaufort the following evening my father's wound was giving him a great deal of pain; although he tried to pretend all was well, the cut seemed to have widened. It was black and purple round the edges and oozing yellow pus. He couldn't raise his right arm.

'It will clear up in a couple of days,' he said, but he was wrong. Two days later the whole of his shoulder was black and he lay on his bed groaning and delirious with a high fever. I watched by his bed day and night, bathed his forehead with cold water and watched while Michel's wife applied a poultice of herbs twice a day to the wound, which by now was smelling of decay. Towards the end he was unable to relieve himself, and I had to help him while he pissed into a bowl. In a moment of lucidity while I was holding him he said, 'I used to do this for you when you were little,' and managed a smile.

We sent for a Perfect from Montaillou, where we had heard Authie was living, but he didn't arrive in time to administer the Consolamentum. We buried my father in a field above the Baise and marked the place with a massive stone. I felt abandoned and desolate, a desolation that persisted even after Authie heard the Confessions of the four of us left from Avignonet and then blessed us.

Bernard sent his son down to Beaufort when he heard the news.

'Beaufort belongs to you now,' said Armand de Roqueville. 'You'll have to swear fealty to my father, then it's yours.'

It was mine, but not for long. We had all of us underestimated the shock caused by the 'Massacre at Avignonet', which reached all the way to Rome. We had killed not just Inquisitors, but Papal Legates, the embodiment, it was believed, of the Pope himself in the Languedoc.

Six weeks later a proper army, again commanded by de Montfort's nephew, arrived in our valley. We were able to warn them at Roqueville, as rumours had reached us three days before that five hundred men were on the way. We had time to move out of Beaufort and into the big castle, all of us together with our few remaining cattle. Roqueville was ready for a long siege.

The siege didn't last long. It was clear it could only have one outcome, and Bernard was persuaded by his wife and sons to negotiate. After a day and a night of bargaining both sides reached an agreement which led to the army's withdrawal.

Bernard paid a high price, a fine of a thousand crowns, and he was forced to hand over half his lands, including Beaufort, to the Church.

'I'm sorry,' he said to me. 'But you hadn't taken possession, and the property reverted to me when your father died.

There will always be a place for you and your men at Roqueville.'

I didn't understand the details of feudal law, but there was little point in arguing, as one of the so-called crusaders had already occupied and garrisoned Beaufort on his way up the valley.

As a final humiliation, Bernard had to perform a public penance in the great cathedral in Toulouse. Naked except for a loincloth, he crawled from the West Door up to the high altar, while the Bishop scourged him on the way with a heavy bundle of birch twigs, refreshed at regular intervals. He was watched by several hundred men and women, laughing and jeering at a great man brought low. There was an extraordinary contrast between the grandeur of the cathedral's soaring Roman arches and the sordid spectacle below that had been arranged for the greater glory of God.

Many years earlier Raymond VI, Count of Toulouse, had been forced to undergo a similar humiliation, but the scourging then was largely symbolic. On this occasion the Bishop, a burly Prince of the Church, laid on with relish and a heavy hand, drawing blood at the third stroke and making Bernard cry out many times. Perhaps worst of all, his wife, his daughter, his son and twenty of his own knights, including me, were made to line the aisles. I watched Blanche, who had been made to stand with her daughter on the opposite side of the aisle. She closed her eyes after the first savage blow and kept them closed until it was all over.

We took Bernard back to Roqueville an impoverished, humiliated and broken man. He died a year later.

2

The Dovecote

ROQUEVILLE WAS A different place, quieter, less exciting without Bernard. While he was alive there was always something happening, neighbours invited for a joust, a hunt for wild boar, a feast to celebrate an ancestor's birthday, a horse race through the valley, an evening with a new troubadour. Armand, his only son, took his place. He was only three years older than me, but had little opportunity to show he was as good a man as his father through success at tournaments or on the battlefield. He resembled Bernard in looks, but soon acquired a careworn expression that rarely left him. I could tell he wished he had been with us at Avignonet.

At the beginning much of the power rested with Blanche, who set about rebuilding the fiefdom. The forfeited land lay mainly to the east, a source of rents rather than crops or animals; most of the valley of the Baise still belonged to Roqueville.

For a year the crusader who had been given Beaufort remained in uneasy occupation, an alien figure from northern France who spoke no Occitan. His taste was for warfare, not husbandry. He killed most of my pigeons and then lived off the cattle, ignoring the need to breed as well as to slaughter.

No one would work for him apart from his soldiers, and they were all warriors as useless as their lord. After twelve months he left; his parting gesture was to fill the hall with straw and torch the place. Beaufort burned for several days. It was no longer mine, but it was the place where I was born and raised, and I found its loss and later destruction hard to bear.

Armand, I suspect at Blanche's suggestion, asked me to go back.

'Thank you, but it's sequestered land now, it no longer belongs to Roqueville, so it cannot belong to me. I'd rather remain here.'

Armand grunted.

'I suppose you're right; you'd be vulnerable to the next crusader who came along once you'd rebuilt Beaufort. My father promised you a place here and we'll honour that.'

Gradually Blanche replaced the lost cattle, buying heifers in the market at Carcassonne; she found two good bulls at Aubiet. At first much of the land was ploughed for corn, which gave us plenty of bread, although meat was scarce in the early years. The vineyards continued to do well and we sold or bartered a third of the wine.

I was one of more than thirty Roqueville knights; half of us lived in the castle, the rest in their own houses or in the little hamlet close to the river, although even the outliers looked to the castle for food and drink. I was the youngest and would probably remain so, as it seemed unlikely that more knights would be created.

In the castle I shared a room with three others. Although they were polite enough, they were ten or fifteen years my senior, and were less than enthusiastic about having someone allocated to their already cramped accommodation. After some months I moved out to a small house in the village, vacant for some time as the previous occupant had died of a black fever. It seemed safe enough to me, although I took the precaution of cleaning the place thoroughly and burning what little furniture was left behind. Its bareness suited me; I had a bed, a chair, a table, a rushlight and a fire in the ground-floor room, where I slept in the winter. In the heat of the summer I needed the cool breeze in the upstairs chamber.

'We have more than enough men who can handle a sword or a lance,' I heard Blanche grumble to Armand. 'All they do is practise for imaginary battles, develop healthy appetites and go through our larders like locusts.'

Blanche was right. Every morning there were men in the tilt-yard or practising swordplay in the armoury. Two of Bernard's former comrades in arms were in charge of the knights. Geoffrey de Goncourt had been a famous jouster, fighting with my father in tournaments when they were young men. He could still unhorse an opponent when he wanted to demonstrate the right way to carry a lance, and could parry the fiercest attack on foot with deft use of his sword and shield. He was fond of me and took particular care that I knew how to handle my weapons. Armand valued his advice, and on more than military matters.

He was Roqueville's source of chivalric wisdom. He knew the fine points of etiquette, of challenge, acceptance, surrender, ransom, when it was appropriate to kill an opponent in battle and when to allow him to yield. He made it clear to me that he regarded Avignonet as insignificant and unworthy.

'Your father deserved a better death,' he once said to me.

He was an expert on heraldry, and liked to refer to himself as Roqueville Pursuivant. He was dismissive of the simple Beaufort coat of arms.

'If your mother had been an only child you could have

added the Malet arms to your own. Eight quarterings, one of them the Duc de Beaujeu.'

After a while I found this an unsatisfactory way of life. We were practising for battles that would never be fought, and the days of tournaments were over. I knew from my experience at Avignonet that fighting was a messy, confused affair that took no account of the courtesies of the armoury. My companions regarded the crossbow as an inferior weapon, best left to the men-at-arms. I did not share this view, and most of my practice hours were spent in the butts. I improved my accuracy and speed until I could regularly get seven or eight bolts into the centre of the target within three minutes.

Although I fulfilled my obligations as a soldier, on many days I would ride down the valley, taking my crossbow in case I came across a roe-deer, and I made a contribution to the table after most of these outings.

I never went to Beaufort, although I visited the great stone that marked my father's grave. The place which now sheltered the bodies of my father and mother was well chosen. It looked out over a grassy valley that in the spring came alive with flowers and clover, the river just visible through the willows and scrub oak that marked its course.

I spoke to my father regularly, more often than when he was alive. I had to imagine his replies, which wasn't difficult as he had been a man of few words.

'I suppose you're already reincarnated,' I said on an early visit, half expecting a wolf or a hawk to appear. I was disappointed but not surprised when nothing happened, and rode off wondering whether my failure to find Authie in time for the Consolamentum had condemned my father to an unhappy new existence.

On another occasion I asked him about Avignonet. 'Was it worthwhile? Killing those Inquisitors has brought nothing but trouble. You'd be alive and Beaufort would still be standing if we'd stayed at home.' Again I got no answer, although a kestrel was hovering above me as I asked the question. It flew off as I left, and it may not have been my father.

There was no dovecote at Roqueville, and I suggested to Armand, as much from boredom as from a desire to replace the past, that I build one.

'I'll ask my mother what she thinks,' he said, and later that day told me that she approved of the idea.

'You can use the field where we used to grow turnips,' he said. 'I'll lend you three men to help with the work.'

We levelled the ground, baked the bricks, mixed the mortar, felled ash trees to erect scaffolding. I sent two of the men to Beaufort to see what they could find among the ruins, and they came back with roof tiles from our old dovecote. It took six months to complete the work; at the end we had a handsome little circular building sitting eight feet above the ground on four curved arches which we built from cut stone. The rest of the building was brick, with an oak floor and chestnut roof beams. Inside there were nesting hollows for three hundred birds. Just above the arches I set long strips of tin projecting outwards and downwards so it was almost impossible for rats to get inside. The dovecote was capped with a round of copper providing eaves over the entry and exit holes, and above the cap I instructed the blacksmith to make a weathervane of a wolf, the de Roqueville crest.

Armand brought Blanche down to inspect the work when we had finished.

'It's very pretty,' she said. 'I'm glad you can work with more than the sword and the lance. But where are the pigeons?'

'There are still semi-wild birds around Beaufort. We'll trap them, bring them here and feed them inside until they are used to their new quarters.'

'I would be happy to live here if I were a pigeon. Perhaps that's how I'll be reincarnated. What do you think, Armand?'

Armand frowned at his mother's indiscretion and said only, 'I look forward to pigeon pie and squabs.'

As I watched them ride back to the castle I thought that was an incautious remark about reincarnation, although I was pleased that Blanche trusted me to be discreet. There was an understanding that Catharism in the valley, though widespread, was not to be talked about and not to be practised openly. The fiction that we were Catholics since Bernard's penance was maintained in the only church in the valley. The priest, an old friend of the de Roquevilles, was happy to see a large congregation every Sunday and turned a blind eye to the fact that the attendees were mainly Cathars who didn't take Communion or go to him for Confession.

The Perfect Guillaume Authie was a regular visitor. I always knew when he was about to appear because I was asked to produce fish from the stew pond, which I had built beside the river when we had finished the dovecote. Authie wore his green robes only within the castle walls and heard our Confessions in a small private chamber off the main hall.

The moment of greatest danger was when a Cathar lay dying and a Perfect had to be found to administer the Consolamentum, followed by the Endura, the fasting to death that ensured Perfection. The Endura was sometimes too much for the relatives of the dying man or woman, as it often guaranteed a painful death. It made people unsure in their faith, too ready to gossip and grumble, which was all right in the valley but risky with strangers and at distant markets or fairs.

Blanche was a strong believer, and always insisted that a Perfect be there even if the dying person was an uncertain Cathar. 'It's my duty,' I once heard her say to Authie. 'I need to save more souls than my own.'

Nevertheless, she wore her religion lightly and was admired and loved. I worshipped her for her beauty, her energy, her gaiety, her subtle ability to manage Armand without undermining him, her determination to restore Roqueville to its former glory.

I saw her once a week at the feast that all Roqueville knights and esquires were expected to attend. On other evenings she dined in her chamber with her daughter and her son. At the feast there was always music, and often a troubadour who would pay tribute to Blanche in words that I, besotted as I was, never thought too fulsome. There were moments when she seemed to pay me special attention, would call for me to sit beside her at or after dinner, would sometimes touch my hand to make a point, or pinch my cheek gently if I tried to outdo the troubadour in her praise.

I watched jealously if others received similar favours; my passion was chaste and honourable in theory, fiery in practice. I had never known a woman. I embraced Blanche many times in my dreams and always awoke from them both exhilarated and ashamed.

My only close friend at Roqueville was Etienne de Vallieres, who had been knighted with me on the same day at Chauvency. He lived with his widowed mother at Barraigne, a small castle much like Beaufort further up the valley. He shared my admiration for Blanche and we would speak appreciatively to each other of her virtues, both trying hard to believe in the purity of the other's courtly love.

Etienne would often ride with me in the valley, although

he was a poor shot with the crossbow and always left it to me to bring back a roe-deer or a partridge for the table. I was Blanche's favourite, he told me.

'She calls you her useful servant; she remembers how well you did at the tournament and at Avignonet. Admires you for bringing food to the table, for building the dovecote and the stew pond.'

This was sweet music, although I told Etienne it was simply her affectionate way of speaking. Secretly I hoped it was more, although I had no way of finding out.

I became more than a troubadour and perhaps less than a knight when, one day, she rode down to the dovecote alone.

'My daughter's horse cast a shoe and she's returned home. I've always wanted to look inside.' She dismounted and tied her horse to one of the iron rings set into the nearest column.

'The floor is covered in droppings and the smell is sharp.'

'I'm a woman. I'm used to dirt and smells.' She sat down on the bench, pulled her riding skirt above her knees, took off her soft brown boots and rolled down her stockings. I looked away. 'Women have feet and ankles and calves too,' she said. 'We just keep them well hidden. Now I'm ready.'

She followed me up the ladder and stood beside me barefoot, her skirt hitched up, her feet half covered in pigeon droppings. She looked up at the hundreds of birds sitting, or flying up to the roof and out, or dropping down from the top and going unerringly to their nests.

'It is a strong smell, but no worse than cattle. I love the sound they make.'

For the first time I thought of the low, rippling coos of the pigeons as background music to love, a feeling intensified when Blanche took my hand. 'It's a magical world in here. I shall be glad to come back as a pigeon.' She let go of my hand

and climbed down the ladder. I followed her down; she was sitting on the oak bench holding her stockings and looking down at her feet, white and grey with pigeon droppings. Two little grey feathers had caught in her hair.

'Now what can I do? I can't put on my stockings, and I can't ride back barefoot.' She was annoyed with herself.

'There's a rainwater butt,' I said, got the leather bucket, filled it and knelt down before her. I took off my scarf, dipped it in the water and began to wash her feet. She had neat ankles and long, elegant toes, although the skin on her heels was tough and the balls of her feet were calloused. Her skin elsewhere was white and soft to the touch. I took my time, not daring to look up, using my scarf to wash carefully between each toe. She had a small white scar halfway up her left calf; it looked like the relic of some childhood accident.

I dipped my hands in the bucket and rinsed her feet clean, stroking them in turn gently from heel to toe and pressing my hand up under her high arches. There was only the odd speck here and there on her calves, but I washed and rinsed them too. I breathed on my hands to warm them, then stroked her feet dry. When I had finished I held a foot in each hand, pressed them with my thumbs over her insteps, my fingers under her arches, and looked up for the first time. Her head was back against the wall, her eyes shut. She opened her eyes, smiled, leaned forward and touched my cheek.

'You are my most useful servant. Now I can ride back in comfort,' and she put on her stockings and boots.

I followed her out from the dovecote, helped her into the saddle and watched until she was out of sight. At the top of the hill she turned, gave a wave and rode on.

I had never touched a woman intimately before, never seen a woman's legs, never stroked a woman's skin. And while I tried to persuade myself that washing Blanche's feet was in the tradition of courtly love, my body told me something entirely different. I went back to my house in the village on fire and lay down on my bed. There I sought relief in my imagination, taking Blanche against the wall of the dovecote while the pigeons fluttered and cooed above us.

There was no one I could confide in. Etienne, my friend and rival, would have been envious. He would not have believed that this was a simple duty, simply performed. And he would have been right. I did not want to share with him the images of Blanche's feet and ankles and calves or tell him of the softness of her skin. These belonged to me.

I could not bring myself to tell Guillaume Authie either when next he came to hear our Confessions. For the first time I had something to confess, and yet I was unable to get the words out.

For a week or more I spent more time at the dovecote than was strictly necessary, hoping that Blanche would visit me again. She did not return, and at the feast at the end of the week she treated me as she had always done, with gentle affection, as though I was a son or a younger brother. I took confidence from the fact that she didn't mention, or joke about, her visit to the inside of the dovecote. I hoped that was because my attention to her feet had more than a routine significance. I closed my eyes many times every day and thought of her foot between my hands, her elegant toes, her soft skin. It was a torment, a delight.

In the spring Armand, who until then had ignored his father's traditions, organised three days of hunting for wild boar. He asked his neighbours to bring their hounds; each day we quartered the woods with sixty men and almost as many hounds. We left our horses and crossbows at home. The boar's charge was too swift, too fierce for more than a single shot. There was no chance of stopping a four-hundred-pound boar with a crossbow bolt even if the shot was accurate. We used strong ten-foot ash spears with a sharp iron point and a crossbar three feet from the tip. It was not unknown for a charging boar to break the crossbar.

We killed twenty-two boars in three days' hunting; the boars loved the acorns from the oak trees and they were plentiful that year. There was no place for the faint-hearted, men or hounds. We lost half a dozen dogs, and three of the hunters had severe wounds from charging boars which they had failed to take on the point of their spears.

I was one of the wounded, and it was my own fault. I had seen no boars on the first day, but had taken two on the second, kneeling down to receive the charge and keeping my point straight. They were brave beasts, evenly matched with a man on foot, and I was happy that I had been steady facing the charge.

On the third day a group of a dozen hounds had a heavy boar at bay, a determined beast. He had already gashed two hounds, which had retired whimpering, and he seemed ready to take on the rest. I dropped my spear and drew my sword, thinking he wouldn't charge me through the mass of snarling, barking hounds. I was wrong. He came for me as I walked forward, tossing two hounds out of the way; my sword caught him on his right side, and he returned the favour as he charged past. A boar's curved tusks don't seem very threatening – a large pair would be no more than ten inches long – but they are razor-sharp. I had an eight-inch gash along the top of my thigh that went through to the bone, luckily missing an artery on the way.

Two other hunters, one of them Etienne, had heard the cry of the hounds and arrived within minutes. They bandaged the gash and staunched the bleeding. We were close to Roqueville and they carried me home sitting between them on an improvised chair made from a couple of stout branches. They left me on my bed, Etienne saying he would tell them at the castle, and there I lay, uneasily remembering my father's fate, the wound throbbing, my head aching, drifting in and out of consciousness.

Blanche arrived in the early evening with her daughter. I was making little sense by then; Blanche ignored my foolish modesty and pulled up my undershirt to reveal the wound.

'This will hurt,' she said, 'but it has to be clean.' I managed to stifle most of my groans. She had brought strips of clean linen to swab and dress the cut, and when she was happy it was clean her daughter Stephanie smeared the wound with a sweet-smelling yellow ointment.

'Now for the sewing. This will hurt more, but Stephanie is a skilful seamstress.' Blanche pulled the edges of the wound together while Stephanie used a sailmaker's needle and strong thread to sew the gash together. It was painful, so painful that I couldn't concentrate on the closeness of Blanche's hair and shoulders and waist as she bent over me.

'You'll live,' said Blanche. 'It's no worse than some of the wounds Bernard brought home from the tournaments. You're lucky the boar didn't turn and come back for more.'

'He had my sword in his guts,' I said. 'They found him dead a hundred yards further on.'

'You're getting better already,' and she smiled, gathered up her things and left with her daughter.

Stephanie came back two days later without her mother. Etienne was with me, and watched as Stephanie inspected the wound, put her face close, sniffed and pronounced it clean.

'You'll be up in two or three days. Make sure you change

the dressings every day and keep the wound dry.'

I was grateful, and said so, masking my disappointment that she was not Blanche. Etienne was impressed by her competence.

'She'll make someone a good wife,' he said and blushed when I told him he shouldn't hold back. Stephanie was her mother's daughter: the same black hair, the same brown eyes, the same slender figure. But somehow – a horse-breeder would blame the sire's bloodline, and Bernard had not been a good-looking man – it all came together in a way that you might at best describe as handsome. But not beautiful, not as Blanche was beautiful.

I sensed that Stephanie was well aware of the long shadow her mother cast, and made up for her lack of beauty with a determined, no-nonsense efficiency. This appealed to Etienne, so I was glad I had refrained from pointing out to him that Stephanie hadn't inherited her mother's looks or easy manner.

As predicted, I was up by the end of the week, with a slight limp that soon wore off. A week later Stephanie had arranged to come by to take out the stitches, which was almost as painful as the original sewing. I had told Etienne I needed support, and he was again taken by the way Stephanie dealt with me.

'You'll hardly know it happened in a year's time,' she said to us both. She looked surprised when Etienne offered to ride with her back to the castle.

I continued to spend time at the dovecote, and Blanche did return, this time with Stephanie and Armand.

'We were passing,' she said, not dismounting. 'I hope you're fully recovered.'

'Thanks to your skill and Stephanie's sewing,' I said with a little bow.

'What's it like inside the dovecote?' asked Stephanie, looking at her mother.

My heart skipped a beat, then Blanche replied. 'Messy, I imagine. Ask our pigeon master.'

'No place for a woman,' I said. 'Knee-deep in pigeon droppings.'

I was pleased when Blanche smiled at my reply. It meant something to me that we had a secret between us.

It was a good summer in the valley that year. It rained enough in the spring to provide plenty of grass for hay and for grazing, and the River Baise was high. It was full of trout and the occasional pike. In sunny weather the pike would bask on the surface of the water, and it was then possible to kill them with a crossbow bolt at close range. I attached twelve feet of line to a hole drilled in the end of the bolt after seeing my first transfixed pike disappear down the river.

The pike were delicious to eat, and much appreciated by Blanche and by Guillaume Authie when he visited us. I never understood why fish was acceptable to a Perfect while meat and eggs were ruled out. Guillaume explained to me once that it was because fish mated without contact, which seemed an odd and unconvincing reason.

Etienne and I rode regularly through the valley, and sometimes I would stay the night with him and his mother at Barraigne. We were cantering along a ride in the woods when he pulled up and signalled me to stop.

'I need your advice, your help,' he said. 'I want to marry Stephanie.'

'I thought Blanche was the woman you admired. Above all others, I remember you declaring.'

Etienne blushed.

'Only as her knight, her faithful servant. You feel the same.'

'I do,' I lied. 'So ask Blanche, ask Armand for Stephanie's hand.'

'She's the daughter of a great lord. I'm a poor knight.'

'Nonsense. You're young, vigorous, handsome.'

Etienne looked pleased.

'And you hold Barraigne and the land around it,' I continued. 'You're well born. I remember you had six quarterings on your shield at Chauvency. It took an age for the herald to describe them all.'

'Four of them are from my mother.'

'What difference does that make? Stephanie rides with you often, likes you well enough. Who are her other admirers?'

I knew the answer to my question. In our valley visitors were rare; Etienne and I were the only suitable young men around.

'Be brave. Ask for her.'

I prodded Etienne gently for the next ten days, and eventually he managed to take Armand aside in the tilt-yard and put the question to him.

Armand looked surprised.

'I'll have to ask my mother,' he said. 'And Stephanie, of course.'

The next time I saw Etienne he was beaming.

'They've said yes, they've said yes. We're to be married in a month. You're a good friend and gave me good advice.'

The wedding celebrations lasted a week. The stew pond was emptied, the dovecote's squabs taken for an enormous pigeon pie, and the week before we had killed a dozen roe-deer for the table. There were archery contests and a little tournament with blunted lances and wooden swords. The armorial banners of the guests fluttered from new flagpoles in the courtyard. In the evening there were songs from the visiting troubadours, on this occasion paying tribute not to Blanche but to her daughter. Etienne looked happy all week.

It was hard for me to see much of Blanche, surrounded as she was by wedding guests. One evening I succeeded in dancing opposite her and revelled in her smile and her touch. When the dance was over I bowed, knelt, kissed her hand and looked down at her feet, encased in golden slippers under a long white gown. When I looked up she blushed, something I had never seen her do before, smiled and pulled me to my feet.

Our lives returned to normal once all the guests had departed, although my riding days with Etienne were over, as he spent all his time transforming Barraigne into a place fit for his bride. He and Stephanie were both Credentes, and when I stayed with them a month later we had a long discussion about our faith.

'Not all of us believe everything we're taught,' said Etienne.

'I do,' said Stephanie firmly.

'Even the Endura?' I asked.

'Even the Endura.'

'You know what happened to our armourer's wife? When she became very ill a Perfect was sent for, she was blessed and persuaded to undergo the Endura. Then she rallied and the armourer insisted on giving her bread and water, even though he was threatened with hellfire.'

'That doesn't sound like Authie. Did she recover?'

'She did recover, no thanks to Cathars. And it wasn't Authie; he'd have had more sense. The whole valley knows about it.'

The story, and others like it, spread beyond our valley, and the convenient fiction that we were all good Catholics became harder to maintain. In Rome there was a new Pope, in Pamiers a new Bishop, in Toulouse new Inquisitors. Stories of torture and burnings were widespread. There was a rumour that Minerve was under siege, and later Authie brought the news that the town had been captured. He told us that the eighty knights defending the town were hanged, as was Count Aimery; the victors threw Aimery's sister Geralda down a well and stoned her to death. All the Cathars in the town were burned at the stake.

It was clear that our valley would not be spared. The Bishop of Pamiers sent for our priest; he was not replaced and did not return. Later we heard that he had been tortured.

'He was a good man,' said Armand over dinner. He had asked all his knights to a council of war. 'But he won't have been able to stand up to torture – how many of us could? He will have told the Inquisitors that none of us took his Communion bread, or went to him for Confession.'

The table was silent until Etienne asked, 'What do you think they will do next?'

'They will send for me and my mother,' said Armand. 'We won't answer that summons, and sooner or later they will attack Roqueville.'

He showed an unexpected determination that impressed us all.

'There's no point in negotiating. Look what happened at Minerve. We need to prepare for a long siege. Prepare now.'

3

The Inquisitor

The Inquisitor

AFTER AN ARDUOUS and unproductive morning my clerk Jean and I were sitting in my small library. The room had bookcases on three walls and a generous window on the fourth that overlooked one of Carcassonne's many squares. The square was deserted. No one willingly passed the doors of the Inquisition unless there was no alternative. We needed to be feared, and I had succeeded in that part of my mission through relentless questioning and condign punishments. It had been my idea to dig up the corpses of dead Cathars and burn them; if we could reach beyond the grave we would have less difficulty with the living.

The fear was, of course, accompanied by hatred, and I am sorry to say that it was not only the heretics who hated us, but also those otherwise good Catholics who for too long had been used to a quiet life. I was in the process of changing that.

I asked my clerk to read out the testimony of the morning's witness. Robert Duvernoy had been accused of communicating with the dead, and he himself had denounced several as heretics, including some members of his close family. He had not been tortured; there was nothing he would not say or do in order to escape punishment. So he was useless as a witness, and I dozed as the clerk read his notes slowly back to me, paying closer attention when I heard his sharp intake of breath.

'My lord, this section is truly frightening,' and he read on:

'I have often seen dead Jews, some of them walking backwards. I have never seen them go into a church. They wander through the roads, not among Christians, walking bent like pigs. I could tell they were Jews, because they smelled and stayed apart from the others. They practised their cult on the mountains; we Christians laughed at them and called them dogs.

Nevertheless, many of them were saved, as Mary would intercede on their behalf with the Lord. He would spare them, because they belonged to Mary's race.'

When he had finished the passage he looked at me, clearly expecting a comment.

'Jews will not be saved unless they abjure their faith and become good Catholics. But where did he get the notion about dead Jews walking backwards?'

'Many people have seen this,' said Jean.

'Including you?'

He looked frightened and uncertain for a moment.

'No. But I have talked to many who have seen what Robert Duvernoy has seen.'

I got up, left the room without replying, went downstairs and called for my guards. Ignorance and superstition are not the exclusive preserve of heretics, I thought as I walked round the square.

I was a reluctant Inquisitor. I had been a contented member of my Order, and happy when I became Abbot of Flaran, a post I had held for eight years. Then the call came from the Bishop.

'We need a good theologian who can argue with the heretics,' he told me. 'And you have the reputation of a man not easily deceived.'

I was contented among my manuscripts, my treatise on 'The Destiny of the Souls of the Departed' was only half finished, and I was in the middle of a long debate with William of Ockham. I was well aware that two groups of Inquisitors had been murdered – Peter of Castelnau many years ago when crossing the Rhône, and most recently Stephen of St-Thibery and William Arnald at Avignonet. I might have withstood the Bishop's pressure, but when he produced a letter from the Pope himself asking me 'to pick out the tares of heresy from the wheat of religion' I felt unable to refuse.

It was a good analogy. As a farmer's son I knew how difficult it was to pick out tares from healthy wheat, and I had been long enough in the Languedoc to know how Cathars had infiltrated our Church and perverted our doctrine. They had been allowed to flourish for too long. This was, I had to admit at the risk of the sin of pride, a task for which I was well equipped.

Four times round the square, flanked by my silent guards, did me good and cleared my head of all that 'dead Jews walking backwards' nonsense. Some stories I was prepared to tolerate, not because I believed them, but because they deterred good Catholics from the Cathar heresy. So I did what I could to encourage the rumours that Cathars were sodomites, sacrificed small children and fornicated on Christian altars. As, for all I knew, they may have done.

When I returned to my library I began the final chapter of my Inquisitor's Manual. My success is directly related to the techniques of questioning that I have developed during the last five years, and I wish my knowledge and experience to be preserved and disseminated. Many of my colleagues think it is a matter of asking simple, direct questions that need only to be answered yes or no. They are unwilling to devote the time to the argument which a genuine conversion requires, preferring to rely on the threat of further torture and the stake. Then they are surprised when, two years later, the same suspect reappears.

I have developed a little dialogue that demonstrates how persistent questioning can force a heretic into a corner from which he cannot escape. It goes as follows:

Q. You are accused as a heretic, that you do not believe and teach that which the Holy Church believes.

Lord, I am innocent. I have never held any faith other than that of true Christianity.

Q. You call your faith Christian, for you consider ours as false and heretical. But have you ever believed in a faith other than that which the Roman Church holds to be true?

I believe the True Faith which the Roman Church believes, which you preach to us.

Q. Let us test the accusation. Do you believe in God the Father, and the Son, and the Holy Ghost?

I believe.

Q. Do you believe in Christ born of the Virgin, suffered, risen, and ascended to heaven?

I believe.

Q. Do you believe the bread and wine in the Mass is changed into the body and blood of Christ?

I believe whatever you order me to believe.

Q. Will you swear that you have never learned anything contrary to the faith which the Roman Church holds to be true?

If I ought to swear, I will willingly swear.

Q. I don't wish to force you to swear, as you believe oaths to be unlawful, and thus you will transfer the sin to me who forced you.

Why should I swear if you do not order me to?

Q. So that you may remove the suspicion of being a heretic.

Then he will stumble along as if he cannot repeat the words, avoiding an absolute oath. If the words are there, they are turned around so that he does not swear, and yet appears to have sworn. A vigorous Inquisitor must not allow himself to be deceived in this way, but proceed until he makes the heretic publicly abjure heresy. If he is subsequently found to have sworn falsely, he may be abandoned to the secular arm.

I have achieved great success through this approach, which recognises two things: that the Cathars believe themselves to be Christians, and that they will not swear an oath.

Questioning on its own is not always successful, so I am not opposed to torture. The Pope in his Bull 'Ad Extirpanda' made it clear that this is a legitimate weapon in the battle against heresy. Torture, however, often achieves little more than the production of whatever the suspect believes will stop the pain. I subject many of my suspects to half an hour of the rack and the strappado without any questioning. This gives them a taste of what awaits them if they do not answer me fully and truthfully.

Most of those who appear before us are convicted of heresy and rightly so, but relatively few, perhaps one in five, suffer the ultimate punishment. I regard it as my duty to attend the executions. The gleeful and vindictive mob who turn up in great numbers to watch the burnings need to know that it was I who sent the victim to the stake.

'Does it not horrify you, the screams, the struggle to break free of the bonds, the smell of burning flesh?' the Bishop asked me once over dinner. He was too fond of good food and a quiet life, and had been heard to express sympathy for elements of Cathar doctrine.

'I am not unmoved, but my sorrow is for our failure to persuade a heretic back into the path of righteousness. It is medicine ordained by mercy. The pain of the stake is as nothing to the pain of eternal hellfire that awaits these unhappy men and women.'

I said men and women, but where possible I avoid questioning the latter. I have in the past been often tormented by the sin of lust, and in my student days in Paris fell from grace only too often. Indeed, it was partly due to the need to remove myself far from temptations of this kind that I became a Dominican. In the enclosed world of the Abbey of Flaran I felt safe. I was safe, although the occasional succubus continued to appear in my dreams.

In Carcassonne it was different. I saw women every day, and there were many who appeared before us accused of heresy. Fortunately most were old and ugly. The younger ones fell into two categories – those who would never forswear their beliefs, and those who would do anything to avoid punishment, and were able to make it clear to me, without speaking, what that might involve.

It was a great temptation. The contrast between me, robed and sitting in the Inquisitor's chair, and the trembling, weeping creature brought before me after half an hour on the rack, clad in the white shift that we give them, had a strong erotic force. I found that the best way to avoid such an occasion of sin was to absent myself from it, and to let one of my colleagues, either more thick-skinned or less concerned about the sin of lust, to take over. I often reminded myself of the words in Ecclesiastes, *I find woman more bitter than death; she is a snare, her heart a net, her charms are chains. He is pleasing to God who eludes her.* I knew how easily I might be ensnared, netted, enchained. I wanted to remain pleasing to God.

Nevertheless I enjoyed my work, God's work. I delegated the interrogation of the women that were brought before us, and in any case the great majority of suspects were men. I obtained most satisfaction from those cases where I was able to obtain not simply a confession of error but a genuine decision to return to the true path of faith, even though these were not common.

The most interesting of the heretics was Baruch the Jew, who had been baptised, but subsequently returned to Judaism. Baruch's original conversion was in Toulouse, when a gang of shepherds, who had killed 152 Jews, had been brought there for trial. The shepherds were freed by the mob, and together they rampaged through the streets to the Jewish Quarter, where, according to Baruch's original testimony to the Bishop:

'They arrived at my house shouting, "Death to the Jews. Be baptised or we will kill you."

'I replied I would rather be baptised than die. They took me to the Church of St Stephen, where I saw the mob kill the Jew Asser from Tarascon and two others. I was dragged before the priest at the font and told to say that I came in good faith to Baptism. So I said the necessary words, was baptised with water and given the name John.

Then some priests took me home, and there I found my books torn to pieces, my money stolen and only seven pieces of cloth left. Some other pieces of cloth, which did not belong to me as they had been pawned, and my silk coverlet, had all been taken. The murder and pillage of the Jews went on until late that same night.'

The Bishop accepted this testimony without further questioning. He was only too willing to accept Baruch's Baptism at face value. Six months later Baruch was arrested and brought before me, accused of reverting to his former faith. As he freely admitted to being a Jew there was no need to torture him. He claimed that his Baptism was invalid; it had taken place under the threat of death, so he had not been required to perform the ritual of purification to return to his faith.

My interrogation and argument went on for many weeks. Baruch's knowledge of the Scriptures was profound, almost the equal of mine, and he was genuine in his questioning and argument.

Our longest and most difficult dispute was whether the Messiah promised in the Law had already come, and was indeed God and man, composed of divinity and true humanity.

In the end Baruch, defeated by the force of my arguments, agreed. It was then easy to show him by the Law and the Prophets that Christ was conceived and born of the Virgin, that he had suffered death for us and our salvation, that he descended to hell and awoke the third day, was ascended to heaven and will come again to judge the living and the dead. Although he resisted the sacrament of the Mass for a while, and it was difficult to demonstrate to him the immortality of the human body after the Resurrection, in the end he consented to all of this.

After three weeks, in a moment of triumph for the faith and for me, he said in front of the Bishop (whose earlier questioning of Baruch had proved entirely superficial) and the assembled dignitaries of the church and the city:

> 'I believe and confess that the Catholic faith, its articles and sacraments are all true, and I abjure the Jewish perfidy, its superstitions and ceremonies and I will pursue all heretics, especially those belonging to the sect to which I held.'

There was a spontaneous cry of *Deo gratias* from several members of the congregation when they heard these words. Afterwards at lunch the Bishop was less gracious.

'Almost four weeks to obtain the so-called conversion of a single old Jew – it would have been simpler and quicker to send him to the stake.'

I did not consider this remark worthy of a reply.

In spite of this success, which became widely known among the faithful, progress was slow. The obstacles were many – the time required to conduct proper investigations, the poor calibre of some of my fellow Inquisitors, lethargy among the clergy. Denunciations were often motivated by spite or the desire to settle old scores.

Perhaps the greatest obstacle was the attitude of many noblemen, who saw the Cathar heresy as the perfect justification to avoid paying tithes. The income of the Church in the Languedoc had diminished by a third in the twenty years before I arrived. Although it had begun to rise again it was still far below the level required to maintain bishops, priests, cathedrals and churches and pay a proper contribution to Rome. Many nobles resented the power of Toulouse, feared France and were in effect presiding over little kingdoms where they made their own laws. And their own religion.

I was appointed soon after the Massacre at Avignonet. This was widely rumoured to be the work of Bernard de Roqueville, who had paid no tithes for fifteen years. He was the count in charge of the kind of little kingdom I have just described. The priest in his valley reported good attendance at Mass and no evidence of heretical practices. He told us that he had never seen a Perfect at Roqueville. This seemed unlikely, given Bernard's aversion to tithes.

The expedition after Avignonet, which I accompanied, was entirely successful; an earlier, smaller raid had only come back with cattle. This time we sent a force of over three hundred crusaders, commanded by Guy de Montfort, nephew of the great Simon. The show of force was enough to avoid bloodshed and obtain, through a negotiated settlement, all that was due to the Church from the last fifteen years in gold or in land. And I insisted that Bernard perform an appropriate penance in Toulouse, which almost brought the negotiations to a halt. I stood firm and eventually it was agreed.

On the way back we installed one of our crusaders in a little castle called Beaufort, where the leader of the band responsible for Avignonet had lived; he died from his wounds not long after the massacre. Beaufort and his land were rightly forfeited. We were able to establish through some forceful questioning where the man had been buried.

We dug up what was left of his body and for good measure that of his wife and burned the pair of them for the heretics they were. We used damp wood to make a great pyre, not because the pitiful bundle of bones and scraps of flesh required it, but because I wanted the smoke to be seen for miles around and recognised as the implacable retribution of the Church.

Perhaps more important than the confiscation of land and gold, although these took precedence in the Bishop's mind, was the public humiliation of Bernard de Roqueville in the Cathedral in Toulouse. Almost naked, he had to crawl from the entrance to the high altar, all the while being thrashed by the Bishop, who plainly enjoyed his work.

I was one of those watching. Most of the onlookers, who drowned the prayers and chanting by their shouts, were moved not by religious fervour but by the same voyeur's instincts that made them turn out in great numbers to watch a burning. In this case they had the added pleasure of watching a nobleman reduced at the end of his crawl to a bleeding, whimpering wreck. It was an exemplary punishment, and Bernard died a year later, as much from shame as from illness.

In the Cathedral I stood opposite Bernard's wife Blanche, their son Armand, Stephanie, their daughter, and twenty of his knights, all of whom had been forced to watch. I studied Armand de Roqueville closely; he showed no signs of remorse or repentance, but stood clenching and unclenching his fists, muttering to himself. I doubted these were prayers.

Blanche and her daughter shut their eyes after the first blow, and covered their ears when Bernard cried out. Blanche de Roqueville was a famous beauty, much praised by the troubadours, and, I could see, rightly so. Even in distress her face was beautiful, and I had to turn away my glance, close my own eyes and pray for forgiveness for the sin of lust, not for the first time. Nor the last.

Despite the fines, despite this penance, despite the death of Bernard, the rumours that Roqueville was a nest of heretics continued and strengthened. I decided to send for the valley's priest, in spite of his regular reports that all was well. He arrived looking sleek and confident; all that vanished after an hour on the rack. He admitted what we had long suspected – that although attendance at his church was excellent no one took the Sacrament and he never heard Confessions.

He also said that there were regular visits to the castle by Guillaume Authie and other Perfects. He knew they were expected when fish from the stew ponds were brought up and he was told that his presence at dinner was not required. He said that the most fervent Cathar was Blanche de Roqueville.

He was a pathetic, craven creature when we had finished with him, concerned only to save his own skin. He asked to return to Roqueville.

'By all means,' I said. 'But only after ten years of repentance in the dungeons. Think yourself lucky to avoid the fire, and prepare yourself through prayer and penance for the next world.'

His evidence made it clear that Roqueville was a hotbed of heresy and could no longer be ignored. We sent a messenger demanding that Armand and Blanche present themselves to us for questioning; the messenger returned, having been rudely treated, with the reply that neither had any intention of complying. This was no surprise, and led to our decision to capture Roqueville and deal decisively with the Cathars in that heretical valley. For too long we had allowed the Church to be undermined and cheated.

The Bishop

I FOUND OUR DOMINICAN difficult to fathom. He was tall, dark-haired, a beaky Norman nose, and he had, I noticed both at the table and in prayer, long and well-kept fingers, which he would clasp and unclasp as he spoke.

He had been a good Abbot at Flaran, and there was never a breath of scandal about that abbey. His scholarship flowered there. He engaged in writing and disputation at a level that, to be honest, was well above my head, and it was that intellectual rigour that made him my predecessor's and Rome's choice to lead the Inquisition in the Languedoc.

It was said that he had been wild when a theological student in Paris, and I could see, by the way he looked at them, that he loved women. As do I, though my shape and button nose, *Deo gratias*, spared me the occasions of sin that often presented themselves to our Inquisitor through the nature of his work.

He always seemed tightly controlled. He took little pleasure in food or wine, and I always felt silently criticised when we dined together, as he would drink only water, push away his plate half finished and watch in silent disapproval when I drank a second or third glass of our excellent wine.

'You might as well be Cathar,' I once said to him. 'They believe that our world was created by the Devil, and has no substance, although they seem to survive well enough.'

He looked shocked. 'My abstinence isn't a turning away

from the real world, which I know God created. I see abstinence as a gift to God, and as a way of disciplining myself. The Cathars believe – well, you know what they believe.' To prove me wrong, he poured himself a glass of wine, although I noticed it remained unfinished at the end of the meal.

He was a patient and thorough Inquisitor, rarely relying on torture, preferring to use the considerable powers of his intellect to reason heretics back into the path of righteousness. This was impressive, though time-consuming – as I pointed out, half an hour on the rack produced a conversion in a morning, whereas he would happily take several days to achieve the same result.

His great disputational triumph over Baruch the Jew took even longer, took weeks. Time wasted, in my opinion, and I told him so.

'I would have let him burn.'

'I have saved him from the flames of this world and from the fires of hell in the next,' and he smiled, then quoted those overused words from St Luke's Gospel: *There is joy over one sinner that repenteth, more than...* I didn't allow him to finish.

Nevertheless, irritated though I was, I admired his intellectual rigour, his dedication and his self-control. When he later fell from grace I was glad that after all his feet were made from the same clay as mine, and yet deeply disappointed that he was no better a man than me.

Of course in some ways I was just as forceful as the Inquisitor in defending the Faith, although my methods were less reliant on intellect and the powers of persuasion. My greatest success was as effective as his conversion of Baruch. I had received a message from Esclarmonde de Fauga, widely rumoured to be a heretic, that she was on her deathbed and wished to see the Bishop. When I called on her the same day it was clear that a mistake, fatal for her, had been made. She expected the Cathar Bishop, was horrified to see me and stubbornly persisted in her heresy.

So I sent for the magistrate, who pronounced summary judgement on her. She was carried on her bed to the Pré du Comte and forthwith burned at the stake. This was more effective as a warning of the dangers of heresy than Baruch's conversion had been, and took less than a day, not weeks, to achieve. I did not attend the burning, but returned to the refectory, gave thanks to God and to St Dominic and ended a good day's work with an excellent meal. We had oysters from northern France, lamb from the Pyrenees and grapes from my own garden, all gifts of God.

4

The Siege

Francois

As armand had predicted, a messenger arrived a month later from Carcassonne. On behalf of his masters he demanded that Armand and Blanche present themselves before the Inquisition to answer allegations, 'from many reliable witnesses', that they were both Cathars and had encouraged the practice of heresy in and around Roqueville. There was no mention of our unfortunate priest in the summons, but the messenger told us that he had confessed and was now in the hands of the civil arm for sentencing.

The messenger was not treated with the normal courtesy shown to our visitors. He and his four armed guards were kept in the courtyard, refused food and drink and told to water themselves and their horses in the river.

Armand's reply to the summons was brief.

'Tell your masters,' he said, 'that I and my mother have no intention of coming to Carcassonne. We have seen what happens to those who appear before the Inquisition, and we have no intention of joining their number. My father's penance and the gold and land you extracted from him should have settled matters for good. Get you gone.'

I watched Blanche as Armand spoke; she looked proud of her son. The messenger, a young priest of about my age, appeared frightened and expected further punishment. He was relieved when he was allowed to depart unharmed, although we heard later that he claimed he had been beaten.

Immediately we began preparations for the siege we knew must come. It was late summer, so we had time to fill our grain stores and slaughter more cattle and cure more meat than usual. To my great sorrow, all but a dozen of my pigeons were killed and the stew pond emptied. I was able to persuade Armand to let me take those birds that were spared to an old disused dovecote in the top of one of Roqueville's four towers. They became used to their new surroundings after I had confined and fed them there for three weeks, and they later began to breed.

All our meat and fish was dried, salted and hung in the long storerooms that flanked one of the walls of the inner courtyard. Rough huts were erected for all those who lived outside the castle walls. I was given my old room, but I had to share it with two others; later I would move into the former stables.

We spent some time discussing the water supply.

'Our well has never dried up, even in the drought years,' said Armand. 'It's clean spring water, inside the walls.'

'What feeds it? Where does the water come from?' asked Etienne.

'There's an underground spring.'

'Could they cut it off at source?'

'There is no source. It's all under the earth, hidden in the hills.'

Gradually Roqueville was turned into a small village; the tilt-yard, archery butts, riding school and pleasure gardens became space for men, animals and arms. Inside the castle we mustered thirty knights, although six of these were too old or infirm to be of much use, about a hundred men and the same number again of women and children. Anyone who wanted to leave was not discouraged from going, but there were few who had anywhere else to go. It was a daunting task to house and feed such numbers within the castle walls.

'We need to hold out for four months,' said Armand. 'After that the crusaders will lose heart and their soldiers will start to go home. Winters in our valley can be fierce. They will bring carpenters, blacksmiths, engineers as well as archers and knights and greedy priests. They'll all need to be fed. We've left them nothing to live off; everything will have to come in on their wagons.'

I asked him about the horses.

'We can keep ten at the most. The rest we will kill for meat.'

Etienne suggested that we should try to ambush the crusaders at the narrow entrance to the valley below Beaufort.

'That's only possible if they send an advance guard. We can expect a substantial force, bigger than last time. We have no chance of defeating them in the field,' said Geoffrey. Armand agreed.

Etienne and I were given the task of preparing a plan; this we did, but its success depended entirely on surprise, the value of which I had learned at Avignonet. And on reliable intelligence about the arrival of the crusaders, so we posted good men well beyond the valley entrance to warn us of their approach.

The warning came in September, a month after the corn had been harvested. Our scouts estimated that their total force numbered about three hundred, moving towards Roqueville at the slow pace dictated by their supply wagons.

'Perhaps a hundred knights, or at least mounted men. They have half a dozen priests chanting as they march along. With an advance guard, forty strong, half on horseback, half on foot, a mile in front of their main force.'

Fifteen of us, all well mounted, trotted down to the wooded area beyond Beaufort where we had buried my father. There I saw for the first time the great circle of scorched earth where they had burned the bodies of my parents. The two empty graves were open to the sky and half full of water.

Our instructions had been agreed with Armand.

'A quick attack, kill as many as you can, and withdraw before the main force arrives.'

The advance guard were taken by surprise. We were concealed by the crest of a little hill, charging down it as they passed across fifty yards of open ground. The slope gave us added impetus as we struck into them with our lances; it was the first and last time all that practice in the tilt-yard was of any value. We killed ten or twelve of their mounted men and perhaps six foot soldiers, although the rest of them scattered at our charge and ran back to join their main force. We did not pursue them, withdrawing after twenty minutes of hand-to-hand fighting on horseback. We lost only one man and two horses, such was the value of surprise.

'That will teach them something,' said Etienne as we cantered back to Roqueville.

'They have enough men and horses to replace the ones we killed,' I said. 'But it will show them that we mean business, that we won't surrender easily.'

'Not like last time when they took Count Bernard to Toulouse.'

'Not like last time.'

As we arrived back at Roqueville the drawbridge was

lowered; Stephanie was in the courtyard, relieved to see that Etienne was safe. Only a small cut on his forehead and a bloody forearm showed he had been in a battle.

'Stephanie is having a baby,' Etienne had told me on our ride back. I told him he should not have come on our sortie.

'I had to. It was my idea, remember?'

Blanche was there too; she held my horse's head as I dismounted, put her hand on my shoulder and said, 'I am happy to see you back safe, happy that you won't need my nursing skills,' and moved on to speak to the other horsemen. At that moment I wished I had been wounded; my shoulder burned from her touch for the rest of the day.

Three hours after our return the main body of crusaders arrived at the head of our valley. They kept a respectful distance from our walls. Armand had told everyone, men, women and children, to man the battlements.

'We want them to believe we are three hundred strong,' he said. 'They won't be able to tell women and boys from armed men at that distance. You did well to surprise the advance guard for the loss of only one man.'

He looked at Etienne and me.

'That's our first and last sortie; we need to keep our force intact. They will try to starve us out. They won't succeed.'

We watched them set up camp in and around our village, using their now empty supply wagons as a wall between the village and the castle. They kept their horses in lines not far from the river. There were many crusaders, over three hundred it seemed, although it was hard to be precise. In the evening we could hear the priests chanting as they celebrated Mass in front of a large wooden cross they had brought with them. They did not use our church, perhaps because they regarded it as tainted with heresy.

The next morning a small party emerged from the village and came to within a hundred yards of our walls under the protection of a white flag. Their herald blew a fanfare on his trumpet, shouted words we could not hear and then they waited. After an hour Armand and a dozen men-at-arms emerged carrying a white flag and went to meet them. The meeting did not last long.

'It wasn't a negotiation. Guy de Montfort set out his demands – my mother, my sister and me to the Inquisition. The rest would be offered the chance to repent and return to the True Faith. I told them we were the Good Christians, we didn't rely on the sword and the flame to show we were right. We knew they were in our valley for money and land. We had paid them once and they would get nothing more.'

This was our last close contact with the crusaders for many days. They initially concentrated in the village, then spread out in a vast semicircle surrounding the front and sides of Roqueville. And sat there, doing nothing.

I was surprised at the strain of waiting for something to happen. Etienne, always eager for action, suggested a quick sortie on horseback; we still had eight horses, although all the rest, including Blanche's beloved grey palfrey, had been killed.

Armand would have none of it.

'They are ready for us now, and this time we could lose five good men. Remember, they would like us to come out. It is a war of nerves, a war of waiting.'

Waiting produced disagreement and conflict within our walls, often over trivial matters. Although there was plenty of water from the well, food was strictly rationed and shared out twice a day. One of the men-at-arms was caught stealing from the storerooms and was publicly flogged in the courtyard. Arguments broke out over trivial matters: a piece of bread, a bottle of wine, an encroachment on a bed space. The rota of manning the walls, four hours on, eight hours off, took its toll, especially if you were on guard from midnight to four in the morning. The eyes constantly played tricks and created imaginary bodies of men advancing in the darkness. There were several false alarms.

I saw Blanche every day; she lived in the keep, while I had moved into the stables, now no longer required for their original purpose once we had killed most of our horses. She and Stephanie would walk round the courtyard every day, and I would cross their paths as often as I dared. Blanche always seemed glad to see me and greeted me warmly. She looked careworn, and thin, as we all did on our restricted diet, but she still retained the beauty so many troubadours had praised in song. I felt I had become her protector, not of course on my own; I longed to be more than this and to close the chaste and courtly distance that separated us. There was no such opportunity, and the memory of washing her feet, on which I had drawn many times for solace, had lost its relieving power.

One morning the crusaders advanced their longbowmen to within eighty yards of the gate and sent an arc of arrows over the walls and into the courtyard. We cleared the courtyard quickly, and the only casualties were a dead bullock and one of our men struck in the shoulder, but it reminded us of the importance of keeping alert.

They had no siege engines. They had tried to bring a massive trebuchet from Carcassonne, but it was stuck in the boggy entrance to the valley.

'Sooner or later they'll dismantle it and bring it close enough to batter our walls – and then we'll have to come out,' said Armand.

It was possible, though dangerous, to leave the castle by night through a small postern gate and cross the crusaders' lines. Even with three hundred men they were not able to surround the castle with an impenetrable ring, and there were big gaps in their lines. We sent out scouts and learned that the crusaders were, as Armand had predicted, bringing the big trebuchet up the valley in pieces.

'They call it The Bad Neighbour. It can throw three hundred pounds of stones over four hundred yards, well out of our range. Our walls wouldn't last more than a week,' said Armand. 'It will take them a month at least to bring it into position. Then we'll need a response.'

After ten days of inactivity we could see trees being felled in the woods by the river, and we heard the noise of hammering and sawing by day and by night. They were building a trevise in which to mount a battering ram.

'First they'll use the trevise as cover to fill in the moat, then haul the ram close enough to start on our main gate.'

They brought the trevise up at night and began to fill in our dry moat with gorse and brushwood. We were able to burn this, but not the stones and earth which followed. After three days, during which we were able to pick off fifteen of their men for the loss of three of our own, they had a solid platform for the trevise. Inside the structure they had slung a great oak beam with an iron tip and with this they battered our gates. The courtyard was filled with its thudding noise, and the gates creaked and groaned. We threw burning bundles of twigs and brushwood onto the trevise, but the roof had been covered with hides soaked in vinegar and we could do no more than scorch it. Eventually, and inevitably, our gates would yield.

Etienne came up with a bold solution, which, after some hesitancy, Armand adopted. Our outer gates were strongest, but we had a second gate of half the thickness forty feet beyond the first. This was normally open; closed, it created a square room below the gate tower. After the second day, when our outer gates were still withstanding the regular pounding, we took away the bars and let their ram appear to blast our gates open.

They rushed through this breach, fifty of them, to find the second gate blocking their way into the courtyard. The bravest of them charged the second gate, while others tried to retreat. We fired at them through slits on either side and poured boiling water on them from two trapdoors in the ceiling. Not one escaped. By the time they had brought up reinforcements we had burned the trevise, rolled the ram down into the moat and closed our outer gates. We allowed them to collect their bodies under a flag of truce.

This was an important success for us, and we celebrated with a feast in the Great Hall that night reminiscent of Count Bernard's days. I hoped to sit close to Blanche, but had to gaze at her from the far end of the long table. Etienne, as her new son-in-law, sat next to her, but he had eyes only for his wife. It was a waste of that place.

A further assault on our gate now seemed unlikely. We had cleared away the stones and earth that bridged the dry moat, and we burned the ram. We kept the iron head as a trophy, placing it on our battlements where the crusaders could see it; their blacksmith had fashioned it into a crude version of a ram's head, curling horns and all.

The crusaders were quiet for several days thereafter, although they celebrated Mass with louder than usual chanting. The ceremony gave them an opportunity to bury their dead. They made a few attempts to scale our walls using great ladders under covering fire from their archers; wooden screens protected them from our crossbowmen. We built our own screens on the battlements out of wood salvaged from their trevise. And our own small mangonel was occasionally effective against the archers, despite its unpredictable accuracy. A well-placed volley of a dozen stones could kill or wound four or five archers, or at worst slow down the rate and accuracy of their fire.

These escalades all failed. I had to admire the courage of the first men up the ladder. We allowed them to get close to the top, then came out from behind our screens and killed them with accurate crossbow fire. It was hard to miss at such close range, and any wounded men were killed when they fell into the moat. Covering fire from their archers came as soon as we emerged from our screens, and we lost three men as a result.

'They may build a wooden tower now their ladders and the ram have failed,' cautioned Etienne.

'That will take too long. They are more likely to rely on The Good Neighbour to batter down our walls. They have been moving materiel up the valley for three weeks now. It won't be long before it is ready,' I said.

For two more weeks we watched them reconstructing the trebuchet on flat ground near the river, just beyond my now empty dovecote. It was well within range of our walls, completely safe from crossbows and our own mangonel.

'They have almost finished,' said Armand to me. 'I would like you to take half a dozen men at night and destroy it.'

I picked Michel, who knew the fording places on the Baise, two of the younger knights and six men-at-arms. Etienne wanted to come but Armand said, 'You've done enough. You've a child on the way and a wife to worry about.'

We left the postern gate at midnight when there was no moon. Each man carried a flagon of oil, a bundle of dry brushwood, a short sword and a dagger. We crossed the river a mile above their camp; I believed they would not expect an attack in their rear across the river, and we had seen that the far bank was unguarded.

We recrossed the river just below their site; one of our knights dropped his brushwood, but the rest was kept dry. The frame of the trebuchet was higher than a small house, its throwing bucket twelve feet across, and there is no doubt that The Bad Neighbour would have lived up to its name. We came across a sleeping sentry propped up against a wheel and killed him quietly enough not to disturb the main camp. He was their sole guard.

Then we piled our brushwood under a cross-beam and soaked the pile with oil. After several agonising failures to produce a flame strong enough to set fire to our kindling, we found their fire store, and carried barrels of tar, sulphur and saltpetre to the great frame. This caught at once, spread rapidly and soon lit up the sky and our retreat across the river. The whole camp was alarmed, and we were pursued by half a dozen men as we retraced our steps back to the postern.

We were saved by the darkness and Michel's knowledge of the terrain, although we lost two men as we retreated. A hundred yards from safety Michel took an arrow in his thigh, and I had to half carry him to the little gate. Once we were inside his wound was dressed by Stephanie, and the rest of us watched the blaze from the ramparts, seeing the scurrying crusaders, lit by the flames, form a chain to bring water up from the river. At dawn we could see that we had destroyed half the frame of the trebuchet, the great bucket and everything in the fire store. Several of the heavy counterweight stones had split from the heat of the fire.

'It will take many weeks to replace those beams with seasoned oak. Green wood isn't strong enough,' said Armand. 'We've dealt with the ladders, the battering ram and now The Bad Neighbour is in ruins. Some of their knights and soldiers will begin to drift away. They're well past their forty days of service.'

All of us in Roqueville had a new confidence; we had supplies for six more weeks and water from the well. The crusaders' camp showed few signs of activity, and they made no attempt to repair the trebuchet.

Two days later Blanche sent her page to call me to her room in the keep. I had never been to her room, although I had seen her sitting at its window many times. Stephanie was with her; both women were sewing.

'I wanted to thank you for destroying the trebuchet. It was a brilliant coup. It means the end of the siege.'

'We were lucky to find their fire store. We'd crossed the river twice, and I don't think our damp kindling would have been enough to set those great beams alight.'

'God was on our side. I know you are a good Cathar, as your father was before you.'

I did not reply. My longing for Blanche had far outstripped the limits of courtly love and the most liberal interpretation of our faith. It was not the moment for the declaration that I had rehearsed many times in my mind. Our conversation was interrupted by Armand entering the room without ceremony, agitated.

'The well is dry. We are without water. They've found the source and cut it off.'

'I thought it was underground,' said Blanche.

'About four miles upstream there's a carrier flowing out of the Baise that then goes underground. That's our source, and I thought no one knew that save me. They've found it, blocked or diverted it. And we've not been storing water. All we have is a couple of barrels.'

This was a greater setback for us than the destruction of the trebuchet had been for our enemies. We sent out a scout the following night, who reported that the crusaders had indeed blocked the carrier and were guarding it with a tight ring of seventy men. An attack, even by night, would fail.

I had always taken water for granted; now we had to exist on half a cup a day apiece. After a week the two barrels, all we had in reserve, were empty. We had to kill our remaining horses, which were going mad with thirst. Our dry faces and blackened tongues and lips were not pretty. We put canvas sheets out to catch the rain, and barrels below the drainpipes, but apart from one brief shower the rain didn't come. Our women and children were allowed to lick the dew off the canvas in the morning, but that was not enough to save several of the smaller children.

Our position grew more obviously hopeless; two weeks after we had run out of water, Etienne and I were sitting in the armoury, searching for answers to our predicament and failing to find them. The sun was just beginning to rise, illuminating the pitiful supply of crossbow bolts and stones for our mangonel.

'We could surrender, ask for terms,' said Etienne. 'They are not likely to be generous. Convert or burn, prison for the men, convents for the women. They know we're desperate.'

'We might as well go down fighting as die of thirst,' I said, and then remembered that Etienne had a wife and unborn child to think about. An honourable death was an easier option for me.

We were still talking when we heard shouts and the clash of steel on steel coming from the western wall.

'It's the postern gate,' said Etienne; we were both in our chain mail, and had only to pick up our swords and run to the source of the noise. We were too late. The gate was open; two of our guards lay on the floor, both face down, one with a crossbow bolt through the body. One of the guards was dead, the other able to speak: 'A traitor stabbed me in the back, shot Alain, let twenty crusaders through the postern.'

We were not only too late, but in the wrong place. The enemy were able to cross both courtyards and unbar the gates before we could organise any proper resistance, and a hundred men rushed in. There was a good deal of confusion in the half-light, and it was at least ten minutes before enough of us had formed a little group, several still without chain mail, to slow down the assault. It was then that I was wounded, a deep cut just below my right shoulder blade that I hardly felt at the time, a cut that could have been inflicted by friend or foe, so great was the confusion and so close the combat.

We managed to hold off the first assault, then retreated from the outer courtyard, and defended the inner courtyard as best we could. For a while a dozen of our crossbowmen on the ramparts were able to pick off several of the attacking crusaders from the flank, but our men were all dead after half an hour. The mêlée in the courtyard was fierce, but we were weak in body and low in numbers. We did our best to defend the keep, and formed a semicircle of perhaps thirty men around its gate. I was at the front of the semicircle, Etienne on my right, Geoffrey on my left. The crusaders didn't press home the attack for a few minutes, believing that we would surrender once enough of their bowmen were up on the ramparts.

There had been no sign of Armand since the gates had been opened. And then he appeared down the stairs and out of the door of the keep, in full armour, plumed helmet, armorial shield and long sword, for all the world as if he was going to a grand tournament. It was a magnificent, ridiculous sight. He pushed us aside at the front of our defensive semicircle and walked slowly towards the mass of our opponents.

For a moment the crusaders were astonished at this apparition, and some of them began to laugh. Armand strode on and began to lay about him with his great sword, which stopped the laughter. He scattered the men-at-arms, killing several of them with sweeping blows and clearing a space around him. Then they regrouped and swarmed all over Armand, finding the chinks in his armour with their small swords. He was beaten to his knees, lost his great sword, then fell slowly backwards and lay dying on the blood-stained floor of the inner courtyard. I had to hold Etienne back as we watched while several of the crusaders ripped off Armand's armour and began to squabble over the spoils. Then they turned their attention to us.

By now dawn was breaking. Eleven of our knights and forty men-at-arms were dead and many more wounded, including Etienne and me; Etienne had an arrow through his left arm and a heavy blow to the head, and I was beginning to feel the gash below my shoulder blade. Geoffrey, the only one of our older knights still standing, told us 'That's enough', stepped forward out of our semicircle, saluted his enemies with a final flourish drawn from his chivalrous past, laid down his sword and instructed us to do the same. We obeyed. So ended our resistance.

The surviving Roqueville fighting men were penned and guarded in the stables, the women and children herded into the Great Hall. To celebrate their victory the crusaders brought their wooden cross up from the camp, erected it in our courtyard and held a Mass at midday. The chanting of their priests was hard to bear.

After Mass they took all the surviving knights, nineteen of us, outside the curtain walls and made us sit in the moat, guarded by a dozen men with crossbows.

'They are going to kill us here,' I said to Etienne. I did not feel ready to die; I remember how green the grass seemed on the edge of the moat, how unconcerned the sparrows that were nesting in the great, useless wall that towered above us.

'Kill us in cold blood? In breach of every law of chivalry? Not even demand ransom?'

'I don't think they are in a chivalrous mood.'

I stopped talking when one of the guards cocked and pointed his crossbow at me. We sat or lay there for three hours, the loudest noise the rasping breath of one of our number who had been wounded in the lung. Then they came and took us, one by one, back into the castle. I believed they would kill us there.

Etienne was taken early and I said a final farewell. They left me to the last, and, as I walked through the gate, a soldier holding each arm, I tried to remember the words of the Consolamentum, with little success. My wound was painful; worse, I was very frightened.

My fear was justified. As I was manhandled through the outer gate I heard a sound I had never heard before and hope never to hear again – the sound, somewhere between a scream and a groan, of men trying to hold on in the grip of unbearable pain. Once through the inner gate I saw the bodies of dead crusaders laid out neatly against the western wall, and the bodies of our own dead piled high around an unlit bonfire of wood in the middle of the courtyard.

Against the eastern wall, sitting or lying, were our surviving knights, covered in blood. Now I understood the reason for the sounds I had heard. Each one of them had been blinded, each one of them had had his right arm cut off above the elbow. The severed arms lay, one still twitching, some palms open as if in supplication, around a wooden butcher's block red with blood. I saw Etienne with his remaining hand over his eyes, over the place where his eyes had been. Geoffrey lay dead; he had not survived the torture.

A few of the crusaders stood watching; most of them had taken off their armour, and one or two were leaning on their swords. We were no longer difficult to guard. A tall monk, standing a little apart from the soldiers, seemed to be in charge of the proceedings, although clearly he had not been involved in the fighting; he wore the habit of a Dominican monk, with over it an immaculate white tunic, a crusader's red cross in its centre. Our victims at Avignonet had been similarly dressed.

I struggled to break free, was too weak, shouted, 'Call yourselves Christians? Where's your mercy, where's your chivalry? Bloody butchers, bloody…' and was pushed to the ground. I lay there for a moment until my two guards brought me to the block and held my right arm down; the executioner took it off with a single blow then dipped the stump into a pot of warm pitch.

The pain doubled that from the wound in my back, but this was as nothing to what followed. The executioner produced his dagger and thrust it into my right eye, and I made the noise I had heard as I came through the outer gate.

He was about to do the same to my other eye – my knees were buckling and I could only stand because I was held up by my guards – when the tall monk stopped him.

'He'll need one eye if he's to lead the rest to Montségur.'

That afternoon I was revived with a bucket of water and forced to watch as the bodies of our dead comrades were consumed by fire. It was the first time I had smelled burning human flesh or seen the contortions, almost as if they were coming alive again, of the bodies of dead men in the flames. One corpse seemed to stand up and take a pace towards us before collapsing back into the fire.

The Dominican who had spared my eye watched the burning with a dispassionate interest. As the fire burned down he walked over to our guards and gave them careful instructions. We were forced to our feet and the fifteen surviving knights, all blind, were lined up behind me. Our guards placed the left hand of each man on the shoulder of the man in front, prodded me, their half-blind leader, and told me to lead this procession out of Roqueville.

'Take them to Montségur,' the tall Dominican said to me. 'Tell them God is not mocked. Tell them his vengeance is terrible.'

5

The Inquisitor and Blanche

The Inquisitor

THE WEEKS AND months after my success with Baruch the Jew were an anticlimax. My colleagues were slow to adopt my techniques of interrogation, preferring to rely on torture and brief questioning followed by the handing over of the heretic to the civil arm. True, not many heretics escaped detection, but there were few genuine conversions. The Languedoc remained a fertile breeding ground for heresy. In two years we had only succeeded in taking one so-called Perfect, Jean Tremiere, who quickly confessed and then had the audacity to challenge me to a public debate. This I declined, not because I feared losing, but because, as I told him, 'The True Faith cannot be a subject of debate.'

The Bishop slyly pointed out that I had been prepared to debate with Baruch the Jew; I told him there was a difference between a public debate and a private argument, an argument which I had conclusively won.

There were several fiefdoms in which, our informers told us, the Cathar heresy was actively encouraged, Romieu, Roqueville and Montségur being the most blatant examples. The heresy provided an intellectual justification for their continued refusal to pay tithes and taxes. Roqueville was well known for having instigated the killing of two Papal Legates and subsequently harbouring the culprits. Although Count Bernard had paid hefty fines and done penance in Toulouse Cathedral, according to numerous accounts the valley had reverted to its former heretical ways. If, indeed, it had ever abandoned them.

So we sent a young priest with an armed escort to demand the appearance of the new Count Armand, his mother and sister before us in Carcassonne. He returned with their defiant message and told us that he had been roughly handled. After a delay while permission was sought from Rome for the incentives of a Crusade – indulgences, the remission of past sins, the right to forfeited property – a strong force of over three hundred men was sent to Roqueville.

The delay had given the heretics too much time to prepare for what they knew was coming, and our crusaders suffered early setbacks. Their advance guard was ambushed, their assaults by ladder all failed, and, worst of all, their great trebuchet was destroyed. When the news reached Carcassonne that Guy de Montfort was thinking of abandoning the siege, I decided I should go there in person.

I found the camp in considerable disarray. The ruins of the trebuchet were a daily reminder of failure. And the conversations round Guy's campaign table were not about the holy nature of the cause but about the extent and division of the land and treasure that would be acquired. If we succeeded, which, given the pervading air of defeatism, seemed unlikely.

'They have enough food and a good well within the castle,' said Guy de Montfort. 'Our prisoners have confirmed that. We have no spies within their walls.'

'What feeds the well?'

'Underground springs.'

I left the tent and went for a long walk up the River Baise. After four miles I was about to turn back when I noticed – and this was God's work, I am sure – a small carrier flowing out of the Baise that disappeared underground after half a mile. I knew at once that this was the source of the castle's water, knelt and said a *Te Deum*, then hurried back to the camp to tell Guy what I had seen. He was sceptical at first, perhaps annoyed that a monk had discovered what his soldiers had overlooked, but he had no alternative plan other than admitting defeat and returning to Carcassonne.

'I suppose we have nothing to lose. We'll divert the carrier and see what happens.'

'And you'll guard the diversion properly?' I was aware that the site of the trebuchet had not been properly secure.

'Of course,' he said with a frown.

Nothing happened for a few days. Then we captured a scout sent to discover what had happened to their source; he confirmed that their well was dry. We bribed him handsomely and told him to return to Roqueville. It was this man who let our small force in at the postern gate. Treachery is a powerful force in sieges of this kind, but I knew, as God knew, that it was the shortage of water as much as the money that persuaded the scout to turn his coat.

Our attack took place just before dawn; their resistance was fierce but futile, ending in the bizarre appearance of Armand de Roqueville in full armour. He was quickly cut down by our troops.

I went up to the castle when the fighting was over. I decided on condign punishment of the surviving knights, overruling Guy, who had some absurd notion that as they had surrendered the code of chivalry should prevail.

'We should demand ransom,' he said.

'From whom? These heretics belong to God, and must be punished in His Name.'

I devised their punishment, and decided that the surviving knights, blinded and one-armed, should be sent as an awful warning to Montségur. I saved the single eye of the last young knight, who was thus able to lead them there, although he was an angry blasphemer. We burned all the dead heretics, including Count Armand, gave our own dead Christian burial, and sent sixteen knights on their way to Montségur. We marked our triumph with a Mass and *Te Deum* in the castle courtyard, although I noticed that many of the men-at-arms and even a few knights were absent, ransacking the castle for the spoils of war.

After Mass, Lady Blanche and her daughter were escorted out of the keep and into the cart that was to take them to Carcassonne. The cart was laden with two heavy chests that contained the Roqueville silver and even a little gold. I insisted that this belonged to the Church, although Guy de Montfort was far from pleased.

As Blanche walked across the courtyard I was struck, not for the first time, by her beauty and composure; I had first seen her when her husband performed his penance in Toulouse. She held her head steady, her eyes looking neither to right nor left but into the distance, not glancing at the heap of ash and bone where we had just finished burning the body of her son. The smell of the pyre still hung in the air.

She was wearing a long red gown, her hair tied up in a knot from which a few strands had escaped. Her feet were bare, and covered in dust and ashes by the time she climbed the makeshift steps into the cart. As she did so I made the Sign of the Cross, but whether in blessing or as exorcism I could not tell.

Her daughter followed a few steps behind, pregnant, bedraggled, a pitiful sight if an unrepentant heretic can be said to deserve pity. She stopped by me, looked back at the pyre and said, 'Where is my husband? What have you done with Count Etienne?'

'We have sent him to Montségur with the other knights.'

As the cart pulled out of the great gate neither woman looked back. I watched Blanche until she was out of sight.

I returned to Carcassonne a day later. I knew that I had to delegate the questioning of Blanche, but I did interrogate the daughter. Stephanie agreed, without the need for torture, to abandon her heretical ways and I sent her to the civil power for sentencing with a recommendation for mercy. Not because she deserved it, as her conversion was unconvincing, but because she was carrying an unborn child that could in due course become a child of God.

Then my deputy, an earnest Dominican from Spain, fell ill, and I was unable to avoid Blanche. I was well aware of the danger. I had dreamed of Blanche several times walking across the courtyard, but in my dream she stopped, turned and came towards me.

In the real world Blanche was brought in by a single guard to the small hall we used for interrogation. She wore a smock of coarse brown cloth that reached below her knees. Her hair had been cut short and her feet were bare; her ankles had been chained together, and I could see the red marks where the iron fetters had chafed the skin.

I sat on my throne-like chair, raised on a foot-high dais, flanked by my secretary taking notes. It seemed appropriate that our prisoners should have to look up to the voice of authority. I tried to be brisk and businesslike and did not offer Blanche a chair. All our prisoners were made to stand, unless they were so weak from recent torture that they had to be seated. Blanche had not been tortured.

'You acknowledge you are a heretic, a Cathar,' I began.

She replied in a surprisingly clear, strong voice, the first words I had heard her speak, 'I am Cathar. I am only a heretic in your eyes.'

'Not just in my eyes, but in the eyes of the Catholic Church, the source and guardian of the True Faith.'

'It is we who are the true, the Good Christians. There can be no heresy in truth and goodness.'

'So you profess. I can demonstrate through Holy Scripture that you are wrong.'

'I have heard such arguments many times before.'

'Not from a proper theologian. Will you listen to me?'

She made no reply, looked at and through me, then closed her eyes and seemed to pray for a moment. There was a long silence; I nodded to her guard and she was taken away.

Later that morning I took my customary walk around the square. I was troubled by Blanche's unshakeable faith, and by her distance from her surroundings and from me. Normally an hour on the rack would have removed all traces of such remoteness, but I was not yet ready to send her down that path. I found her physical beauty, despite her shorn hair and bleeding ankles, utterly compelling. It was a compulsion that an hour on my knees in our little chapel failed to remove.

Two days later I sent for Blanche again. On this occasion I told her guard to unlock her fetters, provided her with a chair and invited her to sit.

'I prefer to stand.'

'We can cure such stubbornness,' despising myself for uttering such a crude threat.

'I am not afraid of torture, or the stake.'

'There is no need for either if you will only listen. Do you not wish to see your daughter?'

These were the first of my words that made any impression. Blanche looked at me for the first time and began to weep soundlessly, then said, 'One of my guards told me she was dead, that she and her unborn child had been burned.'

'Stephanie is not dead. She has been condemned as a heretic, but she has not been sentenced. I can arrange for you to see her again if you agree to listen to me.'

Blanche thought for a moment, brushed away her tears with her sleeve, then said, 'I agree.'

As she was taken away I felt overjoyed, not because I thought Blanche could be convinced, but at the prospect of a series of conversations with this woman. Beyond that I did not allow my thoughts to travel.

The next day I went to Flaran where I had some business to complete at the abbey, hoping that a return to my old surroundings might free my mind from thoughts of Blanche. I found no such freedom there. Walking round the gentle arches of the cloisters failed to produce the comfort I looked for. The reverse; I thought of Blanche by day as well as by night, and even at the holiest of moments, when I was giving the Host to those who had been my monks, the image of her face appeared.

It was as if a spell had been cast on me. Although most accusations against witches are nonsense and informed by malice or ignorance, yet witches do exist and have strange powers. Was Blanche a witch? I did not think so. After all, she had done everything she could to put distance between us. And I had to admit that if I was bewitched I had no desire to exorcise the spell.

Three days later I returned from Flaran and ordered my clerk to prepare the disused storeroom on the ground floor of my house as a makeshift cell.

'She is a noblewoman,' I explained. 'She has agreed to receive instruction from me. I have high hopes of a conversion as notable as that of Baruch the Jew.'

'Lord, it will be hard to make that room secure. Where will her guards sleep?'

'She will not try to escape. She wants to see her daughter.'

Moving Blanche into my house sealed my fate. I knew what I was doing. The interrogations were occasions of sin, and dangerous, but circumscribed by the presence of my clerk and a guard. The moment Blanche was living two floors below me, in a room to which I had the key, I was lost. I remembered, and ignored, the words of Bernard of Clairvaux, *To be always with a woman and not to have intercourse with her is more difficult than to raise the dead.*

I convinced myself that I wanted Blanche to abjure her heresy. So I went down to her cell – her chamber, as it had a proper bed, two chairs, a high window and rush matting on the floor – to begin the dialogue that had worked with Baruch.

Blanche still refused to sit, so I had to look up to see her eyes. She kept her distant expression as I spoke, and my weighty arguments were neither accepted nor countered. Occasionally she would nod her head, not in agreement, but simply to signal that she had heard what I had to say.

I thought I had broken through when I asked her if she believed in transubstantiation, in the miracle of the blood and the wine.

'I can believe in that if I must,' she said, the first words she had spoken during this session. 'But I cannot swear an oath. Cannot I say that I believe? Will that not do?'

'Not swearing means you are still Cathar.'

'Perhaps I will always be Cathar, oath or no oath. Give me time to think about all you have told me,' and she gave a little smile.

I left the room more troubled than ever, clutching her words and her smile to myself, uncertain whether I was on the brink of achieving a conversion that I did not really seek. Or on the brink of something I had wanted since I first set eyes on Blanche in the cathedral.

I allowed a day to pass before visiting her again. On this occasion she sat facing me and her distant look had gone.

'I will swear an oath if that will allow me to see my daughter.'

I did not reply. Minutes passed that seemed like days. Blanche said, 'Tell me what I have to do to save Stephanie.'

I looked away, my heart pounding, my throat dry. I told her what she had to do. Then she stood up, pulled her smock over her head, walked over to the bed and we did what she had to do.

6

Montségur

Sybille

I WAS THE FIRST to see it. I have the best eyes in the castle, better than any of our sentries. It looked like a small brown worm moving slowly across the valley road, stopping now and then, curving round the last sharp bend, once breaking in half and re-forming. I ran to tell my mother what I had seen, and together we climbed the tower to get a better view.

'Perhaps it's a worm,' I said, remembering how it had broken and come together again.

My mother said nothing until the worm had reached the bottom of the steep path up to Montségur.

'They are men, probably pilgrims. Take some water down to them.'

I and one of the men took two large leather buckets of water halfway down the path to meet the pilgrims. The path is rocky as well as steep and takes an erratic course through the scrub oak and bushes, so they made very slow progress. Several times two or three of the men stumbled and fell, and their leader went back and helped them to their feet; he made sure that the hand of each man was on the shoulder of the man in front, which seemed strange. Only the leader carried a staff. They were all dressed in rags.

We waited for them where the path broadens into a small, flat clearing. When they got close I had to put my hand over my mouth to stop crying out; I could see they were all blind save their leader, and he had only one eye. All of them had lost their right arms. Several of them were old, older than my father, although they were so battered and dirty that it was hard to tell. They smelled of their journey and their wounds.

Their leader was a young man, perhaps two or three years older than me. His single eye was bright blue, and there was a bloody mess where the other had been. His right arm had been cut off above the elbow, and ended in a bandaged stump. I burst into tears when I saw him close.

He and our sentry took the water and gave a cup to each sightless man; drinking wasn't easy. Their leader made sure they all had water before he drank.

'Who has done this?' I asked.

One of the men near the front answered, 'So-called crusaders after they had captured Roqueville. We were betrayed and they were too many. They took my wife and her mother to the Inquisition at Carcassonne.'

'You are safe here. We're all good Cathars,' I answered, and I ran up to tell my mother and father what I had learned.

My father looked worried.

'Claire,' he said to my mother, 'we need warriors, not fourteen more hungry mouths to feed. I suppose we have to take them in?'

'We do,' my mother and I said together.

The new arrivals were housed in the little settlement just below the main outer wall of Montségur. My old nurse, Guillemette, was charged by my mother with looking after the newcomers, helped by me and two of the Cathar widows who lived in the settlement. Guillemette knew about healing and herbs and, according to my mother, much more – potions and remedies that hovered on the edge of witchcraft.

We tended their wounds as best we could, but three of them soon died through a combination of exhaustion and despair. I nursed several of them, including their leader, the youngest of them all. I rebandaged his arm every three or four days and cleaned up his eye socket, packing it with herbs that Guillemette recommended.

His name, he told me, was Francois de Beaufort. In those early weeks I got to know him and his history well – and his body, or at least the top half of it, as he had a deep wound in his back that required regular attention. I didn't neglect the other knights, and the one whose wife had been taken to Carcassonne told me what Francois had done for them all.

'Without him we'd all be dead. He kept us together, making sure that each man held the shoulder of the man in front. If anyone stumbled and fell Francois would go down the line, pick him up, replace the hand on the shoulder, and off we would go again. It took us ten days to get here.'

'How did you survive?'

'Water was easy to come by, but the countryside around Roqueville had been ransacked by the crusaders and there was little food to be had. What there was Francois found for us. We must have been a frightening sight stumbling along the road, although we were incapable of doing any harm, incapable of doing anything other than begging. Two of the older knights died on the way.'

He stopped, swallowed, covered his face with his hand, and said, 'We weren't able to bury them, and we had no Perfect with us to ease their passage into the next world.'

A few days later, when I was putting ointment on his back, Francois asked me if I was Cathar.

'Claire, my mother, is a Perfect. My father's a believer, but less passionate in the faith.'

'And you?'

'I'm Cathar. And you?'

'I'm Cathar.'

He had been holding my hand tightly as I attended to his back, which was still painful, and he didn't drop it for a minute. I had to pull my hand gently out of his grasp.

'They dug up my parents' bodies and burned them,' he continued. 'I hate the Catholic Church for what they've done to us. Look at me. I'm a wreck of a man.'

'You're getting better, your eye is healing over, the wound on your back is closed, you've got one arm, and you're still alive, still young.'

'You're right. I need to stop feeling sorry for myself.'

I didn't feel sorry for him – but I was beginning to feel more than just admiration for the way he'd led the blinded knights to Montségur. As part of my nursing duties I'd seen and touched Francois's body, his smooth belly, the strong muscles of his back, the firm grasp of his fingers when he held my hand. I'd never touched a man before. He was – and it seemed a strange word for someone whose body had been so battered and maimed, but I could find no other – beautiful.

I changed the subject. 'They'll come to Montségur next. But look at our castle, perched on top of this sharp little mountain. You'd need an army of crusader goats to attack us.'

He laughed at the thought of crusader goats.

'They'll try to starve us out.'

'They can't encircle the bottom of the mountain unless they bring twenty thousand men.'

'I hope you're right. We thought we could defend Roqueville...' and he fell silent.

It took about three weeks for Francois's wounds to heal and his eye socket to stop weeping. The other knights were slower to recover, and three more died not long after they arrived at Montségur.

'I can't say I'm sorry,' said my father. 'Three fewer to feed. The rest of them just sit below the walls looking miserable.'

'You'd look miserable if you were one-armed and blind,' said my mother.

My father merely grunted.

A couple of days later I saw Francois talking to our blacksmith. Curious, I walked over to see what was going on.

'I've asked him to make an iron tube that I can bolt to the bottom of a crossbow. What's left of my right arm will fit nicely into it, and I'll cock and fire it with my left hand. The crusaders cut off the wrong arm. I'm left-handed.'

'Make the tube wider than your stump,' I said. 'I'll sew a padded sleeve to stop it rubbing.'

Francois looked surprised, then pleased. I took a lot of care over the sleeve, filling a doubled length of linen with cotton and sewing it tight with my best stitches. I made him an eyepatch out of a black silk remnant I found in my mother's sewing basket. I presented him with my work a few days later, and he put on the sleeve at once.

'It fits perfectly.'

'I've dressed your arm often enough to know the measurements.'

Then he tried on the patch. It gave him an additional ten years and made him look like a brigand.

'I'll wear it on formal occasions.'

'We don't have many of those now at Montségur.'

I watched him from my window practising every morning in the butts. At first he was clumsy, swearing quietly to himself when the crossbow slipped off his ruined arm. After the second day I went down to see him; he didn't look pleased to see me, as he'd just failed twice in a row to keep his weapon in place.

'You need a leather strap that goes round your shoulder. Then it won't fall off. Tell the saddler what you need.'

Francois looked doubtful, but did as I suggested. My idea worked, and he was soon adept at cocking and firing the crossbow single-handed. He went to see my father soon after and asked to be included in the roster of fighting men.

'Minus your right arm? What can you do single-handed?'

'I'm left-handed, good with the sword. Geoffrey de Goncourt taught me. And I've adapted a crossbow. Let me show you.' He made no mention of my contribution; perhaps he was afraid my father would think we had become too close.

He persuaded my father to come down to the butts, and he put five bolts into the centre of the target in three minutes. My father was impressed.

'You're as quick as some of my men with two arms. We'll make good use of you when the time comes.'

The time didn't come that winter. 'It's not the season for a siege,' said my father. 'They wouldn't be able to keep their men warm and fed.'

It was a particularly cold winter. Every morning we looked out over a white sea of mist, Montségur alone rising above it; only the Pyrenees in the distance, white with snow, were higher. On most mornings a wintry sun would burn off the mist by noon, but sometimes we would remain marooned on our island all day. I had little excuse or opportunity to see and talk to Francois, although he always seemed glad to see me when we did meet. He only wore the eyepatch on the rare occasions when he was invited to dine in our Great Hall, usually eating with his fellow knights from Roqueville in the little encampment below the walls.

I watched him on a couple of occasions practising in the butts. He was quicker with his crossbow than most of the men. My father organised a competition in the New Year, and my mother and I were part of a little gallery of spectators looking on. Francois came second; he was as accurate as the winner, but loosed off one less bolt in the time allowed.

Afterwards he came up to me and my mother, bowed and said, 'I wouldn't have done nearly as well if Sybille hadn't created the sleeve,' and showed her my careful sewing. 'The leather strap was her idea.'

'You need a replacement,' I said. 'It's worn in several places and the padding has flattened. I'll make you another.'

Francois smiled, thanked me and walked away to talk to his fellow competitors.

'He's very handsome,' said my mother. 'In spite of everything.'

'One eye and one arm thanks to the crusaders. Etienne told me without him they all would have died.'

'I knew his mother; she was a good Cathar, died giving birth to, to...'

'Francois,' I said, too quickly.

I made him another sleeve, this time with stronger fabric and more padding, and I quilted it in little diamonds. I took a week to make it. When I had done all this I went to my chamber and sat on my bed. I had been told many things by Guillemette, most of which my mother dismissed as superstition. I was less sure; I thought my old nurse was a wise woman. I remembered her advice; when I had finished I turned the sleeve inside out and used it to touch myself between my thighs until I was wet, as Guillemette had suggested. At the end I was shaking with a new and unexpected pleasure, which I hadn't been told about.

I hoped this would be a spell that would make Francois love me. I put dried lavender inside the sleeve for two days to make sure that what I had done wasn't detectable by my mother or by Francois.

Francois

I TRIED HARD TO banish the memories of the fall of Roqueville, the maiming that followed and the terrible journey to Montségur. I had nightmares long afterwards, and would wake shouting just as the torturer's dagger came towards my left eye. I was, of course, the lucky one; the Inquisitor who saved my right eye did so not out of charity but so that I could lead fifteen blinded knights to Montségur. He was clever. He knew the story of our punishment and our journey would spread throughout the Languedoc.

We reached Montségur after ten days; we lost two of the older men on the way, as much through despair as through loss of blood from their wounds. There was little food from the countryside on our journey, and the two villages we passed through locked their doors against us as though our wounds were somehow contagious. One elderly Cathar farmer allowed us to stay in his barn for a night, although he begged us to move on in the morning in case word got round that he had sheltered heretics.

We were uncertain of our reception at Montségur, but we need not have worried. Raimond Roger was Cathar, and his wife Claire was even more devout than him; there was room for us in the little settlement below the castle walls, and we were told we could remain there as long as we wished. Which meant forever, as we had nowhere else to go.

We were all still suffering from our wounds, and Guillemette was put in charge of nursing us back to health. She was a wise woman with something of the witch about her, and talked as though she was a less than convinced Cathar.

'I can't see there is a huge difference,' she said. 'Certainly not enough to risk the stake.'

I didn't contradict her, and secretly agreed, although it seemed impolite to say so in front of our hosts. Guillemette knew enough about herbs to help us heal; although we lost three more of our number within two weeks, the rest of us gradually recovered, at least in body.

Etienne got better quickly, but was in despair over the fate of his wife, his unborn child and Blanche. I promised him that when we had both recovered we would go to Carcassonne and find them, and the thought gave him some comfort, although I had little idea how I could keep that promise.

I often thought of Blanche walking across the Roqueville courtyard past the pyre on which the crusaders had just burned the body of her son. She needed to be rescued from the Inquisition, but a single, damaged knight was unlikely to be up to the task.

Guillemette was helped by Raimond Roger's daughter Sybille, a young woman of around seventeen with a slender figure and a direct gaze. Her long auburn hair was gathered in by a gold clasp at her nape, then widened to flow down to her waist. Her eyes were brown and she had gentle hands; Guillemette asked her to dress my wounds and look after the slash in my back, which was the last to heal.

Sybille questioned me about the siege and the journey; my replies were brief and almost discourteous. The pain of memory made it hard to revisit those terrible days and describe what had happened to us. As I recovered I told her that I wanted to be more than just another hungry mouth to feed. She encouraged me in this; I persuaded the blacksmith to make a metal sleeve that enabled me to hold a crossbow, and Sybille sewed a protective cover for my arm.

As the memories of Roqueville faded I found myself thinking of Blanche less and Sybille more. She seemed to like my company, although her mother was careful to make sure we were rarely alone together.

I confided in Etienne.

'I thought Blanche was the woman you admired. Above all others, I remember you declaring.'

I laughed, remembering these were my exact words when he first told me about Stephanie.

'Only as her knight, her faithful servant. Wasn't that your answer?' I said. 'And I'm one-armed and one-eyed.'

'You told me to be brave and I won Stephanie.' And then he broke down and it was hard to comfort him. I renewed my promise that we would find them, hollow though that seemed.

Late in that winter I was able to show Raimond Roger that I could handle a crossbow almost as well as the best of his men. He asked me to move into the castle and take my place in the roster of sentries and scouts; he sent the latter out at regular intervals to collect intelligence. Raimond Roger allowed Etienne to come with me and thereafter he worked every day in the armoury, sharpening and straightening bolts and repairing crossbows. Inside the castle I saw more of Sybille, although I was uncertain how to further my cause.

'Is she promised in marriage?' I asked Guillemette.

She laughed.

'There's a shortage of Cathar noblemen, and the rest wouldn't dare marry a heretic. Why do you ask?'

'Curiosity.'

'All I can tell you is that she insisted on nursing you, and doesn't seem to mind that you are missing an arm and an eye. I assume they left your manhood intact? That's the limb that matters.'

This exchange left me half angry, half amused and not much wiser. I pretended to be shocked by the coarseness of her reply, but in reality I was pleased that she seemed to be, if not on my side, at least not about to put obstacles in my way.

Sybille

IT WAS A long and difficult winter. We had two months of snow, and we came close to running out of logs, so the fires were rationed. I was no longer allowed a fire in my chamber, and any number of blankets couldn't keep the cold from penetrating the castle walls.

When spring finally arrived it did so with a vigour that soon put the winter out of my mind. The brown valley turned green, and our little mountain was carpeted with wild flowers by early April, snowdrops, primroses, hellebores and later gentians. Guillemette taught me their names when I brought bunches of wild flowers back to her, and would ask me to seek out herbs as well as flowers that she dried and used for medicines. And, no doubt, spells. The butterflies didn't interest her; yellow, red and blue was all she knew.

The glory of the spring made it difficult to accept one of

our basic Cathar beliefs, that everything in this world is a snare and a delusion. Evil I understood, but why had all this beauty been created?

'It's a deception,' my mother said. 'It's transient; the real, eternal world is not this, but the next.' She continued with a long and careful explanation of why this was so, but my attention soon wandered and she caught me looking out of the window. She laughed.

'I can see it will be some time before you become a theologian. Enjoy your ride.'

Riding through the valley was a constant source of delight. There were clear, grassy paths through the woods and along the streams, and wide meadows that were good for galloping. I loved the birch trees in the winter for their slender, vein-like branches and the papery silver of their bark, which looked as though someone had begun to peel them and then abandoned the task. In the spring they turned green early, their smaller leaves a sharper, shinier green that contrasted with the deeper green of the oaks and poplars.

I always saw roe-deer, and once in the distance a bear, although my father scoffed and said they never came this far down. I didn't argue, but I and my horse, who wanted to turn for home at once, knew what we had seen.

My father insisted that I rode with an escort in spite of my protests.

'There are marauding bands of vagabonds, former soldiers, throughout the Languedoc. If you want to ride in the valley you must have an armed escort with you. Don't try to persuade me otherwise. If you don't like it, stay in the castle and help your mother.'

I argued for ten minutes, sulked for two days and then accepted my father's decision. It was never easy to get him to change his mind. And I thought that sooner or later Francois would be given the task of escorting me.

When this didn't happen I sought Francois out in the archery butts.

'How well does the new sleeve fit?'

He looked pleased to see me.

'Even better than the last. You've made the padding thicker.'

That's not all I've done, I thought, remembering my spell.

'Tell me when you need a new sleeve. And why are you never my escort in the valley? Can you not ride?'

'I've ridden since I was six. You have to be able to ride in tournaments. I was never unhorsed in a joust.'

'How many tournaments?'

Francois looked a little embarrassed.

'Only two. But five opponents. And four finished up on the ground.'

'I'll tell that to my father. There's no reason for you to be excused escort duties.'

He smiled, took my hand and said, 'It will be a great pleasure. To be on a horse again, I mean.'

I spoke to my father a day later, introducing the subject casually when he was talking about the other blind Cathar knights. He was not easily deceived.

'Have you taken a liking to Francois? There's little enough of him left. And it's hard to ride a horse one-handed.'

I blushed.

'It's not that. He's the only one of them who is any use to you, he's good with the crossbow and he wants to do his share of the work here. He says he can ride.'

'Very well. He can ride Octavian.'

I was about to protest, then thought the better of it. Octavian was my father's warhorse, a black, headstrong stallion with an iron mouth. Most of our knights refused to ride him, and they had two arms. My father was testing Francois, it seemed to me, and there was no sensible way to stop it.

Three days later Francois met me at the main gate.

'Raimond Roger's given me escort duties today, put me on the roster. He says I can ride his horse.'

He looked pleased at the double privilege. I didn't tell him that only my father dared to ride Octavian, who was fresh, strong and hadn't been properly exercised for a month.

Our stables are down in the valley, next to the village. Mules and goats are the only animals that can make the climb up to the castle. We talked as we descended the path; he told me about Avignonet and the long siege of Roqueville.

'They cut off our water. And then we were betrayed. They will try to do the same to Montségur this summer.'

'We are all loyal Cathars here. And our cisterns are full, they go deep down into the mountain. My father says we have water for eighteen months, even if it never rains.'

We'd reached the bottom of the mountain. I took his hand and turned him to look up at the mountain. The slope was so steep that only the zigzag of the path made it possible to climb up to our walls.

Francois looked at the mountain for a long time, still holding my hand.

'You're right. They'll need crusader goats.'

We reached the stables, and the stable boy brought out Marie, my grey mare.

'She's very pretty,' said Francois. 'A good match for you.'

This was the first compliment he had ever paid me; I thought Guillemette's spell was beginning to work. Then Octavian was led out from his stable, snorting, pawing the ground, turning his head to try and bite the stable boy. I felt suddenly afraid for Francois, and in need of another spell.

'He's a handful,' said the boy, looking doubtfully at Francois's single arm. 'I can't stay on him. There's a mounting block in the corner.'

'No need. Just hold his head.'

Francois walked up to Octavian, patted him twice, put his only hand on the reins and vaulted into the saddle. This surprised the horse, the stable boy and me. Octavian bucked twice as he felt his rider's weight, but Francois barely moved in the saddle. My father seemed at one with a horse the moment he was mounted, made it clear he was in charge and wasn't frightened, gave the horse his own confidence. And Francois was the same.

We trotted out of the yard, Francois unaware of my secret pleasure and, I had to admit, relief. I looked back at the stable boy. He hadn't moved, his mouth still open.

We began the morning with a good gallop, Octavian outstripping my mare Marie very quickly. When we reached the end of the meadow I said, 'I hadn't realised it was a race. I thought you were my escort.'

Francois laughed.

'I was never far away. I'll always stay within range,' and he patted the crossbow slung over his shoulder. 'Octavian needs a good gallop. If you stay here I'll take him across the meadow again.' He set off without waiting for a reply.

He shared my pleasure in the valley and the spring as we rode that first morning. We stopped in a little clearing for our lunch of bread and cheese and wine. A roebuck appeared; Francois immediately unslung his crossbow and began to cock it. When I said, 'Please,' and put a hand on his arm, he stopped at once, and we watched together as the buck trotted away, paused to look back at us on the edge of the wood, then disappeared.

If my father was surprised that someone else was able to handle Octavian he gave no sign. So every five days Francois and I rode out together, which gave him every opportunity to – I didn't quite know what – pursue his suit, I suppose. But nothing happened, other than the riding and friendly conversation.

I asked Guillemette what I should expect.

'He's still only a boy,' she said. 'Probably never known a woman. You'll have to show him what to do.'

'What do you mean?'

'I'll tell you.' And she did, in great, and at first embarrassing, detail. I listened carefully, asked a lot of questions, and didn't sleep that night, thinking about Francois and me doing together what Guillemette had described.

'You'll have to pick your moment,' Guillemette had said at the end of our conversation. The next time we went riding together it drizzled all morning, we and our horses were wet and uncomfortable, and nothing happened. I had to wait another five days.

The next time we rode out together was a perfect spring morning. There had been a slight frost the night before, and we waited until the sun burned off the mist that hung over the valley. As usual Francois was on Octavian, who no longer thought it worthwhile to buck. Francois had been riding him regularly even when he wasn't my escort.

'He's been well schooled by your father,' he said. 'Capriole, courbette, levade, all the battlefield movements.'

'Show me,' I said, and when we were out in the field he put Octavian through his paces. I'd never seen these movements before, and thought them beautiful but useless; in the capriole

Francois had Octavian leap in the air and strike out with his hind legs. I kept well clear.

We rode for two hours, then stopped at the end of a long meadow covered in butterwort and the occasional purple orchis. There were white irises by the river. We dismounted and sat side by side, our backs against a mossy bank, the perfect opportunity, I thought, to put into practice Guillemette's advice. I put my hand on his knee, and he covered it with his own, turned towards me, then suddenly jumped to his feet.

'Get on your horse. Quickly,' he said, and as I, angry and disappointed, stayed where I was, continued in a stronger voice, 'Look down the meadow.'

I mounted Marie quickly; I could see what had alarmed Francois: three horsemen trotting towards us. They broke into a canter.

'We've been seen, and we'll not outrun them.'

By now Francois was on his horse, crossbow cocked; he had half a dozen bolts in the quiver strapped to his saddle. 'Stay beside me until they are close, then gallop back to the stables as fast as you can when I give the word.'

When the little group were twenty yards away they stopped and drew their swords. They were all three in chain mail, bearded, dirty. I heard one of them laugh, say something in French about Francois's single arm.

'They've stolen two of the horses from our stables,' I said. 'That's Destiny, and Magic.'

Francois said nothing and kept Octavian between me and the three men, who were by now riding slowly towards us, the spring sun glinting on their swords. Francois said, 'Ride now, as fast as you can,' and I did as he said, kicking Marie straight into a gallop that took them by surprise. As I passed them, crouched low over Marie's neck, one of the men turned and galloped after me.

I didn't look back, heard the twang of the crossbow being fired, and though I had twenty yards' start could hear the hoofbeats behind me getting closer, closer and then alongside me. I turned my head and saw the rider was slumped forward, a crossbow bolt buried in his back. Horse and rider together went on past to the end of the meadow, then the horse pulled up and the rider toppled slowly out of the saddle onto the ground where he lay still.

I was very frightened for myself and for Francois. I looked back and saw Octavian cantering towards us with Francois on his back, a riderless horse on each side. As he reached me I saw he was bleeding from a sword cut to his bad shoulder and I burst into tears.

We both dismounted and I hugged him with joy.

'I was sure they would kill you.'

'One of them did his best. Octavian is a real warhorse. He did a perfect capriole when I asked him. That knocked one of them over, horse and rider both. The other man slashed my shoulder, but I killed him before he could get in another cut. They're all dead now.'

He smiled as he spoke, then sat down suddenly. I bandaged him with a strip torn from my underskirt and we rode back to the stables.

We expected to find the stable boy dead, but he had managed to run up to the castle, and there were half a dozen men, including my father, in the yard when we arrived.

'Sybille,' he said, holding me as I dismounted. 'I was afraid they had taken you.'

I hugged him, said, 'Francois killed all three of them,' then turned and saw Francois had fainted.

We carried him up to the castle and dressed his wound properly. It was a deep cut, but clean, and hadn't reached the bone. We made up a bed in my mother's sewing room and there he stayed. On the third night I went into the room and into his bed and put into practice what I had learned from Guillemette. 'It will hurt a little at the beginning,' she had said, 'and then it will be what it will be. That depends on the two of you.'

It did hurt, but not for long; I was careful with Francois's shoulder, and he was careful with me. As Guillemette had said, what happened afterwards depended on the two of us. We both wanted it to be good, which it was, and then even better on the nights that followed. And days, when my mother was elsewhere in the castle. My mother knew what had happened just by looking at me after our first night together, but said nothing, and allowed Francois to stay in her sewing room until he was fully mended. During the day I sat by his bed sewing; we talked, we laughed, and we made love when we were sure we would not be disturbed.

I knew the top half of Francois's body well from my first days of nursing him, and discovered the rest of him as we lay in the makeshift bed. 'They left me alone below the waist,' he said, and pulled me down on top of him, covering my face with little kisses. He was at first uneasy about his missing eye and arm, but I convinced him that I loved him as he was. That was not difficult: his body was white and smooth and it gave me pleasure stroking and touching him everywhere.

'I was married to two strong men for fifteen years each,' Guillemette said. 'I can tell you what they like.' She was a good guide.

Francois

OUR RIDE COULD easily have ended in disaster. We were dismounted when we saw the marauders, and by the time Sybille, who was angry when I took her hand off my knee, had realised why, it was too late to disappear into the woods. Her grey, Marie, was pretty but slow.

They had swords only, no crossbows or longbows. When they came close I told Sybille to go and she galloped past them down the meadow. One turned to follow and I shot him in the back. I had several nightmares afterwards thinking about what would have happened if I'd missed.

I didn't miss, but the other two parted and came at me one from each side. I made the mistake of trying to reload my crossbow and control Octavian at the same time. The horse was snorting and pawing the ground; he seemed to sense what was going on. I failed to reload and was slow to draw my sword. It was Octavian's capriole that saved me; he did a massive leap, struck out with his hind legs and bowled over one of the marauders, horse and rider both. The other struck me in my right shoulder, but I was on the stronger, bigger horse and a simple parry and thrust did for him. I reloaded and killed the third man as he tried to remount.

Sybille was shaking when I caught up with her. She'd heard the hoofbeats getting closer and closer, not realising she was being pursued by a dead man. We both dismounted and held each other for a long time, then cantered back to the stables, leading the two stolen horses.

Raimond Roger was there with half a dozen men, about to begin a search. He was relieved to see us both safe, but questioned me closely about what had happened.

'I'm glad you're a good shot with the crossbow. But if you'd not been on Octavian it could have ended very badly.'

I agreed, and then to my dismay fainted. They carried me up to the castle and put me in the sewing room on the second floor of the keep.

'Guillemette and Sybille and I will look after you,' said Sybille's mother as I fell into a deep sleep. It was two days before I was back to normal.

On the third day, late in the evening, Sybille came into the room and into my bed. I had never seen a woman's naked body before. Indeed in that dim light I saw little of Sybille, as her hair was brushed forward over each shoulder and hung down to her waist, and she was quick to blow out the candle in the little niche above my bed.

We held each other for a long time. I was very aware of my missing right arm, but Sybille told me it didn't matter, nothing mattered now, kissing me everywhere, even touching my empty eye socket very gently with the tips of her fingers.

Then she told me what we had to do next, told me Guillemette had been her instructress, and all went well, even the all-too-brief moment when our bodies were first properly joined. Later she allowed me to relight the candle, and I was able to look at her as she lay back, smiling, on the bed. The images of Blanche, all-powerful in my mind for so long, were banished forever. My feeling of disloyalty lasted only a moment and never returned.

I was allowed to convalesce for two more days, and then returned to my shared quarters. We made love wherever we could: in the grain store, in Sybille's chamber, very quietly as her mother slept in the adjacent room, in my room which Etienne left free for us with characteristic generosity, and in the valley when I was her escort. That opportunity came round only every five days, and on the other four I felt a stab of jealousy when she rode out with another knight.

This couldn't go on for very long. I consulted Etienne, and his advice mirrored mine to him eighteen months earlier.

'Ask Raimond Roger for her hand in marriage,' said Etienne. 'He'll hardly refuse. If he doesn't know what is going on he's the only one in Montségur, he's as blind as I am. Remember, you're Francois de Beaufort, you saved her life.'

I went to see Raimond Roger, who was kind.

'I must consult Sybille and her mother. If they agree she is yours. You can handle Octavian, you've proved yourself as a man, and that's good enough for me.'

I blushed, then realised he was referring to my skills with the crossbow and on horseback. Or perhaps he knew what Sybille and I had been doing.

Her mother was more direct.

'Of course you must be married. You are married already in all but name. We'll organise the wedding the next time Guillaume Authie comes to Montségur.'

It was a simple ceremony. Raimond Roger entrusted her to my care, Authie blessed us both, Etienne made a brief and flowery speech and Sybille's mother smiled and cried. Thereafter we were together at night in Sybille's chamber, and in the daytime I was her only escort when she chose to ride in the valley.

Which was often. It was a marvellous summer in the Languedoc, sunny days broken only by the occasional brief downpour from black clouds sent from the Pyrenees that stopped the countryside turning brown. The rivers and streams were full from the melted snow.

After our earlier adventure I was cautious. Whenever we stopped I made sure that we could see around us for half a mile at least, which often annoyed Sybille, who wanted more than our bread and wine when we dismounted. Against my better judgement, and because I too wanted to love her in the open air, we would sometimes stop in one of the little copses that studded the valley, or by the river, and make love on the grass. Or standing up, Sybille leaning back against a tree. Or even once in the river, when it was so hot that Sybille stripped off her clothes and jumped in. I followed her, our wet bodies sliding together in the bracing water of the pool. Afterwards I felt I had not been responsible.

'What if those three marauders had found us like this?' I said, trying to appear stern as we lay drying on the bank.

'I saw you left your crossbow cocked with five bolts beside it. Even though overcome with passion. And you can reach it now if you roll over.'

She silenced me with kisses, and I did roll over, but not towards my crossbow. Later we sat drying in the sun, the river gleaming, its surface broken by the occasional trout rising to one of the blue-winged olives drifting down on the current.

I caught one and showed its gauzy-winged, curved body to Sybille.

'They hatch from those little discarded nymph cases you can see drifting by, then mate in the air and lay their eggs on the water.'

'Like us,' said Sybille, letting the fly settle on her finger, then blowing it back into the river. 'And then?'

'And then they die.'

Sybille

'And then they die,' Francois said. We were lying on the banks of the Adour, a small stream that branches off the big river that keeps our valley green. Narrow for most of its journey, the Adour widens into pools deep enough to swim in, deep enough to hold trout. The river flows over gravel and is very clear, clear enough to see the fish if you look carefully. The water is always cold, even when the sun is shining, as it comes from the mountains, always capped with snow.

It was very hot; we had taken off our clothes, swum in the river and made love. I teased Francois when, just before he came into me, he made sure that his crossbow was cocked and within reach of his left, his only arm.

Afterwards we watched the little flies hatching, clouds of them dancing against the blue sky, so many that the trout seemed sated and only occasionally broke the surface of the water to feed.

Francois caught one and let it settle on my finger, explaining that their birth, mating and death all took place within a day. I found it strangely disturbing that these thousands of tiny creatures had been created for so brief a moment.

'I suppose that as this world is an illusion, created by the Devil, that explains it,' I said, but Francois had gone to sleep. I fell asleep; when I woke I looked at his beautiful, battered body for a while, tracing very gently the scar that I had nursed. Francois must have felt my caresses and sat up with a start, grabbing his crossbow and scolding me for letting him doze. I kissed him to put him into a better mood, and that succeeded well.

We rode slowly back to the stables, tired, not talking. My

mind was full of the dancing flies, rising, falling, mating, laying their eggs, then dying in the river or in the stomach of a trout.

The next morning I was sewing with my mother in her chamber.

'How is it that this world is an illusion, the work of the Devil? How can Francois and I be so close, so happy if that is true?'

She put down her sewing and looked out of the window at the bustle in the courtyard below; the men-at-arms were busily preparing for the siege that Raimond Roger had told us would surely come.

'God allows us, some of us, moments of great happiness in this world. You and Francois are fortunate, for the moment, bringing each other joy. But nothing, not even that joy, lasts forever. If we look around us, we can see evidence of the Devil's work – the fires of the Inquisition in Toulouse and Carcassonne, the blinded knights, the marauders in the valleys. Look at Francois's body, as I am sure you do,' she said, beginning to smile and putting her hand over mine. 'He is living proof of the cruelty that disfigured him, that disfigures the world.'

'So we're like those flies?'

'We have a longer life and a greater consciousness. But our life is, in the end, equally impermanent. We should, I believe, use it to prepare ourselves for the next, the perfect, world. And you can only arrive there if you become more than a believer, become a Perfect.

'I could give up meat, I never swear an oath, I tell the truth. But I could never give up Francois.'

'You don't have to do that yet,' said my mother, picking up her sewing and kissing me on the cheek. 'You have years ahead of you to think about these things, to read the Gospels, to listen to Guillaume Authie. And to discover, as I have, that it is possible to love someone without making love.'

I thought about my mother's remarks for many days and began to understand and worry about the impermanence of our lives. Until our discussion I had thought our castle at Montségur, and the valley, and the Pyrenees beyond, as part of a secure and settled existence. I began to realise the threats to our world that even the arrival of the knights had failed to show me. I had been aware only of my love, my passion for Francois.

I said this one evening to Francois as we were lying in bed. He dismissed it with a joke.

'We have several lives to prepare ourselves for the next world,' he said. 'I'd be happy to come back as a dapple-grey palfrey for you to ride.'

I pushed him away and turned my back on him during the night, but I was unable to resist him when he apologised in the morning. And even that short abstinence seemed a waste.

Francois

I BEGAN TO UNDERSTAND Sybille better, to realise she was thoughtful as well as playful, that she worried about much more than her sewing and her horse. She read a great deal, knew Latin and French, and would always attend the services when visiting Perfects arrived at Montségur. She was, I knew, greatly influenced by her mother Claire, a serene woman who had become a Perfect several years before, although she made no attempt to persuade Sybille and me into the rigorous way of life she had adopted.

I had been marked, in mind as well as body, by war. I had killed men, and men had tried hard to kill me. I had ignored our Cathar belief that human life is sacred, albeit for good reasons. Now a curtain had been drawn between that life and the consuming passion I felt for my wife, making me want to think of nothing but the present, nothing but Sybille.

I was born Cathar, which I took for granted. Unlike my wife I was not naturally contemplative, took no great pleasure in studying Cathar texts, and I found reading difficult, as my Latin was poor. I was easily out-argued or bored when Authie spoke to us on one of his regular visits to Montségur.

I told Sybille she made me so happy that I could think of nothing else, and that the idea of abstinence, from meat and eggs and above all from her, filled me with dismay. I told her that, yes, I was born Cathar, hated the Catholic Church, but was happy to trust in the promise of reincarnation to ready myself for heaven. I also said that while I understood our dualist doctrine in theory, in practice I found it impossible to believe that this world in general and our marriage in particular had been created by the Devil.

I foolishly tried to make a joke of all this, and told Sybille that I would return in my next life as her horse. This made her angry, and she pushed me away, although my apology the next morning put things right between us. She knew better than to argue with me – she knew that I would lose the argument without changing my mind – but she continued to worry about the conflict between the life of a Perfect and our happy, passionate existence. Sybille stopped eating meat and eggs, but happily our lovemaking resumed, although I had to explain to her that a man was, as I had discovered, not as quickly recharged as a crossbow.

7

The Fall

Sybille

FRANCOIS AND I avoided theological arguments thereafter and became closer than ever. It was a cold winter, and we were fortunate in having our own small chamber with a fireplace; we kept each other warm during the night and often during the day. I no longer needed Guillemette's advice, and we continued to find new ways of giving each other pleasure. Francois was self-conscious about his missing eye and arm but I was able to convince him that I had helped to heal these wounds on his arrival at Montségur, and that I loved him then and loved him now.

Spring came early and we began to ride through the valley again, a constant source of pleasure for us both. On a couple of occasions my father and mother, at my suggestion, rode with us.

'Octavian has become your horse,' my father said to Francois. He had just tried and failed to get Octavian to perform the capriole that had saved us from the brigands a year earlier.

'You were the man who broke him and trained him,' said Francois. 'He'd get used to you quickly enough if you rode him regularly.'

'Perhaps. Anyhow, these riding school manoeuvres are not likely to be useful when the crusaders come. Their preparations are well advanced, and we'll have them here by the end of the month.'

Soon afterwards their scouts were seen in our valley, and that put an end to our riding. I felt confined as a result; I was deprived of Francois's company during the day, and spent most of the time with my mother. My father had put Francois in charge of our crossbowmen, and when they weren't practising in the butts they were making new weapons, repairing old ones and forging an enormous supply of bolts. Francois took his responsibilities very seriously and would not allow me to distract him.

The valley, I knew, was now barely cultivated, and many persecuted Cathars were inside Montségur or in the ramshackle buildings that clung to the rocks below the walls. We received regular reports of the work of the Inquisition in Toulouse and Carcassonne, and my father had repeatedly warned us all that it was only a matter of time before they came to Montségur.

Francois was always tired, sometimes too tired to make love, which I found hard to understand at first, until Guillemette told me I had nothing to worry about.

'How often?' she asked me.

'Until now, every night and most mornings.'

She laughed. 'Think yourself lucky. My two husbands managed once a week, then once a month if I insisted. Francois is doing well. As are you.'

Francois

RAIMOND ROGER ASKED me about the lessons to be learned from Roqueville.

'Water,' I told him. 'Once they had cut off our water supply it was all over, although the end was hastened by treachery.'

'Our cisterns go straight down hundreds of feet into the mountain. We've never run out of water even in the driest of summers. And they aren't supplied by external streams; that was your undoing at Roqueville. They will think they can starve, or dry us out. The Count of Toulouse failed ten years ago and so will they.'

Montségur's great strength was that the shape of our mountain made it impossible to cut us off completely from the outside world. The castle was perched on top of a massive limestone pyramid that broadened as it descended into the valley, so that at its base it was fully five miles around. On three sides the approaches were sheer. On the fourth side the approach to the castle was steep – I remembered toiling up the path with my Roqueville knights on that first day – and we had cleared away any small trees and bushes that offered cover.

Inside the castle we were well prepared. Our crossbowmen, forty in all, were fast and accurate, and we had a good supply of bolts.

'Adequate,' I told them – Raimond Roger had made me their commander – 'provided you don't loose off at long range and don't miss your targets.' They accepted me after some initial grumbling; I was as quick and accurate as all but the best of them, a grizzled old warrior who had no wish to command. And they knew I had good reason to want to kill crusaders. We had three good trebuchets and stones for them in abundance; the slope up to the castle was so steep you could roll the stones down on any advancing troops.

When Hugues d'Arcis arrived from Carcassonne he had a force of, we estimated, around 8,000 men. Our garrison was 450 strong, but only 250 of these were fighting men. The rest were women, children, old men and Perfects, all hungry mouths to feed and water.

Hugues d'Arcis did his best to put a cordon round the bottom of our mountain, but even with his numbers the cordon was easily permeable. He left the village alone, and was clever enough to encourage farmers to come to its market and sell him supplies, but that also meant that we were able to divert some of this to Montségur. For three months very little happened; boredom was our greatest enemy, as we needed to keep constantly on the alert for any attack.

By the end of July the crusaders realised they were not going to be able to starve us out. They attacked at dawn up the southwest slope with perhaps a thousand foot soldiers, behind wooden shields on rollers that they pushed slowly up the hill. Our trebuchets smashed these to pieces and then did tremendous damage to their troops; not many soldiers got close enough to trouble our crossbowmen. We made a brief sortie to collect weapons from the fallen, and then allowed the crusaders to collect their wounded under a flag of truce.

'They wouldn't have extended that charity to us,' said Guillemette to me. 'I can't believe you didn't slit the throats of any who weren't already dead.'

'They will have to feed and nurse the wounded,' said Etienne, who had been listening to my account of the skirmish. 'That's the difference between Cathars and Catholics. We take life only when we have to. They kill for pleasure and the glory of God.'

There were no more attempts at a frontal assault, and when the rains came and our cisterns filled we thought we were safe. However, they didn't abandon the siege, and were reinforced by a further 1,500 men, which enabled them to strengthen the blockade. Our search for reinforcements was less successful, although we were joined by twenty or so Cathar soldiers over the summer months. Our supplies continued to trickle in.

The Bishop

Hugues d'Arcis had a reputation as a brave commander, a man who had led half a dozen successful campaigns and sieges. I could see no evidence that this reputation was deserved, and when he announced his plan for a frontal assault up the slope I expressed my disbelief.

'It's suicide up that slope. Completely exposed, and no chance of surprise.'

He was angry and said so.

'What do you know about such things? You're a man of the cross, not the sword. We've been building stout pavises for the last two months that will give us cover. And a two-storey tower which we will use once we get close to the walls.'

I reminded him that I had been sent to advise him because I had ten years as a soldier before I became a priest.

'I designed one of the first trebuchets for the great Simon de Montfort,' I said. 'I know what damage they can do, and the Cathars have the high ground.'

He didn't change his plan, with calamitous results, sulked

for a week, then asked my advice. It was clear to me that our only chance of success lay in the possibility of getting men up the northeast side of the mountain.

'It's a series of precipices, almost vertical,' Hugues said.

'They are managing to climb down them and back up again with supplies. That approach appears to be very lightly guarded. If we can get a foothold on the plateau and capture the barbican we have a chance of success. Otherwise we might as well go home.'

He was persuaded that it was worth trying, especially since I was able to recruit a dozen Basque mountaineers who were afraid of nothing and ready, for the appropriate reward, to try and find a way up.

'They are like mountain goats,' I told Hugues, who grunted when he first saw them, squat, swarthy men who paid him no deference and spoke no French.

The Basque goats spent several nights reconnoitring possible routes, watching men arriving and leaving by the cliff, always by the same route. They were clever enough not to kill or detain these men. They made little sketch maps of the path, if path it could be called; it zigzagged up the limestone, and a missed footstep or handhold would have been fatal. Looking up at the route gave me vertigo.

My Basques waited until there was a full moon and led the way up the mountain, hammering iron pegs into the rock which they then linked with ropes to help the less experienced climbers who came later. We were only able to persuade twenty men-at-arms to make the ascent, money again being more important than glory or God's cause.

It was enough. Our little band had the advantage of surprise, took the lightly guarded barbican, killed the dozen Cathars who were inside, and beat off the counter-attack in the morning. We were now only sixty yards from the main fortress, linked to it by a razor-sharp ridge along which it was only possible to travel two abreast. This meant that a counter-attack was difficult; it also meant that an assault on the castle was equally hard.

It took us a further two weeks to haul a trebuchet, one of my own designing, up the cliff. We dismantled it at the bottom and used ropes and pulleys to bring it into the barbican. It took another week to bring enough stones for the trebuchet and begin firing. During this part of the siege we lost only two men, neither of them Basques. We began to batter at their walls every day, but the walls were twelve feet thick, more in places, and it was slow work. However, it put an end to patronising remarks from Hugues d'Arcis.

Francois

IT IS ALWAYS the unexpected that leads to defeat in a siege. In our case we did not believe the crusaders could attack the barbican by the cliff to the northeast, so it was lightly guarded; we kept most of our men in the castle and patrolling the slopes to the northwest. We were wrong.

Once they had captured the barbican the odds shifted in their favour, decisively so when they succeeded in bringing a trebuchet and ammunition up the side of the mountain. We had to admire their bravery and determination, which matched ours.

For two weeks we exchanged stone for stone, neither side making much impression on the thick walls. Each side sustained perhaps a half a dozen killed or wounded every day, but they had the advantage of numbers. More importantly, we were beginning to run short of food, as our main supply route was cut off. The castle and forecourt were impossibly crowded, as the huts below our walls had been abandoned. Wounded and healthy, men and women, and the few children that had survived, crowded into a space designed for a fifth of that number.

Raimond Roger sent for reinforcements from Aragon, and we learned that Corbario, a famous mercenary, was on his way with twenty men. They never arrived; they were intercepted and persuaded to change sides. This failure encouraged one of our commanders, Imbert de Salis, to leave the castle and try to negotiate with the crusaders. He returned empty-handed.

Raimond Roger was furious.

'It is pointless trying to negotiate. The only messages to send to those people are stones from our trebuchet or bolts from our crossbows.'

We stamped the floor and hammered the table when he gave this defiant message, but we all realised our situation was desperate. And that night two of our Perfects left Montségur with our Cathar treasure, which did nothing to boost the confidence of those who knew they had gone.

Two days later Raimond Roger asked for volunteers to try to retake the barbican. I offered to go and was rejected. Raimond Roger told me I didn't have enough arms for the sortie; he made a joke of it, but I knew he was right and it probably saved my life. The plan was to crawl along the mountain just below the ridge at night, and hope to surprise them as they had surprised us.

From the castle we could hear the shouts and screams of the fighting, which lasted perhaps an hour; then all was silent apart from cheering from the barbican. For a moment we thought it was our men. It was not. Of the forty men that set out, only five returned, two of them badly wounded. Two days later the crusaders stormed our outer wall, and we had to retreat into the main keep, leaving our wounded and stragglers behind.

8

The Burning

Francois

THE NEXT MORNING Raimond Roger called us into the Great Hall. There were only a dozen commanders left standing, and I was one of the few who had not been wounded, though I was as dirty, tired and hungry as the rest. We sat at the long table, on which there was no bread, no water, and listened to Raimond Roger standing on the dais at the end of the chamber. He spoke slowly and carefully, making no attempt to conceal the emotion he felt. Throughout we could hear the crash of the crusaders' stones against our walls.

'We can no longer defend Montségur. We have fewer than sixty fighting men, and some of you can barely lift a sword or aim a crossbow. We have two choices. A final sally, not in the hope of victory against three hundred men, but to show only death can defeat us. Or to surrender on the best terms I can negotiate. Which is it to be?'

It was clear Raimond Roger wanted to die fighting – it was equally clear that there was no general appetite for a last defiant stand. Most of us were too tired to speak coherently, never mind fight. I said nothing, but my silence made it apparent, to my father-in-law at least, that I wanted to live. The thought of leaving Sybille was impossible to contemplate, even in exchange for a noble death, and I had seen enough to realise that death in battle was rarely noble and little better than dying of hunger or disease or old age. I also made up my mind at that moment to do what was necessary to escape the stake.

'Very well,' said Raimond Roger after listening to those who were able to speak. 'I was ready to lead you in a final sortie, but not at the head of only six or seven men.'

He managed to smile as he made a jest of his disappointment, looking at me as he spoke, then continued, 'I'll negotiate the best terms I can, in spite of the weakness of our position. And I know, you all know, that any Cathar who does not convert will be burned.'

Normally we would have pounded the table and stamped our feet after a speech from our leader, but we were too tired, and some of us were too ashamed, to respond. We left the chamber and returned to our posts; as we went into the courtyard we heard the crash as the crusaders' stone-gun continued to batter our outside wall.

As it turned out, Raimond Roger was able to negotiate generous terms; our opponents were as anxious to end the siege as we were. The main headings, as far as I can remember them, were:

Hostages would be exchanged, and we were to remain in the castle for two weeks.

We would be pardoned for all our past sins, including, to my surprise, Avignonet.

Anyone prepared to abjure the Cathar faith and confess before the Inquisitors would receive only a light penance and remain at liberty. We would have two weeks to make up our minds.

Anyone who remained a Cathar would be burned at the stake.

It seemed strange that we would be left in a kind of limbo for fourteen days, although as it turned out some of that time was used by the Bishop and the Inquisitors to persuade as many as possible to recant. At the same time our Bishop, Bertrand Marty, was equally active in encouraging his Cathar flock to remain faithful.

And to be burned alive as a result. I was not interested in the theological arguments of either side. I was, quite simply, prepared to do whatever was necessary to survive, and I was determined to persuade Sybille to do the same. I avoided most of the sessions of prayer that took place, and refused the Consolamentum.

I discussed this with Etienne soon after the terms had been agreed. He was of the same mind; he still clung to the hope of finding Stephanie and holding his child. If they were still alive, I thought to myself, as I agreed that he and I and Sybille would go to Carcassonne to search for his family once we were allowed to leave Montségur.

I did not feel a physical coward, as I had been as active as any of the defenders, lucky to escape being wounded again, and I had nothing to prove after Avignonet and Roqueville. Secretly I admitted to myself I had a horror of the stake, to which any end seemed preferable. I felt uneasy about recanting; as Sybille pointed out, in our early days I had stated firmly and proudly that I was Cathar. I contented myself by deciding that swearing an oath and becoming a Catholic was a conversion in name only. My inner beliefs, feeble though they were, would remain the same.

Towards the end of the truce it became clear that around two hundred of our number would remain Cathar and face the stake rather than recant. I was astonished at this bravery, a courage quite different from that shown in battle. Many of these faithful were men-at-arms, whose faith I had thought simpler than mine; they turned out to be more steadfast. Sixty knights, most of the female Credentes and all the wounded and elderly refused to recant. Sybille's mother was already a Perfect, and I never doubted that she would die for her beliefs.

In the final days there was a moving, and for me unsettling, distribution of gifts from those who were about to die to those who wanted to live. Their possessions were pitifully small, but Bishop Bertrand gave me oil, salt, a piece of green cloth and a blessing. Sybille received from her mother some money, an embroidered purse and a pair of shoes with gilt buckles. We both looked on these gifts as relics.

The crusaders had stripped the castle of anything of value, including the tapestries in the Great Hall. I saw two of their men-at-arms coming to blows over the hangings in Claire's room. Their disappointment and surprise that there was no silver or gold was evident.

Sybille

FROM THE VERY first Francois made it clear he was determined to recant, and that he wanted to live, wanted us both to live. I knew he was no coward, but I was disappointed that he took this decision immediately without listening to the arguments put forward by my mother and by Bishop Bertrand.

I spent many hours with my mother during the truce.

'I love him. He is my husband and I feel bound by his decision, however speedily it has been taken,' I said to her. She was gentle in her arguments, but forcible in saying that I should think long and carefully about recanting.

'You are not bound, in the eyes of God, to follow Francois's lead. Think whether the prospect of eternal life, which beckons me and of which I am assured, is not more attractive than anything this imperfect world can offer. Even to you, young and in love as you are.'

I told her I was torn apart by her words and the prospect of losing her forever, but that the strongest of my conflicting feelings was my love for Francois. This she seemed to accept.

My mother had decided to die. She was already a Perfect, and I never thought she would choose any other course. On our last morning together she gave me her embroidered purse and some money, which made me realise that in less than a day I would see her for the last time.

Images of her being consumed by fire haunted me. As I touched her arm I was unable to stop myself imagining the flames blackening her soft skin.

'How will you bear the pain when you are burning at the stake?' I asked, hardly able to speak these terrible words through my tears.

'God will take the pain upon himself, of course.' And she drew me to her and hugged me as I cried.

Francois

FOR FOURTEEN DAYS only priests and monks entered the castle on their errand, as they saw it, of mercy. They made no impact on the Perfects and the Credentes, and those of us who had decided to live did not require their attention.

We, the new Catholics, were brought in batches before two magistrates, were required to swear an oath and profess the abandonment of our heretical ways. The sincerity of our conversion was not questioned; few of us would have responded accurately to a detailed catechism. Cathars and Catholics had the Lord's Prayer and the Gospels in common, but little else. Then we were all sentenced to make the pilgrimage to Compostela; it seemed unlikely that this journey would be made by many of us or monitored by our judges.

Early on that last morning the soldiers came in and separated converts from Cathars. We were allowed to make our final farewells. Sybille was distraught, in tears, and had to be pulled gently away from her mother's embrace. Claire did not weep, or smile, and the look in her eyes told me that she was already on her way to her final destination. I felt incapable of speech. Raimond Roger was not there. He had been taken to Carcassonne the night before, which added to Sybille's distress.

I looked among the soldiers for any of the Roqueville torturers, but these men were mainly French, a few English and the Basque mountaineers who had been our undoing. They looked as tired, hungry and dirty as the men they had overcome. As we left the castle they were fettering the arms and legs of those who were about to die.

We were led down the mountain until we came to the flat field where the burning was to take place, and made to line the path for the final journey of the Cathars. We had heard the sounds of hammering and sawing all week, but the field was not visible from the castle. I had expected to see two hundred stakes and pyres; instead the crusaders had built a palisade from wooden stakes perhaps a hundred feet long and forty feet wide. Inside they had piled brushwood and firewood along the palisade walls and down the centre, creating two separate channels no more than three feet wide into which the Cathars would be herded. As we arrived soldiers were soaking straw in each corner with oil and pitch.

We stood there for perhaps an hour, the four of us opposite the gate into the palisade. Sybille looked at it once, then shut her eyes. I could feel her whole body trembling, and although she was beside me she clung to Guillemette.

First came the priests and the monks, led by their Bishop, chanting the *Te Deum* and then, in supreme irony, the *Nunc Dimittis.* As they moved past us a little way down the hill I could see that, unlike the fighting men, they were well fed and well clothed.

Then came the procession of two hundred Cathars, first the men led by Bishop Bertrand, then the women, Claire the last of them. They were walking slowly and awkwardly because of their fetters. Half a dozen wounded or elderly were carried down on stretchers. Their heads were bowed and they prayed as they walked, although their words were drowned by the chanting of the monks. When he reached the gate Bishop Bertrand stopped, uncertain what to do, until a soldier pushed him into one of the narrow aisles.

The women were last. When Claire came almost to the gate she stopped, turned, saw her daughter, opened her arms and gave a smile of great sweetness. And at that moment Sybille raised her head and saw her mother.

Guillemette

I WAS ALWAYS A 'Castle Cathar'; if my mistress Claire had become a Mohammedan overnight I would have followed her. Our Cathar religion seemed no worse than any other, although I never aspired to be a Perfect and the Endura seemed a thoroughly bad way of ensuring a prolonged and painful death. I had always made it clear that I would follow Claire anywhere except to the stake. I was happy enough in this imperfect world and in no hurry to risk the uncertainties of the next.

Francois, Sybille, Etienne and I were sentenced, as were all the converts, to make the pilgrimage to Compostela. We got off lightly. After Roqueville, after Bram, after Puylaurens, we expected prison. So relief rather than sorrow, I am ashamed to say, was my main emotion as we were led down to the Field of the Burned, as it came to be known. There I marvelled at the cruel ingenuity of the crusaders in their construction of the palisade.

It all seemed slow and strange, the chanting of the monks, the clumsy walk of the fettered Cathars, the indistinct sound of their prayers. I wanted the grim ritual to be over as soon as possible. Francois, Sybille, Etienne and I were opposite the gate, Sybille quietly crying, her eyes closed.

Then something happened that I find difficult to understand or to describe. Claire, the last of the women, stopped by the gate, turned, opened her arms and smiled. We were no more than ten feet away. At that moment Sybille looked up, saw her mother, let go of my arm and ran to join her. They were through the gate, which was closed and barred behind them, in less than a minute. Etienne and I instinctively grabbed Francois's arm, but he made no attempt to follow Sybille, whether out of shock or fear I do not know.

The drums began to beat, the Bishop gave a signal and four soldiers plunged their burning torches into the piles of brushwood, straw and kindling at each corner. There was a breeze strong enough to fan the flames and very soon the whole palisade was blazing. The chants of the priests were not loud enough to drown the screams of the victims.

We had to move down the hill to escape the heat and the black smoke, although we did not escape the smell of burning human flesh. The fires burned for two days. Francois was in a daze, and neither Etienne nor I could comfort him. We reached the bottom of the hill, while the soldiers remained on the upper slopes. There Francois seemed to come out of his trance and wanted to go back to the Field of the Burned.

'Sybille's gone. There's nothing left. You'd be wasting your time,' I said to him, then turned to Etienne. 'Where do we go now?'

'To Compostela. But first to Carcassonne.'

9

The Price

Blanche

I knew exactly what he wanted, exactly what I was doing. I walked over to the bed, pulled my shift over my head, lay back and let him come into me. At that moment I ceased to be a Perfect, or even a believer, but it seemed a price worth paying to see Stephanie and my grandchild.

That first time was painful; Bernard had been dead for several years, and although I had flirted innocently with the young knights at Roqueville, I had become a Perfect and accepted abstinence from sex as part of my new, more ascetic life. And the Inquisitor was not gentle. It did not last long; he rolled off me, adjusted his long robes and left the room without speaking.

For the rest of that day and for many days thereafter I was concerned that now he had obtained what he wanted he might not keep his side of our bargain. He visited me again that night; he did not speak, although he cried out as he came, leaving my room soon afterwards.

It continued like that for the rest of the week; he would come to my room, I would take off my shift, lie back on the bed and raise my knees as he entered me. I managed to withdraw myself from the act, closing my eyes and making no noise, not even of protest. I would look at the shutters, always drawn in the evening, and concentrate on the little crack that ran down one of them, causing the light blue paint to bubble and peel.

Although the act, mechanical and brief as it was, disgusted me, my disgust was as much at myself as at the Inquisitor. To my relief, he bathed regularly and as a result smelled only of the walnut oil soap that, I learned later, was made at his old abbey of Flaran. He did not try to kiss me, although I noticed his breath was sweet.

He spoke to me only once, to ask whether I had enough to eat and drink. I asked him when I could see my daughter.

'As soon as I can make the necessary arrangements,' he replied as he left the room.

I discovered his name from the elderly attendant who brought my meals to my room – it could no longer be called a cell, as it had rudimentary furnishings and a close-stool outside the door, which was not locked. Arnaud was the Inquisitor's given name, although he had changed it to Mathieu when he became a monk. He was a farmer's son from the north, plucked out of his abbey by the Pope to root out Catharism from the Languedoc.

After that first week his secretary came to see me.

'Thank God, Lady Blanche,' he said. 'I am pleased you have been convinced by my master to return to the True Faith. You are welcome indeed.'

'Am I free to go?'

'You are to move from this little room to a house that befits your station. You are free to leave that house, but not Carcassonne. Eventually you must appear before the magistrates, but your penance will not be severe. My master has said to them that your conversion is sincere, your repentance absolute.'

I asked him who was paying the rent for the house.

'It's Church property,' he said, and I left it at that. It seemed he had no knowledge of my bargain with the Inquisitor, although it was unlikely that his visits to my chamber and their purpose would pass unnoticed for long.

The house was in an adjacent square; small, a single bedroom above a ground-floor room for living and cooking. It had been whitewashed inside, and the walls were of the warm stone of the region, with two windows at each level and a blue-painted door. There was a courtyard at the back shaded by a plane tree. The secretary gave me a key and a purse containing a small sum of money. 'You are free to leave the house, but you must not go outside the walls of Carcassonne,' he repeated as he left.

I had no wish to stray far from my house, going only to the twice-weekly market to buy food and wine. As I was no longer a Perfect I bought and ate meat and eggs for the first time for many years. I had to admit to myself that the change in my diet was a change for the better; I had endured the monotony of vegetables and the occasional fish for a long time, and I enjoyed the strong red wine of the region, which I had not tasted for twenty years or more. It was better than I remembered from the old days at Roqueville.

On my fifth night in the little house the Inquisitor told me that Stephanie was living in a small community of nuns not far from his old abbey of Flaran. He had heard that morning she had borne a healthy son. He went on to tell me what I had already assumed, that she too had recanted, though Stephanie was always a convinced Cathar and would have found it hard to swear an oath. Suppressing my tears, I asked him what had happened to Etienne and the other Roqueville knights.

'As far as I know they are at Montségur,' he said, then rose and left the house without leading me upstairs, for which I was grateful.

Mathieu

AFTER I FIRST possessed Blanche I thought I would find it easy to return to my celibate ways. This was not the case; the more I had, the more I wanted.

Blanche kept both parts of the bargain. She gave me her body without protest or resistance. She appeared in front of the Bishop, his retainers and many of the nobles of Carcassonne, swearing the necessary oath in a clear, unfaltering voice, and then joined in the celebratory Mass which followed without any outward show of reluctance.

Afterwards the Bishop congratulated me.

'Blanche de Roqueville is an even more important conversion than Baruch, and achieved in far less time. Your powers of persuasion have not diminished.'

I looked at him closely as he spoke these words, wondered if he knew of my bargain with Blanche, and then realised that I did not care. I knew his own life was far from blameless. He was rumoured to be a regular visitor to the brothels of the city. I was safe so long as I was discreet, so long as word of my conduct did not reach Rome. The Bishop was in no position to act against me. I accepted his compliment at face value.

'Now that she has converted she will be able to petition the Church for the return of her lands. It will be difficult to refuse her.'

The Bishop looked thoughtful for a moment.

'Well, it is a price worth paying. The tithes are flowing more freely now that Béziers and Bram and Puylaurens have fallen.'

The Bishop was my confessor, and until now I had little to tell him, which he had found disappointing. I was unable to reveal my relationship with Blanche even in the confessional, and I continued to celebrate Mass and take Communion in a state of mortal sin. This perhaps accounted for my increasing leniency towards those heretics that came before the Inquisition. As the Bishop had pointed out, these were diminishing in number, and the need for exemplary punishments seemed to be a thing of the past. This made me more comfortable with Blanche, although we avoided talking about such things.

She pressed me after two weeks about Stephanie. I hesitated, then said, 'I am afraid that once you have seen her you will not return here. You will have to go under escort.'

'Where would I go? You have made me – I have made me – whatever I have become. I did not choose the path that brought me here,' and she gave a slight smile, 'but here I am.'

These words and the smile brought me a little guilty happiness which I found hard to conceal.

'I'll make the arrangements for you to visit the convent next week. It's a day's journey at most.'

Stephanie

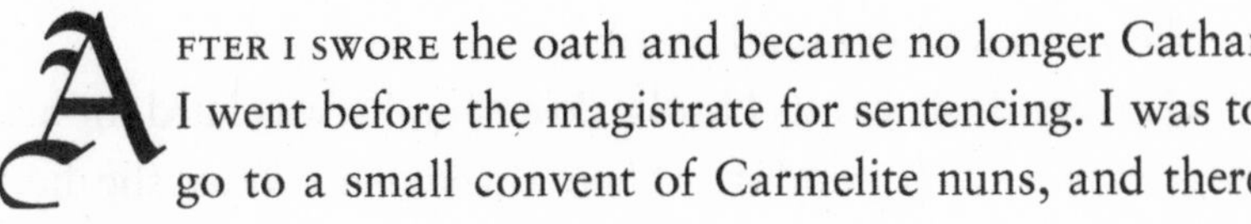

AFTER I SWORE the oath and became no longer Cathar I went before the magistrate for sentencing. I was to go to a small convent of Carmelite nuns, and there my son was born. At that point I did not know whether Etienne was alive or dead, and my mother and I had been separated the moment we arrived in Carcassonne.

She had been a Perfect for many years, was steadfast in her faith, and would, I was sure, find it impossible to swear an oath and recant. I had found it hard enough. So she would be tried, convicted and burned, a fate which she could accept in the confidence that eternal and glorious life awaited her. No such prospect awaited me. I had sworn, I had converted, I was no longer Cathar. I had abandoned the faith into which I had been born. Holding my baby son was my consolation.

News was hard to come by at the convent. It was not a closed order, and the nuns were friendly enough, but we had few visitors. Then came word, via the abbey, that Blanche, my mother, would visit us in a few days' time. I was overjoyed, and surprised, at the news that she was still alive.

As soon as she arrived she was shown into my small chamber; Bertrand was sleeping in his cot. We hugged each other for a long time, cried, found words hard to utter. She held Bertrand as soon as he had finished feeding at my breast. My son seemed instantly at home in her arms.

'He looks like my father,' she said, able to discern a resemblance to her father that had escaped me. I was desperate for news of Etienne.

'I am told he and the other knights were led by Francois to Montségur, and have found shelter there. Etienne was strong, he will have survived the journey.'

'Are you sure he is still alive?'

She paused. 'I cannot be sure.'

Hearing those words I broke down, and it was hard for her to give me much comfort. Then I asked her how she had managed to escape the full weight of the Inquisition. She told me everything, sparing no details.

I was shocked, and showed it. My mother, the Perfect, who had taught me and many others the Cathar faith, had sworn an oath and recanted. Far worse, she had allowed herself to be violated by the monster who had ordered the blinding and maiming of Etienne.

'Better to have burned,' I said. 'You have become the Inquisitor's whore.'

These were unforgiving, unforgiveable words. Behind them lay my jealousy of her beauty ever since I had reached womanhood, jealousy of the way in which she allowed the younger knights at Roqueville to make courtly love to her. Including my Etienne.

Blanche was silent for a moment, then replied, 'How else could I see you, see Bertrand? You recanted. Were your reasons any better than mine?'

I could not reply. She handed Bertrand back to me, gave me a kiss which I was unable to return and left the room. In the morning she was gone.

Blanche

I WAS IN DESPAIR after seeing Bertrand and Stephanie. I found her unkindness to me shocking. Her rejection was cruel and unwarranted; we had both recanted, and for good reasons. She had saved her unborn child, and if I had not given myself to the Inquisitor I would never have seen her or my grandson again. I would have been handed over to the secular authorities for sentencing, and could well have spent the rest of my life in jail. As it turned out, I was in a prison of a sort, and it seemed my sacrifice had been in vain.

On the evening of my return to the little house in Carcassonne the Inquisitor came to see me. He asked about my visit to Stephanie and my grandson, and I broke down in tears, unable to answer for several minutes. I had never before shown such frailty of spirit in front of him.

Then I said I had been rejected by Stephanie, not for recanting, but for sleeping with him.

'You had no need to tell her,' he said.

'I am still enough of a Cathar to tell the truth. She hates me now. I'll never see her again.'

He put his hand on my shoulder and stroked my hair for a moment, and this show of sympathy made me cry even harder. Then he said, 'She'll change her mind in time. I'll leave now, and come and see you later in the week.'

I had not believed him capable of possessing, never mind displaying, the gentler human emotions, but his sympathy was genuine and I had no one else to turn to. In the weeks that followed our relationship began, very gradually, to change to something more than one-sided sex. I would give him supper – fish, bread, wine – two or three times a week. And on these evenings we would talk, eat and then go upstairs. Sometimes he would stay until dawn.

Our conversations were circumscribed. I would ask him about his early life on the farm and in Paris, and he in turn would listen to me talk about my childhood at Villeneuve-Comtal before I came to Roqueville. We were careful to avoid theology, or talk about the siege and the events that had preceded the fall of our castle.

From time to time I would fall silent, reminded in spite of myself that Mathieu had ordered the burning of my dead son's body and the blinding of Etienne. Stephanie and my grandchild were his hostages. Our first sexual encounters were as part of a bargain. I could not easily forget what he had done to my family and my fellow Cathars. I had done my best to withdraw myself from anything but passive participation in the act.

I could not help noticing he was tall, striking rather than handsome, with beautiful, expressive hands, surprising in a farmer's son. He had the lean, ascetic body of a man who fasted regularly. He approached the act of love as though he was making up for years of celibacy; at the beginning he was as brief, and as powerful, as the stallions I had seen shuddering into our mares at Roqueville.

I for my part, after separating myself from the act in those early nights, was increasingly unable to avoid being caught up and taking pleasure from our coming together. I used oil on myself and on him and raised my knees to make the act easier. And he began to notice my body, to caress me, to take enough time, at my whispered requests, to give me pleasure too.

I rarely regretted the changed nature of the bargain nor the changed response of my body – the latter at least did not seem to be within my control. We had a saying in the Languedoc: 'As well be hung for a sheep as for a lamb.' And I was no longer a Perfect, no longer Cathar.

I understood that this was the ultimate betrayal, not just of my faith but of my dead husband and son. Yet I could not, in the end, ignore my body and I no longer pretended I was an unwilling victim. I stopped thinking of him as the Inquisitor and began to call him Mathieu.

10

To Carcassonne and Barraigne

Guillemette

I BECAME BY DEFAULT the leader of our little band. Etienne was blind and Francois might as well have been for all the use he was in those early days. I was struck by how helpless knights were without a horse, a sword or a crossbow. Without me Etienne and Francois would have starved.

Etienne wanted to find his wife and child, although secretly I doubted that they were still alive. Carcassonne, where they had been taken after the fall of Roqueville, seemed as good a destination as any, and it was one of the many starting points for the pilgrimage to Compostela.

'Remember, we are pilgrims now. Devout, humble and penitent. Warriors no longer,' I told them both on that first evening. We were only three miles away from Montségur and could still see the smoke from the fire that had destroyed two hundred Cathars. Francois kept looking back; I looked once and never a second time.

We had sheltered in a small copse as night fell; we had no food and no means of making a fire. We had detached ourselves from the other converts; there was no safety in unarmed numbers and we would travel faster without our former friends. To mark our pilgrim's status I spent the evening sewing scallop shells on the cloaks we had taken as we left Montségur.

At dawn we were stiff, cold and slow to get moving. We walked all morning and just before noon we had our first stroke of luck. We came across the corpse of a soldier lying in a ditch. He had been dead for some time judging by the smell, and his face had been partially eaten away, probably by foxes. I searched his body, gagging at the smell, and found a tinder box and some flints.

Francois wanted to take his sword. I would have none of it.

'We are peaceful pilgrims on a holy journey. Downcast eyes and silence are the best weapons.'

He reluctantly agreed, although I found out later that he had taken the dead man's dagger and hidden it in the lining of his coat.

We were retracing the journey that Francois and his fifteen companions had taken after Roqueville had fallen. 'We should avoid Roqueville. We'll find no friends there,' said Etienne. 'Better to go via Barraigne. My mother may still be alive.'

The rolling countryside along our journey was uncultivated and empty, the farmers having been killed or driven out, their crops taken and their animals slaughtered. Many of the buildings had been burned, though we were usually able to find some kind of shelter and build a fire. We lived off what little was left of the land. I was the provider; we saw the occasional roe-deer, hare or partridge but had no means of bringing them down. I set snares every evening once we had halted, but they were always empty in the morning. What saved us were the mushrooms in the woods. The crusaders had stripped the land bare, but if you knew where to look there were plenty of ceps, girolles and trompettes de mort to be had.

'We're living like kings,' I told Francois, who was incapable of telling a mushroom from a toadstool. The mushrooms were delicious, although after a week a diet even of ceps became monotonous. But we did not starve.

Etienne

I HAD ALWAYS BEEN a little wary of Guillemette. It was thought in Montségur she was something of a witch, even though she had helped many of us to recover with her poultices and infusions. She became our leader, as Francois had, at least for the time being, withdrawn into an inner world. Her knowledge of the countryside and her down-to-earth attitude to our plight was exactly what we both needed, and she spent little time dwelling on the terrible things that had happened to us.

I asked Francois to describe her to me on the first night of our journey. Guillemette was asleep, untroubled by the cold and the hard ground.

'She's a typical Languedoc farmer's daughter; doesn't use two words when one will do, says what she thinks, unimpressed by rank, tough – she's buried two or three husbands. She looks like she sounds. Earthy.'

'Is she a witch?'

'I hope so. She's on our side.'

I was determined to find out what had happened to Stephanie and our child. If indeed the child had been born, if both had survived childbirth. Stephanie was a devout Cathar, far stronger in her faith than I. I feared she would have been prepared to face the stake rather than swear an oath and recant. Except for the child. And when she and Blanche had been taken away she had not received the Consolamentum, would not have been prepared to face the next world. I struggled with hope and fear as we walked along; although my hand was on Francois's shoulder, much of the time he seemed far away.

I made a few attempts to console him but soon gave up. Our roles had reversed. I was sustained by the possibility that Stephanie might still be alive. He had lost Sybille forever.

Francois

I BRUSHED AWAY ETIENNE'S well-meant attempts to console me. His hand on my shoulder gave me some kind of contact with reality, but was not enough to stop the turmoil in my mind.

What should I have done differently? Run after Sybille and pull her back? Join her and her mother in the flames? Sybille and Claire were inside the palisade within a few seconds; and it was only as the gates closed that I realised Sybille was joining, not bidding a final farewell to, her mother.

She had not looked back. Perhaps she had planned her escape, although that is a strange word, as we walked down the path to the Field of the Burned. It was painful to realise she preferred to die with her mother than to live with me.

I found it hard to banish terrible images of Sybille burning, screaming, perhaps wanting to change her mind and leave the palisade. Were the screams I had heard, the burning flesh that I had smelled, Sybille's?

I wished I had joined them in the Field of the Burned.

I shared these tormenting thoughts with Guillemette.

'Nonsense,' she said. 'Better a live dog than a dead lion. It was a sudden impulse, she was determined to join her mother. All three of us were taken by surprise. It was over in a moment.'

'She had sworn an oath, she was no longer Cathar, she had no hope of eternal life.'

'You must think that the God of the Cathars is as uncaring as the God of the Catholics. Of course she will be with her mother in heaven.'

Guillemette's confidence gave me some respite from the terrible dreams I had by day as well as at night. Fatigue and hunger played their part in dulling my pain, and I gradually found I still had the desire to live, a desire that had brought me, battered but alive, through two sieges. It was to live that I had abandoned my Cathar faith, sworn an oath and persuaded Sybille, for a brief moment, to do the same. On the last part of the journey I acquitted myself of cowardice, began to torture myself less, and recognised that Sybille was gone, was ash and bone on the Field of the Burned. Did I believe in reincarnation? I wasn't sure.

Guillemette

IT TOOK US some time to find our way to Barraigne; Etienne was of little value as a guide, and Francois, who was beginning to regain his interest in this world, took us along several wrong paths. We got there in the end, meeting a woodcutter on our way who gave us good directions. We must have looked like harmless pilgrims, for he did not run away the moment he saw us.

'There's nothing and no one there any more,' he said. In spite of this disappointing news, we decided to press on. We would at least find a roof for a few nights.

Barraigne from the hill above looked small, a square block of a castle without towers and an apology for a courtyard whose walls were crumbling in several places. There was a gatehouse; one of the gates was hanging off a single rusted hinge. All in all, the place did not measure up to Etienne's many quarterings, which he had been kind enough to list for me when I was nursing him and the others in their first days at Montségur.

The courtyard was deserted. The ground floor of Barraigne had a single chamber at the front; we paused at the door and I gave a shout, 'Anyone there, anyone there?' We waited for a minute or two, and then an old woman appeared at an upstairs window.

'There's nothing here, they've taken it all. Go away.'

'We're looking for the Comtesse de Vallieres,' Francois said. His voice was more reassuring than mine, for the woman left the window, came downstairs and appeared at the door. She looked at us beadily.

'I can see you are pilgrims,' she said. 'Although some pilgrims I've sheltered overnight have robbed me in the morning. You can spend the night here, but I've no food to offer you.'

Etienne had been listening carefully as she spoke, took a pace forward, stretched out his good arm and said, 'It's me. Your son. Etienne.'

His mother seemed about to faint, steadied herself by taking Etienne's good arm, and said, her voice little more than a whisper, 'I thought you were dead. I heard Montségur had fallen.'

She sobbed as she spoke and clung to her son for a long time.

We spent four days at Barraigne recovering from our journey. It turned out that the Countess's sensible claim 'There's nothing here' was not entirely true. In the stable block, which looked even more decrepit than the castle, there were four milking goats, several hens and, to Francois's pleasure, sixty pigeons in the dovecote.

I continued to forage for ceps, but the Countess was generous with her eggs, encouraged Francois to take squabs from the dovecote and was dissuaded only with difficulty from killing one of the goats in our honour.

Etienne spent many hours with his mother. She had been living entirely on her own since Roqueville was taken, helped only by an elderly retainer who later emerged from the stables.

'They tried to throw me out, said my land and this place were forfeit,' she told us over our first supper. 'I would have none of it, said I had never been Cathar, unlike you and your father. I said that we held this land not from Roqueville, but from the King of Aragon. That scared them off, I can tell you.'

I was surprised that greedy crusaders paid any attention to who held what from whom, but there she was, living proof that some feudal laws occasionally commanded respect. Or perhaps Barraigne was too poor to bother about.

She was distressed when we decided to move on.

'I must find Stephanie and your grandchild,' Etienne told her.

'If they're still alive. Carcassonne is a dangerous place. The Inquisitors are there; you'll find vagabonds and thieves in the city and on your route. Promise me you will come back.'

'We'll come back.'

11

In Carcassonne

Francois

ETIENNE'S REUNION WITH his mother was moving; I even saw Guillemette shed a tear as they embraced. We were able to stay at Barraigne for several days in some comfort and build up our strength for the rest of the journey. Our diet of mushrooms had kept us alive, but not much more. And we hadn't seen eggs or milk or cheese at Montségur for many months.

The journey to Carcassonne was uneventful. As we neared the city we met more travellers, most of them heading in the same direction. Some of them were friendly, some would happily have slit our throats if we had appeared to have anything worth stealing. Guillemette's insistence that we looked and behaved like poor and humble pilgrims was sensible. And I had the comfort of my dagger if poverty and humility failed.

I had never been to Carcassonne, and I was astonished at its size and the extent of its walls. It was a castellated city; the fortifications had been rebuilt after the capture of the city by Simon de Montfort. A village had sprung up below its walls, and we began by finding shelter there. Etienne's mother had given us money which she had successfully concealed from crusaders and from vagabond bands. Guillemette guarded this little hoard carefully, never showing she had more than a few coins when we bought food or paid for our lodgings.

The village was a source of endless, unreliable rumour. It was known that Montségur had fallen, and that hundreds of Cathars had refused to recant and been burned. There appeared to be no Cathars in the village, which was hardly surprising given the widespread fear of the Inquisition. Gossip was common in our lodgings and the tavern which I visited in search of information; but the moment I asked questions I was greeted with silence.

'People use the Inquisition to settle old scores,' we were told by our innkeeper. 'You are denounced, then you are tortured, then you confess to whatever sin they require of you. You are lucky if you escape the stake. You cannot be too careful, too devout in your attendance at Mass.'

We heeded this advice; the pilgrim's scallop shell wasn't enough to ensure our safety. We took care to go to Mass regularly in the great church in Carcassonne, which was always crowded, the congregation swelled by those who saw attendance as security against arrest and interrogation.

After a week we moved from the village into the city; closer to the Inquisition, but also closer, we hoped, to better information. Our new inn was more expensive; Guillemette, our treasurer, kept warning Etienne and me that the money would soon run out. She tried to persuade Etienne to beg.

'Blind, one arm, you'd melt the hardest heart. Francois is too healthy-looking, and they would never give money to a woman.'

Etienne refused indignantly, and Guillemette gave up trying. In truth, begging in Carcassonne was already an overcrowded profession.

Guillemette went off to the market and came back with food and a cousin from her village, a cobbler who had moved to the city five years before. He showed us where the Inquisitors were based, pointed out the prison and where heretics were taken to the stake; he seemed disappointed that there hadn't been a burning for several months. I also found out where the Inquisitor lived, the man who had blinded Etienne, half blinded me and maimed us both. I put my hand on the hilt of my dagger, a reassuring feeling, when I saw his house.

Then I saw Blanche. I had gone to the covered market to buy bread, cheese and wine for our midday meal, which the three of us usually took in the big square by the church. She was talking to the man who sold melons. A striking figure even in that crowd, she was wearing a simple grey dress, her hair coiled up above her neck, and she wore an amber necklace; I didn't remember her wearing jewellery of any kind at Roqueville. Any doubts I had were dispelled when she spoke; her accent always revealed that French, not Occitan, was her first language. She looked older than I remembered, tired, still beautiful. She looked directly at me, then turned away to bargain with the melon-seller.

I felt a moment of shock that she did not recognise me, then remembered that when she saw me last I had two eyes and two arms. My hair had been shorn by Guillemette down to a stubble, I was unshaven and dirty, my cloak torn – I was the picture of a poor pilgrim. Uncertain what to do, I kept my distance and watched her disappear out of a corner of the market square.

I went back to the melon man, waited till he and I were alone, and bought his last three melons.

'The lady in grey,' I said, 'I think I used to…' Love her, I thought, then: '… serve her husband.'

He looked at me carefully, lowered his voice to the whisper in which most people in Carcassonne answered direct questions.

'She's from Roqueville. So are you by the look of you. She lives in the Place des Pénitents. Good customer. They say she's the Inquisitor's woman.'

'The Inquisitor's woman?'

'That's what they say.'

'It's not possible, not Blanche,' said Etienne when I told him. 'Do you remember the troubadour's song, praising her "virtue and wisdom and beauty"?'

'*I cannot find another one as fair.*'

I remembered the words well, remembered those feelings, pure at first, then passionate when I washed her feet below the dovecote.

'We were both her admirers,' said Etienne with a smile. 'In the finest tradition of courtly love.'

Guillemette snorted. 'Courtly love? What's that? Something you knights have dreamed up to cloak your lust?'

The three of us were suddenly silent, unsure what to make of this news. We had thought Blanche was certain to have been burned as a Perfect, and found it hard to believe that she, of all women, had recanted.

That evening I went to the Place des Pénitents and shared a shadowy corner with two beggars, neither welcoming until I gave each of them a coin to keep them quiet. I waited and watched; no one entered or left the house. The next night was the same. On the third evening I saw a tall man come to the blue door, knock and go in. He was still there two hours later.

I went back and told Etienne and Guillemette what I had seen. Feeling sick as I spoke, I said, 'I cannot be certain, it was too dark to see his face, but he was the right height and came from the right direction. He didn't leave. And my new beggar friends knew all about the two of them. I'd like to kill him.'

'Don't be foolish,' said Guillemette. 'You killed two Inquisitors at Avignonet. I don't think the Montségur pardon would stretch to a third.'

'How could she do this? Look at Etienne – she's given herself to the man who took his eyes and his arm. And burned the body of her dead son.'

'You can't eat that piece of bread a second time,' said Guillemette. 'Nothing will bring back your eyes and your arms. Blanche sounds like a sensible woman to me, not like Claire and Sybille. She's used her body to save herself, and perhaps your wife and child as well.' She looked at Etienne as she spoke.

'She'll know if they are alive and where they are.'

'You two should call on her in the morning. Leave me behind. We don't want her thinking I'm your shared fancy woman,' and Guillemette laughed for at least a minute at this idea. Etienne and I were not in a joking mood.

The next morning the pair of us called on the house with the blue door, knocked and waited till Blanche appeared. She saw us, looked uncertain, then put her hand to her mouth, swayed and steadied herself by holding the door. We stood there and said nothing.

'I'd heard you were dead, that they'd killed all the Cathars at Montségur. Thank God you're alive,' and she stepped forward and embraced Etienne, then turned to embrace me. I took a pace back, and her face changed.

'You've heard the gossip in the city, I see,' she said to me. 'Perhaps you won't want to come inside.'

'We want news of Stephanie,' said Etienne, reaching out to Blanche. 'Lead me into the house.' I followed him in. The room was simply furnished; we sat at a small table and waited while Blanche left the room, returning with a pitcher of water and three glasses. Etienne wept when Blanche told him that Stephanie was alive and had borne him a son.

'He's called Bertrand, after his grandfather, looks exactly like him. They are being well looked after by the nuns. Stephanie and I parted on bad terms. I told her I had recanted, and of my bargain with Mathieu.'

Mathieu. She called him Mathieu. How could she use his Christian name? What had she become? I left Etienne and Blanche to do the talking; I watched Blanche carefully, aware of her beauty and of the power it once had, perhaps still had, over me. Her face had a few more lines than I remembered at Roqueville, but her hair was still glossy and black and her skin unblemished. She didn't look like a victim, a prisoner. Only her hands, which she clasped and unclasped, showed she was nervous.

'Stephanie thought I should have chosen to burn as a Perfect. I would never have seen her again, never held my grandson. She felt it was a price I should have paid.'

'Perhaps it was,' I said, regretting my words the moment they were uttered.

Blanche looked at me and held me in a steady gaze until I looked away.

'You don't know what it is to have children,' she said. 'Etienne is about to find out.'

That was a sharper blow than she realised. Sybille and I had talked about having children, argued whether three or four was the right number, even discussed names, although she was sure our firstborn would be a daughter, and thus couldn't be named after my father. All these children had perished in the Field of the Burned. I got up, left the room and walked round the square.

When I returned Blanche stretched out both hands to me and I took them, but only for a moment.

'Etienne has told me what happened to your wife. I'm sorry.'

I did not reply and there was silence for a while. Then Blanche said, 'I will speak to Mathieu about the necessary arrangements, and get word to Flaran. It's a day's journey from Carcassonne. Come back tomorrow and I'll give you directions and money for the journey.'

Etienne looked overjoyed, stood up and embraced Blanche. I offered a little bow.

I went back the next day without Etienne. I was stiff and uneasy talking to Blanche, who confronted my unspoken disapproval.

'You make it clear you agree with Stephanie. Yet you recanted quickly enough, as did Etienne.'

'I wasn't a Perfect,' I said. 'You've done more than recant. You've given your...' I didn't finish.

Blanche finished the sentence for me. '... body to Mathieu. That was the bargain. It was a price worth paying. Etienne realises that, and Stephanie will in time, and so will you.'

'I don't think I will. We both worshipped you, would have done anything for you, as you knew.'

'That was courtly love. I was old enough to be your mother, far too old to be your lover. It was a gentle and harmless affection.'

'Not once I had washed your feet and legs beneath the dovecote.'

'I remember that too,' Blanche replied. 'It's all a long time ago. I'd like you... not to forgive me, I've done nothing for you to forgive, only God can do that, but to understand.'

I stood up, bowed, thanked her and left the house with the

directions to Flaran and a purse full of money. I was stiff-necked and unreasonable, but recanting was one thing, sleeping with the Inquisitor another, a different kind of betrayal, coloured by my remembered passion for her. I thought Sybille had banished those images forever, but they had returned with a force that surprised and shocked me. And I made matters worse by thinking of her and the Inquisitor together.

It was an easy day's walk to the abbey and convent at Flaran. We were again in funds; Guillemette whistled in appreciation when she opened the purse.

'Gold, not silver. This will take care of us for several months.'

'Tainted money, Inquisition money,' I said.

'Gold is gold, and never tells whoever had it last or how they came by it. It's repaying a little of what the crusaders took from Beaufort and Roqueville.'

I stayed in the abbey guest house while Etienne and Guillemette went to see Stephanie and the baby. When they came back in the evening Etienne described Bertrand in loving detail and said Stephanie was the perfect mother. His blindness was no obstacle to detailed descriptions of the colour of the baby's eyes, the pinkness of his skin, the brilliance of his smile. I felt great happiness for him, and a secret envy which I was careful to conceal.

The next day I went with them to the convent and was able to see Bertrand for myself. He was a handsome child, and seemed happy to be patted and passed between the four of us.

'Stephanie and I and Bertrand will go back to Barraigne,' said Etienne. 'We'll make a life there. We hope you and Guillemette will come with us.'

'I've nowhere else to go,' said Guillemette. 'I dare say I'll be of some use.'

I was uncertain. The three of us had been together for a long time.

'I'll come with you as far as Carcassonne and decide there. It's a risk. We were sentenced to go to Compostela.'

'They've got more important things to do than check up on the three of us.'

By the time we reached Carcassonne I had decided that Barraigne was not for me. I doubted whether it could support yet another hungry mouth. The next day I walked the first mile of the journey with the four of them, Bertrand gurgling happily in a sling on Guillemette's back, and we took our long and affectionate farewells.

I went back into the city a single man, single eye, single arm, with a little money and no useful trade. I was alone. Alone, and ill equipped to survive in a cut-throat city like Carcassonne. I was used to routine – mornings in the tilt-yard or the archery butts, afternoons in the dovecote or by the stew pond. And during the two sieges we were on watch every eight hours. Until now I had been among friends.

Carcassonne was a city full of thieves, vagabonds, mountebanks and beggars, any one of whom would have cheerfully cut my throat for a silver coin. The crusaders had laid waste the countryside for miles around, burning what they could not steal, and the refugees they had created were scrabbling to survive.

I asked my innkeeper where I might borrow money; I was sensible enough not to tell him I wanted to deposit cash. I went to the man he recommended, Baruch the Jew.

Baruch was famous in Carcassonne. He had converted, relapsed and avoided the stake by recanting a second time, persuaded by the Inquisitor after a lengthy debate. He smiled when he saw my gold.

'That's a tidy sum,' he said, 'Of course the law does not

allow me to pay you interest, only guarantee safe keeping. And perhaps the present of a bolt of cloth when you reclaim your money.'

I asked him about the Inquisitor.

'He is a formidable man with a relentless intellect. He overwhelmed me with his logic, and I was a Talmudic scholar. He only uses torture when all else fails.'

'He was quick enough to use it on us after Roqueville.'

'I see you were one of the unlucky ones.'

'Not as unlucky as the rest. They lost both their eyes.'

Baruch hesitated, then continued.

'Now they say he's mellowed. Has a fancy woman in the Place des Pénitents. Converted her with his cock. Or perhaps it was the other way round.'

The coarse phrase ended our conversation. I purchased a linen money belt in which I concealed enough money for a month, left the balance with Baruch and took my leave.

I began to visit the taverns in the evenings, partly to seek out the company of other men and women, partly to find comfort in drink. Company was hard to come by, as I was a marked man. It soon became well known that I had kept my single eye in order to lead the sorry procession of knights from Roqueville to Montségur. That I had recanted after Montségur's fall rather than burn did not bring me any closer to the men in the taverns, even though none of them admitted to being Cathar.

Through force of circumstance I became a solitary drinker. The tavern I frequented was dirty, cheap and dangerous, a tumbledown shack in the village outside the city walls. They served watery beer, rotgut red wine and a fiery spirit that they distilled themselves. I drank all three in a planned succession to dull my senses and forget the past. I was unable to think about the future.

In the second week I was attacked as I walked unsteadily back into the city. Two of my drinking companions had decided I was an easy target and followed me as I left. I had enough sense to keep my hand on my dagger – I had long abandoned Guillemette's advice to rely on poverty and humility – and I heard them come up behind me in time to turn. They were poorly armed with a single small knife between them; I killed the first with a thrust under the ribs and the second man ran away.

There was no law outside the city walls, and little enough within the city; the starveling body of the man I killed lay where I had left him, unmourned and uncollected, for several days. This served as a warning to others who might have sought to rob me, but it did not encourage other drinkers to seek me out as their companion.

I retreated to the city and drank there in greater comfort. Carcassonne was beginning to recover its former energy. The Thursday market was crowded, and the countryside around was again beginning to produce enough vegetables, fruit and meat to satisfy those who could afford the prices. There were several merchants doing good business in textiles and leather, and even a stall selling relics from the Holy Land, although the old woman in charge had plainly never left Carcassonne in her life.

There were many former crusaders in the city, mostly mercenaries from the north or from Catalonia. These men either no longer had enough money to return home, or had become used to a scavenging, transient life. Some were expecting another Crusade to begin, although there were few Cathars left to kill. After Montségur had fallen the smaller castles that were still intact swiftly came to terms.

I found myself drawn to the Place des Pénitents, even

though my motives were unclear. I was careful to avoid being seen by Blanche, although I managed to watch her from a distance in the Thursday market which she always visited in the middle of the day. I longed to speak to her, and yet had no idea what I wanted to say.

I also watched the Inquisitor arrive to visit Blanche on a number of occasions, sitting with my beggar friends in the corner of the square until he left at dawn. This was a dangerous, self-imposed torture, fuelling my images of the two of them together. One of the beggars must have informed on me; I was visited in my lodgings one morning by two armed monks who took me in for questioning.

'You are meant to be on your way to Compostela,' the Inquisitor said to me. This was only the second time I had heard him speak; his last words to me had been 'God is not mocked'. He was a formidable figure, robed in black, looking down on the accused from a throne-like chair on a dais. I was sentenced to a week in prison and told to leave the city by the end of the month.

'You know the alternative if you do not comply?' he asked me.

Only too well, I thought, but said nothing; instead I nodded my assent and was taken to the cells.

A week in prison was enough. Four of us shared a cell twelve feet square; the others were thieves, pimps or beggars, dirty, flea-ridden, fighting over the meagre rations we were given twice a day. It was unbearably hot during the day, freezing at night. I was glad to be let out after seven days; I went immediately to see Baruch and reclaimed half my gold.

'I heard you were arrested,' he said. 'Not many are let out after only a week.'

'I'm on my way to Compostela, the penance they imposed

on me after Montségur. Keep the rest of my money safe until I return.'

'It's a long and arduous pilgrimage. What if you don't come back?'

'I want to collect my bolt of cloth. I'll be back.'

I spent the rest of the day in preparation for the journey, from which there now seemed no escape. Strangely, I had begun to welcome the pilgrimage, not because I believed I would receive numberless indulgences and years of exemption from Purgatory – I was too much Cathar to believe such nonsense – but I had been given a destination and a purpose. And I had never been out of the Languedoc.

It was a journey of at least sixteen weeks from Carcassonne. I had my money safely stowed in my money belt, and my dagger, both of which, to my considerable surprise, had been returned to me when I left the prison. I bought a pair of good boots in the marketplace, a stout staff against dogs and vagabonds and a spare set of outer clothes. I found a good leather water bottle, a canvas sack and a hat to keep off the rain and the snow. I looked like the pilgrim the scallop shell on my cloak identified.

On the way back to my lodgings I passed a little chapel dedicated to, among others, St Christopher. I needed the patron saint of travellers on my side and went in. It was empty, simple, with plain windows and a single wooden cross above the altar. There were no pews or chairs. I stood for a moment, then knelt and prayed – for forgiveness, for understanding, for my parents, for Sybille and Claire and Blanche. And for my dead comrades. I felt unburdened when I rose to my feet.

I had one more self-imposed task before I left. I called on the house with the blue door; Blanche answered my knock.

'I didn't expect to see you again,' she said.

We sat once more in her downstairs room. I apologised for my intemperate words when we last met, and she told me how she regretted her clumsiness about Sybille.

'Etienne and Stephanie couldn't bring themselves to see me again,' she said. 'But they sent Guillemette and Bertrand to say goodbye.'

'They'll understand in time.'

'Perhaps. Do you?'

I thought long and hard, then looked at her and did not turn my gaze away.

'I do understand. I know myself well enough to realise that jealousy, not righteousness, made me speak as I did.'

Blanche said nothing. I took a deep breath and continued.

'I want you to come with me to Compostela. I need company. It's a pilgrimage, a good way of breaking the bonds that hold you here.'

Blanche looked astonished, then laughed, laughed until I stopped looking offended and laughed with her.

'You have changed. Two weeks ago you couldn't bear to be in the same room. Now you want me as your...'

'... companion,' I said quickly.

'Are you sure?'

'I'm sure.'

'It's an endearing offer. But the bonds that keep me here are strong. And breaking them would carry grave risks. I can't say yes.'

'I leave tomorrow at dawn from the Western Gate. I'll wait for you there.'

'Don't wait too long – but I am very glad you called.'

Blanche rose, gave me her hand, which I held in mine for a moment, raised it to my lips, and left.

The next day at dawn I waited for half an hour at the gate, but Blanche did not come. I set off on the long journey to the Pyrenees and to Compostela on my own.

Blanche

I HAD NOT EXPECTED to see Francois again. His revulsion at my conversion and my relationship with Mathieu was very clear. I in turn was angry with him, Etienne and Stephanie for their lack of understanding and sympathy.

His call was a welcome surprise. We talked for a long time, and the barriers between us began to fall away. He told me about the last days at Montségur; I was aware of how young he was and how much he had suffered.

Nevertheless, when he asked me to come with him to Compostela I was first astonished, then amused and, much later, thoughtful. I was living in the moment with Mathieu. I had deliberately given no thought as to where our relationship might lead. It was dangerous for both of us, and it was hard to see a happy ending. Mathieu could be excommunicated; I could be imprisoned or burned.

When Francois spoke of 'breaking the bonds' he made me think about a future in which Mathieu and I were no longer together. To my relief Mathieu didn't call that evening; I went to bed, but not to sleep. I was still awake at dawn, but I did not go to the Western Gate.

Mathieu

As I feared, Blanche's trip to the convent, followed by the arrival of that strange trio in Carcassonne, was unsettling. The understanding between us had grown and was strong, but when Etienne and Stephanie refused to see her again Blanche began to question her growing affection for me.

I had, of course, ordered the maiming of Etienne and Francois and the others. I believed it was a brutal necessity if the Catholic Church was to survive. It was now clear that heresy was in full retreat, for which my methods deserved much credit.

I could say none of this to Blanche. She had recanted with apparent sincerity, but I was not foolish enough to believe that she did so other than under duress in order to see her daughter and grandson. Our relationship began with a… rape, no other word will do, and then gradually changed. Not to love, that is too strong a word, but affection based on a shared physical passion.

My informers told me that Francois was spying on the house in the Place des Pénitents. I had him arrested and confined in prison for several days. I warned him that he had better be on his way to Compostela soon after his release if he wished to stay alive. I knew the others had gone back to Barraigne, and I wanted them all out of the way, so that my relationship with Blanche could resume its steady course.

The Bishop

THE SPECTACULAR CONVERSION of Blanche de Roqueville had enormous resonance within the Languedoc, a blue-blooded Perfect being worth twenty Baruchs. Soon after I learned, at first through innuendo, later by Mathieu's secretary, of the relationship between this unlikely pair.

I was pleased. No longer could Mathieu look down on me from his high horse, no longer could he criticise me, albeit largely through looks rather than words, for my fondness for wine. And for women, although I tried to restrict that weakness to one or two visits a month. Unlike Mathieu; my spies told me he visited Blanche two or three times a week.

She changed him for the better. He became far less stiff in my company, less censorious, less ascetic. And in due course he told me, as his confessor, everything.

He wanted to go further; he told me he was about to contact Rome and asked to be released from his vows.

'Don't be a fool,' I said. 'They will never agree. They'll make an example of you. And burn Blanche as a witch. *Quieta non movere*, my friend.'

My advice was forceful, and Mathieu did let sleeping dogs lie. His intellect was his worst enemy, and it was clear to me that he might crack under the strain. In the end it was Blanche who decided to end the relationship.

Mathieu was called away to Toulouse for a convocation of Church dignitaries that lasted a week. I learned that Blanche had left him a long and affectionate note which suggested that she had gone to Barraigne.

12

Pilgrimage

Francois

IT TOOK ME a day or two to get over my disappointment that Blanche had not appeared at the Western Gate and had decided to stay in Carcassonne with the Inquisitor. It took longer for my feet to get used to the demands of the pilgrimage, but by the time I was two weeks into my journey my blisters were beginning to heal and I was walking ten or fifteen miles every day depending on the terrain. At first I seemed the only pilgrim, but once I had reached Toulouse there were small groups all along the way that formed and dissolved, providing company and advice about routes and way stations that welcomed pilgrims. Some were on horseback, some on mules; there was one elderly and infirm lady carried in a litter by her retainers, but most were on foot.

I was able to choose my companions each day, but was careful not to form any permanent alliance, easily and politely done by leaving early the next morning. I often preferred to walk alone. I seemed to be the only pilgrim sentenced to Compostela as a punishment; although I would have liked to conceal this fact, my single arm and eye identified me to anyone from the Languedoc as the man from Roqueville.

Once we had reached Le Puy we were joined by a stream of pilgrims from the north, including some from Germany. One pilgrim, Brother Simon, a friar from Lyon, was shocked when I admitted to knowing little about the saint I was walking towards. He made it his business to teach me.

'He was James the son of Zebedee, one of two James among the disciples. Jesus called him and his brother John the "Sons of Thunder". After the Resurrection he preached all around the Mediterranean, and was beheaded in Jerusalem by Herod Agrippa.'

'How did he finish up in Galicia?'

'Through miracle after miracle. His body was placed in a stone boat that was later washed up, through the grace of God, on the Galician shore.'

'A miraculous story,' I said; I did not speak cynically. The friar believed every word, and there seemed little harm in such simple faith.

'And then he reappeared at the Battle of Clavijo and helped to expel the Moors. So he is also known as Matamoros, the Moor-slayer.'

'I didn't think saints and martyrs went to war.'

'Only when they have to, only when the True Faith is threatened.'

Brother Simon detected a note of disapproval in my voice, as well he might. I had lost an eye, an arm and many friends at the hands of defenders of the Faith. We changed the subject to less controversial matters and, like all pilgrims, talked about the next meal and the state of our feet. Simon was suffering from terrible blisters and badly fitting boots that were rubbing his heels raw; two days later I gave him the money for a better pair of boots, which made him see me in a less censorious and more friendly light.

Most of us rose early and walked before the sun was high, resting at midday and completing our journey in the late afternoon and evening. The refuges varied; sometimes in the bigger places there was supper to be had in the refectory. A lively business in relics, indulgences, food, wine and clothing had grown up along the route.

There was almost always a service in the evening, and again in the morning before the majority of the walkers set out. I normally attended, partly because I did not want to draw attention to myself, partly because it was part of the pilgrimage routine to which I was now committed.

I had been on my journey for two weeks, and the Pyrenees and the pass at Roncesvalles, where Charlemagne fought and Roland died, were in plain view, when my journey took on an entirely different complexion.

I was joined by Blanche.

She arrived on a grey mare, leading a sturdy gelding; she was matter-of-fact about her decision, ignoring my surprise and evident delight.

'You were right about the need to break free. I had to walk for three days before it felt safe to buy a horse. I wanted Mathieu to think I had gone to Barraigne. I hope you like the horse I picked out for you.'

'I do. He looks well up to my weight.'

It seemed at once extraordinary and natural that she should arrive in this way. We rode together, not talking, for the rest of the afternoon. That evening we ate bread and smoked fish that Blanche had brought with her, and over that supper she made her position clear.

'You said you wanted a companion, and that is what I will be. Not your mistress.'

I protested that I had no such thoughts – I was deceiving

myself, though not Blanche.

'There seemed no point in replacing one set of bonds with another, even if you had wanted a woman as old as I am as your lover. I'm glad that's not the case. And I wish to become a Perfect again.'

Thereafter I had Blanche as a companion; and the dormitories that we slept in were not designed for sex. I had more than the occasional pang of desire for her, but the fatigue we both felt after a day in the saddle was a useful dampener on such feelings. She became an older sister, a friend, as opposed to the idealised object of Etienne's and my courtly love at Roqueville. I had wanted her then, of course, and again in Carcassonne, but less and less as we rode together.

Blanche was the best of companions. She had a keen eye for the flowers, birds and animals along our route, and would stop to point out a rare orchis in the grass or an abandoned hawk's nest in the woods that from time to time flanked our route.

She had a keen eye, too, for the foibles of our fellow pilgrims, including the friar, who produced his version of the St James legend for her.

'I've never heard such nonsense. Stone boat indeed.'

'So why are we going if we don't believe in St James?'

'You're going because you have to, because you don't want to burn. I'm escaping a life that was leading nowhere.'

'Is that all?' I asked. The disappointment in my voice was obvious.

'Of course it's not all. You are my old friend, a good companion, and I love sharing the journey with you. We both may find something we need along the way. I just don't expect three hundred years' remission from Purgatory and forgiveness for all my sins thanks to touching St James's bones.'

On our journey she asked me to tell her about Sybille, and I told her everything, including the passion we had felt for each other. I said I still found it impossible – I broke down at this point – to understand how she could suddenly run away from me and towards a certain and agonising death.

'Can you explain that? You are, you were, a Perfect.'

'She loved you. You have no need to doubt that. She also loved her mother, loved God.' Blanche reached across and held my hand in hers for a moment, and we rode on in silence.

The next day I asked her about the Inquisitor, about how he had forced himself upon her.

'It was the only way I could be sure of seeing Stephanie again,' she said. 'And women's bodies aren't as important as men think.'

'He raped you.'

'Not really. It was as though I had become a prostitute at that moment, not for money but for my daughter. Gradually it changed. Mathieu needed me, not just my body; he'd never known a woman in any sense before, apart from the women of the street when he was a student in Paris a long time ago. I was entirely dependent on him. There seemed no point in not making the best of it. So I did.'

'Even...?'

'Even that. I had been celibate for a long time. You think of him as the Inquisitor, cruel, a torturer by proxy, and he is all of these things. He felt he should do anything to preserve the Catholic Church, and those terrible acts were sanctioned by the Pope. He believed in the cause, however mistakenly. There is more to him than the side the Cathars have seen. At heart he's a scholar. He would have been a happier man if they'd left him in his abbey at Flaran with his books.'

And so would I, I thought, but kept the words to myself.

Blanche worried that the Inquisitor – I never felt able to think of him as Mathieu – would pursue her and force her to return.

'He'll believe I have gone to Barraigne and do nothing for a week, then send a messenger there and discover… discover where I haven't gone. He'll work it out for himself in the end. We've passed enough returning pilgrims, and one or two will have noticed us. There aren't that many of us on horseback, and you are…' she smiled and patted my stump as she spoke, '… particularly distinctive.'

She was always on the alert for trouble, for strangers arriving after us in the refuges or catching us up during the day. She was a light sleeper; we were usually on adjacent beds and I would hear her tossing and turning during the night, sometimes crying out.

Once through the pass of Roncesvalles and into the Basque country Blanche relaxed. She continued to take pleasure in our journey, once spotting a hare lolloping away from us across a meadow and seeing the form it had just left, in which there was a single leveret.

'He can't be more than a day old. Look, his fur still seems damp.'

I asked her how she could reconcile this joy with the Cathar view, something I never fully accepted, that all this world is the work of the Devil.

She laughed. 'I find that hard too. Authie used to explain it to me. I would grasp the argument for half an hour, then forget. I'm happy to think that not everything we see and experience is the Devil's work, although there is enough, as you know, to blame him for. But that's not good Cathar dogma.'

It had been cold as we climbed up the pass, and there were many traces of snow on the peaks. On the other side it was warmer and we made good progress. Our horses were able to travel twenty to thirty miles a day, twice as far as I had managed on my own. There was always forage for the horses at the refuges, and they remained sound, although we had to pause for three days to allow my gelding to recover from a badly bruised foot.

As it turned out, that was a fatal delay, and Blanche was wrong to believe we were safe in the Basque country. Her Inquisitor had a long and determined arm.

We were eating in the refectory at Jaca when four burly monks in Dominican habits came through the door. They didn't sit down but stood scanning the room. Blanche pulled her hood closer around her face and looked down; I stared at them for a moment too long.

'That's him, the one-eyed man,' said their leader. 'The woman's beside him.' I recognised him; he was the man who had put out my eye at Roqueville.

They came over to us, pulled us to our feet and began to march us out of the room. I struggled, but eight arms against one was an uneven contest, and a knee in the groin silenced me for a few minutes.

'These men are robbers, not men of God,' said Blanche. 'They are kidnapping us.' One of the monks put a hand over her mouth, which she bit hard, and was slapped twice for her bravery. None of the other pilgrims raised a finger to help us, save Brother Simon, who had caught up with us that day.

'What are you doing? We are all pilgrims here; this is a peaceful place,' he said, until a blow from one of the monks brought silence. He was a brave man; I had underestimated him.

Outside they had their horses. 'We are to take you back to Carcassonne for sentencing,' the leader said to Blanche.

She looked distressed but calm, turned to me and said, 'I'll go; I was afraid he wouldn't let me escape.'

The two men holding me started to lead me away from Blanche towards the stables; one of them drew his sword. It was clear they planned to kill me, until Blanche broke free, ran to me and held me in a tight embrace.

'Haven't you done enough to him? Look at your handiwork. If you want to kill him you'll have to kill me first.'

By now the refectory had emptied and the other pilgrims were watching from the door. The friar had recovered from his blow and a little group began to form at his urging. They were armed only with their staves, but outnumbered the monks three to one. The leader of the monks looked at them for a moment, then said, 'He was only to die if he resisted. We'll take his horse and let him go.'

I looked hard at him as he spoke, noting for the second time every line and wrinkle in his face. He was plumper than I remembered. 'You've grown fat since Roqueville,' I said. 'Fat on what you stole. One day we'll meet on equal terms. And then I'll kill you.'

He looked angry for a moment. He didn't like my words. Then he laughed. 'We'll never be on equal terms; you're missing an eye and an arm. Lucky for you I haven't the time to finish the job.'

Blanche held on to me for a moment, then was prised loose, taken to her mare and they were gone.

Once more I was on foot and alone. I had no means of following them, and even if I had caught up with the kidnappers it is difficult to see what I could have done. I stood there listening to the hoofbeats growing fainter, then went into the dormitory; the friar put his arm around my shoulder for a moment when I thanked him, but the other pilgrims, perhaps alarmed at the possible consequences of their momentary bravery, gave me a wide berth.

I tried to sleep and failed; I persuaded myself that Blanche would not be condemned. The Inquisitor's affection for her would outweigh his rage at her attempt to escape. He would try to get her to resume their old relationship. Unless he thought that Blanche and I had become lovers, but she had truth on her side to buttress her natural persuasiveness. He would no longer bother with me.

I thought about abandoning my pilgrimage and of returning to Carcassonne, but I would certainly have been rearrested and given a harsher sentence, probably the fire. There was no sensible way of rescuing Blanche; she would be more likely to deal with the Inquisitor without any assistance from me, whatever feeble form that might take. And for what would I be rescuing her? Not a life with me, that was clear, and her daughter and Etienne had disowned her. I felt sorrow and anger at what had happened to both of us, coupled with a realistic recognition that there was nothing sensible I could do.

We had moved on to a little village called Villa de Lobo when the monks found us. But it was unlikely that a one-armed, one-eyed knight without a horse (the monks had made off with my gelding) and with a strong taint of heresy would be welcomed there for very long. So I decided to continue to Compostela.

The next morning I again thanked the friar, who had done his best to protect the two of us, and indeed had saved me from a severe beating and perhaps death. I told him the story of Blanche and the Inquisitor and of Montségur and Sybille as we walked along. We were the same height, and although he was perhaps ten years older than me he was lean and energetic, so we were well matched.

'That's typical of the Dominicans,' he said. 'They believe they can do what they like, where they like.'

'I thought you were all the same.'

This was ignorant and tactless. Brother Simon explained that he was a Franciscan, sworn to poverty, chastity and obedience to the Rule of St Francis.

'You could be a Perfect, Cathar, if that's what you believe.'

'I could not. I also believe in the supremacy of the Pope, in the doctrine of the Catholic Church, the True Faith as expounded by our founder Francis of Assisi, may he rest in peace. And we don't believe in the equal and opposite powers of good and evil, or that this world and all that is in it was created by the Devil. And nor should you.'

'I'm now a Catholic,' I said. 'Although the threat of fire had something to do with my conversion. I'm on my way to Compostela to atone for my heretical past. Why are you on this journey? Not as a punishment, surely?'

Brother Simon laughed. 'For me this is a pilgrimage of joy. I've always loved the story of St James, and received special permission to make this journey, provided I preached along the way.'

'How do you pay for food and lodgings if you're sworn to absolute poverty?'

'Through the generosity of those I meet and preach to along the way, and from fellow pilgrims. Your friend Lady Blanche gave me some money, enough to get me to Compostela, you gave me new boots, and the Lord will provide for my return.'

I told him I would be able to help again, and he seemed pleased. We walked along together, mainly in silence, although he extracted my life story from me. He understood my continuing anguish over the loss of Sybille, and accepted that there was no consolation he could offer.

'I've never known what it is to love and be loved by a woman,' he said. 'But I can see how glorious it must be, and how terrible to have it destroyed.'

'Do you believe in the fire?'

There was a pause, and then he replied, 'I believe in the Rule of St Francis. There is no mention of torture or hanging or fire in the Rule.'

I was happy with that reply, and we walked on in silence for the next two hours. Our days continued in the same way, although by the time we were fifty miles away from Compostela Brother Simon had attracted a small following through his preaching, which usually took place after supper in the pilgrims' lodgings.

He was a good and convincing preacher, even though his French wasn't very strong, as he was born in Italy, near Urbino, and spoke with the heavy accent of northern France. He had spent the last ten years in a Franciscan house in Lyon. Like me he had little Spanish. In spite of this eight or nine fellow pilgrims attached themselves to Brother Simon, who told the story of St James so vividly that even I wanted to believe in its essential truth.

There was, of course, the added security of being in a small group. The hilly countryside in Navarre and Castile was poor, and there were stories of pilgrims being attacked and robbed, although our little band was left alone. Simon had learned by rote most of a Pilgrim's Guide called the Codex Calixtinus, and was able to warn us which villages to avoid and which rivers, a surprising number, were unfit to drink from. The Navarrese, he said, reciting the words he had learned so well, are 'malignant, ugly of face, debauched, perverse, faithless, corrupt, lustful, drunken, skilled in all forms of violence...'

'All of them?'

'All of them. And they hate the French.'

'I'm from the Languedoc. I'll look after you.'

Nevertheless, we passed safely if speedily through Navarre, although Simon continued to make little detours to the shrines of saints on our way. At Sahagùn it was the blessed martyrs Facundus and Primitivus. On the banks of the river some of the lances of the Frankish knights miraculously took root and put out leaves before one of Charlemagne's battles, the knights receiving in advance the palms of martyrdom. I did not point out that those leafy lances would have been useless the following day, content to admire the fine poplars along the river bank that Simon believed were proof of his story. And in León we had to visit and venerate the remains of the Blessed Isidore, who Simon said had 'adorned the Holy Church with his fruitful writings'. I had never heard of Isidore, nor have I since.

Not all the members of our group were as devout as Simon. One, a merchant from Paris, made sure he ate as well as the little villages and towns we passed through could provide. When we were in Rabanal he discovered a house of ill repute, and urged me to join him. I was annoyed he had picked me out as a fellow sinner, and said so.

'I thought this was a holy journey. Going with a prostitute isn't right.'

He laughed. 'You've missed the point. When we reach Compostela we receive absolution for all our sins, and I've plenty of those, I can tell you. One last night of pleasure down the road will be wiped out along with the rest of my transgressions when I kiss the foot of St James. Come along; they won't mind that you've only one arm and one eye so long as you can pay.'

I declined. Even when Blanche was my close companion I had felt only the occasional flash of desire, and once she had been taken away I found it easy to be as celibate as Brother Simon.

'You'd better not die before we get there,' I said unkindly. 'You don't look that healthy to me.'

He did have a red complexion and a prominent belly that he hadn't managed to walk off.

'I'll take my chance on that. I'll tell you what you missed in the morning.'

And so he did, evidently pleased with himself and his encounter, until I strode on ahead of his conversation.

At Lavacolla in the wooded country two miles from Compostela, we took off our clothes and bathed in the river. I avoided looking at the Parisian merchant as we washed ourselves. We spent the night before we reached Compostela in an open field. This was Brother Simon's idea. It was late spring, and warm enough to sleep outside. He told for the last time the story of St James and his miracles; by now I was beginning to believe in the stone boat that floated. We lay on our backs and looked up at the Milky Way – Compostela means the Field of Stars – and it was easy to believe in an all-powerful God, hard to believe that such beauty was the work of the Devil.

The end of our journey was something of an anticlimax. The church and its nine towers were magnificent, a manifestation in stone of the power of the Catholic Church and the Kings of León. Outside the North Door, where Brother Simon told us French pilgrims normally enter, there was a splendid fountain, a huge circular stone basin with a bronze column in its centre topped with four lions out of whose mouths flowed a steady stream of the purest drinking water.

But in the main square we were surrounded by beggars and pickpockets in a noisy, sweaty confusion, stalls selling wineskins, shoes, purses, belts, all kinds of medicinal herbs (I saw the Parisian merchant making a thoughtful purchase). And moneychangers and whores.

By the South Door, next to the Temptation of Christ, one of the many guides was careful to point out to us the depiction of a woman holding in her hands the stinking head of her seducer, cut off by her own husband, which, compelled by him, she had to kiss twice every day. I could not believe we had come so far just to see this.

Brother Simon was oblivious to such contradictions, ignored the commerce and was in a state of near-ecstasy. Tears streamed down his face as he touched the pillar just inside the doorway of the church; a deep groove had been worn in the stone.

We were able to get close enough to kiss the foot of the statue of St James, see the marble tomb that held what was left of his body, and then our pilgrimage was over.

Simon came with me to get the certificate that showed I had completed the journey. I needed this as proof that I had served my sentence if I ever returned to Carcassonne, and he vouched for the gaps where my document had not been properly stamped on the way, looking so horrified at the suggestion of a little extra payment that the clerk quickly abandoned the idea.

Once this was done, we embraced. Then he set off on his long journey back to Lyon, while I took a room in an inn not far from the church where I could think about where to go and what to do with the remainder of my life.

The pilgrimage to Compostela, although I had undertaken it under compulsion, changed me. I was a Catholic only because of the threat of the stake – the abduction of Blanche by the so-called holy men reinforced all I had experienced at the hands of the Catholic and Apostolic Church. And the greed along our route and in the square outside the cathedral suggested that Christ might have expelled the moneychangers from the temple, but they hadn't moved far away.

It was the simple and determined faith of Brother Simon, a man as good in his own way as Guillaume Authie, that made me realise there were many roads to salvation. Or, if not salvation in the next world, at least peace of mind in this.

Once my pilgrimage was over I was left suddenly without a purpose. For several weeks, weeks interrupted by the arrival and then the kidnapping of Blanche, I had been a pilgrim with Compostela as my destination. Now I was a free man, but with no clear idea of where to go or what to do.

I still had some money left, and used this to travel slowly and cheaply across Spain, augmenting my slender capital by buying, training and reselling horses. There were skirmishes and little wars between the endlessly squabbling feudal lords everywhere along my route, and this created a regular demand for sturdy, well-trained chargers that would carry a man in full armour.

I never spent more than three or four months in any of the towns and villages on my way back to the Languedoc. That was normally long enough to find a half-trained horse, bring it on and resell it for a modest profit. But I felt no desire to settle; the pull of the Languedoc was powerful. In my heart I believed that was where I belonged, and I still felt Cathar.

In Aragon, where there were many Cathars living half openly in villages and towns close to the mountains, I had been given the name of several towns and villages in the foothills on the other side of the Pyrenees that would be likely to provide me with shelter and possibly even a living. Of these

Montaillou appeared the most promising, but by the time I arrived there I was penniless.

I had been robbed, something that had happened several times before, in spite of my pilgrim's scallop shell, but previously they found and took only the half-dozen small coins I kept in my purse as, I thought, an adequate robbers' offering.

This time it was my own fault. The inn, just below the peak on the Aragon side of the mountain, was crowded. Instead of going outside into the cold to find the coins for my supper I reached, cautiously I thought, inside my cloak and took the money from my money belt.

Not cautiously enough. I was followed by three men the next morning as I climbed up to the summit of the pass, and they were not happy with small coins. They pushed me to the ground, fumbled inside my cloak, found the belt and took it, along with the dagger that had been my reassuring companion ever since I looted it from the body of a dead soldier in a ditch not far from Montségur. I couldn't understand their dialect, but they seemed to debate among themselves whether they would kill me, decided I wasn't worth the effort and left me penniless with only my staff, looking down on my old homeland of the Languedoc.

Later that day I was overtaken by a fellow traveller who turned out to be Guillaume Authie, one of the few surviving Perfects, whom I had last seen just before the fall of Montségur. I recognised him at once; he asked me if I was still Cathar, and blessed me when I replied that I was, in spite of the pilgrimage to Compostela.

We continued together down the mountain to his first destination, the hut of one of the shepherds who had just moved his flock up to the mountain pastures. The shepherd, a weather-beaten man of perhaps fifty whose name was Arnaud, had spent all his life with his sheep, half the time in the valley, half the time in the mountains, building up his flock from almost nothing to two hundred ewes and five rams.

Guillaume Authie and I spent the night in the shepherd's shelter. I used the opportunity to ask Guillaume how he had become a Perfect; I had heard that he had been a lawyer in a previous life, which turned out to be true. His was an extraordinary story, and the way in which he described his calling made me understand, once again, the difference between the simplicity of the Cathar faith and the elaborate and corrupt nature of the Catholic Church. That Church was determined to make Cathars and Catharism extinct.

13

Returned to Mathieu

Blanche

MY CAPTORS WERE taciturn; when I asked them where they were taking me they said, 'To Carcassonne,' and nothing more. I pointed out that they were kidnapping me, that I had been on pilgrimage, that they had stolen Francois's horse, and got only grunts in reply. It took me a day to realise that they had not been sent to kill me.

They were monks only in name, each of them strong, burly men armed with a short sword and a dagger. They were not from our region and spoke a guttural northern patois that I could not understand. Although I was not ill-treated, I was always only a pace or two away from the nearest guard. It was a long and dismal journey.

When we reached Carcassonne I was taken not to the little house in the square but to the room in the Inquisitor's lodgings – I was no longer thinking of him as Mathieu – where he had first imprisoned and forced himself upon me. His clerk brought me my old smock, which I refused to wear, although my clothes were dirty and needed laundering. He was no more forthcoming than the monks; he brought me food and water, and not much of either, keeping me locked in the room. I was allowed out for only an hour a day, closely guarded by one of the soldier monks.

After ten days of solitary confinement I was brought before Mathieu in the room where I had first been tried. He looked stern sitting on his throne-like chair, and it was clear he wanted to emphasise he was again my judge. On this occasion his clerk was in the room, taking only occasional notes.

'Why did you escape from custody and leave Carcassonne? You were sentenced to house arrest after you publicly recanted. Your breach could result in a further trial and much more severe punishment.'

'I was not aware that the house in the Place des Pénitents was my prison. Nor that I could be punished for going on a pilgrimage to Compostela.'

'You were consorting with a former Cathar, a knight with a known history of rebellion and violence against the Church.'

'He, like me, had been forced to see the error of his ways. He was a friend of my son-in-law and my daughter, and we had known each other since before your so-called crusaders ruined Roqueville. Which, by the way, I claim as mine. Whoever holds it does so against the law.'

Mathieu was both surprised and discomfited by my defence. He clearly expected me, after the kidnapping, the long journey and ten days' solitary confinement on inadequate rations, to be both frightened and penitent. I was neither.

After a long pause he asked me, 'Have you become Cathar again?'

I replied, 'You took me away from a pilgrimage to one of the holiest shrines in Christendom.' It was a clear sign of his uncertainty that he didn't follow up my oblique reply with an insistence that I answer yes or no.

'Very well. I shall adjourn these proceedings and consider

whether you should be handed over to the secular authorities for sentencing.'

This was a clear threat that I could face years of imprisonment or even the fire. As he finished speaking I held his eyes in mine for almost a minute until he looked away, rummaging among his papers as I left the room. I was led back to my cell by the clerk.

As soon as I was alone I sat down on my chair and cried. I had left Mathieu, lost the companionship of Francois, and my daughter and Etienne regarded me as an outcast. I had put on a bold front in the courtroom, but I had no friends in the city, and probably none in the whole of the Languedoc. There was no one to whom I could turn, no one who knew where I was. I was frightened by the civil courts, whose arbitrary and savage sentences – they had walled up an elderly Cathar noblewoman, Adelais de Ventenac, only two years ago – were well known. I knelt down and prayed, to which God didn't seem to matter, remembering some Latin words from the days when I was a genuine Catholic:

'De profundis clamavi ad te Domine,
Domine, exaudi vocem meam.'

I was indeed in the depths.

Mathieu

I WAS UNABLE TO deny the pleasure I felt on seeing Blanche again, although I was careful to conceal this from Blanche and my clerk. I reminded myself of her betrayal; she had given me no indication that she wanted to leave, and had waited until I was away in Toulouse for a week, leaving an ambiguous note that made me believe at first she had gone to Barraigne.

And I was intensely jealous, an emotion I had never before experienced. I had seen Francois de Beaufort several times, saving one of his eyes on the first occasion, although only because that suited the Church. He was ten years younger than me, undeniably handsome and brave enough to survive at Roqueville and Montségur treatment that would have destroyed a lesser man.

They were together, in close proximity, for six weeks on the road to Compostela. I did not believe she would have resisted his advances; after all, she had sought him out. I had feverish, disgraceful dreams of the two of them together, from which I awoke sweating and miserable, wishing I had ordered Francois' death, wishing I had never seen Blanche. I had no clear idea of what to do next.

Blanche

AFTER I HAD spent a further week in my cell Mathieu came to see me in the evening. He began as the Inquisitor, upbraiding me for abandoning our life together. He accused me of sleeping with Francois, that the attraction of a younger man was the reason I had left him.

He asked me the direct question.

'Did you fuck him?' The coarse word, a word that I had never before heard him utter, surprised me.

'That is none of your business. I thought about it.'

'Did you fuck him?'

'No.'

'How can I believe you?'

'I am still enough of a Cathar to tell the truth. I haven't yet learned to lie in the Catholic way.'

The look of relief that crossed his face made me realise that simple, powerful sexual jealousy was behind his words and actions. I smiled.

He saw the smile, misinterpreted it and threatened me again. I was confident enough to resist.

'You have no right to hold me here. If you send me to the secular arm the true facts of our relationship will come out.'

'That sounds like blackmail. You won't be heard, only sentenced. My clerk is loyal.'

'Francois and Etienne and Stephanie and Guillemette knew. And who is your confessor? The Bishop?'

This struck home, and he looked at me with despair, turned to leave the room, turned back, knelt in front of me and buried his head in my lap.

'I'm sorry,' he said after a minute. 'Those were all empty threats. I missed you while you were away, I need you, I want you to return to our house, I want to live together again.'

'As your prisoner?'

'No. As my...' He couldn't find the right word and began to weep silently, burying his head in my lap again. I said nothing, but held his head between my hands for several minutes. It seemed I was renewing the bargain between us, but on better terms.

The Bishop

MATHIEU WAS MISERABLE after he had lost his woman. I suggested other ways of compensating for her loss, but he would have none of them. He disappeared for a couple of weeks on a retreat to his former abbey at Flaran, but was no less miserable on his return. He began to delegate his duties to men ill-equipped for the task and I told him so.

'For God's sake, get her back,' I told him one evening over supper.

'She won't come.'

'She's a fugitive. She's broken house arrest. Send some of your tough monks to bring her back to Carcassonne. And they can deal with her one-armed fancy man while they're at it.'

My crude reference to Francois de Beaufort distressed him, and he got up and left the room. Nevertheless, after two days he took my advice, and many weeks later Blanche de Roqueville was back in Carcassonne.

'Take care how you handle her,' I told him. 'You're on shaky legal grounds even by Inquisition standards.'

I enjoyed my new relationship with Mathieu. I had become his counsellor. Now he sought my advice and acted on it. And soon, without any public scandal, all between Mathieu and Blanche was, more or less, as before.

14

The Last Perfects

Guillaume Authie

My BROTHER AND I and were prosperous notaries. We were comfortably off, well known and sought after for advice ever since we negotiated on behalf of Roger Bernard, Comte de Foix, over his castles in the Sarbarthés. This was a long and complicated dispute, eventually resolved in Roger Bernard's favour after several years of argument. This success established our reputation throughout the Languedoc.

I was married to Alazais, by whom I had seven children. I loved her dearly, although after our last child we rarely, if ever, made love. And I also, to my subsequent shame, had a mistress, Monete Rouzy. She was the widow of a colleague and bore me a daughter. Our family and that of my brother Pierre were quiet Cathars, not eager to draw the attention of the church and the Inquisition to our heresy.

All this changed when, on a sunny spring afternoon in Ax, I was reading to my brother from St John's Gospel. '*In the beginning was the Word, and the Word was with God, and the Word was God...*' it began. It was a passage later on that struck home: '*Ye have not chosen me, but I have chosen you, and ordained you, that ye should go and bring forth fruit.'*

As I read, it seemed to me in a flash of revelation, painful in its intensity, that if these words and the words that followed were divinely inspired we had no choice but to follow them. I said as much to my brother, and he replied, 'I feel that we have lost our souls. Our lives are empty, an emptiness that we cannot any longer fill with material possessions or by the pleasures of sex and food and wine.'

We talked late into the night; we had always been close, and it was not surprising, to me at least, that we should have arrived at this turning point in our lives at the same moment. It was clear that we needed to look for salvation together. We decided to go to Lombardy where our faith was still alive, and where we could learn, with God's grace, enough to become Perfects ourselves. We planned to return to the Languedoc, where the Word was threatened but not yet extinguished.

Our families found it difficult to understand what inspired us to leave. Pierre and I had all heard and read this passage from St John many times before, and it was hard to explain why, in middle age, we had both been struck by the same lightning bolt. I told my wife that recognising that these words were more than rhetoric, were an imperative, had overcome us both with a near-physical force. It was impossible to ignore the words, but it was difficult to convince her or my children of what had happened.

Alazais was angry. 'Your life will be in danger, you'll end up tortured and then burned. You'll never see me or the children again. And we will no longer be safe.'

All this was hard to contradict, other than by saying I felt I had no choice.

'It is something I have to do. Being a believer is no longer enough, particularly when our faith is under attack throughout the Languedoc.'

In the end, after talking long into the night, Alazais realised she was arguing not with me, but with the Holy Spirit, and she gave me her affectionate, if reluctant, blessing. I would not see her again for over two years.

My brother and I were in Lombardy for eighteen months in a Cathar seminary with others like us. There we began not only to understand the detailed doctrines of our faith, but to practise the severe rules by which we would be bound forever. We no longer ate meat, animal fats, eggs, cheese or drank milk. We fasted on bread and water for three days in every week and kept three Lents in every year. We did not kill. We did not lie. We did not touch women. We did not swear oaths.

This was a gruelling regime both mentally and physically, and after the powerful revelation that had brought us to Lombardy began to wear thin, we were both occasionally tempted to give up and return home. But we were sustained by each other, and by those simple words that had changed our lives. Several others fell by the wayside. Of the fourteen that arrived at the beginning of the year only six received the Consolamentum and became Perfects. Pierre and I were of that number.

The final ceremony was moving in its simplicity, in marked contrast to the elaborate rituals that accompanied any Catholic ordination. It took place in the room where we gathered every day to pray. The whitewashed walls were bare, and the only furniture was the dozen benches and a table at the far end of the room, on this occasion covered in a white cloth. The room was illuminated by dozens of white candles symbolising the tongues of flame of the Holy Spirit at Pentecost.

On the table was the Gospel of St John whose words had brought us there, and a basin of water in which the officiating minister washed his hands before reading from the text. He was a famous Perfect, Bishop Bertrand Marty, whom I was to meet several times afterwards, and who died in the Field of the Burned at Montségur. He was a good Christian, a good man in every sense of the word. To be in his presence was to feel strengthened and purified.

Bishop Bertrand recited the Lord's Prayer, the six of us repeating the words after him, and then we abjured the Catholic faith. We asked permission to enter the True Church, swore to give ourselves to God and the Gospel, and promised never to renounce our faith through fear of death by fire or any other torture. Finally Bishop Bertrand put his hand on each head in succession, asking God to receive us and send His Holy Spirit upon us. When I received the kiss of peace from Bertrand I became a new man at that moment, born of the spirit.

The following day Pierre and I began our journey back to the Languedoc. We travelled through the plains of Lombardy and the rivers and woods of our own Languedoc, seeing the countryside through the eyes of the Perfects that we had so recently become. And the name itself, Perfect, which we had hitherto understood as a label attached to only a few men and women of our acquaintance, had now acquired a new and weighty meaning. I told Pierre that I found it difficult to dismiss our surroundings as the work of the Devil, and he laughed.

'I have the same problem. My conclusion is simple; we can enjoy and even admire the Devil's handiwork, as long as we realise its temporary nature.' Pierre could always find a sensible solution to my overanxious questioning, and it was exchanges like this that made me realise how much I would miss him. We had become very close during our time in Lombardy, our bond of blood strengthened by our new faith and its strenuous discipline. We embraced for a long moment when we finally parted, a parting made more poignant by the realisation that we would never be as close again.

Thereafter I led a nomadic life, sustained by my faith and by the hospitality and prayers of the Cathar believers. In those early days there were many believers, from the great men and women in their castles to the humble shepherds and in the pastures and in the villages. I passed myself off as a travelling pedlar when challenged, and I had a basket of ironmongery which I managed never to sell.

We were wanted men, sought out by the Catholic Church and the Inquisition with ever-increasing ferocity and success. Once captured there was only one end for a Perfect: the stake. Unless he abjured, and in thirty years there were only three who saved their mortal bodies by recanting.

As the power of the Inquisition and its informers grew I became more careful. I rarely wore my green robe, I never risked staying longer than two or three nights in any house or castle, and from time to time would move, guided by shepherds who were Cathar to a man, over the Pyrenees to Aragon, where there were many hospitable Cathars. I preached wherever I could, I blessed those believers who sought me out and I administered the Consolamentum to the dying.

In those early days I enjoyed outwitting those who wished to capture and imprison me, enjoyed practising our Cathar faith under the noses of the well-financed, bureaucratic and stupid Catholic Church. I was less careful then about those whose lives were endangered by my presence in their houses. It was only later that the pressure of being always on the run, of being a danger to others, became a burden that I found harder and harder to bear.

Insofar as I had a base, it was in Montaillou, where both the chatelaine of the castle and the priest were Cathar. I was also welcomed many times at the house of Arnaud Issaurat in Larnat. He had a small room used for storing farm implements, on the same level as his cattle byre, and he made a comfortable bed in one corner that was shielded from view by a small handcart.

The Issaurat family nursed me there for six days when I became sick after climbing the pass from Aragon back into the Languedoc. They were brave and generous hosts and indulged my weakness for good bread and honey.

I was able to see my family very rarely. I met my love child, my daughter by Monete, only once, but was able to bless her during a brief walk in the dusk at Larnat. She of all my children seemed to understand best the path that I had taken.

My wife came, at considerable risk to herself, to the wedding of Bernard Belot and Dominique Benet in Montaillou. I stayed in the Belots' house, officiated at the wedding (it was the last occasion on which I was able to wear my green cloak) and spent the night in a comfortable bed, complete with a silk cushion, in the loft. My beloved Alazais lay beside me. We used this precious time to talk about the children, Alazais urging me to take particular care to avoid betrayal.

'Even in Montaillou, even in Larnat, there are now those who would give you up to the Inquisition,' she said. 'The new Inquisitor has promised eternal and worldly rewards to anyone denouncing a Perfect.'

'But for Arnaud Lizier I could move freely in the square

at Montaillou. I have nothing to fear from the Clergues.'

'Not from the Clergues, perhaps. But there are others who could be tempted by the reward.'

I promised I would be careful. And when Alazais reached across the bed to embrace me I didn't have the heart, or the resolve, to push her away.

Alazais was right about the danger.

To my great sorrow she and three of my children were arrested later that year. They were interrogated in Carcassonne, and after several months' imprisonment were sentenced to the yellow crosses before being allowed to return to Ax. I had crossed into Catalonia and spent three months in friendly houses there before it felt safe to return to the Languedoc. The number of houses prepared to shelter Perfects rapidly dwindled.

Early in the following year I learned that my brother Pierre had been arrested and burned, together with many others of our number. The lightning bolt had struck me and my brother at the same moment: we had been in Lombardy together for a year and a half and were almost as one during that period of trial, instruction and prayer. Ironically, our ways parted almost immediately thereafter, and we were to meet again only twice, briefly and furtively, in the years that followed, although he was always in my thoughts and in my prayers.

He was burned in front of the Cathedral of St-Etienne in Toulouse. I was told that his last words to the Inquisitors were that if he could preach to the people he would convert them all. He was the most eloquent of all the Perfects; needless to say he was not allowed to speak. I hope and pray his death was easy.

His death and that of so many other good souls was hard to accept. If God was on our side, if we were indeed the only

Good Christians, how was the devilish work of the Inquisition allowed to triumph? And how, if there were no more Perfects left alive, could our Cathar faith continue? It seemed that I was about to become the last Perfect, and might not survive much longer.

15

In Montaillou

Francois

ARNAUD THE SHEPHERD sent us on our way to Montaillou after a breakfast feast of sheep's cheese, bread and milk. Guillaume Authie didn't stay in the village, but went on to Ax after giving me a final blessing.

'Ask for Pierre Clergue when you get to Montaillou. He'll find you something to do,' Arnaud had said to me. 'Something to do' turned out to be joining the little group of enforcers that guaranteed Clergue's rule over Montaillou. Montaillou was a small village of perhaps two hundred souls, with a castle at one end and a church at the other. A double row of houses ran down the main street, which was roughly paved with cobblestones. Around the village were well-watered fields which produced enough fodder for the cold winter months. Montaillou was prosperous thanks to its sheep; almost everybody owned sheep or worked with them, from the hired shepherds, the crop-watchers and the owners with two or three hundred animals. There were a few cows, oxen for ploughing and most families kept a pig and some hens.

Montaillou was dominated by its castle and by the Clergue brothers, Pierre the priest and his brother Bernard the magistrate.

Pierre was a powerful man, dark, burly, a head shorter than me, black eyes set deep in their sockets and a squashed nose that looked as though it was still recovering from a brawl. He had a neatly trimmed beard and a mouth full of bad teeth.

Pierre was both priest and Cathar, as was clear from his sermons, although not from his conduct. He was some considerable distance from being a Perfect. It suited him to allow the Cathars to exist in his village in an atmosphere of secrecy, as the fear of denunciation was one of his weapons, although it would have been hard for him to use it without implicating himself. So there were regular visits to certain houses by Guillaume Authie and other Perfects, and Pierre Clergue and his brother would often attend their ceremonies.

He used his position to obtain sexual favours. It was rumoured that he slept regularly with at least three of the wives in Montaillou and had a child by one of these women.

He ensured that everyone attended his church at the bottom of the village and also that every household paid tithes, some of which, enough to keep everyone happy, he sent to the treasurer of the Church in Carcassonne. He explained to his flock that this was the price of being left alone. And as priest Pierre heard everyone's Confession, and knew the intimate details of every inhabitant of Montaillou.

His brother Bernard, the magistrate, dispensed rough justice from which there was no appeal. His powers rested on a document from the Comte de Foix that he would occasionally produce and read out; in practice it was their enforcers who guaranteed the Clergues' position. Two years before my arrival Bernard had cut out the tongue of Mengarde Maurs for spreading rumours about the heretical youth of the Clergue brothers. It was a brutal and effective way of reducing dissent to whispers, winks and nods.

All this I learned later. I sought Pierre Clergue out on my arrival; his house was the biggest in the village with perhaps half a dozen rooms on the first and second floors and a large byre beneath where he kept sheep in the winter. The first question he asked me was 'Are you Cathar?'

'I am.'

'Then why were you on pilgrimage?'

I explained, but the explanation wasn't necessary. He knew exactly who I was, why I had only one eye and one arm, and that I had been sentenced after the fall of Montségur to go to Compostela.

'Have you proof that you completed the journey?'

I produced the battered, stamped document that I kept inside my cloak.

'Let me read it,' Clergue said, glancing at it for a second, then putting it down on his table.

'It will be safe with me,' he said. 'What are you good for? Not fighting, with only one arm and one eye.'

'Try me with a sword against any man,' I said, anger overcoming common sense. Because Clergue knew exactly what I could do.

'That won't be necessary. You can work for me. Food, clothes and lodging.'

I accepted. I had no choice other than to starve. There were four of us in Clergue's little band, the other three all Cathar, former men-at-arms who had learned their trade fighting for little lords elsewhere in the region, or for mercenary bands, or for the crusaders, or in one case for all three. They accepted me soon enough after the inevitable jokes about a one-armed, one-eyed soldier knight being next to useless. We duelled now and again with wooden swords and I was easily able to defeat each of them, for which I thanked the days of practice with my father and at Roqueville.

As it turned out, working for Pierre Clergue involved no fighting. Our principle task was collecting tithes, and the four of us were sufficiently formidable to overcome the doubts of even the most devout Cathar.

'Sending tithes keeps Carcassonne and the Inquisition off our backs,' Clergue would remind the village. 'It's a price worth paying, as is Confession.' He was right. Montaillou was left to its own devices, far enough from Carcassonne for any rumours of heresy to have been watered down to gossip by the time they reached the ears of the authorities.

After two years my way of life in Montaillou changed. Arnaud, who had guided me to Montaillou, was one of three shepherds in the village, all men of substance. He asked me to help him with his flock of sheep, now over two hundred strong, in the move up to the mountain pastures.

'It's too much for one man,' he said, 'I'm feeling my age. And there are more wolves than ever.'

I was bored with tithe-collecting, and told Pierre Clergue I planned to help Arnaud.

He looked thoughtful for a moment, then said, 'Very well. You'll have to find somewhere else to live. And he can't afford to pay you.'

'Neither can you,' I said. 'With Arnaud I'll learn something useful.'

'I dare say you've learned something working for me. You go with my blessing.'

'I'd like to take a crossbow with me. And my pilgrim's certificate.'

'Take the crossbow. The certificate is safe with me.'

I didn't argue, as the certificate seemed a reasonable surety for the return of the crossbow. At that time there were only two crossbows in the village armoury, and both belonged to Clergue. I told Arnaud I came with Clergue's blessing and a crossbow; we agreed that for every wolf I killed I would get a carrying ewe to call my own. He gave me a small room in his house at the bottom of the village.

Pierre Clergue was able to replace me easily enough with one of his cousins, Arnaud Sicre, who had been until that moment a shoemaker in Ax. He had no friends in Montaillou, and collected tithes with a zeal that made him many enemies, although the Clergues were pleased with the increased income. Whenever we met Pierre was careful to tell me how much better Sicre was at the job. I told him I was happy for him, and that I was much better suited to the life of a shepherd.

The flocks wintered in the valley, when we fed them with hay from the meadows, then moved up to the rich mountain grassland once the snow had melted. The journey to the upland pastures was an annual ritual; the three Montaillou shepherds took their flocks to the mountains in a fixed order. Arnaud was last.

Managing the migration of two hundred sheep, including lambs and four rams, was a slow business, even though Arnaud had three fierce dogs to help him. Their instinct was to attack any stranger, and I was careful to earn their affection with titbits and their respect with a blow from my staff if they tried, as they did at first, to bite.

It took three days to reach the grassy plateau where Arnaud grazed his sheep. Spring had begun in earnest; the grass was rich and the pastures were cut with little rivulets that would dry up in the summer but were full of snowmelt in the spring. Mountain flowers – violets, harebells, gentians – were everywhere, the trees beginning to break into leaf. I felt like them, breaking out into a new life.

'It's beautiful,' I said to Arnaud, who only grunted in reply. Our first job was to repair the corral where the sheep were kept at night; luckily it had suffered little damage in the winter. Then we set about rebuilding Arnaud's cabin, doubling it in size. The four posts at the corners were made from young birch trees, and we cut hazel to weave the walls. We needed a fire only in the first month, and there was wood left over from the previous year.

I dug a pit thirty paces away for our latrine. Arnaud thought this unnecessary, but I pointed out there were now two of us, and once it was built he was happy enough to use it for his daily business. I hammered four strong forked posts into the ground by the lip of the pit, each with a sturdy crossbar, the lower to sit on, the higher for a handhold. This meant Arnaud could sit rather than squat, which at his age he was finding difficult.

Once we had finished building my job was to kill wolves. This, I soon discovered, was not easy. Wolves would regularly take a lamb from the edge of the flock, drag it some distance away to the edge of the woods that bordered our pastures and eat as much as they could before dawn. If I touched the carcase, or went near it, the wolf would not return.

So I built half a dozen high seats in trees that bordered the pasture and sat up over the lamb after each kill, hoping the wolf would reappear at dawn or at dusk. I was often disappointed: by a breeze carrying my scent the wrong way (I didn't bathe often in the mountains), or by one of Arnaud's dogs scenting the wolf and barking. They wouldn't attack a wolf, having learned from painful experience that they were outmatched.

I learned my crossbow had to be cocked, that the wolf would disappear at the slightest unfamiliar noise and that I had to be thirty paces away and high in a tree to have any chance. I tried powerful snares, but they were useless for wolves, although I regularly caught mountain hares in them, which enriched our diet.

I think Arnaud expected to part with one or two ewes at the most; after all, he had never seen me use a crossbow. I had lost the iron tube that the blacksmith had forged for me in Montségur, but I was able to replace it in Montaillou. I had kept the padded sleeve Sybille had sewed for me, and the eyepatch, although I never used the latter. Both had survived the long journey to Compostela and then across Spain. After we were married Sybille told me what she had done, at Guillemette's bidding, to the sleeve. I laughed and said she had indeed bewitched me. It was the only possession I had to remind me of her. The sleeve smelled faintly of lavender, but of nothing else.

In the first month I had one shot, and missed; in the second I killed three wolves; and in the third month eight, including two cubs. Arnaud didn't know whether to be glad or dismayed.

I was pegging out two wolf skins to dry in the sun; I had made him a present of the first two I cured.

'Perhaps I made a poor bargain,' he said.

'How many sheep did you lose last year?'

'Twenty-one.'

'This year?'

'Twelve.'

'And you're warm at night into the bargain.'

He laughed and made no attempt to renegotiate.

Although we hardly talked, for he was unused to company, he liked my presence in the little hut and the hares and the occasional roe-deer I brought to our table. I had learned enough from Guillemette about mushrooms to pick and eat them, but

Arnaud either disliked the taste or thought he would be poisoned. Otherwise we lived off bread, sheep's milk, sheep's cheese and the occasional cup of rough red wine.

One of the Belot boys, Andre, arrived every two weeks with flour, wine and sometimes a few eggs. I once gave him a wolf's skin in return for the food and his trouble.

'I'd have given him nothing,' said Arnaud. 'Now he'll be greedy, expect something every time he comes.'

'You've given him nothing, I have. Perhaps he'll come more often, with more and better provisions.'

Apart from young Belot and the occasional Perfect, whom we welcomed and fed in exchange for a blessing, we had few visitors. I was always glad to see Authie, to whom I could talk about Roqueville and Montségur and Sybille. He came at least twice every season.

The solitary life suited me well; until now my pilgrimage and the need to make a living among strangers as I travelled from Compostela back to my own country had given me little time for reflection.

My sorrow at losing Sybille, my failure either to rescue her or join her, the almost unbearable memories of our happiness together, which at the time I imagined would continue forever, weighed heavily. I had terrible nightmares about what had happened to Sybille, to Claire and the other brave Cathars in the Field of the Burned. I could still hear the screams, smell burning flesh. I thought, too, of Blanche, regretting my feeble defence of her on the way to Compostela.

In the mountains the nightmares came less often, and I tortured myself less frequently with what I might have done. It was partly the serenity of the landscape, partly the preoccupation with sheep and wolves, partly the dig in the ribs from Arnaud if I groaned in one of my dreams, that gave me the beginnings of peace. And I felt I had left my recantation behind, had become Cathar again.

The rhythm of the seasons was comforting. The lambs were born in the spring, and that was a stressful time for Arnaud and me. We got little sleep. He taught me how to deal with a stuck lamb, and after that kind of birth I was covered in more blood than after any of my battles. Inevitably we would lose some ewes, which was always disappointing, although we kept the fleece and the meat. And often enough we would have ewes that produced, quickly and efficiently, twins or even triplets. Pyrenean sheep are tough; they have to be to make the long journey to and from the mountain pastures.

We castrated the male lambs soon afterwards, a business that required a sharp knife and a hard heart. Although it was simple enough to make the cut and extract the two small testicles, I was never able to do the work without feeling a twinge, a retraction in my own groin. Arnaud selected one every three years or so to be spared the cut and replace the oldest and least active ram in his flock.

'How do you choose?' I asked.

He looked surprised.

'I don't choose. He chooses me.'

And I had thought he just took the one nearest to him at the time.

The lambs were weaned in May, and then the milking began – milk for ourselves, milk for cheese. It took me some time to get used to the taste of sheep's milk – Arnaud told me he had never tasted milk from a cow – but the hard tangy sheep's cheese was easy to enjoy.

We had a small brick oven by our cabin where Arnaud taught me how to bake bread. At the bottom of our great meadow there was a stream that held small trout, but these were difficult to catch, as the stream was too big to dam. Arnaud had hooks, but had never used them; I borrowed these to extract one or two fish using a pellet of our bread as bait. My rod was a long willow branch with a line of spun thread which often broke. We smoked any fish I was lucky enough to catch and kept them for a visit by one of the Perfects.

Cheese-making was an art I was slow to master. We had a separate cabin where we made the cheese and kept a stock of two or three rounds from previous years. We sold most of our cheese in the valley at the same time we sold our wool.

When in May I saw four rough-looking men coming towards our cabin my immediate reaction was to reach for my crossbow. Arnaud restrained me.

'They're the sheep-shearers. From the Basque country.'

As they came closer I could see they were not from the Languedoc. They were short, wiry men with weather-beaten faces and blue eyes, almost comically identical. It didn't seem appropriate to enquire whether they had the same mother. Each had a pair of shears and a whetstone dangling from his belt. Their single mule carried half a dozen wineskins.

'By the time they have finished the shearing they will have drunk all the wine and replaced it with fleeces,' Arnaud told me. 'They will have a sober journey back to the Basque country.'

We didn't have a language in common, but that didn't matter. We corralled our flock and then let them out two at a time. The shearers, working in pairs, would take off the fleece in less than ten minutes, pausing only to sharpen their shears. They had the knack of holding each sheep on its back, completely immobile after a brief initial struggle, and managed to avoid anything but the occasional small nick in the flesh.

'How do they do that?' I asked Arnaud.

'They're strong. And they have a word.'

He clearly believed there was witchcraft involved. I looked closely while the shearing was going on, and they seemed to have a grip around each animal's head or throat that effectively paralysed it. The sheep were unharmed by the process and were happy to be relieved of their heavy burden in the hot weather.

The Basques were with us two days and one night, and it was the only time in the year that we butchered and roasted one of our lambs. The Basques drank their own wine, making it clear that they thought ours inferior stuff. I tried a mouthful and decided it was an acquired taste. They slept in the open, covered in thick brown cloaks that the dew seemed not to penetrate. I remembered Sybille saying Montségur could only be taken by mountain goats, and wondered whether any of these men had been one of the band that had climbed the steep path up to our castle. They looked tough enough for the task; perhaps luckily, I hadn't the language to ask them.

Arnaud paid them on the second evening with a mixture of coins, cheese and fleeces and then they left, touching our hands first, for the next pasture. Two days later Andre Belot appeared, riding one mule and leading two others.

'One of them is mine,' said Arnaud. 'The other two are borrowed from Clergue. I'll go with Andre to the market. You'll manage.'

This was high praise. I watched them leave, the three mules looking like comical, mythological beasts under their woolly burden. My main concern was for Arnaud's three dogs, but they seemed to know by instinct what to do and rounded up the sheep each evening without paying much attention to my mimicry of Arnaud's cries and hand signals. I enjoyed being on my own in the mountains, and after a nervous first day realised that the dogs and the sheep between them knew enough to keep us out of trouble. At any event, I didn't lose any animals, although I noticed Arnaud counted them all into the corral on the first night with particular care.

'How was the price of wool?

'Terrible. Worse than last year. I presented a fleece to St Francis and to the Virgin Mary of Montaillou as usual. Never seems to have much effect.'

'I thought you were Cathar.'

'So I am. But no harm keeping in with the others.'

That seemed to sum up the Catharism of Montaillou, and certainly that of Clergue. It was a pragmatism that appealed to me. I distrusted the narrow righteousness of Catholic or Cathar zealots, and I had learned that some of the Perfects, like many abbots and bishops, found it easy to fall from grace, especially where women were concerned.

Authie alone seemed to be consistent and undeviating. Belibaste, on the other hand, another Perfect whom we saw occasionally, had broken most of the rules at some time or other. He always travelled with a female companion who was also his mistress. Or so it was rumoured.

In my first year Arnaud and I were celebrating a successful sale of wool with perhaps too much red wine from a fresh wineskin. It loosened his tongue.

'I became a shepherd when I was twelve,' he told me that evening.

'Always here?'

'No. I was involved in a brawl when I was fifteen and had to leave Montaillou. I worked for five years for Brunissende de Cervello in Puigcerdà.'

'And then?'

'Saved some money, bought ten sheep on my return, and here I am, thirty years later. Most shepherds move about, never stay in one place for more than two or three years. Hire themselves out this side of the Pyrenees or in Catalonia, doesn't seem to matter. Content to live in cabins. Don't need a house. Neither did I at the beginning.'

This was a long speech for Arnaud. I thought he would ask me about my past, but lack of curiosity or good manners prevented him.

After three years, and many dead wolves, and good fortune with twins during the lambing season, I had built up my own flock of thirty-seven ewes and one ram. I continued to work with Arnaud, both for the company, taciturn though he was, and for his great experience, particularly at cheese-making. Our cheeses always commanded the best price in the market.

It was later that third summer that the accident happened. He'd gone to the far end of the pasture to cut down a tree for next year's firewood, and when he didn't return in the early evening I went to look for him.

I found him under the tree that he'd been felling. It had toppled the wrong way and even though he'd managed to avoid the main trunk one of the branches, as thick as my thigh, was crushing his chest. I couldn't see his face, as it was covered with leafy side shoots; it seemed unlikely he was still alive, but I tried to shift the weight of the tree off him, cursing my lack of a right arm, then hacked away at the branch on either side of his body with the axe he had been using to chop down the tree. This took an hour, an hour during which Arnaud made no sound. When I finally freed his body I could see that he had been killed at once, his chest completely caved in.

I carried him back to our cabin; he weighed no more than a young boy. I laid his body out on his bed, closed his eyes and crossed his hands over what was left of his chest. Then I wept; I had seen many bodies, and many gruesome deaths, but this accident of nature, killing my only friend in Montaillou, seemed a violence as unfair as it was unpredictable. Arnaud had taught and helped me. As I looked at his body I realised that he and I, together with the dogs and the sheep, were all that either of us had as family.

It was two days before Andre Belot arrived with our regular supplies. I explained what had happened, showed him the tree – Montaillou was the kind of village where you needed a witness to a sudden death – and we decided to bury him on the edge of the meadow where he had spent most of his life. We dug a deep grave to keep Arnaud safe from wolves and foxes and said an Our Father together, a prayer used by Catholic and Cathar alike. Andre left to carry the news back to Montaillou, leaving me with Arnaud's sheep and mine, and his three dogs, until the end of the season.

When I returned to Montaillou I went to Bernard to ask about Arnaud's house.

'There's no one to claim it. Take it. He owes my brother a year's tithe and me...' he looked at some documents and then said, '... six livres Tournois. Pay us off and you can keep the house.'

'And the sheep?'

'They belong to the Church.'

'Forty of them are mine.'

'Settle with Pierre. He'll give you time to pay.'

I was able to agree a price with Pierre, and to pay the brothers off in wool, cheese, sheep and money. I knew where Arnaud kept his coins and had left them in the mountains, buried in a crock under a big stone. The Clergue brothers didn't need to know about that little fortune.

So I found myself owner of a house in Montaillou, over 200 sheep and grazing rights. I was transformed overnight from a share-cropping shepherd to one of Montaillou's richer citizens, although I was no rival to the Clergues, the Benets or the Belots.

I mourned for Arnaud. I was saddened by the brutal accident that caused his death, and even more by the fact that there was no one to regret his passing but me. His dogs had transferred their allegiance quickly enough. The next spring I asked Authie to say a prayer over his grave, and that was all that marked his passing.

The Montaillou that gave me shelter and a living was an unusual village as it lacked a lord. It had a small castle occupied by a few dozy old retainers and an ineffectual steward who collected rents when he needed cash. The de Planissoles had married up and out; nobody had seen Beatrice, the heiress and nominal chatelaine of Montaillou's castle, for several years. This state of affairs had created a power vacuum that was quickly and effectively filled by the two Clergue brothers, Pierre and Bernard. Between the two of them, Pierre as priest, Bernard as magistrate, they controlled every aspect of village life through Confession and the court.

This balance of power changed when, in the year that Arnaud died, Beatrice de Planissoles returned to reclaim her castle. Barely thirty, she had lost her husband, who had been unlucky enough to be killed in a tournament. She was rich, richer than the Clergues, through inheritance and marriage, and had left behind her stepson in her husband's fiefdom.

Pierre Clergue dealt with any possible challenge quickly and efficiently by taking Beatrice as his mistress. She told me much later that the first time was close to rape, but Pierre was attractive to women and you could sense his power the moment he entered a room. Even in the castle that power accompanied him, and his humble origins (his father had been a herdsman, and Clergue's manners had been learned in the field and the sheep pen) made him attractive to a noblewoman like Beatrice.

In those early days I saw little of her, although enough to know she was tall, fair-haired and used to being admired and obeyed. I kept my distance. Pierre Clergue was not a man to cross in love, or anything else for that matter. She did once see me bathing at the washing-place in the early morning; I was naked, and she made a coarse remark about my manhood that I found disturbing. And provocative, although I did nothing about it. As it turned out, I didn't need to.

16

Summoned to Carcassonne

Francois

PIERRE CLERGUE WAS summoned to Carcassonne, 'on Church business' he told the few who dared ask him why; he looked uneasy when he used those words to me. We thought that rumours of Catharism in our village may have reached the level at which they could no longer be ignored. All the great Cathar castles had been taken: Bram, Puylaurens, Roqueville, Montségur; their lords imprisoned or burned, their lands confiscated and given to the Church or one of the crusaders. The Crusade itself was over.

Montaillou survived for two reasons. Its closeness to the mountains made it easy for the few surviving Perfects to come and go discreetly. And Pierre Clergue was skilful in maintaining an outward show of devout Catholicism.

'Perhaps it's money, not doctrine,' I said to Agnes Belot, the mother of Andre, who still supplied me with flour and wine and eggs during the summer months. 'Perhaps they've found out he's taking more than the priest's share of the tithes.'

'Speak quietly,' she said, looking around her in case we were overheard; the main street was almost deserted, but those habits die hard. 'I don't want to suffer Mengarde's punishment. She can hardly speak, and nothing tastes of anything, poor woman. Although she always did talk too much.'

She looked around again.

'Pierre may have left. But Bernard's still here.'

'Better if it is the money,' I said. 'That might clip his wings, and the rest of us won't be involved.'

Agnes nodded, feeling she had said enough, and walked on to her house. I had only just begun to understand the strange and furtive atmosphere in Montaillou, a combination of fear of the Clergues, the secret Cathar rituals and the sheltering of Perfects, and the complicated family feuds, many of them generations old, that intersected the village. I understood the first two and carefully avoided asking about the feuds. I knew that the Clergues hated the Maurs, and that was knowledge enough.

I was on my way to the castle to pay my feudal dues for my house and for the grazing rights over the upland pasture. The mountain meadows that first Arnaud, and then I, used were the property of the de Planissoles, who in turn paid, not often I suspected, dues to the Comte de Foix. Or perhaps the King of Aragon. The patchwork nature of ownership throughout the foothills of the Pyrenees was never clear, and in the end reduced itself, for a tenant like me, to paying whoever demanded payment and could back up their claim with force.

Soon after her return Beatrice's steward came to see me, set out his view of the position and asked for payment.

'Arnaud never paid you. Why should I?'

He looked unhappy.

'We don't expect you to pay Arnaud's arrears. You have the protection of the castle. And it isn't a big sum, you needn't pay in coin.'

‘And if I refuse?’

He looked even less happy.

‘Then, then…’ he thought for a moment, ‘… then we’ll take you before Bernard Clergue.’

That appealed to neither of us, and to his evident relief I agreed to pay. We agreed a price of one livre Tournois, a ewe and two cheeses.

I arrived at a castle in need of repair and of mine and others’ feudal dues. It consisted of a long courtyard with a substantial keep at one end. Along both sides of the courtyard were buildings, some in stone, some ramshackle. Everything was on a much smaller scale than Montségur or Roqueville, more the size of Beaufort.

There was a *pigeonnier* in the north corner, but no pigeons that I could see. Half a dozen elderly retainers were sitting in the courtyard, two women spinning or carding wool, four men dozing happily in the sun. A few chickens scratched a living from the courtyard grass, and there was a sow and some piglets in a pen just by the entrance.

‘The protection of the castle’ mentioned by the steward seemed not worth a sou, never mind a livre Tournois. I was directed to the steward’s quarters in one of the better stone buildings, where he took my money and my cheese gratefully.

‘Now that you’ve paid I’ll find it easier to persuade the rest.’

‘I hope I had an abatement for being the first. Taste the cheese.’

He cut off a generous slice which we shared. It was hard, but not rock-hard, didn’t crumble, and had a salty, creamy taste that made it stand out from all the other cheese in the valley. Arnaud had always used more milk than the other shepherds in the making of each cheese, let them ferment longer and never sold a cheese less than a year old.

'It's the best in the valley,' I told the steward, and his mouth was too full to disagree. When he had finished (I was glad to see he picked the crumbs off his jerkin and ate those too) he said, 'Lady Beatrice will wish to thank you.'

He escorted me across the courtyard – I noticed the dozing retainers didn't stir – and we climbed a winding, worn stone staircase to the first floor. Walking down the passage we could hear the sound of a sweet, true voice singing one of the best-known troubadours' songs, one I knew well, composed in honour of Blanche de Roqueville. As we entered the singing stopped, and I completed the last two lines:

'In you lie all my happiness, all my desire,
I cannot find another one as fair.'

I have been told I have a decent voice. Beatrice looked surprised for a moment, then said as I bowed, 'Of course. You were at Roqueville before Montségur.'

'And Beaufort before that, my lady. I've been chased from castle to castle by the crusaders.'

'I hope they won't follow you to Montaillou.'

'I've completed the pilgrimage to Compostela and I have a certificate to prove it. Absolves me from all my past sins. Pierre Bernard Clergue has it for safe keeping.'

'Safe keeping? He probably regards it as surety for good behaviour. Or else he'll change the name on the document to his own. My steward tells me you have agreed to pay your dues.'

'He has, my lady. One livre Tournois, a carrying ewe and two cheeses.'

The steward had brought a generous slice of my cheese

which he offered to Beatrice. She broke off a piece, tasted it with caution, then greedily and quickly ate the rest, licking her fingers when she had finished.

'Good. Who made the cheese?'

'I did, using Arnaud's methods. It's still the best in the valley.'

'They make good cheese in Laroque.'

'Mine is better. And I've brought you these in settlement of past dues.'

I unwrapped the bundle under my arm from its cloth covering and spread two wolf skins out on the floor. They were my finest skins, cured so well that they smelled only of herbs and oil. The fur, silver and grey and black, was thick and soft. I had even stitched up the holes made by my crossbow bolts.

Beatrice looked pleased, rose from her chair, picked up one of the skins and pressed it to her cheek.

'I've never seen or held a wolf skin. Much softer than I expected. Shepherding, cheese-making, skin-curing, you're resourceful for a former knight. And you have a good voice. Visit me again and we'll sing together.'

She held out her hand in dismissal. I took her hand, bowed over it and left the chamber with the steward. It was clear that I had made a good, if different, impression at our second meeting, and I found that exciting, although the dangers were obvious. Still, I thought, Pierre Clergue is in Carcassonne and may never return.

Less than a week later I sang my way into Beatrice's bed. Her steward called on me again, inviting me to a feast the following day, a feast to celebrate St Someone or Other. He mumbled the name, and, anyway, Cathars don't believe in saints. Martyrs we have in abundance.

The feast was in the Great Hall. The sentry was asleep and I had to kick chickens out of the way as I crossed the courtyard, but the Great Hall, decked out for the feast, was in marked contrast to the rest of the castle. It was early evening, but the room was well lit with rushlights, dozens of candles on the table, a blazing fire. There was a splendid tapestry on each of the long walls; I recognised Diana and Actaeon in one, and the other was a myth I didn't know. Zeus in a shower of gold coming to Danae, Beatrice later explained. The colours were bright, and although the room was smaller than the hall at Roqueville the overall impression was far richer than you would have imagined from the courtyard, richer than our very occasional display at Beaufort. There was enough silver on the table to make a dazzling display.

'If you bury a rich husband you are likely to have enough silver for one castle, although not for two. I didn't leave much behind for my stepson,' Beatrice said as we moved to the table. 'You are looking at the de Planissoles silver and the silver I inherited from my mother, all in honour of St Eustacius.'

'Who was he?'

'Ask my steward. He knows about such things.'

I thought there was enough on display to deserve better guarding than a sleeping sentry. The silver would become common knowledge through the valley within days.

Beatrice sat in a throne-like chair at the head of the table, her steward on her left hand. To my surprise and Bernard Clergue's annoyance I was placed on Beatrice's right. She had decided that I was not only more than a shepherd, but deserving of promotion, calling me the Comte de Beaufort all evening, in spite of my explanation that I was only a knight, and a landless one at that.

The other guests were an assortment of Clergue cousins, Belots, three of Beatrice's elderly retainers, a knight on his way to Carcassonne, and Guillaume Authie. Authie was silent throughout the meal and tried not to draw attention to the fact that he was served with fish. The rest of us feasted on pork, venison and mutton and drank our local red wine, of which there was a plentiful supply.

After dinner a troubadour entertained us. He had composed a flattering but disappointing song in honour of the Lady of Montaillou, which pleased Beatrice in spite of its trite words and uneven rhythm. Later we all sang the best-known songs, the knight recited a long poem about the Battle of Roncesvalles and then fell asleep, and we finished with local ballads, none of which I had heard before, but were funny and frequently bawdy. I noticed Authie had left the room at this stage; I learned later he had gone to administer the Consolamentum to Mengarde Maurs, who had been ill for many weeks.

Then Beatrice, ignoring the troubadour, asked me to sing, with her, the song to Blanche de Roqueville that I knew so well. I had been careful not to drink too much wine and so my voice was true, as was hers. Then she rose, her guests took their leave and as I moved to follow them she put her hand on my arm.

'Let me show you how well your wolf skins look in my chamber,' she said, taking a candlestick from the table and leading me up to the room where I had visited her the week before. There was a wide bed in an alcove; a small fire lit the room, and the wolf skins were red and silver in the firelight. Beatrice slipped out of her clothes as I watched, then lay back on the bed as I undressed and joined her.

That was the first of many nights with Beatrice. She was unashamed about sex and proud of her body. She was intrigued by mine, by my scars, and took a strange pleasure in being touched by my all but vanished right arm.

She had slept with her husband, with Clergue and perhaps with others; at any rate she was in charge when we made love. That suited me well. Apart from some mechanical couplings with whores as I crossed Spain, I had known only Sybille, who was as innocent as I was. So I was happy to follow her adventurous and exciting suggestions. I left the castle at dawn, passing a different sentry whom I had to wake to get the drawbridge lowered, went to my own house and slept till noon.

At the beginning I felt I was simply filling a vacancy caused by Pierre Clergue's absence in Carcassonne. Beatrice would send for me once or twice a week and we would make love, or, rather, couple, in her chamber. Sometimes she would arrange our meetings so that we could eat afterwards. The meal was not much more elaborate than the bread and cheese I ate in the mountains.

It was then that we talked. She wanted to know about Beaufort, Roqueville and Montségur, and about my journey to Compostela. She was intrigued by my relationship with Blanche.

'You lay beside her for six weeks and didn't sleep with her?'

'The rooms were crowded and we were all on pilgrimage.'

'Was she still beautiful?'

'She was.'

'Yet she slept with the Inquisitor, not with you.'

'That was a bargain she had made, not one that made me happy. Had it been you beside me...' and I showed her how it would have been.

I asked her about Pierre Clergue.

'The first time he forced himself on me, here in this room. I could have cried for help, but part of me wanted it to happen. Otherwise I wouldn't have allowed him in my chamber.'

'And afterwards?'

'He's not like you. He smells of the farmyard, he's rough, he talks only when he has to. He's used to getting his way with women. He takes as long as he needs to get his own pleasure, and I have to hurry to keep up. You're slower, more gentle. You talk before and after we make love.'

'Which is better?'

'Both are better,' and she laughed. 'Why should I choose?'

'He is a priest.'

'That's part of the attraction. Once we made love…' and she put her hand over her mouth.

'… behind the altar in the church,' I said.

'How do you know that?'

'In time everyone knows everything in Montaillou. Whoever saw you there says Pierre was angry, shouted, "You bastard, you have interrupted an act of Holy Church."'

Beatrice found it hard to stop laughing. 'It's true, it's true, all of it. That's why I like Pierre. He is without shame.'

She took a long drink of wine, drummed her fingers on the table, then continued, 'He's shameless, and also dangerous. He's been several weeks in Carcassonne. He'd betray any of us to save his own skin. If the Inquisitors have got hold of him, and I was a member of the Maurs family, I would leave for Spain at once.'

'Why does he hate them?'

'Some insult long ago that everyone has forgotten. Except Pierre.'

'Are you safe?'

Beatrice looked out of the window.

'I'm safe. I still have friends in high places. You, on the other hand...' She did not finish the sentence.

It was a mild autumn, and although my sheep had been down in the valley for several weeks it was still warm enough to ride up in the foothills. Beatrice owned the only horses in Montaillou, and lent me a big gelding so we could ride together from time to time.

'The gelding's too strong for me,' she said.

'I'm good with horses. I made my living buying and selling them as I crossed Spain.'

'But you've only...'

'... one arm. I know. But the legs matter more. And he's been cut, he's not a stallion.' I told her the story of Octavian and his life-saving capriole.

'What happened to Octavian?'

'We ate all the horses.'

We rode up to my meadow, her meadow, and I showed her the sheepfold, the place where I and young Belot had buried Arnaud, and the little tree platforms where I waited for wolves. We tethered the horses outside my cabin, went inside.

'It must be cold in the winter. But it's warm enough now.'

'Warm enough for what?'

'For this,' and she pulled me over to the bed of pine branches.

Afterwards she insisted on trying my latrine.

'It's a clever design,' she said as she pulled up her undergarments and skirt. 'Better than squatting.'

I was glad I had covered my summer leavings with a thick layer of earth.

Back in Montaillou I discovered that Bernard Clergue had been looking for me. The messenger who brought me the summons was one of Pierre Clergue's enforcers, a man I had worked alongside for two years.

'What does he want?'

He rolled his eyes and didn't answer. It was never likely to be good if either Pierre or Bernard sent for you, and my first reaction was that he was about to punish me for usurping his brother's place in Beatrice's bed.

I went to see him as soon as we had dried, fed and watered the horses. Beatrice was also uneasy.

'You've done nothing wrong, nothing to challenge their authority,' she said, then added, 'as far as I know. You're in the mountains half the year.'

'Becoming your lover in Pierre's absence might count as a challenge. But it would be difficult to frame a charge around that.'

'I'm sure Bernard could think of something.'

Bernard's office was separate from his house. I met him in a large room that also served as the court where he dispensed his summary justice. The village jail and the armoury were on the ground floor. I noticed he had framed his authority from the Comte de Foix and hung it on the wall behind his chair.

He asked me to sit and there was no one else in the room, both encouraging signs. And as it was early evening he offered me some bread and cheese. The Clergue cheese was famously bad, but I complimented him on it anyway.

'It's my brother, it's Pierre,' said Bernard. 'They've imprisoned him in Carcassonne for holding back some of the tithes.'

'And did he?'

Bernard looked indignant. 'Only the twenty per cent due to him as priest and collector.'

'I thought...' but I was sensible enough not to continue. Twelve per cent was the most that could be deducted.

'They've fined him twenty thousand sous.'

'Can you pay?'

'We can,' Bernard said, trying to suppress a look of satisfaction. 'We can. I want you to take the money to Carcassonne and make sure he is released.'

'Why don't you go?'

'I've never been to Carcassonne. Neither has anyone else in Montaillou except Lady Beatrice. And I trust you.'

That came as a surprise, but was only a measure of how far he distrusted everyone else in the village. I had been careful not to cross either brother, at least until I slept with Beatrice, and that piece of recent gossip may not have reached Bernard's ears. Or perhaps he knew and didn't care.

'I'll think about it and come back in the morning. I'll need my Compostela certificate, which you have for safe keeping.'

'I'm not sure I know exactly where it is,' said Bernard, lying out of instinct.

'I don't go without it. I'd wind up alongside Pierre if I had no proof I'd done my penance.'

I went straight from Bernard to Beatrice.

'Will you go?' she asked. 'Perhaps Montaillou is better off without him.'

That surprised me, but she didn't mean it.

'I don't like Pierre Clergue,' I said, 'but I don't like the idea of him in a Carcassonne jail. If the Inquisition take an interest in Pierre's conduct of his priestly duties he'll betray any of us, you included, to save his own skin.'

'You can borrow the gelding.'

'Thank you.'

'You can thank me now,' and Beatrice, never one to miss an opportunity, led me over to the alcove and the wolf skins.

I told Bernard the next morning I would carry out his errand, and set out my conditions.

'Two livres Tournois for my trouble and expenses. One of Pierre's men as escort; there's a lot of money involved. And my certificate, which I don't plan to return.'

Bernard accepted at once, gave me my certificate, which had, mysteriously, turned up overnight, and suggested Pons as my escort.

'Pons can have our strongest mule. He should be able to keep up with your gelding. Come back this evening and I'll have the money ready.'

'Don't tell Pons about the money. He'd cut my throat and make off with the cash if he knew how much I was carrying. Tell him I need an escort because... you come up with a good reason that isn't twenty thousand sous.'

The journey was uneventful. Pons was a man of few words, and I slept in my cloak, my hand on my dagger, in the two little inns where we broke our journey. When we reached Carcassonne I found a decent inn with good stabling and sent Pons back to Montaillou, keeping the mule.

'I need it for Pierre's return journey.'

Pons grumbled at the prospect of a five-day journey on foot but accepted the logic.

It took me several days to find my way through the labyrinth that had Pierre in jail at its centre. There were several clerks and jailers who were ready to receive the money, but I knew only a release order would do. I called on Baruch the Jew, and was relieved to find he had remained a sufficiently devout Catholic to stay alive.

'I hold four hundred livres Tournois to your account,' he said the moment he saw me at his door. 'I am glad to see you are able to claim it.'

As we went upstairs he said, 'I heard the Inquisitor's men had beaten you when they seized Blanche de Roqueville.'

'They thought about killing me, but I wasn't beaten, thanks to some friendly pilgrims. I got to Compostela.'

'I congratulate you. You must be almost without sin. The Lady Blanche is back in the Places des Pénitents. They say the Inquisitor is very ill. I am happy to say the Inquisition has been very inactive of late. No burnings.'

'Not many Cathars left to burn.'

'There are still Jews, and witches, and sodomites. Luckily I am none of those things.'

I told him why I was in Carcassonne, and came back the next day to hear the result of his enquiries. We ate in his room, which was full of pictures, manuscripts and bolts of cloth. We ate roast pork.

'I make a point of eating pork as often as I can,' Baruch said. 'It means I cannot be a Jew. We're the same, you and I, converts. In my case twice. Once at the point of the sword, the second time persuaded by the silver tongue of the Inquisitor.'

'It was the fire that convinced me.'

'I find my new faith remarkably attractive when I consider the alternative. I am a diligent attender at all their rituals, which I enjoy. They are nothing if not colourful, especially in the cathedral. And they have no knowledge of what goes on in my head.'

'I'm the same.'

'The rumour is that Perfects pay regular visits to Montaillou. Is that why they are holding Pierre Clergue?'

'He's been keeping back money from the Church.'

'Much worse than heresy.'

'I have the funds from his brother to get him out, if I could find the right person to authorise his release. Plenty of people want to take the money.'

Baruch knew exactly whom I must see, what I should pay, and how I could guarantee Pierre's release.

'You go to the chief magistrate's office, show him the money and wait there until Pierre Clergue is produced. With his fetters struck off. Here – take two bolts of silk. I've been able to put your money to work in the last three years.'

Baruch's advice was good. Pierre was produced the next morning, I handed over 20,000 sous to the magistrate, his fetters were struck off and we were free to go.

Pierre was surprised and not particularly grateful to see me.

'I expected my brother.'

'He thought it best to stay in Montaillou. Two Clergues in prison wasn't a risk worth taking.'

'What took you so long? I've been in prison for almost twelve weeks.'

'You must ask your brother that.'

We went back to my inn, round to the stables and I gave him his mule.

'Isn't that Beatrice de Planissoles's horse?' looking at the gelding in the adjacent stall, then looking at me. He knew Beatrice well.

'It is.'

'I'll take him.'

'No, I'd look foolish on a mule, wouldn't know how to control him. He is yours; you're used to each other.'

Pierre didn't care for this argument, but was in no position to disagree. He left for Montaillou after a silent meal. Three months in jail, the same jail where they had locked me up for a week years before, had made Pierre thin and hungry, though he bore no signs of torture. I gave him half a cheese and a little money for his journey, and received a reluctant grunt of thanks in return. His displeasure at our new relationship was clear.

I told him I had business to attend to in Carcassonne and would return to Montaillou at the end of the month. In fact I had finished my business with Baruch and was intent on seeing Blanche again, to whom I felt strong ties of loyalty and affection, although no longer love, courtly or carnal.

I felt able to walk around Carcassonne freely; I had my Compostela certificate safe in an inner pocket. I used some of my livres Tournois to buy good clothes, a new dagger and a sword, and as a result looked less like a shepherd than when I had arrived in the town. I went to the Thursday market to buy a horse, but they were a rough lot that day, not up to my weight, beyond mark of mouth, barely sound and without any signs of breeding.

I extended my stay in my lodgings and visited the taverns round the centre of town to discover more about Blanche and the Inquisitor. Although it was clear the Inquisition was less active – as Baruch had suggested, there hadn't been a burning for well over a year – old habits of circumspection die hard. It was not easy to find useful information.

I did find something in those taverns that surprised me. I had become well known, as had all the knights from Roqueville. There was an inaccurate, heroic ballad celebrating the march to Montségur and our part in its gallant defence. The ballad was only sung in one or two taverns with Cathar sympathies, and only late in the evening, but there I was treated as a hero.

I soon gave up explaining that all I had done was to lead a group of blind and maimed men on a long and depressing march, and accepted compliments with a good grace. Several late-night drinkers insisted on touching my stump for good luck, and I began to feel for a moment like a living Cathar relic. Which indeed I was, although I was careful to go to church regularly.

My dilemma was solved when Baruch told me over dinner that the Inquisitor had died two days earlier.

'He had a fatal wasting disease,' he said. 'The Church have claimed his body, taken it to his old abbey of Flaran for burial. He won't be mourned by many.'

'Not by me. I'm one-armed and one-eyed thanks to him.'

'Nor by me. Although I had a healthy respect for his intellect, even if it took him to some cruel places. You know what he said after the fall of Puylaurens? They were unable to distinguish between Cathar and Catholic prisoners. "Burn them all," he said. "God will recognise his own."'

'That's the man I knew.'

'And yet Lady Blanche stayed with him for his last years and nursed him through his final illness.'

'His monks took her away from the pilgrimage, and from me, and brought her back to Carcassonne by force. She had nowhere else to go. Her daughter and son-in-law had disowned her.'

'Nevertheless there was something between them. The Inquisition became far less fierce when she came back. And now she is a rich, or at least a landed, woman again.'

'How did that happen?'

'Partly through me. I advanced her money to fight for the restitution of the Roqueville lands. I acted as her advocate. I argued that it was a powerful and proper incentive to conversion if expropriated property was returned to its original owners. And in this case the Bishop agreed.'

'Has she been back to Roqueville?'

'I have no idea. I hear you were looking for a horse at the

Thursday fair. Complete waste of time. Try my friend at Montcalm, outside the city. He usually has something decent to sell, took some good horses off crusaders who had gambled or whored their money away. He's not cheap.'

17

Back to Barraigne

Francois

I went to see the horse dealer in Montcalm, but first I called on Blanche. She was astonished to see me; we hugged each other, she cried and we talked until late over several glasses of good wine.

'I completed my pilgrimage, reached Compostela. I have many thousand days' remission from Purgatory, and a certificate.'

'I had no news of you from the moment I was taken back to Mathieu. I couldn't ask him about you.'

'I travelled through Spain for several years buying and selling horses. Ended up in Montaillou. I'm a shepherd now, no longer a knight.'

'Much more useful.'

Blanche got up to light the fire, which had already been laid. She was still beautiful, but now she looked worn, older than her years. When she sat down she refilled her glass, then said, 'You know that Mathieu died three days ago,' and as I began to speak she went on. 'No need to say anything. You only saw that fierce and unrelenting side of him.'

'I and many others.'

'Francois, I know. But he was different when I returned – no burnings, no savage sentences, no exhumations. He continued to argue and achieved enough conversions to keep everyone happy. And he was a good lover.'

Blanche laughed when she saw the shocked look on my face.

'I'm sorry, I shouldn't have said that. But it's true.'

I wanted to change the subject.

'Any news from Barraigne?'

'I might as well be dead as far as Stephanie and Etienne are concerned. I haven't seen my grandson since Flaran. I send little presents of money and wine, which I suppose get there safely, but they are never acknowledged. And now I have to move out of this house within the week. Mathieu's body has been taken to Flaran. They won't let me attend the burial.' She began to cry. I got up from my chair, tried and failed to comfort her and promised to come back the next day.

Early the following morning I rode out to Montcalm and found Baruch's friend, a horse dealer much as I had been in Spain. He trotted half a dozen beasts in front of me, and I bought the best after cantering him round the field. He was an eight-year-old, sound in wind and limb, the dealer said; it was an expression I had often used myself, in most cases truthfully. I paid a fair price after a little haggling and rode him back into Carcassonne.

When I called again on Blanche, later than planned, she asked me to sit down.

'I have a favour to ask you.'

'I'll do what I can.'

'I now own Roqueville, thanks to Baruch's advocacy and money. I'd like you to escort me there, see if anything has survived.'

I thought for a moment, realised Pierre Clergue would already have had a week to reinstate himself in both Beatrice's affections and her bed, and agreed.

It was a two-day, unhurried ride. We found a tavern in Castelnau, shared a chaste bed and arrived at Roqueville that afternoon.

It was a desolate place, one that had bad memories for both of us at the end. I had lost an arm and an eye there; Blanche had seen her son killed and his body burned, along with the bodies of many of her retainers and friends. The earth was still black where the crusaders had built their great fire in the courtyard and the outer walls were mostly demolished. When we went into the keep pigeons scattered out of the windows, and the floor of the Great Hall was covered in bird droppings. There were signs of rats, no signs of humans. One corner of the roof had caved in, and rainwater had caused several of the floor beams to rot.

We stood in the Great Hall for a moment, remembering the splendour of its feasts.

'We celebrated for a week when Stephanie and Etienne were married,' said Blanche. 'Now look at the place – you'd think it had been abandoned fifty years ago. No wonder the Church didn't fight very hard to keep it.'

'Was there a steward?'

'I don't know. If there was he didn't know his job or want to stay.'

We rode down to my dovecote, now a tumbled pile of stones and wood. I remembered washing Blanche's feet there, but didn't remind her. The fields around were uncultivated, and the little village by the river was deserted.

'The whole place has gone to ruin,' Blanche said. 'It's a lifetime's work for a young man to restore its glories.' She was silent for a moment, then looked at me. 'Would you take it on?'

'It's not mine, it's Stephanie's. And the happy memories have been blotted out by what happened after we lost our water and were betrayed. I'm a shepherd now.'

We cantered down the valley to Beaufort, which was in no better state. There were signs that somebody was living in the little castle, but they didn't appear. We went on to the stone that marked my parents' grave, dismounted and said the Lord's Prayer.

'They dug up their bodies and burned what was left.'

On our way back past Roqueville it began to rain. We hadn't seen a human or an animal all afternoon.

'Now where do we go?' asked Blanche.

'To Barraigne.'

As we approached Barraigne, Blanche grew increasingly nervous and critical.

'The place is almost as run-down as Roqueville,' she said. 'They haven't done much to improve things.'

'You should have seen it when we first returned. It was far worse than Roqueville, worse than my old home at Beaufort. Remember your son-in-law is blind in both eyes. They have replanted the vines, and they look healthy enough.'

We had pulled up our horses on a small hill half a mile from Barraigne. The meadow in front of us was uncultivated, but between it and the walls of the little fort vines had been planted in neat rows right up to the walls and stretched round the fort as far as we could see. Their leaves looked green and glossy from a distance, and as we rode up to the gate between the vines we could see that they were free from mildew and rust and bore many clusters of grapes, although they were still green.

'You go first,' said Blanche. 'I don't know whether they will be glad to see me. You're sure of a welcome.'

I took her advice and rode into the courtyard, disturbing, I was pleased to see, many pigeons. The courtyard was cobbled, and a horse stuck an inquisitive nose out of a low range of stables on the left. In the corner of the courtyard a woman was playing with three children. It was Guillemette. She stood up, leaving the children, ignoring their protests and almost pulling me off my horse to embrace me.

I felt equally moved. 'It's been years since I left the three of you here. You haven't changed.'

It was true; she had always looked older and been wiser than her years.

'Stephanie and Etienne will be overjoyed to see you. She's in the Great Hall, Etienne's checking on last year's wine.'

We went inside, leaving the children playing, and Stephanie's embrace was as warm as Guillemette's. Until I said, 'I have Blanche with me. She's waiting outside. The Inquisitor died five days ago.'

Stephanie's face changed when I mentioned her mother's name. 'That woman is not welcome here. She can go back to Carcassonne, or to hell, for all I care.'

'Then I must leave too. You seem to have forgotten that you and Etienne would not be together but for her.'

'She didn't have to sleep with him.'

'That was the bargain. She did the best she could. And why do you think Etienne's sentence, which was the same as mine, was never enforced?'

The last was a guess, and at that moment Etienne came in. I embraced him clumsily, laughing as I did so – there is something comic, as well as tragic, when two one-armed men with one eye between them try to hug each other.

'I'm not staying. I've Blanche with me outside the gates, and Stephanie doesn't want her here. Even though the Inquisitor is dead.'

'I'm not unhappy to hear that,' said Etienne. 'Of course Blanche is welcome here. She's your mother, for the love of God. Bring her in, bring her in.'

'But she's a harlot, a prie—'

'Enough. I said she is welcome here, and you'll have to make the best of it. If my wounds and Francois' have healed so can yours.'

He and I went outside and found Blanche in the courtyard, dismounted, playing with her grandson. She looked up at Etienne and said, her voice unsteady, 'I'll go away if Stephanie doesn't want to see me. I heard what she said.'

'We both want both of you here. My mother died two years ago. The children need a grandmother.'

We went inside, little Bertrand nuzzling Blanche's shoulder, the other two girls holding Guillemette's hands. Stephanie stood up, tried to maintain her stern look, and then collapsed sobbing into her mother's arms, the child almost squashed between them.

I stayed for three days, telling them about my pilgrimage, my long journey across Spain and my new life as a shepherd in Montaillou.

'I'm rich these days, with my own house and over two hundred sheep. We make the best cheese in the valley. I've saved one round for you to taste. The rest I used as bribes.'

'We'll drink some of last year's wine,' and I watched as Etienne, without a stick or a handhold, walked out into the courtyard, reappearing with a large wineskin.

'I've learned painfully every cobblestone and sharp corner in Barraigne,' he said on his return. 'And I learned how to make decent wine by trial and error. The first year we threw away, the second we drank ourselves and the third we sold well in the Carcassonne market. Here, what you think?'

'It's as good as my cheese,' I said, and it was. We ate and drank well for three days, Etienne and I doing most of the talking, while Blanche contented herself with the children, competing with Guillemette for their affection, a competition which she easily, if unfairly, won. And by the third day Stephanie had come to terms with her mother, no longer rejecting her embraces, although they were not returned with quite the same warmth.

Etienne walked with me to the gate. 'I hope you look after your pigeons,' I said.

'Why don't you stay and look after them for me? Montaillou sounds a strange and dangerous place to me.'

'Strange, but not dangerous. I've just obtained the release of Pierre Clergue from the Carcassonne jail. That gives me some protection. And I need to get back to my sheep.'

Which was true. I also wanted to get back to Beatrice. We parted with another clumsy embrace, we agreed to exchange wine for cheese every autumn, I mounted and rode off. I was impressed, not only by the vineyard and the wine, but by the way Etienne was clearly master of Barraigne. I no longer had any fears for Blanche.

18

In the Village

Pierre Clergue

I WAS SURPRISED AND not altogether pleased that my brother had sent Seigneur Francois de Beaufort – to give him his full title, although he was now only a shepherd – to extract me from the Carcassonne jail. Bernard believed he was the only man we could trust with 20,000 sous. He was probably right.

This was a reflection on how little my work was understood or appreciated in the village. I alone enabled Catharism to survive, I made it possible for the Perfects to visit regularly, I allowed the Consolamentum to be administered to dying souls. All this at considerable expense to my own conscience. It was I who had to preach carefully worded sermons, conduct the Mass which I no longer thought a real sacrament, impose penances and collect tithes.

I did not expect to be loved. Ordering the cutting out of Mengarde Maurs's tongue guaranteed that. Her incessant gossip about my youth as a believer threatened not only me but the whole of Montaillou, and meant there was only one remedy. Which, by the way, worked. As did the killing of Arnaud Lizier, who hated all Cathars, and was often heard reciting the disgraceful ballad composed by the troubadour Pierre Cardenal:

Clergue pretends to be a priest, a shepherd of his flock,
But really he's a murderer, though he seems of great holiness,
When you see him in his clerical habit.

Lizier's body was left for all to see on the green in front of the castle, and the ballad wasn't heard any more in Montaillou.

I wanted to be feared, and my brother and I achieved that at least. I also thought I would be understood, and I was wrong. The women were to blame. Bernard told me that he had overheard two of them gossiping to each other that Montaillou would be a better place if I never returned from Carcassonne. He gave me their names, Alazais Faurs and Gauzia Maurs, the latter the sister of the tongueless Mengarde. I decided against applying a similar remedy, but the next time they or any member of their families came to me or Bernard for a loan, or for some cloth, or to borrow one of our mules, they received short shrift. We made the reason for our rejection clear.

I hated all the Maurs clan and for good reason. It was Mengarde's father who, soon after I became the priest, called me 'little man' in front of half the village. I smiled and did nothing at the time, but it did not take me long to become richer and more powerful than the rest of them put together. My stature I can do nothing about – I am of medium height, not small – and later I had no objection to being known as the 'Little Bishop'.

My other offence was to love and to be loved by the women of the village. I need a woman regularly, and my attentions were not unwelcome once I had explained that priests were much like other men. I could offer subsequent absolution for those who wanted it.

Bernard laughed when I told him this.

'Most of us make do with one woman. You've had half the village.'

He was exaggerating; it was no more than six or seven of the wives and daughters in Montaillou, and they were willing enough and even grateful, some of them. I tried to be discreet, but that was difficult in a small village where we all lived on top of each other.

'On top of each other? You take that too literally,' said Bernard. 'One day a jealous husband will stick a knife in your ribs.'

'They should be delighted. I teach their wives how to please men. Most of the husbands are too tired to perform more than once a week. And Beatrice is a widow.'

Beatrice was different from the rest of my women. For a start she was of noble birth, and when she returned to the village and her castle she kept her distance from the rest of us. I was persistent in my attentions, and the first time had to use force, but only because I could tell her reluctance was feigned. Thereafter she couldn't get enough of me. There's no doubt in my mind that part of the attraction was my priesthood, and the fact that I was a peasant.

'You smell of the farmyard, not the vestry,' she said to me. On one occasion I even persuaded her to make love in my church behind the altar.

'How can we do such a thing in the Church of Notre Dame?' she said. It was easy to convince her that St Peter wouldn't mind. I had prepared a makeshift bed of old church vestments on which we spent an exciting night. And many other nights, usually in the castle, with her maidservant guarding the door.

Most of the time, however, Beatrice was the dominant partner in our relationship. She wasn't afraid of me, unlike the other women, and took occasional, cruel pleasure in refusing me when I wanted her most.

So when Francois de Beaufort arrived in Carcassonne on a horse he had borrowed from Beatrice, sending me back on one of our own mules, I at once wondered whether Beatrice had yielded to his charms. For although he was one-armed and one-eyed he was still handsome, confident, well born. And tall.

The moment I got back I asked Beatrice whether she had taken him as her lover.

'That's none of your business. But the answer is yes. I like him. And we all believed you would never return from Carcassonne. But since you are back...' and she took me there and then, standing up in her antechamber, not caring whether we were interrupted. I felt much better after that. I had been three months without a woman, something I had never known before.

Francois had arrived in Montaillou three or four years earlier, with no money. Bernard and I, out of kindness to a fellow Cathar, made use of him as one of our collectors. Perhaps that was a mistake; anyhow, he didn't stay working for us very long. He became a shepherd, taking over Arnaud's house and flock when Arnaud was killed – by a falling tree, Francois said – and soon prospered.

He was never a rival to Bernard or to me even when rich. He came to church regularly and confessed, at least until he had slept with Beatrice. And he sheltered the Perfects in his own house and on the mountain. Authie told me Francois was genuinely interested in discussing the finer points of our religion, and was, in Authie's view, close to becoming a Perfect himself.

My time in the Carcassonne prison, even though I was eventually released, had disturbed more than my relationship with Beatrice. My influence was diminished. Tithes became harder to collect. Pons, the most reliable of our men-at-arms, left to visit a cousin in Pamiers and never returned.

Worst of all, a new and more zealous Inquisitor came to Carcassonne. Montaillou was the last redoubt of Catharism, and I was no longer sure that I could preserve the illusion that we were all good Catholics. Or preserve my family's wealth and power.

Francois

BACK IN MONTAILLOU I soon found, as I had expected, that Pierre Clergue had re-established himself as Beatrice's lover. She was happy to love me too, and when I grumbled about the arrangement she was absolutely clear.

'It's my body we're talking about, not yours, mine to dispose of as I see fit.' We had just made love, we were eating my cheese and drinking Etienne's wine, and I was tired by my journey, by our lovemaking, and by that sadness that one of our poets says always comes after physical ecstasy.

'I know it's your body, but it's mine too. I feel I belong to you when we're together, when I'm inside you.'

'I'm happy when you say that', and she took a long sip of her wine, 'but when you're in the mountains I still need a man.'

'Need a man? Is that all I am to you?' I was about to say that I loved her, but that was so obviously self-serving, and only a little true, that I stopped myself, saying instead, 'You know he has other women?'

'Of course I know. He's a man who has a hunger for sex, that's part of the attraction.'

I was silent for several minutes, afraid to ask why I wasn't hungry enough for Beatrice, and angry at the way the conversation had gone.

Gone nowhere; it was clear I had to share Beatrice with Clergue if I wanted her at all. I left her chamber depressed, and for a few days tried to live without seeing her, days which passed without her reaching out for me. Days which ended with a visit to her chamber bringing two of my best fleeces, some cheese and a clear, if unspoken, acceptance that I had no exclusive right to Beatrice's affections or her body.

I wasn't afraid of Clergue, but I understood very clearly what he was trying to do in Montaillou. Maintaining his and Bernard's wealth came first, but he was genuine in his protection of Catharism and the Perfects that visited us, although that in turn gave him the ability to denounce almost the whole village to the Inquisition if he chose. This was a two-edged sword; anyone he sent to Carcassonne could try to incriminate the whole Clergue family, and they might well have been believed.

It was fortunate that his imprisonment had been for skimming too much of the tithes, a common enough offence, and not seen in the same light as heresy. By the standards of the Languedoc the Clergues were not brutal. The mutilation of Mengarde Maurs and the killing of Arnaud Lizier, both of which happened several years before I arrived in

Montaillou, had been enough to enable the Clergues to rule thereafter with only the petty sanctions of penances or fines. And at one level all in Montaillou understood the rules, and abided by them.

19

The English Band

Francois

SOON AFTER HIS return from Carcassonne, Pierre Clergue asked me about Montaillou's defences. The Crusade was over, but not all the soldiers went home, some because they had nowhere to go, most because they were used to living off the land and liked fighting, often among themselves. So the remnants of those armies continued to threaten the Languedoc, forming and re-forming into little bands of mercenaries, anything from ten to a hundred strong.

'I've heard several villages not too far away have been attacked in the last six months,' said Pierre. 'Could we defend Montaillou?'

'The village walls are useless. You would need two hundred men to defend them, and there are no more than fifty in the village.'

'What about the castle? How many men would that need?'

'The castle is strong enough. Twenty men would be adequate, if you had provisions, and the well stayed full, and you had a dozen crossbows, two hundred bolts, a mangonel and a good supply of stones,' I told him. 'We'd be safe until they'd filled in the moat, built a siege engine and rolled it up against the walls. If they took Béziers, and Cabaret, and Montségur, an army would deal with Montaillou easily enough. But we could withstand anything less than a long-drawn-out siege if we were properly organised and equipped.'

Clergue looked thoughtful; I had undermined his faith in his village walls and the castle. The next morning at dawn I saw him, his brother and a cousin leaving the village on horseback towards the northwest, leading four of the mules we used to take supplies up to the mountains in the summer. Clergue was a man who made up his mind quickly.

Four days later they were back, the mules almost buried beneath the clutter of beams and iron, one poor beast struggling under two great sacks of stones and crossbow bolts. After they unloaded the cargo in the middle of the village it looked as though a small ship had just been wrecked there. Everybody surrounded the debris and waited for Clergue to speak. He was pleased with himself.

'The spoils of war,' he said. 'From Cabaret and Montségur.' Then he pointed at me. 'You're the one who can get this done. The blacksmith can handle the ironwork, and we're all carpenters after a fashion.' Nobody grumbled, which is rare in Montaillou, and I thus became the armourer.

It took us three weeks to build the mangonel from all the bits and pieces, but the frame was almost intact and we managed to find a piece of oak straight and strong enough for our throwing arm. We didn't use counterweights. Clergue extracted half a dozen cowhides from our herdsmen; these we cut into long strips, twisted them together, pushed the bottom of the throwing arm through the middle, secured it with an iron band and finally pissed on the strips to tighten them and give some torsion. The blacksmith put together a crude pawl and ratchet to crank the arm down, and remembered after it sprang back on him to put in a locking fid. On our first dry test the arm smacked into the stopping beam with a satisfying clunk.

I'd never made anything like this before, although I had been on the receiving end of siege engines. In our first test the stone failed to clear the outer wall and took a great piece out of it. We persevered, lengthened the bucket at the end of the arm, and at our third attempt threw a big stone two hundred feet down the main street of the village. I paced out the distance, and we brought the stone back to use again.

Crossbows I knew about. Clergue had found a dozen stocks in various states of repair, enough horn to fashion the bows and leather for the strings. After a couple of botched attempts the blacksmith made good copies of my goat's foot lever to cock the weapons.

'The crossbow is effective only at short range, forty or fifty yards,' I told them. 'It's not like a longbow which will kill at three times that distance. Watch', and we stood at the seventy-yard mark in the tilt-yard, 'and you'll see how quickly the bolt drops down. But at forty yards it will penetrate chain mail, and even some armour. So until the attackers get close, hold your fire. You will be on the ramparts either side of the gatehouse tower; we'll mark the distance.'

We went outside the castle walls, paced out forty yards, and marked the spot with a large whitewashed stone.

'Wait until they have passed this point, and then fire. That means you'll only get one or two shots at the most before they are at the gates. So make sure those shots count. There are twelve of you, so I want twelve men dead after the first assault. Accuracy is more important than speed.'

The men, particularly the younger ones, were keen to practise and were soon able to get off at least two bolts in less than five minutes. After all this we felt prepared, felt better.

'Talk about it through the valley,' said Clergue. 'We want marauders to go for easier targets than Montaillou.'

For several months that worked, but in the end we were tested. Clergue always had a herdsman doubling as a sentinel at each approach to our valley, which gave us two hours' warning before strangers arrived in our village. On the morning we were attacked it had been a crisp dawn after a frost, and our valley was covered in a narrow blanket of mist that burned off later in the day. As I walked back from the washing pool the village was beginning to wake up and the cattle were moving out of their byres below the prosperous houses to graze in the fields to the south. The dung heaps were steaming, their strong smell staining the air, brown rivulets flowing down the gutters either side of the street.

I was almost back in my small house when a young shepherd, one of the Belots, came running up the street, shouting as he ran, 'They've killed my brother, they're coming.'

He ran on to Clergue's house; I followed him and listened as he told us what had happened.

'Alain had been at the far end of the big field, the one we call A la Cot. He saw the strangers but only when they were very close. He shouted to me, and then they killed him,' he said, sobbing. 'And then I ran away, ran to the village.'

'How many?' asked Clergue.

'Forty or fifty. They weren't speaking our language.'

'We should get everyone and all the cattle and sheep we can round up inside the castle walls. It sounds like the English.'

The English band is what they called themselves. They were well known in the Languedoc. Some of them had been de Montfort's men, there were a dozen pikemen from Genoa, several French from the north. They had nurtured their reputation for butchery, and for two or three years had managed to get what they wanted – cattle, sheep, money, women – without too much fighting.

We watched the little band move towards us down the valley in the early morning. We were all of us, villagers and beasts, inside the walls of the castle when they entered the far end of the village. There were forty of them, walking quite slowly, only one on horseback. There they stopped, drinking from the cattle trough, their voices indistinct and foreign; we could just hear the occasional French word. They seemed in no hurry. They dug a fire pit, butchered and roasted a sheep and shared it out.

We were standing at the top of the keep, Beatrice a pace in front of Clergue and me. She was wearing a long dark red dress with a gold belt, her fair hair kept in place by a silver band. She looked every inch the chatelaine, and only Clergue and I could see her fists clenching and unclenching.

We were unsure what would happen next, and Clergue, usually decisive, was quiet.

'Perhaps the castle will put them off. Perhaps they know we have a mangonel,' said Clergue.

'They've got half a dozen pack mules, all unladen. I doubt they plan to keep them idle for long.'

Then they formed into three columns and marched towards us like a little army. Their blue flag had a gold fleur-de-lis and a couple of drummers were beating time. They halted two hundred feet away from our moat, well out of crossbow range. Their captain, the only one in chain mail, sitting easily on a strong charger, swept his right hand from his face down to his hip, as though holding a hat. Perhaps it was mockery, but it was no less than Beatrice deserved.

'Lady, we're not here to stay,' he shouted, first in English, then in French. 'Let out the animals and we'll be off. No need for bloodshed.' He came a little closer to hear the reply.

We had a dozen crossbowmen on the walls, weapons cocked; I had told them to fire when the mangonel was released. I tried to talk to Beatrice, but she was past listening. Clergue asked her a question, got no answer, went down to the gate, and I followed to the courtyard, crowded with animals and people. We had fenced off the mangonel from the sheep, and the cattle were penned in the far corner

When the captain shouted again Beatrice answered in Occitan and then in French. Her voice, normally deep and clear, was unsteady. Then she called down to Clergue to open the gates and let out the animals. As the drawbridge chains began to clatter down, the English cheered and ran forward. And I fired the mangonel.

Two sounds, one after another: the smack of the throwing arm into the stopping beam, then the sharp song of our crossbow bolts. I watched the big stone curve, slowly it seemed, over the wall and out of my sight. Then a third sound, a splash, and the cheering stopped.

The fifty-pound stone had taken their captain full in the chest, lifting him out of the saddle and leaving him a bloody heap in the middle of his men. I wished I had seen that. We killed eleven of them with our crossbows and the rest ran away.

'What did you think would happen if they'd come in through the gates?' I said to Clergue. 'They would have rounded up the animals and left quietly?' He didn't reply. Beatrice by now had gone to her chamber. He stood there for a few minutes, looking at the bodies in the square, the flies already round them.

Then he said, 'It was a lucky shot,' and walked back to his house, saying nothing to our crossbowmen, who found it hard to believe what they had done, especially the Credentes, to whom all human life was meant to be sacred. He was right; it was a lucky shot. It meant I would have Beatrice to myself for several weeks thereafter.

Pierre Clergue

IT WAS A few months after my return from Carcassonne that we were attacked by the English band. On Francois's advice, I had greatly strengthened the village defences. My brother and I had gone away for four days to find crossbows, bolts and the materials for building a mangonel, and on my return I put Francois in charge.

When we were eventually attacked Beatrice lost her nerve. We both believed that the marauders would be satisfied if they took our livestock, and when she gave the order to lower the drawbridge I didn't countermand her instructions.

Francois knew better; he fired the mangonel, his men, my men, on the ramparts loosed off their crossbows, the English commander was killed and the survivors ran away. They were not used to resistance from a village as small as ours. And it was a lucky first shot from the mangonel that killed their leader. I said so to Francois.

'I paced out the distance and used the stone we had tried in practice. It was going to kill half a dozen men if it missed the man on horseback. And we'd been training hard with the crossbows.'

The village agreed and gave Francois all the credit, treating me as though I was a coward, even though I had organised the materiel which made our victory possible. And it was Beatrice, not I, who gave the command to lower the drawbridge.

She shared the village view about the attack and took none of the blame herself. Instead, she devoted herself entirely to Francois thereafter and was barely civil to me. When I accused her of abandoning me, she said, 'Our understanding is at an end. Besides, I know and the whole of Montaillou knows that you are sleeping with Gaillarde Benet. And Grazide Rives. That ought to be enough for any man.'

I was so angry that I tried to force myself upon her, but her resistance wasn't feigned on this occasion. She scratched my face, kneed me in the groin and cried out for her steward, who came into her chamber and I was forced to leave. That was the unhappy end to our affair; even when Francois took his sheep up into the mountains she was no longer interested in my attentions.

Beatrice

IT IS STRANGE how a single incident changed my perception of two men I thought I knew well.

The appearance of the English band in Montaillou was terrifying; we had readied ourselves for the possibility of an attack, but without really believing it would come about. And in the preparation both men, Pierre and Francois, did what I would have expected. Pierre quickly obtained the materials we needed for our defence, and as quickly delegated the responsibility of making a mangonel, and crossbows, and training the young men in their use, to Francois.

'He may have only one eye and one arm,' Pierre said, something he never lost an opportunity to point out (a blue eye, and a strong body, and a charming voice, I replied – but only to myself). 'But he knows about military matters, or so he claims, so let's put him to the test.'

Francois, somewhat to my surprise, had no difficulty taking orders from Pierre. Although he had worked for Pierre collecting tithes during his first two years in our village, since then he had built up his own flock of sheep thanks to his ability to kill wolves with his crossbow, but he was still an outsider.

Montaillou felt unable to place a knight in its precisely ordered village hierarchy, even one whose heroic deeds after the fall of Roqueville were well known enough to be commemorated in a ballad. When he arrived Francois had no money, no horse, no wife, and no weapons apart from a crossbow borrowed from Pierre Clergue.

Francois told me later that he had never built a mangonel, but I wouldn't have guessed that. Pierre had managed to obtain all the necessary materials, or almost all, and our village carpenter and blacksmith were well able to follow Francois's rough drawings scratched out with a stick in the mud of the courtyard. They only tried two practice shots. After the first took a piece out of my castle wall I was tempted to tell them to stop. The second practice shot, after some adjustment to the throwing arm and the bucket, was better, clearing the wall without damaging it. The third, when it was later fired in anger, saved our lives.

Francois trained the young men of the village, a dozen or so, to use the crossbow in our old tilt-yard. At first they were reluctant to pay much attention to a one-armed man, but he quickly showed them how he had managed to kill so many wolves. I used to watch them from the window of my parlour.

We were well prepared when the English band came to our village. Nevertheless we were all terrified. We knew their reputation. And I, who should outwardly have appeared fearless, was as frightened as anyone. I wanted to believe they were only after our cattle and sheep and told Pierre to lower the drawbridge. He should have known better, he should not have paid any attention to me, but he was as frightened as I was.

Only Francois was sensible enough to ignore my order. I will never forget that moment when the stone from the mangonel sailed over the wall a few feet away from where I was standing and struck the English captain out of his saddle, leaving him a bloody mess on the ground. And our young men, apart from one or two, held their fire for just long enough to make their shots count, getting in a second shot as the mercenaries ran away. I stood there rigid with fear, scarcely believing we had won with such apparent ease, until my steward came up and led me to my chamber.

The events of that day made me reassess my opinion of Pierre, Francois and myself. My loss of confidence in my own judgement and, perhaps unfairly, that of Pierre Clergue, was counterbalanced by a new and profound admiration for Francois. I was wise enough not to let the latter show too obviously, although I made it clear to Pierre that he was no longer welcome – in my bed, I said, but our coupling had only rarely taken place in my chamber. Still, he understood that it was over between us, although he protested and tried to take me there and then until I shouted for my steward.

Francois

THE ATTACK BY the English band changed two things. First, and perhaps unfairly, I received all the credit for our victory. I had trained our crossbowmen, built the mangonel and given the order to fire just as Beatrice, and an acquiescent Pierre, had lowered the drawbridge. It was clear in that moment that the English band would take more than our livestock, but then the mangonel killed the English commander and the weeks of crossbow training paid off.

Pierre immediately arranged and presided over a service of thanksgiving in the church. He made it clear in his sermon, while he didn't mention himself by name, that it was his vision and preparation, using Church money, that made victory possible.

All perfectly true. But I released the mangonel, the slow arc of the stone that struck the English commander was etched on the minds of all the men on the ramparts, and later on every man, woman and child in Montaillou believed they had seen it themselves. Within a month the troubadour composed a ballad about our triumph, a ballad that made no mention of Pierre but sang the praises of the one-eyed, one-armed warrior who had come to save the village from a fate the ballad described in enjoyable, gruesome detail.

Beatrice was also changed. She was a strong, independent woman, but that moment of misjudgement had undermined her confidence. And she blamed Pierre Clergue for failing to countermand the order to lower the drawbridge

'It was down before he could say the word. It's your castle, your drawbridge.'

'He could have stopped me. We'd all be dead but for you.'

I soon gave up defending Pierre. It was plainly useless,

hardly in my interest, and from that moment on I no longer had to share Beatrice. I moved into the castle, lending my house to the young Belot boy, Andre, who brought provisions regularly up to the mountain during the summer. My relationship with Beatrice's steward, an old Planissoles retainer who regarded his primary duty as the protection of his mistress, was uneasy at first. But I was careful never to give him an order, made only occasional requests, and he began to accept I was no threat and a comfort to Beatrice. I became more than her lover: I became her confidant, her counsellor, almost her husband.

'I buried my first husband,' she said, 'I see no need to marry a second.'

'It might be unlucky,' I agreed, and didn't point out I had never suggested marriage. I was happy enough with what we had.

For some time after the abortive raid by the English band the Clergues continued to rule Montaillou. But that power was no longer absolute. It had been undermined when Pierre Clergue was arrested, and although he boasted on his return that his detention was an administrative oversight 'by those penny-pinchers in the Bishop's office' tithes became harder to collect. One or two of the bolder villagers made an automatic deduction of 5 per cent, 'because that was what the Clergues have been skimming off the top. They will have to do without their cream', and then boasted about their boldness in a way that would have been unthinkable in earlier years.

Bernard's authority as magistrate was also challenged. When he summoned Pierre Lizier for allowing his sheep to graze on Clergue pastures, Lizier first failed to appear and then refused to pay the fine of a hundred sous, although that was modest enough.

'I appeal to the Comte de Foix, from whom I understand you derive your authority,' Lizier said when he was manhandled into the court. 'That was always our land until you and your brother stole it.' This was an extraordinary defiance, and soon became widely known throughout Montaillou.

Nevertheless Bernard continued to defend and encourage Catharism in the village. His faith appeared to be genuine. At considerable risk to himself he arranged for Guillaume Authie to visit Montaillou and sheltered him in his house for several days while Authie administered the Consolamentum to the dying Alamande Guilabert.

Until that moment visiting Perfects had been sheltered in other friendly houses; the stream of visitors that followed Authie's arrival in the village was a risk even for a Clergue. This was a defiant gesture by Bernard, and perhaps an attempt to recover some of the ground he and his brother had lost.

Beatrice and I watched this slow decline in the powers of the Clergue family first with a detached curiosity and then with alarm. Montaillou appeared to be exchanging the certainty of despotism, and its protection, for a freedom that seemed unlikely to last very long, and would not include the freedom to practise Catharism.

The Inquisition had a long reach, and Montaillou had survived partly through distance, partly through the ruthless suppression of gossip and rumour by the Clergues, and partly through the repeated assurances by Pierre Clergue that his flock were good Catholics, attended his church regularly and received absolution for their sins.

'There are no heretics in Montaillou,' he claimed have told the Bishop in Carcassonne, 'only good Christians.' As the Cathars often referred to themselves as Good Christians, in contrast to the follies and venality of the Catholic Church, this was a comment that could reassure both the Bishop and the Cathars in Montaillou. It is uncertain whether even Pierre Clergue would have dared to use these words to the Bishop, but the village took considerable comfort from his repeated claim to have defended his flock, whatever words he may have used in Carcassonne.

In spite of Pierre's claim, and in spite of the fact that he had returned from Carcassonne apparently unscathed, the boldness of those who had been damaged by the Clergue family – and there were all too many in Montaillou – increased. It was rumoured that Raymond and Jean Maurs had sworn a ritual oath over bread and wine to kill Pierre Clergue and had gone as far as hiring two assassins to carry out the task. Pierre heard the rumours soon enough and thereafter never went far from his house or the church without two of his men-at-arms to guard him. And he abandoned his usual trip to the market at Ax, where the would-be killers waited for him in vain.

Pierre made his displeasure known to Beatrice and me on the way back from Mass a few Sundays later.

'The Maurs family are my eternal enemies,' he said, 'and I will do what I can to destroy them. They hired some ruffians to kill me in the marketplace in Ax. We should have cut off Mengarde's head, not her tongue, and walled up her son, or burned him when we had the power.'

'He's gone to Catalonia,' said Beatrice. 'He can't harm you or your brother now.'

'He's not gone far enough. We'll see if we can't reach him once we know exactly where he is.'

'Why bother?' I said.

Pierre Clergue looked astonished and didn't reply

Later over supper in the castle Beatrice and I discussed the feud.

'It wouldn't matter, but Pierre seems to have lost his judgement along with some of his authority. He'd become a full-blown Catholic overnight to strike at the Maurs, or to save his own skin. It won't be long before someone denounces him to the Inquisition, and they'll take it seriously now. There are too many cuckolded husbands and discarded mistresses for him to feel safe,' I said.

'At least I discarded him. But that doesn't make me feel safe. Nor you. He'd betray us in a moment if it suited him.'

'There are easier targets. You never had a Perfect stay overnight in the castle. And you have friends in high places in Carcassonne and Toulouse.'

'My lands are worth seizing, and they will know or soon find out that almost everyone in Montaillou is Cathar, or complicit. If they send for Pierre they won't need to torture him for very long.'

'I go to the mountains with my sheep in three days' time. Come with me. It's cooler there in every sense, and perhaps Montaillou and the Clergues will have calmed down when we return.'

Beatrice seemed doubtful, took a sip of wine and looked down on the village for several minutes. The main street was deserted, apart from a couple of stray dogs, and the smoke of the cooking fires rose straight in the still air. Every five minutes a donkey brayed from one of the common pastures.

'It looks calm enough this evening. Perhaps I will come in a week or two. I do like it in the mountains. I've even got used to your latrine.'

20

The Raid

The Bishop

MONTAILLOU HAD LONG been the source of rumours about its selective attitude to doctrine, although earlier we had assurances from their priest that nothing was amiss. The previous Inquisitor had taken these words at face value, but I am sorry to say that he had become lax in his prosecution of heresy. I attributed this to his liaison with a former heretic, the noblewoman Blanche de Roqueville. It was sad to see a great and, on his day, penetrating intellect softened by sexual congress.

In the end it was the priest himself, Pierre Clergue, who informed us that he was unable to check the spread of heresy within his congregation without assistance from Carcassonne. He went as far as naming forty or fifty citizens of Montaillou as potential heretics worthy of thorough investigation. For the moment I was happy to rely on him as an invaluable source, although I made a mental note that, in due course, we would need to enquire how he had allowed his flock to stray so far from the true path.

I organised the operation in great detail, and accompanied our little force to make sure that everything went according to my plan. Montaillou was the last redoubt of the Cathar heresy in the Languedoc. All the great castles had fallen and their heretical masters burned or converted. Only this little village remained, an insult to Almighty God and a continued challenge to the authority of the Church. If we could extinguish the Cathar heresy in Montaillou our long task, first taken up by the crusaders many years ago, would have been accomplished.

The raid took place in the early morning of the feast of the Nativity of the Virgin, a day when the whole village attended Mass. Our men-at-arms, directed by Jacques de Polignac, who was normally in charge of the prison in Carcassonne, blocked up the main tracks out of Montaillou to Camurac, Ax, Prades and Gazel, two men on each track. The rest went from house to house rounding up men, women and children over the age of fourteen and taking them, some of the men protesting vigorously, many of the women and children crying, into the castle courtyard.

Beatrice's steward watched in the courtyard; he was saved from our attentions only by virtue of his mistress's rank and her friends in high places. Beatrice herself was, we were told, in the mountains. She had not been accused, although her companion, Francois de Beaufort, had appeared before us some years earlier and had been sentenced to go on a pilgrimage to Compostela.

In the castle yard Bernard Clergue was in charge of the roll call. I heard one of the Maurs shout out when his name was called, 'It's the Clergues you want, not me. They've turned a blind eye—' and was knocked to the ground by one of the soldiers before he could continue. It was perhaps a pity that we didn't hear then what he had to say, but I made a mental note to investigate in greater detail the activities of the Clergue family.

Pierre had recently been found guilty of taking more than his share of the tithes, a frequent offence I am ashamed to admit, and one that was rarely punished with enough severity. But he was the priest, he had instigated the raid and there had only been rumours and gossip about his attitude to the heretics.

There was an immediate hearing of those accused of minor offences. Pierre Clergue made the selection, and they were forthwith sentenced by me – I had the power of summary judgement in such cases – to wear the double yellow cross on their cloaks and tunics for at least three years. Some of the rest were given dates to attend the court, and the most serious offenders were escorted in fetters by de Polignac and his soldiers to Carcassonne, leaving in the early evening.

Francois

BEATRICE AND I were in the mountains and received a detailed account of what had happened from her steward on our return. Pierre Clergue had been in charge of the process, occasionally allowing one or two of his friends, although there were few enough of these, to escape arrest. This treachery dismayed the village, although it came as no surprise to us. It seemed like a last, desperate throw of the dice by the Clergue family

'Mersende Maury managed to bluff her way past the guards on the road to Prades,' the steward told us. 'She carried a loaf of bread on her head, with a sickle in her hand, claimed she was only in Montaillou to help with the harvest, and was on her way home.'

'How did Andre Belot get away?'

'He was taken to the castle, but managed to slip away in the crowds and confusion. He avoided the main tracks and crossed the fields to the woods on the mountain side of the village.'

'It was Andre who made his way up to our pastures and told us what had happened,' I said.

'And one of the Benets was flushed out of the secret passage between the Rives and Benet houses, betrayed by Pierre Clergue. He was taken to the castle and later to Carcassonne.'

The raid was the ultimate revenge for the Clergues, who immediately began to confiscate the fields of those who had been charged or taken away. By the time we returned from the mountains, it was to see a Montaillou in which almost every citizen was wearing a double yellow cross and tunic, a Montaillou missing forty or fifty of its most prominent men and women.

They had been taken away to Carcassonne or Pamiers after the round-up. Although they trickled back in the following year, the lucky ones sentenced only to the wearing of the double yellow cross, four of their number had been burned and several more given long sentences of The Wall – bread and water in a tiny cell from which they were unlikely to emerge alive.

I would have expected the Clergue family to have behaved with greater caution under the circumstances, but the reverse was the case. It was clear that both Pierre and Bernard believed they were now beyond the reach of the law or the Inquisition, and their Cathar sympathies were more in evidence than ever.

Later in that same year, the year of the raid the year of the roundup, Pierre Clergue's father Pons died, but not before he had been consoled by Guillaume Authie, who was sheltered for three days by the Clergues. The body was laid out in the kitchen. The dead man's face was splashed with water, and hairs and nail clippings were taken to ensure the good fortune of the Clergue family. A large number of villagers, mostly wearing their double yellow crosses thanks to Pierre and Bernard, came to pay their respects, more from fear of the Clergue family than from love of the patriarch. And when Mengarde Clergue died not long after, Pierre buried his mother next to the altar in his church.

'As though she were a saint,' said the Maurs family among themselves, although only when they were confident they were in no danger of being overheard. The power of the Clergue family in Montaillou, which seemed to be on the verge of collapse a year earlier, had been triumphantly, brazenly, reasserted.

It was not to last much longer. Four of the early victims of the round-up were turned over to the secular arm and burned, long sentences of bread and water were given to several more, and out of fear and revenge the denunciations of Pierre Clergue came thick and fast. Bernard had been right when he suggested his brother's promiscuity represented an enormous risk, and former mistresses now incarcerated in Carcassonne felt more frightened of the immediate, terrifying power of the Inquisition than the distant authority of Pierre and Bernard.

The new Inquisitor was now assisted by an able and feared Dominican from Pamiers, Brother Gaillard. Both took a detailed, almost prurient interest in the amorous affairs of Pierre Clergue and there was no shortage of witnesses eager to implicate him. The two judges were astonished by the extent of Pierre's promiscuity, and his ability to use his position to convince so many women that they were committing only the mildest of sins, easily pardoned, if they slept with the priest of Montaillou.

The Bishop

THE MAN IN the courtyard was right. No less than four women, Grazide Lizier, Alazais Faurs, Alazais Azema and Esclarmonde Fort, who appeared before us in Carcassonne, claimed to have been mistresses of the priest. And they spoke of many more. The Inquisitor and I, used as we were to the frailty of clerics, were astonished by the promiscuity of Pierre Clergue.

But there was worse. Grazide Lizier made it clear that Pierre, at least for the purpose of seducing her, had declared that all visible and tangible matter, sky and the earth and everything that lives there were created by the Devil, the ruler of the world. And that therefore she needn't worry about committing the sin of adultery, a sin from which in any case he could absolve her in Confession the following Sunday.

This was dualism at its worst, rank heresy, a far more serious crime than even the seduction of married women. It explained the many, hitherto unsubstantiated, rumours about Montaillou. And Esclarmonde Fort went so far as to allege that Clergue had intercourse with Beatrice de Planissoles behind the altar of the church itself, although she admitted that she had not witnessed the sacrilege, which we accordingly discounted.

I did, however, make a mental note that the chatelaine of Montaillou, who had powerful friends, should perhaps be brought to Carcassonne when we had finished with our current crop of prisoners.

We had more than enough evidence to arrest Pierre Clergue; he was charged with heresy, taken to Carcassonne, and then to Pamiers.

Francois

BERNARD CLERGUE MADE expensive and unsuccessful efforts to free his brother.

'I spent fourteen thousand shillings on bribes,' he told me months later. I was the only man left in Montaillou to whom he could speak in confidence.

'They took my money and kept Pierre inside. I gave a mule to the daughter of Roger Bernard of Foix so that she would intercede with the Bishop. I gave three hundred pounds to Gui de Levis who was on his way to the Curia in Avignon. I persuaded four Cardinals to write to the Inquisitor on my brother's behalf. All useless. We are finished in Montaillou. We have lost the head of our family, the best a clan could hope for. I'll never see him again in this world. And there's a new priest in the village.'

'What will you do?'

'There's nothing left for me to do except wait until they send for me. I'll be lucky to escape the stake.'

The following year Bernard submitted himself to the mercy of the Inquisitor. He was found guilty of heresy and impenitence and handed over to the secular arm.

21

After the Clergues

Francois

THIS TIME PIERRE would not return. When Bernard was arrested and taken away, replaced by a new magistrate who brought a dozen men-at-arms with him, tough men from the north who spoke little Occitan, it was clear that the Clergue rule over Montaillou was at an end.

Wild rumours circulated in the village about what had happened to the two brothers – they had been burned, they had been tortured, they had escaped, they had been pardoned and were on their way back, they had been sent on a pilgrimage to Compostela. In the end, to silence the rumours, the new magistrate produced a copy of their sentence, ten years in The Wall. A few months later he told the village that neither had survived the Pamiers prison diet of bread and water.

The Maurs clan rejoiced, and Andre Belot returned from Catalonia. 'I hope they burn, both of them. It's the least they deserve,' he said to Beatrice. 'Montaillou is a better place without them.'

Most of the village seemed to agree. But it soon became obvious that although much had changed, it was not necessarily for the better. Two-thirds of the village wore double yellow crosses, and this badge of heresy was rigidly enforced by the new magistrate, a humourless lawyer from Toulouse. The yellow cross could have been worn with pride; instead, it was regarded as a shameful reminder that its wearers had all recanted out of fear of imprisonment or the stake. I understood the feeling only too well.

Catharism had been effectively extinguished in Montaillou. We all continued to go to church, but the new priest's sermons had none of Pierre Clergue's subtle ambiguities, and he kept a careful record of all those who failed to come to Confession. There had been no sign of the two surviving Perfects, although they were rumoured to be in hiding in Catalonia.

Beatrice and I went to Mass and Confession, but were careful and selective about our sins. We were not anxious to follow the Clergues to Carcassonne or Pamiers.

'At least our wives and daughters are safe,' said Andre one evening.

'True. With the new one perhaps it's your brothers and sons that you need to worry about. But he seems the sort of priest who is sexless. I see they've made no attempt to return the confiscated meadows.'

'The Benets tried and failed. No one convicted of heresy has any chance of restitution. We must all make do with what we have, and thank God we're still alive.'

In this uneasy atmosphere I told Beatrice that I thought we should leave.

'They'll come for us sooner or later. The Church would love your land, they've never been convinced by my conversion, and we're the most prominent targets left in the Languedoc.'

'We're not exactly counts or dukes, with all due respect to your lofty, landless status, Seigneur Francois,' she said, laughing. 'We have abided by their rules, you served out your sentence on the road to Compostela, and the Inquisition make some attempt to abide by the rule of law. They don't trump up charges themselves. They rarely act on gossip and rumour alone, which is why the Clergues survived as long as they did.'

'I still think we should leave for Catalonia while we can.'

Beatrice became angry at my persistence.

'I belong here, even if you do not. These are my people, this is my village, and it would be the act of a coward to leave unless there was no other choice.'

'I've never been called a coward,' I said. 'You believe you are safe, untouchable, like the Clergues. Look what happened to them. Who knows what Pierre said about you when he was interrogated?' I got up and left, sleeping in the Great Hall alone for two nights until we both calmed down.

Life in Montaillou continued in this new, uneasy fashion, and over the year all but the four condemned to the stake, and two of the young girls who had died in prison, trickled back to the village in ones and twos. They had all recanted, they all wore the double yellow cross and several had been tortured. They were reluctant to talk about their experience or the fate of their friends, or even to rejoice at the deaths in captivity of Pierre and Bernard Clergue.

Beatrice pretended not to notice the cowed spirit of the village.

'People are too frightened even to gossip,' I said. 'At least when the Clergues were in charge there were some good jokes about them, and a ballad or two.'

'No one dared sing the ballad, or tell jokes outside their own families,' said Beatrice. 'It wasn't exactly a golden age.'

It was the sudden and severe illness of Beatrice's steward Robert that brought matters to a head.

'He's dying, he wants the Consolamentum, and I've sent for Authie.'

'That's foolish. He's too well known in Montaillou.'

'I've sent for him. Robert has served me for forty years. Authie will arrive at night and leave at dawn.'

He did arrive in time to comfort and console the dying man. Robert was lying in his little room in the corner of the courtyard. The airless room, lit only by two guttering candles, smelled sour. Robert's eyes were closed, but they opened when he heard Authie's voice.

Authie laid his hand on Robert, brushed his forehead with a little copy of the Gospels, and told him that the Endura must begin from that moment. He was in a state of grace, could take only water, could no longer be touched by women, and his soul would now certainly travel to meet God in heaven. Only Beatrice and I were present.

Although I was unhappy at Beatrice's rashness and was sceptical about the value of the Consolamentum, it was clear that the ceremony, which lasted only a short time, comforted Robert.

So I joined in the Our Father and felt moved in spite of myself. Robert's Endura, mercifully, didn't last long. I put myself in charge of his feeding, to conceal from the other servants that he was only given water. He died the following evening.

After the ceremony we shared a meal of fish and bread with Authie, and just before dawn I escorted him out of the castle, down past the washing pool and set him on his way back to Catalonia.

The moment the new priest heard of Robert's death he asked why he hadn't been sent for.

'He died in the night, suddenly,' said Beatrice. 'And he'd been to church ten days before. I'm sure he confessed his sins, if he had any, and died in a state of grace.'

The priest looked unconvinced but was not bold enough to question Beatrice. But the village knew Robert to be a devout Cathar who had been lucky to escape arrest. Someone, perhaps Arnaud Sicre, who was a compulsive informer and wished to curry favour with the new powers in the village, had seen Authie arrive in Montaillou and told the magistrate.

Within ten days a warrant arrived for Beatrice's arrest, and she was taken to Carcassonne. The arrest, like the round-up, was carefully timed; I was away at the market in Ax selling cheese and wool. When I returned she was gone.

22

Beatrice in Prison

Francois

I FELT ANGRY WHEN I heard the news. Angry not with the Inquisition, who were doing what they had always done, but with Beatrice, who had risked everything in order to ease the last hours of her steward. And neither of us believed that the Consolamentum made much difference to Robert's chances of eternal life.

It was difficult to find out anything useful about the arrest. Montaillou's state of mind was one of stunned acceptance of whatever the Inquisition chose to do to the village. I asked Andre Belot what he knew.

'Almost nothing. There were a dozen of them; they arrived at dawn on horseback, waited till the drawbridge was lowered, went into the castle and took Lady Beatrice. They spoke to nobody except the new magistrate before they left. And he immediately organised a house-to-house search. "We're looking for the heretic Authie," he said. "There will be trouble for anyone who has harboured him."'

'A dozen men – that's a lot to take a single woman prisoner.'

'They weren't taking any chances, even though their spies

told them you would be in the market in Ax.'

'Spies? You mean Sicre.'

Andre didn't reply. I went to see the new magistrate, who was at first unhelpful, and then threatening.

'She's been taken to Carcassonne. I can't tell you any more than that. We'll be taking steps to sequester her land.'

'Not unless she is convicted; Beatrice holds some of her land from the Comte de Foix, some from the King of Aragon, none from the Church.'

'We'll see about that. And our informant says Authie spent the night in the castle. Were you there when he visited the steward?'

'I've never seen this man you call Authie.'

I had decided I would no longer worry about lying. I went back to the castle and made sure that we were adequately defended against the magistrate and his Basque soldiers. I spent the next week wondering what, if anything, I could do.

During that time my initial anger faded and was replaced by a reluctant admiration for what Beatrice had done. She had been far braver than me; I admitted to myself that I would never have sent for the Perfect, even if it had been Beatrice on her deathbed.

My fear of what might happen to her in the hands of the Inquisition was accompanied by a growing realisation of how much she meant to me as a companion as well as a wonderful lover. And I was aware that I had never declared my feelings for her, except through the act of love itself. That no longer felt enough.

Beatrice

THEY CAME TO take me to Carcassonne when Francois was selling his cheese in Ax. Perhaps that was fortunate; they had a dozen well-armed men, and Francois, out of pride, of which he had more than enough, might have tried to resist them. We had only half a dozen men-at-arms in the castle, all elderly, and Francois had long ago abandoned any attempt to turn them into a garrison.

I was surprised and frightened. Surprised because I thought I was beyond the reach of the Inquisition and the secular arm of the law. I was, after all, a second cousin of the Comte de Foix.

Frightened because on arrival in Carcassonne they put me in a small cell and left me there for three weeks, bringing me only bread and water and porridge in the morning and evening. The cell was cold; little rivulets of water ran down the walls. There was a stone bench to sleep on and a single threadbare blanket which I wrapped around myself all day as well as at night. The chamber pot in the corner was only emptied every other day. The cell smelled; I smelled. And the guards were constantly changed, and were clearly under instruction not to talk to me.

I could read on the wall crude calendars scratched to show how long previous prisoners had been kept there. One man had been imprisoned for three hundred days. There were little prayers to St James and the Virgin, an obscene caricature of a Dominican with a donkey, and, most frightening and realistic of all, a crude picture of a man tied to a post above a pile of faggots. I was not tempted to add my own drawings to their number; indeed, as I had been given neither knife nor spoon, I would have had to use my nails. I thought I would go mad.

I had time to think. Think about my betrayal; the Inquisition would not have come for me without some evidence or a denunciation. Think about my disregard for Francois's advice to leave Montaillou, about my earlier relationship with Pierre Clergue, about the folly of allowing Authie to console my steward on his deathbed.

I had time to think about the charges that would be laid against me, and to prepare some kind of defence. If I were to escape the stake I had to deny that Authie had come to Montaillou and spent the night under my roof. I would be forced to admit that I had been Pierre Clergue's mistress for several years. There were too many witnesses, including Clergue himself.

Beyond that I would admit nothing. After three weeks in the cell I reached the point that I wanted them to come for me, to charge me, if only so I could hear the sound of a human voice again, however hostile.

Francois

AFTER MY INITIAL shock at Beatrice's arrest I went to see Sicre to find out what he knew. He was hard to track down; I eventually found him in his cousin's house in Camurac. I went in without warning, my sword drawn, to find Sicre sitting there alone. He rose out of his chair, and as he reached for the dagger on the table in front of him I struck his arm hard with the flat of my sword, hard enough to hear the bone crack, then swept the dagger onto the floor.

'What did you tell the men from Carcassonne about Beatrice?' I asked. My sword was at his throat, and he could see I was ready to kill him. He was holding his damaged right hand with his left, breathing in short gasps.

'I told them nothing,' he said. 'And I'm under their protection. You'll regret this.'

It was an obvious and foolish contradiction. I pricked his throat hard enough to draw blood and he began to talk. Much of what he said was a patchwork of lies and half-truths, intended to show him in a favourable light, but he admitted to telling the Inquisition about Authie's night in the castle and about Beatrice's relationship with Pierre Clergue. He took some pleasure in describing that story.

'I discovered the pair of them fornicating behind the altar,' he said, hoping for my discomfiture. 'I felt bound to tell them about such desecration.'

'No doubt you were motivated by your faith,' I said. I thought of killing him there, and decided he had already done his damage. 'You're not worth killing. The whole world knows of your treachery. You were a guest at Beatrice's table, you were a professed Cathar, and now look at you.'

He was weeping as I left the room, partly through pain, partly because he knew his life would always be in danger. Four of Montaillou's men and women had been burned at the stake, and many more had died in prison, because of his treachery.

I left the next day for Carcassonne without a clear plan in my mind, but conscious I could achieve nothing in Montaillou. I went straight to see Baruch the Jew, who was glad to see me.

'What have you heard about Beatrice?' I asked him, leaving my glass of wine untouched.

'Nothing,' he replied. 'The Inquisition has clamped down on loose talk, and most of the prison guards are too frightened to reveal who is in their jail. But I am Baruch the Christian now, not Baruch the Jew. Quite a respectable lawyer, no longer a detested usurer, although a few Christians still come to me for money. I'll see what I can discover.'

Two days later he sent a messenger to my inn, and I called on him a second time.

'She hasn't been tortured,' he said. 'She has confessed to having sexual congress with the priest of Montaillou, Pierre Clergue. But she has refused to admit to being Cathar or to harbouring Authie. She claims she was a regular attender at the Montaillou church, both before and after Clergue left, took Communion and confessed her sins regularly.'

'What will they do to her?'

'The Inquisition could try her as a heretic, and if she is found guilty then she will burn.' Baruch was not a man to mince his words, and either did not notice or ignored the look on my face as he spoke. I had already lost a wife to the flames, and he seemed to be telling me they were likely to burn my lover.

'What can I do?'

'Very little. The secular judges are no longer taking bribes, and the Inquisition have never been venal. You can use your money, through me and some friends in the prison, to get Beatrice out of solitary confinement and provide her with decent food and clothes. That's all money can buy in Carcassonne these days. You may be allowed to visit her.'

'So she will burn?'

'Not necessarily. They would burn Authie if they could catch him. But unless they can prove Beatrice was Cathar they may have to settle for lesser charges. If she is tried by the secular arm I can argue in her defence.'

'What are the arguments?'

'I have a month to think of something. They won't try her in a hurry. Meanwhile, let me make arrangements for her comfort and for a visit from us both.'

Baruch's dispassionate analysis was both comforting and depressing. He was not a man to raise false hopes, yet he also made it clear that he was ready to act on Beatrice's behalf. I had great confidence in the power of his intellect and told him so. He looked pleased, smiled and said, 'Your praise is welcome, though I must remind you that I was comprehensively out-argued by the Inquisitor.'

'That was over matters of doctrine, not law. You were able to convince them to release Roqueville and its land to Blanche.'

'True. I am not sure they have yet forgiven me for that. We'll see.'

Later that week Baruch arranged for Beatrice to be moved to better accommodation in the prison. He argued that no charges had yet been brought against her, that she had confessed and cooperated, and she was a noblewoman, the widow of a crusader and a cousin of the Comte de Foix. As always in the Languedoc, it was her lineage that was the most powerful argument.

'She's been moved thanks to her blue blood and five livres Tournois to the jailer,' said Baruch. 'The trial will take place in three weeks' time. The Inquisition have let her go to the civil court to be tried for fornication with a priest. And it will be a public, well-attended trial, which means they are confident of a conviction. They may intend to make an example of her. Although, God knows', and here Baruch crossed himself, smiling as he did so, 'there are few enough Cathars left alive and unrecanted to learn very much from whatever happens to Beatrice de Planissoles.'

'She's confessed. They are sure to find her guilty. What will her sentence be?'

'She won't burn. She could be sentenced to The Wall, as much as ten years' solitary confinement on bread and water in a cell about the size of this table. Not many last longer than two or three years. She could withdraw her confession, but she hasn't been tortured, so they are unlikely to believe that it was other than genuine. As, of course, it was. They plan to call Sicre as their main witness. Luckily Pierre Clergue and his brother are both dead. They lasted less than a year in The Wall.'

I put my face in my hands and wept. Baruch's unvarnished words were too much for me to be able to retain my composure. He let me weep for a minute or two, then put his hand on my shoulder.

'She hasn't been found guilty or sentenced yet. Do you know where she kept the deeds to her properties?'

'I do not. They are unlikely to save her. They will confiscate her lands in any case. I should have killed Sicre when I had the chance.'

'You'd be surprised what legal documents can do. But first we need to find them. We are allowed to pay her a visit tomorrow.'

I spent an unhappy night thinking about a future without Beatrice. Until then I had thought only of our hours of pleasure together, aware that when I first met her I was sharing her affections with a man I feared and disliked. She had banished Clergue from her bed easily enough; I had always thought she might do the same to me. So I had made a conscious effort to restrain my feelings for her, careful to protect myself against rejection. That was now no longer possible. It was also too late.

The jail in Carcassonne was as grim as I remembered: grey, damp, oppressive. I had managed to survive there for a week; Beatrice had been in solitary confinement for three times as long. And she was a woman who was used to comfort, warmth, good food and wine. By the time I had been jailed I had been through two sieges and was hardened and better prepared for that kind of ordeal.

The jailer locked and unlocked three sets of doors, taking us up a winding stair to the top of the jail's square tower.

'That's a good sign,' Baruch whispered. 'The higher the better. As you know.'

The jailer opened a final heavy iron door into what was a room, not a cell. Beatrice was sitting in a chair as we entered. She rose and put her arms around me, holding me tight, and I could feel how painfully thin she had become.

'I didn't know whether you would visit me,' she said. 'I paid no attention to your good advice, and look where that got me. The jailer told me it was Baruch who had arranged for me to move to the top of the tower.'

'I'm proud of you,' I said, kissing the top of her head. 'One week in those cells was enough for me. You've survived three.'

'I wouldn't have lasted much longer. And I confessed to everything except being Cathar and sheltering Authie. What do you think they will do to me?'

I stopped Baruch from giving his dispassionate analysis. 'You're to be tried by the civil courts. Baruch can represent you. He wants to know...'

'... where all the deeds by which you hold your castle and lands are kept,' Baruch said.

Beatrice looked surprised. 'My title isn't being challenged. They'll steal my land anyhow. All those documents are in a locked box in my chamber. I keep the key separately under the big candlestick.'

'Francois must go there and bring them to me. We don't have much time. And if you encounter Sicre and can persuade him...' Baruch didn't finish the sentence.

We spent another ten minutes with Beatrice, who showed us, almost proudly, round the room. She had a table and chair, a bed, a bible, a washstand with a bowl and ewer, and her old clothes had been returned. A corner of the room had been screened, where I assumed there was a chamber pot. I didn't check.

'I can survive in these conditions,' Beatrice said. 'Stand on the chair and you can see over the whole of Carcassonne.'

Baruch, I could tell, was about to explain the probability of The Wall, when fortunately the jailer entered and escorted us out, but not before a final embrace from Beatrice, who kissed me with a warmth and passion which I returned. After a couple of loud coughs from Baruch and an impatient rattling of his keys by the jailer I gently prised loose her arms.

'I need to get to Montaillou. I'll be away for three or four days. The black iron box in your chamber, the key under the big candlestick, the one by the window?'

Beatrice nodded, her eyes full of tears, and we left the room. We walked down the winding staircase, my head spinning with the realisation that this was the first time we had ever kissed, although we had been the most intimate and ingenious of lovers. As we went back to my inn I urged Baruch to shelter Beatrice from the possible severity of her sentence. He looked surprised.

'I always assume it is best to tell the unvarnished truth,' he said.

'Not in Beatrice's case. She won't survive The Wall.'

'Very well. Let us see what those documents have to offer.'

I pressed Baruch to tell me why they might be useful. He replied that it was impossible to tell until he had seen them.

I left Carcassonne that afternoon. I had hired a second, strong horse from the man at Montcalm and I made good time. As Beatrice had told me, the documents were in the iron box and the key was under the candlestick. One look at them made me realise they provided me with no clues. On vellum or parchment, most with a heavy red wax seal stamped on the bottom with coats of arms that I did not recognise, they were in Latin, a language with which I had always struggled. I had to hope Baruch knew what he was doing.

Once I had located the deeds I went in search of Arnaud Sicre for the second time. There was no shortage of information from the villagers about his movements; hatred of his betrayal of so many of the men and women of Montaillou outweighed their fear of the new magistrate and rector. He had moved closer to Montaillou, to Aubiet, a hamlet less than three miles away.

I took Andre Belot with me. Beatrice, at my suggestion, had appointed him as her new steward. The double yellow crosses that three members of his family wore were the result of Sicre's information, and he was as eager as I was for revenge.

We found Sicre in the poorest house in Aubiet. He had a single, sleepy guard whom we were able to disarm without much resistance. Sicre on this occasion made no attempt to reach for a weapon. He held out his right arm, now bound in a crude splint, and said, 'This is your work. You'll find it easy to kill me.'

That had been my intention, but I found it impossible to murder a defenceless man, although Andre showed no signs of any such scruples.

'You burned my aunt, imprisoned my sister,' he said. 'A quick death is better than you deserve.'

I restrained him with some difficulty.

'We'll take him back to Montaillou and keep him in the castle jail until the trial is over. Then the village can do what it likes with him.'

Sicre looked relieved, Andre disappointed. We waited until dark, then returned to Montaillou and locked Sicre in the castle jail. The jail was rarely used, and as uncomfortable as anything Carcassonne had to offer. We were not seen; Montaillou after dark was always deserted, and only the magistrate's men would have taken any interest in what we were doing.

'You are his jailer, not his executioner,' I said to Andre. 'Feed him bread and water twice a day. It's what Beatrice has lived on for three weeks. And you may kill him if he tries to escape.' I left the next morning, unsure whether the two saddlebags would provide any help for Beatrice. My own horse had gone lame on the journey, so I had to rely on the hireling from Montcalm to carry me and a mule for the saddlebags. I took the precaution of bringing several cheeses for Baruch, for Beatrice and for bribes.

The journey back took a day longer than expected, as my horse cast a shoe and it took me a morning to find a blacksmith. I went straight to Baruch and tethered my horse and mule to a post outside his house; he had no stables and went everywhere either on foot or on a borrowed mule. His manservant showed me upstairs to a large room in which almost every surface – tables, chairs, window seats – was covered in manuscripts or documents. Formerly we had met in a room on the ground floor which was full of the fabrics he dealt in. I told him the room looked like a monastery library.

'When the Capuchins closed Mont de Ferrat they were more interested in money than in letters, and I bought their entire library for – well, let us say a very reasonable amount. I expected you two days ago. Let me see what you have found, what treasures are in your saddlebags.'

He cleared a space on the centre table by sweeping the documents that covered it onto the floor. I emptied the contents of both saddlebags on the table, expecting him to look daunted.

'There must be something here,' he said. 'Help me to arrange them in the order they were sealed.'

'They are all in Latin,' I said. 'How good is yours?'

'Excellent, excellent, of course. What did you expect? Occitan? Hebrew? I read Latin as well as I speak it, which is better than most monks, and certainly better than any other lawyer in the Languedoc.'

In a lesser man this would have appeared boastful, but Baruch was never concerned with making an impression.

It took us the rest of the day to sort through over one hundred deeds, wills, judgements, and the occasional letter; by the time we had finished the already dusty air of Baruch's book room smelled of the strange, musky odour of documents that had lain undisturbed in Beatrice's black box for many years.

Baruch was particularly interested in documents with seals, and put them aside in a separate small pile. One or two of the seals were separated from their ribbons.

'That makes them useless. You should have taken more care,' he said.

'You told me to hurry.'

'I did. I assumed you would treat them with respect,' then, seeing the crestfallen look on my face, said, 'but we may have enough.'

He looked again at each of the deeds with attached seals, humming to himself as he used a magnifying glass to inspect the seals closely. One of these gave him particular pleasure, to such an extent that he put the document down and did a little dance of triumph, kicking aside several books as he did so. It was an incongruous and encouraging sight.

'*Deo gratias*, *Deo gratias*, as we Christians say. I lit several candles to St Anthony in the hope we would find something like this.'

His pleasure was unfeigned, although I wasn't sure whether to believe him about the candles.

'Why is that seal so special?'

'Can't you see? It's the seal of the King of Aragon. Although everything will depend on the contents of the deed it is attached to. Luckily it wasn't one of those you shook loose. Leave me to read through all of them – unless you'd like to stay and read alongside me.'

He knew perfectly well that was an invitation I couldn't accept.

'I might as well challenge you to combat with lance and horse,' I said, nettled by his words in spite of myself. 'I'm a knight. I can ride, couch a lance, fight with sword and shield, fire off five crossbow bolts in three minutes.'

'All very useful in certain circumstances.'

'And I can herd sheep, deliver a lamb, kill a wolf, and I make the best cheese in the Languedoc. I brought you some,' and I produced a round of mature cheese from the bottom of the second saddlebag. Baruch was fond of his food.

'That's a much more useful accomplishment. Sit, we'll have some wine, and then you can go and visit Beatrice.'

We went downstairs to the small room where we usually met, and he produced some excellent wine, helping himself to a generous tranche of cheese.

'Excellent, excellent – we don't get enough good sheep's cheese in our market here. The wine, by the way, comes from your friends at Barraigne.'

'Etienne de Vallieres?'

'From Etienne.'

I felt a sudden pang of guilt. I had given no thought to Etienne, Stephanie, Guillemette and Blanche for many months, and resolved to pay them a visit as soon as possible. As we finished the wine and cheese Baruch asked, 'Did you find Arnaud Sicre?'

'I did. We didn't kill him,' adding, as Baruch looked disappointed, 'but he won't be coming to Carcassonne as a witness.' He was careful not to press me for further details.

I went to see Beatrice the next morning, bringing wine from Baruch and some of my cheese. The guard took his usual easement of a hundred sous, and insisted on cutting the cheese in half and tasting an overgenerous slice.

'We've known visitors to bring in knives hidden in loaves of bread and rounds of cheese,' he explained, licking his lips as he spoke.

'Wash it down with a swallow of wine from the wineskin,' I offered. It seemed only sensible to ingratiate myself with Beatrice's jailers. He took several swallows, pronounced it good, if a little lacking in body, and passed the wineskin back to me reluctantly.

He showed me up to Beatrice's prison room, and I felt a surge of joy as she came to me and held me tight for several minutes. She had put on some of the weight she had lost in the dungeons below, although she still looked drawn, still anxious.

We sat down together on her bed (I remember thinking that the Beatrice of old would have seized such an opportunity, guard or no guard); she held my single hand in both of hers, stroking my fingers and intertwining them with their own. I wanted then to declare, exactly what I was uncertain, but I didn't have the words to express my new, changed, intense feelings. When she moved her head to kiss me for only the second time I felt that words were not necessary.

'Were you able to find the documents Baruch wanted?' she said when we had finished our embrace.

'I was. He seemed pleased with what he saw, although he is busy reading through them all. He's a careful man, Baruch. He liked the seal of the King of Aragon – but some of the seals had become detached. Everything was in Latin, quite beyond me. I tracked down Arnaud Sicre for the second time. He told me he was too busy,' and here I looked at the grille in the cell door, 'too busy to come to your trial.'

These words made Beatrice smile, as did the cheese and wine. 'They bring me proper meals twice a day. I'm getting plump again,' patting her stomach.

'I know what a week of bread and water can do to the appetite, never mind three weeks. Much more of that...' I didn't finish the sentence. We both knew that The Wall would bring much more of that, and we both looked sombre for a minute. Then the guard rattled the key in the door and came in.

'I have complete faith in Baruch. You will be free in a few weeks' time,' I said in a confident tone of voice. 'They only allow two visits a week, so I'm off to Barraigne to visit my old friends.'

I had told Beatrice only a little about Etienne, Stephanie and Blanche. She was particularly intrigued by Blanche.

'She slept with the Inquisitor? That's worse than me sleeping with Clergue. How is she free?'

'She was never charged. She tried to break free of him, came with me on part of the way to Compostela, and the Inquisitor sent a gang of monks to bring her back.'

'And, you told me, you never slept with her? '

'I did not. I had always looked on her as an object of courtly love, not of desire. She was old enough to be my mother.'

Beatrice snorted and said, 'A beautiful mother by all accounts. I remember you knew the song praising her beauty well enough to sing it with me.'

We sat in silence until the jailer came to escort me out; we clung to each other for a final moment. As Beatrice turned away I could see she had begun to cry.

I arrived at Barraigne in the late afternoon; it had rained earlier in the day, and the summer sun had polished the leaves of Etienne's vines to an even brighter green. The grapes were beginning to turn purple, although they had another two months of ripening ahead of them. The vineyards reminded me of how long it was since I had last visited Barraigne, as the mature vines I had seen on my last visit had been increased by two more plots, one that looked to be in its third year, one clearly planted that spring. As I rode up to the outer wall the gates were closed by an alert sentry. He called through the slit in the wall and asked me my business.

'I am Francois de Beaufort, come to see my old comrade, Etienne de Vallieres,' and I pointed to the stump of my right arm as proof. After five minutes the gates were quickly unbolted, and Etienne emerged to escort me inside. The smile on his face could not have been more welcoming; his ten-year-old son looked at me with considerable curiosity, holding tight to his father's hand, then said,

'You're like Papa, you have only one arm. But you've got one good eye.'

'I was the lucky one after Roqueville fell.'

'It was Francois who led us to Montségur. Without him we all would have died. He was a great warrior with sword and lance when we were both young, and the best horseman in the valley.'

Stung by the past tense, I said, 'I couldn't handle a lance

today. But I am still a good swordsman, and can fire off…'

'… five crossbow bolts in three minutes,' Etienne said, laughing as we walked together into the courtyard. Some pigeons scattered out of the dovecote in the square tower above the gate.

'Those are my pigeons,' young Bertrand said proudly, reaching across to take my left hand, which was looped through the reins of my horse, in his. The courtyard was immaculate, not a weed to be seen, the cobblestones in good repair. Above the main tower flew the flag of the de Vallieres with its six quarterings. I admired the flag, dug deep into the lectures about heraldry that Geoffrey, who liked to call himself Roqueville Pursuivant, had given us, and said,

'You should have added the arms of Roqueville.'

'Now you are showing off. Not while Blanche is alive. Which I am happy to say she is.'

We stabled my horse alongside three others. There were six stalls in all, fresh straw in each, and a stone water trough running the length of the stable block against the freshly whitewashed wall.

'Barraigne is back to its former glory,' I said.

'I'll show you round. But we must first meet Stephanie and Blanche.'

'Guillemette? Your mother?'

'Both dead. We have had some fierce winters.'

We went into the Great Hall where Stephanie and Blanche were sitting together, Stephanie sewing, Blanche spinning wool. When we had finished hugging each other, both women with tears in their eyes, when they had finished upbraiding me for deserting them for so long, Etienne said, 'Let me show you everything while it is still light. We can gossip to our heart's content over supper.'

'I brought you a sheep's cheese. I'm a shepherd, a cheese-maker now, the best in the Languedoc.'

'It will be a good match for my wine.'

We walked out again into the courtyard, Armand running ahead.

'He's my pigeon master,' said Etienne. 'Although he's too soft-hearted to kill the squabs. He leaves that to me.' On the stable side of the courtyard there was a forge, and next to it a general workshop, both well used.

'Our blacksmith and our carpenter are working in the stew pond.'

'Where did you find them?'

'They found us. They are, or were, both Cathar, one from Puylaurens, one from Carcassonne. But we've been through too much to be Cathar any more, and there are no Perfects left.'

'Authie is still alive.'

'They'll find him in the end and burn him. So we will all die unconsoled. I expect God will understand. We go to the valley church regularly, take Communion, make our confessions, and only we know what is in our hearts. We no longer talk about religion. Armand, show Francois your pigeons.'

We inspected the dovecote. I told Armand I had built the dovecote at Roqueville.

'Yours is better. It is part of the castle and above a busy courtyard, and you won't be at the same risk from hawks.'

Armand looked pleased, then said, 'But we have rats. They come from the stables and take the squabs.'

'Get your father to take several long strips of tin and set them at a downward angle in the brickwork all the way round, a yard below the pigeonholes. That's where they are getting in. Your trapdoor is tight enough. Each tin strip needs to be nine inches wide, three inches to set in the wall, six inches projecting out and down.'

Armand looked pleased at my praise and my suggestion.

'Papa, can we do that?'

'Of course we can. The dovecote at Roqueville was rat-free. Although the hawks took plenty of Francois's pigeons. Now let's inspect my wine.'

The left-hand side of the courtyard was entirely given over to this.

'We bring in the grapes using these *comportes*,' said Etienne. 'The grapes go straight into the press.' The press was almost the height of a man, with an iron screw at the centre of a heavy wooden disc that fitted inside a circle of staves bound with two iron hoops. Around the base of the press was a circular stone trough, a foot above the floor.

'We take the stalks off the grapes – one reason why my wine is better than the rest. It is well worth the trouble. Half the time you're drinking sap from stalks if they are crushed along with the grapes. It makes the wine bitter, even though it increases the volume. Then the juice runs into the trough at the bottom; we catch it in buckets and put it into the stone vats to ferment. After three weeks the wine goes into the barrels, sits there for six months, and then we put it into hogsheads or leather wineskins.' Fifty barrels lined the walls beyond the press and the three stone vats.

'I'm astonished, Etienne. It's even more complicated than cheese-making.'

Etienne looked pleased. 'I'm known as the blind wine-maker. It was an insult at the beginning, as our first two vintages were undrinkable. Now we get the best price in the Carcassonne market.' He unlocked the door of the room at the far end of the barn. There were at least eighty hogsheads, each just light enough for a man to carry, each with a wooden bung, and the same number of leather wineskins.

'We make our barrels and our hogsheads in the carpenter's shop. Our barrel-maker came to us from the Carcassonne jail. We buy the wineskins from Catalonia. Take two with you back to Montaillou.'

Over dinner I explained my presence in Carcassonne, said I needed to return there the following day, and without going into much detail made it clear that Beatrice was central to my life.

'Whether I will ever see her again after the trial is uncertain. She has confessed to enough sins to be sentenced to as much as ten years in The Wall. She wouldn't last two. Baruch's argument may reduce her sentence, but they can hardly find her innocent.'

'He's a powerful advocate, a powerful intellect,' said Blanche, seeing I was close to breaking down. 'He recovered Roqueville for me against all the odds.'

'What happened to Roqueville?' I asked, relieved at the opportunity to change the subject.

'I sold the land and the ruins quite well under the circumstances. The money helped to pay for all this,' and Blanche pointed to the three good tapestries, the solid oak chairs and tables, the silver candlesticks that lit the room.

'And now we live off wine,' said Francois. 'We miss Guillemette and my mother every day.'

We talked of how dependent the two of us had been on Guillemette after the fall of Montségur.

'You lived on mushrooms?' asked Armand, astonished that this was possible.

'We did. We caught nothing in our snares. I had no

crossbow, and I was useless, in a trance. Guillemette was a real countrywoman, and she brought us safely to Barraigne.'

We were all silent for a moment. Then I said to Armand, 'Did your father ever tell you how we routed the crusaders' advance guard? How later we burned their big trebuchet, which they called The Bad Neighbour? Your father and I were doughty warriors; we had four eyes and four arms between us in those days.'

'You are both better off making wine and cheese,' said Stephanie sharply.

I smiled, ignore the rebuke, and went on, 'We were up here, twenty of us,' and I made a little mountain with my napkin, 'in the cover of a wood not far from my old home at Beaufort. The advance guard, fifty crusaders, half on horses, half on foot, came along the valley,' and I made a little column out of breadcrumbs. 'We waited until they were all out in the open, and then your father led the charge. It was the only time we ever used our lances in anger. We killed twenty of them, and the rest ran away.' I swept half the crumbs off the table and spilled a little red wine over the rest.

Armand's eyes were wide, and Etienne looked pleased at his son hearing about his warlike past.

'Great warriors indeed. There should be a ballad to mark it, the Chanson of Etienne and Francois,' said Blanche, smiling.

'I can still sing the ballad in your honour,' I said. 'Etienne will remember the words too.' And we sang the old tribute:

'Lady Blanche, your virtue and wisdom and beauty,
Your elegant speech, your sweet laughter
Draw me to you with a pure and loving heart;
In you lie all my happiness, all my desire,
I cannot find another one as fair.'

As we sang I thought of my old, intense love for Blanche, remembering the extraordinary experience of washing her feet and calves below the dovecote.

'Easy enough to find another one as fair today,' said Blanche. 'But I'm pleased you both remember the words.'

I spent the next morning, with Etienne's blessing and Stephanie's acquiescence, in making a small crossbow for Armand.

'You are only to use it when your father is there,' said Stephanie. 'It won't be a plaything. I don't want you killing your sisters.'

'It's to be used for killing rats,' I said. 'Etienne will be in charge of its safe keeping.'

Stephanie looked somewhat reassured.

Armand was pleased with the finished product. The workshop and the forge were able to produce all the materials we needed, including enough for three iron bolts. We tried it out and it was accurate to about fifteen feet.

'You'll need to get quite close to kill a rat,' I said. 'You will have to ambush them in the stables. And never, ever, point it at anyone, even when it is uncocked or unloaded. Break that rule and it will be taken away.' Armand promised to be careful, and I set off back to Carcassonne warmed by their good wishes.

It was one of those beautiful early autumn afternoons in the Languedoc, with a sharpness in the air just short of frost that heightened the colours and the senses. My gelding felt it too, giving a couple of quick bucks, joyous rather than malicious, when I mounted, and used any excuse, a startled rabbit, a flock of starlings wheeling low to the ground, to skitter sideways. I was in no hurry, as I would have to break my journey at the inn this year; I had left Barraigne too late to make the trip in a single day.

I had time to think. I thought about Stephanie's words, and recognised their truth, that wine-making and cheese-making were both less dangerous and more useful than being able to couch a lance, draw a sword or cock a crossbow. I was, in spite of myself, proud of being a knight, proud of my lineage, even proud of my ability to survive all I had been through at Avignonet, Roqueville, Montségur, and on the road to Compostela.

That was all over. I resolved to stop boasting about my warlike skills and my warlike past (and, God knows, it had ended in disaster every time – my father dead after Avignonet, the blinding and maiming after Roqueville, the burning of the Cathars, including my beloved Sybille, after Montségur). From now on I would content myself with herding sheep and making cheese.

I also thought of the binding strength of old friendships, which was hardly surprising, given all that we had been through. I had known the three of them at Barraigne most of my life, and the terrible times we had experienced together made that friendship unbreakable except by death.

How many friends do you have? I asked myself. *Other than Etienne, Stephanie and Blanche? Guillemette is dead. Andre Belot, no one else in Montaillou. Arnaud the shepherd is dead, but I never knew whether he liked me or simply tolerated me. Perhaps a little of both. The friar, but he's back near Lyon, five hundred miles away. Baruch the Jew, but our relationship has been entirely professional. And, of course, Beatrice.*

I thought at length about Beatrice as I rode. At the beginning our relationship had been founded entirely on physical passion. And there had been moments, for example when I knew she was with Pierre Clergue, when I hated her, and myself, and wanted to break free.

Looking back, all that changed after we routed the English band. Beatrice had dismissed Clergue from her bed, not because I asked her to, but perhaps because – I wasn't sure – perhaps because I had become enough. She had lost some of that confidence in her own judgement, her self-sufficiency, when she gave the order to lower the drawbridge, and she had gained more confidence in me.

My feelings for her had intensified on seeing her in jail, on realising there was a strong possibility that the courts would take her away from me forever. Our kisses, even under the eyes of a jailer peering through the grille, meant something new and strong. Not just to me, I thought, but also to Beatrice. I felt determined to put my thoughts into words when I next saw her.

I saw Baruch the following evening in his book room and presented him with a full wineskin from Barraigne. He was delighted. 'It's in short supply in the market, it sells out as soon as your friend sets up his stall. I'd cheerfully buy half a dozen hogsheads if I could. As it is, you and I drank my last drop a week ago. We should try this crop now.'

We did, and Baruch pronounced it excellent. I knew better than to hurry him. He began by saying, 'I understand they are going to press for a harsh sentence, make an example of her.'

I felt sick. 'She'll be sent to the stake?'

'No. Perhaps ten years in The Wall. But we know that is a living death for someone like Beatrice.'

'What about the documents I brought you?'

'I read them all. Very interesting, very interesting. They show how the de Planissoles estates were assembled through marriage, purchase, forfeiture and conquest over the last hundred years. Almost all useless for our purposes.'

'Useless?'

'There are two that are promising: one with a missing seal; one, the most recent deed, completely intact.'

'What does it say that might be helpful?'

'I'm not going to tell you. You'll tell Beatrice. And I don't want to raise false hopes in either of you. It is not absolutely clear that the court will hear me. The trial will be held in public, as I told you, and that will make it harder to refuse me. They are still trying to find Sicre, their only living witness, but he seems to have disappeared.'

'Indeed.'

'You must tell Beatrice not to wear her own clothes on the day of the trial. She should look bedraggled, downcast, penitent.'

I went straight from Baruch's house to the jail. Beatrice flung herself into my arms and held me tight.

'I expected you yesterday. I thought you had abandoned me.'

I took a deep breath, then said, and for me it was an important declaration, 'I will never abandon you.'

Beatrice looked surprised at the intensity with which I spoke, thought for a moment, then replied, 'I may abandon you if I'm convicted. What does Baruch say?'

We sat down on her bed, my hand in hers, while I gave an account of what Baruch had told me, erring on the side of optimism.

'Only one document out of that great pile is useful?' she said.

'It may be enough. You know Baruch. He likes to be cautious. I didn't press him.'

'Did he say I might burn?'

'He said you won't burn.'

She had begun to shake as she asked the question, and it took a minute or two for my answer to reassure her.

'I'll kill myself rather than go through years of The Wall.'

'You won't kill yourself. If you are sentenced to solitary confinement I'll come and get you out.'

'You'll get me out?' she said in a disbelieving voice.

I had nothing substantive to back up my brave words, but I continued nevertheless.

'This jail is as porous as a sieve. The jailers are bribable, we know that already, elderly, sleepy. I'll get a group of men-at-arms together from Montaillou and Carcassonne and organise your escape. It's not impossible, it's been done before.'

I had no idea whether my last sentence was true, and while I knew the jailers were corrupt I was unsure whether that extended beyond allowing food and wine to be brought to prisoners awaiting trial.

Beatrice managed a laugh as she said, 'My retainers at Montaillou are just as old, just as sleepy. They would find the journey to Carcassonne exhausting, and as for a jailbreak...'

'There are many men-at-arms in Carcassonne who would slit their grandmother's throat for the right price. Look at me.' I looked directly into her eyes for a long moment, and said with all the confidence I could summon up, 'I will get you out of prison.'

She held my gaze, smiled and we kissed for the third and sweetest time. I broke away, gave her Baruch's message about wearing her prison smock and left the room, knowing that whatever happened we would not be together in that place again.

23

The Trial

Francois

I SPENT TWO ANXIOUS days and sleepless nights before the trial planning and replanning Beatrice's rescue. There seemed to be only the faintest of chances that Baruch, brilliant though he undoubtedly was, would succeed in obtaining an acquittal. It was difficult to see title deeds, whatever their seal, having any impact on the judges. Two of the three judges were also priests, and although Beatrice's confession might argue for leniency, Pierre Clergue's deposition, in which by all accounts he named half the women in Montaillou, would have been enough on its own to obtain a conviction. Two of his former mistresses had already received severe sentences. I would have to rescue Beatrice.

It seemed to me that the best opportunity would be on the way back to the prison from the court, a distance of perhaps a mile. Prisoners were always taken there on foot, guarded by never more than half a dozen men-at-arms.

I went back to my old haunts outside the walls, where the rough tavern still seemed to be doing good business, and where the drinkers were all former Cathars or disillusioned crusaders, no lovers of the authorities inside the city walls.

Recruiting such men was not without risk, but they would have only two days in which to turn their coats after taking my money. And I was ready to offer them each 500 sous immediately, 500 sous if they appeared at the agreed rendezvous and a further 500 if the rescue succeeded.

I spoke to the landlord of the tavern on my first night there, and asked him if he knew any men, preferably former soldiers, who were willing to risk their lives for good money.

'Almost anyone who comes to drink here,' he said. 'Those men', and he pointed to a group of five men drinking around a table in the farthest corner of the tavern, 'are believed to be responsible for most of the robberies on the road between Carcassonne and Toulouse. They've never been caught, and their money is good here.'

On the second night they were at the same table. I went over to them and stood patiently while they ignored my presence. Then one of them looked up, took in my missing arm and eye, and said in near-friendly tones, 'I know you. You're the man from Roqueville.'

'I am.'

'What do you want?'

I sat down and explained the plan.

'Short swords and daggers. I'll take the woman and leave you to deal with the guards.'

'You're going to a lot of trouble and expense over damaged goods,' he said.

'That's my business. Do you want the money or not?'

'What if she's acquitted and there's no one to rescue?' said the man who appeared to be their leader.

'I'll be very happy to make the final payment,' I replied. He seemed satisfied, looked at his four companions and they each nodded.

'We'll take the money. But it's one livre Tournois if it comes to a fight. We won't be safe in Carcassonne, even out here, for quite a long time.'

I agreed, paid the deposit and left them.

IT WAS DRIZZLING on the day of the trial. I walked to the court from the inn, my heart beating faster as I went over the plan. I had four horses waiting in the stable yard for Beatrice and me; I had given the leader of the band of ruffians my sword and dagger when we met as planned at noon. He knew where the ambush was to take place. I told him I would join them the moment a guilty verdict was announced.

'And if she's not guilty?'

'Meet me back at the inn for the final payment.'

The courtroom was packed. The three judges dealt with a couple of petty thieves, and then Beatrice was brought in, looking beautiful and vulnerable in her prison shift. The crowd murmured, but I didn't, perhaps fortunately, hear what they were saying.

The presiding judge began by noting that the most serious charge, that of harbouring a Perfect, had been dropped owing to the absence of the key witness, one Arnaud Sicre. He added that this could be reinstated if Sicre was found. There was only one charge left against the Lady Beatrice de Planissoles, that of fornication with the priest, Pierre Clergue. He asked the clerk to read out Clergue's evidence.

It was this that the crowd had come to hear. It was a lengthy deposition, which had been translated into Occitan from the original Latin, describing in considerable detail the number and places of Pierre's transgressions, not only with

Beatrice but also with all his other mistresses in Montaillou. Fortunately for Beatrice he had not confessed to sex behind the Montaillou altar.

The judges looked appropriately shocked; the crowd, on the other hand, were both unsurprised at this behaviour by a priest and, I suspect, impressed by his voracious sexual appetite. At the end of the recital Beatrice was asked if she had anything to say.

'The first time he forced himself upon me. After that I was willing.'

Then Baruch stood up. He was sitting at a table opposite the clerk, wearing a long black gown and with a wooden cross hanging from his neck.

'I am Lady Beatrice's lawyer, and I would like to plead on her behalf.'

'Hear him, hear Baruch the Jew,' the crowd muttered as the judges conferred.

'There seems little more to be said, but you may say it.'

'With the greatest respect,' said Baruch, 'I would like to present this title deed to the court.'

'What bearing can a title deed have on these charges?'

'My client has confessed to the error of her ways and is truly penitent. But this deed confirms that Beatrice de Planissoles not only holds her lands from the King of Aragon, and owes him allegiance, she is his subject, not the subject of the Count of Toulouse or the King of France. This court, with the greatest respect,' and here Baruch bowed, 'has no jurisdiction over her. You will note the royal seal of Aragon, Or, Four Pallets Gules. I will, if I may, read the relevant passage.'

Baruch read slowly and carefully from the deed. It was in Latin, and that was enough to impress the crowd, although they couldn't understand a word. Baruch later told me that only the presiding judge had Latin good enough to understand the implications of the deed.

He also understood the importance of maintaining good relations with Aragon. There was a lengthy consultation between the three judges, who then called Baruch to their table, whispered in his ear, and received a nod in return.

'Lady Beatrice is free to go. She must wear the double yellow cross as a sign of her penitence. We will record your agreement on her behalf.'

The crowd was amused and delighted. The discomfiture of the judges was obvious, and although the crowd would have preferred a burning, they had the prurient pleasure of listening at length and in detail to the misdeeds of Pierre Clergue and a member of the nobility.

Beatrice looked stunned. I left the courtroom without speaking to her and hurried to the corner where my ruffians were standing, the citizens of Carcassonne giving them a wide berth.

'She's been acquitted,' I said, and the look of disappointment on their faces made it clear I had chosen my men well. 'Here is a livre Tournois for each of you. Celebrate in the tavern tonight; no need to leave Carcassonne.'

That evening Beatrice and I and Baruch dined happily together, Beatrice still barely able to believe she was free.

'The court was, of course, quite wrong to sentence you to wearing the yellow cross,' said Baruch. 'But it seemed a price worth paying, and it saved the judges' faces.'

'I thought tonight,' said Beatrice, taking a deep draught of wine, 'I would be on bread and water. Instead, we are free to return to Montaillou.'

'We leave tomorrow. We don't want to risk any second

thoughts.' I decided not to describe my rescue plan; the glory rightly belonged to Baruch.

'You must come and visit us in Montaillou,' said Beatrice. 'We will have a proper feast in your honour.'

Baruch looked uncertain. 'It would take me a week to get there on my mule. I'm happy to celebrate in my own home on the evening of your acquittal.'

He rose and held up his glass.

'I'd like to propose a toast. To the King of Aragon.'

'To the King of Aragon.'

24

The Calm

Francois

WE RODE BACK together to Montaillou, taking our time, stopping in small inns twice to break our journey. We rode side by side where the road permitted, singing from time to time and holding hands – my horse was amenable enough to walk on with a loose rein. Beatrice knew the words of all the great troubadour songs and taught me some of them; I hummed, usually in tune, during the rest. In exchange I taught her the words of the least bawdy of the tavern songs, although there was little new to Beatrice in either the language or their sentiments.

I called it a road, but it was paved for perhaps a mile outside Carcassonne, and then became a track, well used by farmers coming into the Carcassonne market on every second Thursday. Otherwise we saw no one.

The two inns we stayed in reflected this lack of trade. The beds were lumpy, the blankets coarse, and on the second night we were well bitten by fleas and bedbugs. Both innkeepers needed a little persuading to take us, as they were deterred by the yellow crosses and my missing arm and eye. My careful explanation of the court's verdict and an inflated sum in advance eventually succeeded. There were no other guests; we ate with the innkeeper and his wife on the first night and alone on the second. The meals were identical, potatoes and gravy and hard black bread. We had our own cheese and a skin of Etienne's wine, which kept us happy during the day as well as in the evening.

On the second night we both fell asleep immediately, and the next day I realised that this was the first time Beatrice and I had shared a bed without making love. Neither of us commented on this, and it seemed, to me at least, that our relationship had settled into a less ardent, but arguably more affectionate mode.

'You would think we were eighteen,' said Beatrice the next morning as I gave her a little bunch of wild flowers.

'I wish we were. I'd have my eye and arm back again.'

'I like you as you are. I loved you from the moment I saw you at the washing pool. And now I can settle for one man in my life, something I never thought possible.'

'As long as I'm that man,' I said, astonished that she had used the word love for the first time in our relationship. I leaned across and kissed her. I didn't want to risk asking her to confirm that it wasn't a slip of her tongue. 'I'm happy with the way things are between us.'

Three hours later, when we could see Montaillou and Beatrice's castle in the valley below us, she asked, 'What would you have done if I had been sentenced to The Wall?' shivering as she spoke the last two words.

'I would have set you free,' and I explained my plan with the band of ruffians I had recruited outside the walls of the city. Beatrice leaned across, took my hand, pressed it and let it go. I could see there were tears in her eyes.

'Would it have worked?'

'You should have seen my ruffians. They were disappointed at your acquittal only because they didn't have a chance to kill a few dozy prison guards, most of whom they knew well. But we would be heading for Spain by now if it had turned out like that. The courts and the Inquisition would have followed us a long way.'

As we entered the village the sun came out and turned the walls of the little castle to gold. Beatrice's flag was flying over the gate, and Andre Belot came out to meet us, smiling broadly as he helped Beatrice to dismount.

'We heard the good news yesterday evening,' he said. 'I've organised a feast in the Great Hall for tomorrow night. I thought you needed a day to recover from the journey.'

I was impressed at Andre's initiative. He had come a long way from the young man who used to deliver provisions to Arnaud and me in the mountains. Then I remembered.

'Arnaud Sicre?'

Andre's smile disappeared, and he unconsciously put his hand on his sword.

'He tried to escape, and nearly succeeded. He'd almost reached Ax when I caught up with him. I left him dead in a ditch. He'll not be missed. And no one in the village knew he was a prisoner.'

Beatrice had gone into the castle when this conversation took place. I patted Andre on the shoulder.

'His testimony would have convicted Beatrice in front of the Inquisition, that's certain. You did well. I won't miss him. He was a deceitful, traitorous bastard.'

'He and the Clergues betrayed the whole village, and then he betrayed the Clergues, who thought he was their man, their informer. I lost a mother and sister thanks to him. He had a quick and easy death compared with the stake or The Wall.'

The feast the following evening was a joyful affair. Andre had arranged it all, butchered two hogs, even found a troubadour to entertain us. All of Montaillou was invited, with the exception of the new magistrate, his henchmen and the priest. Everyone there was wearing the double yellow cross, which served as a badge of admission, and we drank and sang late into the night, finishing with a toast to the King of Aragon.

I had a headache the following morning – we had not been drinking Etienne's good wine the night before – and when I recovered and went out into the courtyard I found Beatrice and Andre, who had both clearly drunk far less than I, talking about the evening.

'We should celebrate like that more often,' said Beatrice.

'I don't think my head could take it more than once or twice a year. And no doubt a version of the event will soon be on its way to Carcassonne.'

'As long as we go to church and pay our tithes promptly they have nothing to grumble about.'

'The Inquisition will think that you and I have escaped proper punishment. There are not fools. They will know Sicre's disappearance wasn't accidental.'

'What happened to him?' asked Beatrice, saw the look on our faces and didn't press for an answer.

After the excitement of the feast Montaillou settled into a calm routine. The petty feuds between various families flared up and died down, but never reached the point of denunciation to the magistrate or the priest. We all went to Mass on Sundays, confessed often enough to keep the priest happy, and we all wore our double yellow crosses proudly.

Indeed, I heard one of the Maurs children, an eight-year-old, point to the magistrate as he left the church on Sunday and say, 'Look, Mother, he doesn't have a yellow cross.' His mother laughed and hushed him; our magistrate was not amused.

I continued to look after my sheep, the flock now three hundred strong. I hired two of the younger boys in the village to help me on the trip up to the mountain pastures in the late spring, but once there found I was able to manage on my own, although I now kept a horse to help with the evening round-up. Beatrice would visit me every ten days or so, and our lovemaking on that primitive bed of wolf skins and pine branches was as passionate as ever. She helped me bake bread and make cheese, both new skills for her, and she turned out to be a good bread-maker.

'I've never done anything useful before,' she said to me. 'Only sewing and embroidery.'

'Neither had I. It was thanks to Arnaud taking me under his wing that I'm now a man of substance in Montaillou, no longer a useless knight.'

'Those skills saved the village from the English band.'

And displaced Pierre Clergue from your affections and your bed, I thought, but wisely kept those thoughts to myself.

'The Languedoc is calmer now. The big bands of marauders have all dispersed, and we have nothing to fear from the odd collection of half a dozen robbers. They'll look elsewhere. Although we should practise what we learned, and not let the grass grow over our mangonel.'

So once a year we did re-create the defeat of the English band. The young men practised with their crossbows for a week beforehand. And on the anniversary day we set up targets in the village street, including one representing the English commander, and herded all the animals into the castle courtyard and the villagers into the Great Hall. Then we pulled up the drawbridge. On a sign from Beatrice we let the drawbridge down, loosed off the crossbows and fired the mangonel.

It turned into a celebration rather than a military drill, but it was none the worse for that. We included the magistrate, his henchmen and the priest, despite some grumbling from a few who would have preferred to see them as targets, and the day went off well. The whole valley, perhaps the whole of the Languedoc, knew Montaillou was well prepared. And the inclusion of the magistrate and the priest made it plain that we were not planning another Cathar revolution.

Andre Belot was an effective steward for Beatrice. He collected her rents, organised her cattle – she preferred cows' milk to the distinctive taste of milk from my sheep – and paid visits to her other properties once a year.

Her stepson came to see us once to discuss various legal matters about the castle and lands at Planissoles. He was a stiff young man, perhaps five years younger than me, and the relationship with his stepmother was uneasy, at least until she made it clear she had no claim on his inheritance and was more than happy with Montaillou. He disapproved of our yellow crosses and our apparent pride in them; I suspect he was fearful of guilt by association. He left us after a couple of days.

'I don't suppose we will see him again,' said Beatrice. 'I can't say I mind very much. He's like his father, a dull dog with no tournaments to excite him.'

'His father was older than you?'

'Fifteen years older. He was killed in a tournament. They were his obsession, a substitute for real war. I was meant to be heartbroken, but it had been an arranged marriage. I soon recovered after a short period of mourning. And then I came back here. This property was mine through my mother. I was an only child, an heiress, a prize.'

'You're still a prize,' I said, and kissed her warmly, kisses that she returned until we went upstairs to her chamber and the wolf skins.

Beatrice

After our successful defence against the English band my feelings for Francois deepened. I had confidence in his judgement, so when he came to see me with Baruch the Jew in Carcassonne jail and told me he would get me out, one way or another, I believed him. I was desperate by then, in need of the hope that he provided. When he told me later of his plan to ambush my guards on the way back to the prison, I had no doubt that it would have been successful.

Montaillou meant a great deal to me. It belonged to my mother, and she and I lived there until I was sixteen and married off to Berenger de Planissoles. This was a good match, I was told, although he was fifteen years older than me, a widower with a ten-year-old son. Our castles and land were about the same size and value, although Berenger lived in greater style at Planissoles than we at Montaillou.

He was kind enough to me, disappointed that I bore him no more sons; his approach to sex was that of a stallion or a ram. Nevertheless, I was genuinely sorry when he was killed in one of the last tournaments held in the Languedoc before real war took over. His opponent's lance splintered and entered his visor. He was dead, they told me, before he hit the ground.

My relationship with his son, young Berenger, was always uneasy. I tried hard to please him, perhaps too hard, but he understandably wanted only to be with his father, and was devastated by his death. He was at the tournament as his father's esquire and had to bring the body home.

When my stepson was sixteen I was happy to entrust Planissoles to his care; he and I had inherited a competent and reasonably honest steward from his father. Returning to Montaillou was returning home, although in my absence (my mother had died two years after I left for Planissoles) the two Clergue brothers, Pierre and Bernard, had established their total dominance over the village. And very soon, in Pierre's case, of me.

Pierre taught me, at first roughly, then carefully, about sex. I had known only Berenger and, after his death one other lover, a visiting troubadour who, as it transpired, was better at singing about love than making it.

Pierre had no inhibitions, no scruples, and was apparently insatiable. He always had at least one other woman in the village as his mistress. He liked to live dangerously, regarded my chamber as only one of the many places for making love, and persuaded me to organise my undergarments to make sexual intercourse easy – in the barn, in the gatehouse, on the stairs, and once in the church behind the altar. And for a while sharing myself between Pierre and Francois, the latter no less ardent but more conventional, more tender, seemed a satisfactory arrangement.

Sharing came to an end after the attack by the English band. This pleased Francois and disappointed Pierre, although he soon found consolation elsewhere. I was genuinely sorry when I learned Pierre was dead, and found it easy to forgive his naming of me in his lengthy confession. We were told he had been tortured before appearing in front of the Inquisition. Those who attended the trial said he looked a wrecked version of the confident priest he had once been. I was only saved from a similar fate by Francois and Baruch the Jew.

Montaillou without the Clergues was a calmer, more settled village. We all wore our double yellow crosses proudly, and there was nothing and no one left to denounce to the Inquisition or the secular authorities. Montségur had been the last Cathar castle; Montaillou was the last Cathar village. Both had fallen. The Catholic Church had re-established its absolute supremacy, which once appeared under serious threat, throughout the Languedoc. There was only one Perfect, Guillaume Authie, left.

25

Arrivals and Departures

Francois

FOR TWO YEARS there was a good price for wool and the whole of Montaillou prospered – carders, weavers, cheese-makers, shepherds. I had decided that three hundred sheep was the most my mountain pastures would feed. It was also the most that I, together with six dogs all descended from the unruly animals that Arnaud bequeathed me, could safely manage. At lambing time I needed help; I had built two sheepfolds in the valley to shelter my flock in the winter and early spring, but the lambs had a habit of arriving all at the same time, and it needed at least three men to deliver them safely.

I had good merchants in Ax who were eager to buy my wool and my cheese, the latter always commanding a high price. When I realised my cheese was not being sold in the Ax market, but was sent on to Carcassonne, I decided to sell at least half of my production there myself. Beatrice was uneasy.

'Why would you want to go back to Carcassonne? It has terrible memories for us. We know the jail there only too well.

You're easily recognisable; the Inquisition is capable of arresting you again.'

'I've been to Compostela, I wear the double yellow cross, as do you. We have become good Catholics again and neither of us has anything to fear. On my next trip I'd like you to come with me, and we'll go on to Barraigne. It's time we had some decent wine again. The red terror we buy at Ax is bad for my digestion. And I'd like you to meet Etienne and Stephanie.'

'And the famously beautiful Blanche,' said Beatrice.

I overcame her fears, and we planned a trip at the end of the summer once my sheep had been brought down from the mountains. I was talking to Beatrice in her parlour one evening when she said, 'I'm afraid we won't be able to go to Barraigne, at least this year.'

'We have nothing to fear from the Inquisition.'

'It's not the Inquisition. It's for a much better reason. I'm pregnant.'

I looked at her, astonished, then knelt beside her and put my head in her lap, half laughing, half crying.

'I'm four months overdue, so the baby will be born close to Christmas. No bouncing about on horseback for a while.'

Words were hard to come by. I had believed that by now Beatrice was too old to conceive; she had had no children by de Planissoles, and after an early miscarriage any hope either of us had about children seemed to have been extinguished. It was a possibility we had avoided discussing.

'We'll need a nurse,' I said. 'I only wish Guillemette was still alive.'

'We'll need a nurse, not a witch,' said Beatrice. 'This won't be the first baby born in Montaillou.'

'It will be our first. A quiet life for you until he arrives.'

'Or she. I'm not going to stay in bed all day. Cheese-making isn't too strenuous.'

I watched with delight and apprehension as Beatrice's normally elegant figure swelled. I stroked the tight curve of her stomach as we lay in bed together; pregnancy in no way lessened her desire to make love.

'You aren't going to disturb the baby,' she said, laughing as she lowered herself onto me. 'I'll try to be gentle with you. You're strong enough to bear the extra weight.'

I was strong enough, and she managed our lovemaking in a new and stately fashion almost until the baby was born. This happened the week before Christmas; I was in the courtyard when her maid came running out.

'Her waters have broken. Lady Beatrice has sent me to fetch Ermengarde.'

Ermengarde Benet arrived soon afterwards; she had borne five children herself, all still living, and assisted at the birth of many more.

'What can I do?' I asked her as she made her way across the courtyard.

'Nothing. Just keep out of the way. You played your part nine months ago.'

For the next five hours I paced up and down in the Great Hall. The walls were thick, but I could hear the occasional groan from Beatrice in her room on the floor above. Towards the end the sounds became more frequent, then suddenly stopped, and two minutes later Ermengarde came down. She was smiling

'You can go now and see your babies. You have a son and a daughter.'

Beatrice was lying back on her bed, a baby suckling at each breast, her eyes closed. She opened her eyes as I leaned over her and kissed her forehead, which was still damp. She had one hand round each pink, wrinkled bottom. She was too tired to speak.

When the twins had finished feeding Ermengarde wrapped them tightly in linen cloth and gave them to me to hold, one at a time, watching as though I was about to drop the precious bundle. All I could see was a little face and a crown of black hair, and I can remember to this day the smell, the warm, milky smell. It was the happiest moment of my life.

The next two years the babies – Francois and Constance (her mother's name) – dominated our lives. They were christened in the Church of Notre Dame at the bottom of our village. This was a joyful event, attended by most of the village, although it made me realise the double religious life we had to lead in order to conceal our Cathar faith.

'It's another kind of dualism, I suppose. I would have liked to have them blessed by a Perfect,' I said to Beatrice as we walked back up the village street. She carried our daughter and the nurse carried our son; it was not thought appropriate for a knight, or even a shepherd, to carry his own child.

'I'm only surprised that our priest didn't insist on having the yellow crosses sewn onto the christening robesa.'

'We are no longer Cathar, remember,' Beatrice said. 'It's safer that way.'

Not long afterwards, when Beatrice felt able, reluctantly, to leave the twins behind in the capable hands of the nurse Ermengarde had found for us, I decided to visit Barraigne.

'We can call on Baruch on our way,' I suggested, but Beatrice did not want to enter the walls of Carcassonne ever again. Eventually she was persuaded. I wanted to sell cheese in the Carcassonne market on the way to Barraigne. And, as I pointed out, but for Baruch, 'You might still be in

Carcassonne, in The Wall, if you survived that long.'

'What about your gang of ruffians?'

'That might not have succeeded. But even if it had, we'd be in Catalonia now, not Montaillou.'

So we set off, a little caravan, Beatrice and I on horses, my manservant Hugues on a mule which also carried our clothes. Hugues led two more mules, each laden with cheeses, some for the market at Carcassonne, some to exchange with Etienne for wine. We sent Hugues on ahead, and met him at the inn where we broke our journey on the first night.

Carcassonne looked unchanged as we approached the city, powerful, forbidding, austere. We passed the little settlement outside the walls where I had once killed a would-be robber, and the tavern where I had recruited my ruffians.

'Do you want to see if they are still there? I'd like to thank them,' said Beatrice.

'They've had the only thanks they value, ten livres Tournois. They're quite capable of ambushing us on our return journey if they knew we were carrying a precious cargo of wine.'

There were two long lines of travellers waiting to enter and leave the southern gate of the city. An officious sergeant of the guard took his time to question us when he saw the yellow crosses.

'Aren't you the man from Roqueville?' he asked.

I looked at Beatrice, resisted the temptation to give a clever answer, replying, 'I'm one of them, yes. I am Francois de Beaufort and my wife is Lady Beatrice de Planissoles. We've both done our penance, and I have been to Compostela. Here's my certificate to prove it.' I produced the battered parchment with its stamps, which he pretended to read.

'What brings you to our city?'

'Selling cheese.'

'We have plenty of cheese in Carcassonne already; we don't need any more.'

'Not good sheep's cheese from the Pyrenees. Here, try some.'

I cut off a generous section and offered it to the sergeant on the point of my dagger. He tasted it, looked surprised, took another bite and waved us on. He put what was left in the pocket of his jerkin, pleased with the transaction.

We went straight to the inn where we stabled our animals; our route took us past the jail where Beatrice and I had spent too many unhappy, uncomfortable nights. Beatrice closed her eyes until we were safely past.

She came with me to the market early next morning. I borrowed a table from our innkeeper, which Hugues and I set up in a corner of the square. We were twice moved on by indignant sellers whose place, time-honoured they claimed, we had taken, and eventually found a spot which we were able to hold unchallenged.

There was no stampede to buy my cheese, although I made a faint-hearted attempt to cry my wares. 'Sheep's cheese, sheep's cheese, sheep's cheese from the Pyrenees,' I called out, trying to find a lull in the cries from competing stallholders. By noon I had sold a single cheese, beaten down by a tough old woman to the price I would have obtained in the marketplace at Ax.

'The trouble is they look like any other cheeses,' Beatrice pointed out. 'They just taste much better. Here's what we should do,' and she cut off thirty or forty generous pieces of cheese, put them on a large wooden platter and went off into the crowd. She was soon back for more, accompanied by three buyers of whole cheeses at good prices. Within two hours we had cleared our table and went happily back to the inn.

'You've missed your calling,' I said to her. 'I'd still be there with a laden table, shouting "cheese from the Pyrenees" until I was hoarse. I think your sparkling eyes helped.'

She smiled and looked happy.

'I'm not sure my mother, Lady Constance de Villeneuve et de Gaja, second cousin of the Comte de Foix, would have approved. I enjoyed myself.'

That evening we called on Baruch, who was pleased to see us, and even more pleased when Beatrice spent half my cheese money on two beautiful bolts of cloth.

'Woven in Flanders,' said Baruch approvingly. 'Now come upstairs and we'll drink some of your friend Etienne's good red wine.'

'We're on our way to see him and Stephanie,' I said as we settled down in Baruch's study. 'They were both Cathar.'

'We are all good Christians now, good Catholics, I should say,' said Baruch. 'There are no Jews left in Carcassonne, all burned or converted, and only a few by special licence in Toulouse. I carry on my two trades as cloth merchant and advocate quite unhindered, although I am still called Baruch the Jew by most of my customers. I expect the God of Israel will recognise me in due course. There are no Cathars in Carcassonne either.' in Carcassonne

'There are none in Montaillou.'

'The Inquisition has triumphed over both our religions. In my case, by the power of argument,' and he gave a little smile as he said those words. 'In most cases, by conquest, by torture, and by the stake. I find my new religion completely ruthless in pursuing its enemies.'

'And completely successful. Although there may be one or two Perfects left.'

'They burned Pierre Authie in Toulouse. They are still

looking for his brother. He is rumoured to be alive and preaching where he can in the Languedoc.'

'Guillaume Authie came to Montaillou and consoled Alamande Guilabert on her deathbed.'

'They were a strange pair, the Clergues brothers. Almost as ruthless as the Inquisition in the way that they controlled Montaillou.'

'They were ruthless, it's true. But they were genuine Cathars and allowed their version to flourish in our village. This was their undoing, and the undoing of many others in the end. We were lucky to escape, and we all feel safer now.'

'As do I,' said Baruch, getting out of his chair. 'You'll forgive an old man who needs his sleep. I am very happy you called. God be with you.'

I presented him with one of my cheeses, he gave me a bolt of heavy purple cloth for a cloak in return, and we went back to our inn.

As we approached Barraigne the next day I could see the vineyards were more extensive than before. It was early autumn, and the grapes had already been picked.

'I thought Barraigne was almost derelict from the way you described it,' said Beatrice. 'The vines are well looked after, the walls are in good repair and their flag is flying.'

'Etienne is proud of his flag, his six quarterings. And why not? He's even prouder of his wine-making.'

There was the same alert sentry, who on this occasion recognised me (not a difficult task) and opened the gates to our little convoy. Etienne, Stephanie and the children came out to meet us, and I presented Beatrice for their inspection.

Stephanie looked at Beatrice with a keen eye, but was mollified when Beatrice said how handsome Bertrand and his little sisters were. Hugues stabled our horses and mules, and as we went into the Great Hall Beatrice said, 'Francois has told me what Barraigne was like when you arrived. How hard you must have worked to make the place so splendid.'

Stephanie enjoyed the open flattery.

'I'm sorry we felt the journey would have been too much for our twins.'

'Twins?' said Stephanie and Etienne together. 'We hadn't heard. Our congratulations. Come, we'll drink our best red wine over dinner to celebrate.'

'Where is Blanche?' I asked.

Stephanie looked sad. 'She's very ill. She hasn't left her bed for a month. She has the wasting sickness, finds it difficult to eat or drink, talks very little. Visit her in the morning with Etienne. Don't be surprised if she doesn't recognise you.'

This was sombre news, but not enough to prevent us enjoying our dinner and admiring Etienne's wine and my cheese.

'They complement each other perfectly,' said Etienne. 'I propose a toast – to wine-making and cheese-making.'

'And to the King of Aragon,' said Beatrice.

The next morning Stephanie took me to one side, congratulated me on my choice of a wife and the birth of the twins, then said in a worried voice, 'Blanche, in her lucid moments, wants to see Guillaume Authie. She wants to be consoled.'

'And the Endura?'

'And the Endura. She won't last much longer, eats and drinks very little as it is. I don't know what to do. It's hard to ignore my mother's dying wish.'

'Hard indeed. I can't advise you. But I'm sure you will do the right thing.'

Stephanie took my hand and pressed it hard, then kissed me quickly on the cheek.

Later that morning Etienne and I went up to see Blanche. I had been warned, but even so was not prepared for the sunken cheeks, the withered, stick-like arms lying on the light blanket, her once beautiful hair white, sparse, the scalp visible here and there. She opened her eyes as we came into the room.

'It's Francois de Beaufort come to see you,' said Etienne.

Blanche frowned, turned her head with painful difficulty to look at me, then smiled, a smile that transformed her face and made it beautiful once more.

'My true knight, my fellow pilgrim,' she said, lifting her hand a little off the blanket. I took her hand and pressed it to my lips. She closed her eyes again and Etienne took her other hand in his. I found it impossible to speak; we sat there for several minutes, then, quite quietly, I began to sing her troubadour's song, Etienne joining in, and as it ended, *I cannot find another one as fair*, I could feel the gentle, returned pressure of her hand on mine.

We left a few moments later, Etienne saying to me as we went down the stairs, 'She wants to see Authie. She wants to be consoled.'

'Stephanie told me. I couldn't advise her what to do.'

We stayed at Barraigne for two more days, Beatrice talking to Stephanie and her daughter, I walking round the vineyards with Etienne and teaching young Bertrand how to cock and fire a crossbow quickly.

'I can't demonstrate, as I didn't bring my extension,' and I explained how that worked.

'Five in three minutes, my father said.'

I laughed. 'Perhaps in my prime. I'd be slower now. But still accurate, which is more important than speed.' I congratulated Bertrand on installing the projecting eaves of tin around his dovecote.

'You were right,' he said, looking pleased. 'It really works. We've had no more trouble with rats since. We lose the occasional pigeon to hawks, that's all.'

26

The Consolation

Francois

WE LEFT BARRAIGNE early the next morning, sending Hugues ahead, his mules laden with full wineskins.

'They are patient beasts,' Hugues said. 'Perhaps they thought the return journey would be easier once we had taken the cheeses off their backs.'

'One wineskin weighs as much as two cheeses,' I said. 'It works out at about the same load. They are beasts of burden, after all. We feed them well, and their normal work, a weekly trip up to the mountain pastures, isn't a lot to ask. You're light enough, your mule is the lucky one.'

It was an easy journey, and shorter as we skirted Carcassonne; we passed only the occasional farmer going to or leaving the city. At all the major crossroads the Church had erected large crosses, complete with a crucified Christ in agony.

'Ten years ago those would have been taken down,' I said to Beatrice. 'Now they are safe enough.'

At noon we stopped, watered our horses and gave them hay which Etienne had provided. We sat in the early autumn sun and ate our cheese and drank Etienne's wine. Beatrice sighed happily.

'We have all we need. I could live off our cheese and the Barraigne wine. I wonder if Francois and Constance will recognise me.'

'I doubt it. You've been away all of nine days by the time we get back to Montaillou.'

She looked shocked for a moment, until I kissed her. We saddled the horses, and were about to mount when we saw a solitary figure walking down the track towards us. As he drew closer I could see he was wearing a green cloak over a brown tunic; he carried a staff, but had no other baggage.

It was Guillaume Authie, older and more lined than when I had last seen him, but still sturdy. He smiled when he saw us – and both of us at the same moment dropped to our knees, seeking his blessing. He touched our heads in turn, we said the Lord's Prayer together, and then we offered him some bread and wine, which he took, declining the cheese.

'I'm on my way to Barraigne. I heard Lady Blanche is very sick.'

'She is,' I said. 'Although they are Catholics, as we all are.'

He smiled. 'You are Cathar again now that I've blessed you, at least for a moment. And Stephanie has always sheltered me at Barraigne. I'm not sure Etienne knows.'

I looked at the track and back along the path we had taken.

'You need to hurry. She won't last much longer.'

Guillaume saw my look. 'There's no one behind me and I'm not being followed. Thank you for the bread and wine. God bless you both. I'll be on my way.' He strode down the track towards Barraigne without a backward glance.

Beatrice and I resumed our journey, both exhilarated and troubled by this chance meeting.

'I find I like being Cathar again,' said Beatrice. 'I feel better.

Strange that the touch and the words of one man can do that.'

'It is strange. It can't endure – we'll be Catholics once we are back in Montaillou.'

'I should have given him my horse,' said Beatrice.

'No.'

We rode on in silence, and by the evening of the next day we were home, Catholics once more.

Stephanie

GUILLAUME AUTHIE ARRIVED the morning after Francois and Beatrice left us.

'I passed them on my way here,' he said to me. 'I understand Lady Blanche needs me.'

'She does. She has asked for the Consolamentum.'

'And the Endura?'

'And the Endura.'

I knew my mother was not long for this world, and felt that in her case the Endura would hasten her end by only a few hours. I told Etienne that Authie had arrived.

'Did anyone see him?' he asked.

'Only the sentry, and he is Cathar, happy to have been blessed again by a Perfect.'

'We should take him to see your mother at once. And, even if it seems inhospitable, ask him to leave at dawn. He may have been seen arriving in the valley, he may have been followed. He is making no attempt to conceal who and what he is.'

'I'm tired of disguises,' Guillaume said to me as we went to my mother's room. 'They were never very successful; I didn't make a convincing pedlar. God will decide how soon I join my brother.'

Blanche was asleep, her room lit by a single candle until Etienne brought three rushlights from the hall below. She opened her eyes as the dark receded and seemed to recognise Guillaume Authie.

'Do you wish to be consoled and undergo the Endura?' he asked in a kind voice.

'I do,' said Blanche in a faint whisper.

Authie placed his hand on my mother's forehead for a minute, then took a small copy of the Gospels from his tunic and touched her head and breast with the book. We said the Lord's Prayer together, Blanche's lips moving soundlessly to follow us, and then she closed her eyes.

She never opened them again. When I went up an hour later to say goodnight she had gone. I went to tell Authie and Etienne.

'Does that mean she's Perfect again? In spite of recanting, in spite of the Inquisitor?' I asked.

'It does. God doesn't care about such things if you come to him in the end.'

Authie left before dawn, blessing us both, but not the children. 'They are too young to be discreet,' said Etienne, and he was right. 'I only hope his arrival and departure went unnoticed.'

It seemed so – and we resumed our recanted lives as though nothing had happened. We buried Blanche in the churchyard, our priest officiating, and all was as before.

27

The Reckoning

Francois

ON OUR RETURN to Montaillou I spent many hours thinking about our encounter with Guillaume Authie, and the way in which Beatrice and I, unprompted, had knelt down to receive his blessing and say the Lord's Prayer. We felt better for the blessing; we had become Cathar again.

Guillemette used to describe herself as a 'Castle Cathar', saying that if her mistress Claire had become a Mohammedan overnight she too would have converted, if only out of convenience. Her Cathar faith was skin-deep; she had no desire to undergo a painful death by fire to prove her belief in a doctrine about which she was, at best, confused.

'Two hundred good men and women gone forever,' she would say. 'How is the world a better place without them? It's a victory for evil, for brutality, for the power of the sword.' There was little point in arguing with her; the fact that I was still alive demonstrated the weakness of my position.

Born Cathar, I had converted quickly enough after the fall of Montségur. I had made no attempt to follow Sybille into the flames, excusing myself through the suddenness of her action. But I knew that if she had told me of her plans a week beforehand I would have tried to dissuade her, would have used physical force to restrain her if that were possible, but I would not willingly have accompanied Sybille, her mother and the other men and women who had gone, almost eagerly, to their painful death.

Did that mean I was a coward? I had proved myself in battle, I had fought off the little gang of marauders that had attacked Sybille and me, I had played my part in the two sieges of Roqueville and Montségur, I had been prepared to risk my life to rescue Beatrice had she been convicted. But I had readily accepted the penalty of the pilgrimage to Compostela; unlike many who had received the same sentence, I completed the journey. And while I was in the company of the friar I had little difficulty in understanding his version of the Catholic faith.

Now I was back in Montaillou, safe enough for the moment. Arnaud Sicre, the one man whose testimony could have destroyed Beatrice and me, was dead. Yet I felt changed by Guillaume's blessing. He had told me how he and his brother Pierre had been overcome by the words of St John's Gospel. His blessing, unexpected and unsought, had a similar impact on both Beatrice and me. I was not about to become a Perfect, but I had become a genuine believer. I could tell that Beatrice felt the same.

This realisation, discussed at length between us over breakfast, when we were always alone, had no immediate impact on our lives. Life in the village and in the valley continued to revolve around sheep, cheese-making, and wool from fleece to finished cloth. Our seasons were marked by the annual ritual of the transhumance, the journey to the mountain pastures in the late spring and back again at the end of summer.

Our magistrate and our priest were pale imitations of the Clergue brothers they had replaced. The magistrate collected tithes efficiently enough to satisfy his masters in Carcassonne, and resolved the endless boundary disputes over the valley fields and the mountain pastures with, we had to admit, a far greater degree of fairness than the Clergue brothers, who almost invariably had an involvement with one or other side in any lawsuit. And sometimes both; in Pierre Clergue's case he had often slept with the wives of the plaintiff and the defendant.

Our church was well attended, but then it always had been full. The new priest heard Confessions regularly and we celebrated our saints' days with enthusiasm. I once made a joke in bad taste about the priest's expectations in relation to the chatelaine of the castle and the altar of the church, and Beatrice was not amused. I slept alone for ten days afterwards.

Our twins were a constant source of delight, apart from the occasional anxiety that childhood illnesses bring. Beatrice and I were not always in agreement about their upbringing.

'There is little point teaching Francois to be a knight,' said Beatrice; she had been watching me playing with him in the courtyard. 'He needs to know about sheep and cheese.'

'Those were wooden swords. It's never too early to learn the simple parry and riposte. The Languedoc is peaceful now, but that may not last forever. The King of France, and the Counts of Toulouse, and the Church, and all those little kings across the mountains, will always have something to fight about.'

'Little kings? The King of Aragon was big enough when I needed him.'

'Indeed he was. So I'll teach Francois about sheep and swordsmanship. And when he is old enough, lances, crossbows and pigeons.'

Beatrice was happy with this compromise, although we had a further argument when I presented our son with a real sword on his twelfth birthday.

'He's strong and sensible. He's as tall as you now. When he and his sister ride out together it will deter any vagabond who might think of stealing their ponies.'

'And worse. They shouldn't go out without an escort,' said Beatrice – but Francois kept his sword.

'Spoils of war,' I said as I buckled it round his waist. 'Belonged to the English captain who tried to capture Montaillou, good Damascus steel. Perhaps he acquired it on a proper crusade. Remember, it's not a toy.'

Francois looked after his new treasure with great care. The sword hung in its leather scabbard on a special peg in his chamber and was regularly oiled and polished once Francois had removed its years of rust. His sister was allowed to admire the weapon, but only from a distance.

Our carpenter built a quintain in the tilt-yard where we still practised with our crossbows once a month.

'What is that ridiculous object?' asked Beatrice.

'A quintain. Strike the Saracen's head with your lance at the near end of the beam and it swings round, pivoting on the central pole. The sandbag on the far end clouts the rider if he misjudges his speed or fails to duck.'

'Why a Saracen?

'Tradition.'

Our son soon became adept at hitting the target and avoiding the sandbag, but only after he had suffered the indignity of being knocked off his pony a couple of times.

'It looks dangerous to me. It's not a skill he will ever need,' said Beatrice.

'I hope you're right. But a couple of tumbles hurt only his

pride. He'll soon learn.'

Francois and I spent many hours practising simple skills with wooden swords.

'Our master at arms at Roqueville taught us all kinds of elaborate flourishes – feints, disengages, prises in octave. Elegant but useless. All that was instantly forgotten in a real fight. Parry and riposte is all you need. Parry first, to stop your enemy killing you, and then the riposte, to kill him.'

And that is what we practised, until Francois could fend off the strongest attack and make an effective riposte.

'Let's hope it's a skill you'll never have to use,' I told him after one energetic session. 'But if you do you'll be glad we fenced together. I was only a few years older than you when I first had to use my sword in earnest.'

The four of us rode out together every morning, the twins both strong, confident riders. Our annual summer adventure was a trip to the mountain pastures to visit the sheep. They were now looked after, with great confidence and the latest generation of fierce sheepdogs, by Andre Belot.

Francois and Constance enjoyed everything about the trips, with the exception of the latrine. They were astonished by my pride in its ingenious construction, and by their mother's agility in using it. I took the precaution of replacing the cross-pieces with thicker, sturdier branches at the beginning of every summer.

We were visited each year by Beatrice's stepson, who came to seek annual reassurance that his stepmother was happy with Montaillou and had no plans to assert her rights over the Planissoles estates. And we had a return visit from Etienne and Stephanie, together with their children and two mules laden with wine.

We had ample warning of their visit, time enough to bring mature cheeses down from the mountain pastures. Beatrice organised a feast in our Great Hall, we killed several lambs, and found a troubadour who sang a long poem about the sixteen knights from Roqueville. I had heard a version years ago in the taverns of Carcassonne; the more seditious verses had been deleted.

The next morning I saw Etienne's son showing off his small crossbow to Francois. 'Your father made it for me. I've killed seventeen rats with it. You must never point it at anyone, even if it is unloaded and uncocked.'

Etienne and I listened to this conversation with pleasure.

'I'll put Francois in charge of our pigeons now he is old enough to handle a crossbow. I'm impressed by your boy's rat-killing skills.'

'I can teach him wine-making, but not marksmanship,' said Etienne. 'Stephanie tells me that most of your villagers are still wearing the double yellow cross.'

'Beatrice and I both wear it, although I forfeited the obligation once I had completed the pilgrimage to Compostela. In Montaillou it's a badge of pride, not of shame. And it demonstrates to the outside world that we have been punished for our beliefs, and have turned back into the path of the True Faith.'

I didn't tell Etienne, then or later, of our meeting with Guillaume Authie when he was on his way to give Blanche the Consolamentum. I would have trusted Etienne with our lives, but the less that was spoken about Guillaume the better.

Guillaume did visit us two or three times a year, usually on his way to or from Catalonia. We were careful about these visits; he never went into the village, and held a ceremony in the stables attended only by our own people. He arrived late in the evening and left at dawn the following day. Nevertheless, the risks were considerable, although Guillaume no longer wore his green cloak and had long since abandoned his pedlar's collection of pots and pans. Beatrice and I were always pleased to see Guillaume, and felt physically as well as mentally refreshed after his brief visits.

We continued to wear our yellow crosses, went to church regularly, and confessed, although we had little of interest to tell our priest. There was no doctrinal objection to Confession as far as Catharism was concerned; our religion concentrated on telling us how to behave in this, false, world in preparation for the next.

We joked about reincarnation, hoping that we might return together as a pair: 'of swallows,' suggested Beatrice, 'anything but sheep.'

Guillaume Authie had explained reincarnation to us on a number of occasions.

'One life is not enough for the unawakened soul,' he said. 'I have had several previous incarnations and have often been reminded of them. Once I was out walking with my brother years ago when I suddenly realised I was in familiar country, familiar to me not as a man but in an earlier life as a horse. In that previous life I was being ridden by my master on the journey home and lost a shoe between two stones. I stopped, bent down and found a horseshoe where I had cast it off in that earlier incarnation. I have kept it ever since. Here it is.'

He rummaged in his bag and produced an old, battered horseshoe of a type that had not been used in the Languedoc for many, many years.

It was an extraordinary, almost comical story, but sustained by Authie's obvious sincerity and faith, which Beatrice and I found it impossible not to share.

It was easy to feel a good Cathar in Authie's company. Less easy when he was gone, less easy in view of the apparent success of the Inquisition in stamping out our faith through torture and the stake.

'How can our faith survive?' I asked Guillaume.

'God will ensure that it does,' he answered with serene confidence.

And yet the Devil seemed to be winning the battle for supremacy in this impermanent and imperfect world. The monstrous apparatus of the Inquisition, their scribes, constables, bailiffs, warders, torturers and executioners, led by Dominican monks who provided a cloak of holiness, seemed to me at times overwhelming. Deceit appeared more than a match for the Cathar response of always telling the truth.

The concept of live and let live, which allowed Cathars to exist in the Languedoc under the protection of half a dozen feudal overlords, had long gone. The zeal of the Catholic Church for torture, burning, condign prison sentences and yellow crosses was unabated; indeed, it seemed to be fuelled by its successes.

We continued to hear the stories about the Inquisition's activities, but in towns and villages far away from Montaillou. We believed that the death of Arnaud Sicre and the inactivity of our magistrate meant that, provided we continued to pay our tithes, we were safe.

We were mistaken. Early one morning a messenger arrived, in great haste, from Baruch.

'I was sent to tell you that they had captured Guillaume Authie. That was all.'

'No letter?'

'No letter.'

'I suppose it was bound to happen,' said Beatrice. 'He is one of the last Perfects. There is no one to rescue him or to bribe his way out of jail. We are safe enough here.'

'We're not safe,' I said, almost angrily. 'He is bound to tell the truth. He knows they will burn him, and he won't be able to die a Perfect if he lies to save his own skin, or ours. The best we can hope for is that he doesn't tell them about his visits to Montaillou immediately. We need to leave for Catalonia as soon as possible.'

'I'm staying here,' said Beatrice.

'They'll burn you too,' I said. 'And Constance and Francois.'

There was a long silence. Then I continued, 'I'll send Hugues with a message to Andre Belot to take the sheep to Puigcerdà. The four of us will leave tomorrow at dawn. Pack what you can, anything small and valuable, money, jewels. We will need food for five days. Two horses, two ponies for the children, no mules – they'll only slow us down. We'll tell the children it is an adventure, a trip to meet their Spanish cousins.'

I wasted precious time convincing Beatrice, but there was no avoiding the awkward truth. We knew Guillaume too well for that. I told Hugues that Authie had been taken by the Inquisition, and that we were going to Catalonia in the morning.

'Let me come with you. They'll know I'm Cathar.'

'We don't have enough horses. Take a couple of mules, and as many cheeses as you can manage, and head for Lombardy. Here's money for your journey. It's not you they are interested in. They tried and failed to convict Beatrice and me several times already – now they will believe they have us.'

I gave Hugues the money, embraced him and wished him good fortune. There were tears in our eyes as we parted. He left the same evening.

I went to the Montaillou tavern, which was no more than the front room of the Maurs family, selling wine we nicknamed

The Red Infuriator. You needed the digestion of a horse to keep it down. There I let it be known that I was moving my sheep to Catalonia via the southern passes.

'We haven't enough feed for the winter here, and I know I can buy fodder from Beatrice's cousins.' I knew this piece of gossip, unfiltered, would be with the magistrate the next day; the Maurs family love to be the source of information.

It was cold when we left the next morning, barely light enough to see our way, the children still half asleep and complaining. We had saddled the horses the night before. Beatrice organised the food for the journey. She saw me pack two crossbows and forty bolts, and buckle on my short sword and dagger. Young Francois insisted on wearing his sword.

'We won't need them, but it is best to be ready. I think we have two days before they arrive in Montaillou.'

I was wrong. We went past the washing pool, up the track that led to our mountain pastures and stopped on the little col they call Bellevue, which gave us a view over the whole valley and the village. Beatrice and I looked back for the last time, then she put her hand on my arm. Her eyes are better than mine.

'Look at the track from Ax, from Carcassonne.' I could just make out a blurred group coming into our village.

'How many?'

'Three. No, four horsemen. Wearing chain mail.' The sun had glinted on the leading man, enough for Beatrice to see his armour.

'As well we stopped. We've got two or three hours, not two days. And we can only move as fast as the ponies. Still, we know the path better than they do. They may pick up a guide in the village.'

Francois and Constance could hear the tension in our voices.

'Who are they, Mama?'

'Bad men from Carcassonne. But we won't let them catch us.' Francois looked excited; Constance began to cry and was comforted by her mother. We trotted up the track, knowing that our pursuers would have less to carry, although it was not possible to canter on most of the track. Our horses and the children's ponies were tough, surefooted, used to the mountains.

We made steady progress that morning, eating and drinking as we rode. We stopped briefly at the next vantage point where we could see our pursuers, now close enough for my eyes to pick them out.

'We've a two-hour lead. But the gap is closing. We will need to be well into Catalonia before they turn back. The price on our heads will be big enough to override several miles of boundary dispute.'

'What will happen if they catch us, Papa?' asked Francois.

'What did Etienne tell you about me and my crossbow?'

'Five in three minutes, he said.'

'How many did Mama say were following us?'

'Four.'

'There you are. One to spare. But' – seeing the look on Beatrice's face – 'it won't be necessary. They'll not catch us. Your ponies are doing well.'

And indeed they were. Beatrice and I took it in turns to lead, and on the first part of the journey the track was wide and grassy. Later on it narrowed, falling away quite sharply below us, slippery after the early morning rain. And on that track, but for no specific reason, no stumble, no fall, my horse went lame. Properly lame, three-legged lame, not something we could ride off. I dismounted at once, ran my hand down his foreleg, felt the heat, and I could see the bowed tendon that was causing the trouble.

I looked up at Beatrice. 'The tendon's gone. He won't

make another hundred yards.' I swore silently to myself.

'My mare will carry us both.'

'She could – but not for long, and not fast enough. You three go on ahead. I'll go back half a mile to where the path is ideal for an ambush. We'll tie my gelding out of sight here.'

Beatrice knew me well enough not to argue. And there was no alternative other than surrender. I took my short sword, the two crossbows and the quiver of bolts, the children silent and wide-eyed. Then Francois said, 'I'll stay with you, Papa. I can hand you the bolts.'

I didn't know whether to laugh or cry.

'You need to look after Mama and your sister.'

I hugged them both and kissed Beatrice.

'We'll meet again in Catalonia. I'll have the pick of their horses. Now off you go.'

I walked back down the track to the point where a large, overhanging rockfall made it impossible to travel other than in single file. Small trees and shrubs gave good cover. I scrambled to the top of the rockfall, laid out my bolts, selecting the ten best, strapped the extension onto my stump, then cocked and loaded the two crossbows. I was well hidden by the bushes; I planned to take my shots from a kneeling position at a range of not more than thirty feet. I would wait until the first two men were round the corner, kill them both and hope that I could reload in the confusion.

I was about to find out whether I could live up to my legend – in hot blood, in anger, with the lives of my wife and two children dependent on my speed and accuracy, untested in anger since the fall of Montségur. I was many years older; and the wolves I had killed in the mountain meadows had not been armed.

Five in three minutes.

Beatrice

I DIDN'T WASTE TIME arguing with Francois. His quiet confidence that he could handle four armed men calmed me and the children, although young Francois was adamant he should stay and help.

'Your sister and I need you with us,' I told him, and we set off at a brisk trot. I stopped and waved to Francois as he walked down to the narrowest part of the track, but he didn't look back.

We had ridden on for no more than ten minutes when Francois, already some distance behind Constance and me, turned his pony and without a word cantered back down towards his father.

I didn't know what to do; I wouldn't be able to catch him before he reached his father, and then what? Four of us couldn't hide, and Constance and I would only be an encumbrance. Francois at least had his own sword, and might be of some help to his father if he arrived in time. So I calmed Constance and told her with as much confidence as I could muster that they would be all right, and that we needed to press on.

Francois

The ambush went almost as planned, but I had counted on the four of them riding close together, while in the event the second pair were fifty yards behind the first. I was able to kill the first two; at a range of no more than twenty feet the crossbow bolts penetrated chain mail easily enough. The first rider fell, and his horse bolted back down the track. It took the second rider several seconds to realise where I was hidden, and he made the fatal mistake of trying to turn his horse and join his two companions. This left me enough time to pick up my second crossbow, and fire, and kill him.

'Two in less than a minute,' I said to myself – but that left two horsemen unaccounted for. I hoped that they would have the sense to retreat, but they were determined men; they galloped up the track and arrived before I could reload. I dropped my bolt and wasted precious seconds scrabbling for it in the long grass.

By now they had dismounted, and walked slowly towards me with drawn swords. I came down on the track below them on the Montaillou side, a lucky decision as it turned out. Singly I was a match for them, but they separated as they approached. I couldn't parry two swords simultaneously, and the pair of them were not interested in single combat. One of them I recognised as my old enemy, the torturer from Roqueville who had led the group that captured Blanche and returned her to the Inquisitor.

'Can't you deal with a one-armed man on your own?' I shouted. He was too sensible to reply. Half of his party were already dead, and he had no intention of joining them. I backed away down the track, making it as hard as possible for them to come at me together; they were not in a hurry, careful to avoid a mistake through moving too quickly, confident that two against one would have only one outcome. I parried the first attack from the right and jumped back just in time as the man on my left slashed at my sword arm. There was no escape for me down the rough and rocky hillside.

And then my son arrived. The two didn't see or hear him until the last moment, and by then he had spurred his pony into a gallop. The pony was brave, almost as brave as his rider, and the path so narrow that they had nowhere else to go, crashing into the man attacking me on my right and knocking him to the ground.

On my left I was able to step forward into my old enemy's attack, beat his sword to the ground and cut him in the neck. He fell with the force of the blow, dropping his weapon, tried to sit up and failed.

Our other opponent had lost his sword in falling, and yielded as I stood over him, my sword already bloody. Francois and his pony had stopped fifty yards down the track; they turned and trotted back, Francois smiling and crying with relief. As was I. He fell off his pony into my arms and we stood there for several minutes, lucky to be alive.

'I knew you would need me,' said Francois, half angry, half proud.

'I did indeed. You saved the day,' I said. 'Thank the Lord it's over.'

It was over. Or so I thought. I turned back down the track to collect one of the loose horses, when some instinct made me look round. I saw the detested torturer, whom I had left for dead, struggle to his feet and lurch towards Francois, raising his sword to cut my son down.

'Look out,' I shouted, and Francois turned, raising his sword in a parry that deflected the blow and caught his opponent's sword in the vee between guard and blade. It was the torturer's last effort; he fell to his knees and then onto his face, dying without the need for a final coup.

'I should have made sure he was dead,' I said, knowing what Beatrice would have thought of my carelessness. And I found myself being comforted by a hug from my son.

'What will we do with this one?' I prodded the only survivor to stand up.

'Don't kill him,' said Francois.

'No. There's been enough killing already. We'll send him back to his masters in Carcassonne. On foot.'

He made a dejected figure as he stumbled down the mountain towards Montaillou.

'Even if he catches one of the horses, he'll not come after us. He'll be busy concocting a story about how they were overcome by a twenty-strong band of vicious Cathars. Now we'll rejoin your mother and Constance. You've given the troubadours something to sing about; we can sing what we like once we're safely in Catalonia. But it won't be "five in three minutes."'

Author's Note

Cathar is a novel, not history, but I have used the names of real events and places (Avignonet, Montségur and Montaillou) and people (Baruch the Jew, Guillaume and Pierre Authie, and the Clergue brothers) in several instances. I have relied on the novelist's prerogative to ignore the timeline; it would not have been possible to be at the siege of Montségur and later at the raid on Montaillou. Rather than change the names of the people and places which stimulated my fictional account, I have used them in the hope that those interested in the history will read, in particular, *Montaillou* by Emmanuel Le Roy Ladurie, *The Yellow Cross* by René Weis and *Massacre at Montségur* by Zoé Oldenbourg.

Acknowledgements

This is my second novel, notoriously difficult in the publishing trade, so I am particularly grateful to my agent, Michael Sissons, and my publisher, Head of Zeus, for their continued support. Rosie de Courcy has been an exceptional editor, and in particular supplied me with an ending for the book when I had failed to find one.

And I owe an immense debt of gratitude to my wife Jennie – this is her second novel too, and her encouragement has been generous and unhesitating.